lina

"Jill Jones is one of the few authors who can burst onto the publishing scene and create their own special niche. Her talent for combining fact with new historical possibilities is unmatched." —*Romantic Times*

"Jones is especially adept at creating tense plots and authentic characters." —*Publishers Weekly*

Remember Your Lies

A Featured Alternate Selection Of The Literary Guild, Mystery Guild, Doubleday Book Club, And Rhapsody

Bloodline

"Compelling . . . [an] inspired take on the mystery of the elusive Ripper." —*Publishers Weekly*

"A chilling murder mystery." —*Romantic Times*

"A spine-tingling novel that will grip readers and hold them captivated . . . Jones yet again proves herself a force to be reckoned with—amazing." —*New-Age Bookshelf*

"Chilling . . . a wonderful thriller . . . a truly fascinating book—don't miss it!"—Heather Graham, *New York Times* bestselling author of *Long, Lean and Lethal*

the page for more praise . . .

RE

The Island

"[A] fast-paced story . . . [with] well-drawn characters and a few unexpected plot twists." —*Library Journal*

"A magical escape into a realm steeped with legend."
—*Bookpage*

"Top-notch entertainment to die for!"
—*The Belles and Beaux of Romance*

"Mesmerizing . . . a page-turner from start to finish."
—*Old Book Barn Gazette*

Circle of the Lily

"Her clever and compelling plot twists will keep . . . readers riveted." —*Amazon.com*

"Dramatically enthralling . . . another notch to Jill Jones's growing list of surefire hits." —*Romantic Times*

"Impossible to put down." —*Rendezvous*

Essence of My Desire

"A unique and utterly spellbinding story to savor . . . a true original." —*Romantic Times* (4 1/2 gold stars)

"An alluring tale of suspense and erotic enchantment."
—*Publishers Weekly*

The Scottish Rose

"Seamlessly blends the elements of romance, time travel, adventure, and danger with truly spectacular results."
—*Romantic Times*

"Exciting, absorbing, one of the top books of the year."
—*Affaire de Coeur*

"A unique page-turner, sure to win a favored place on bookshelves." —*The Belles and Beaux of Romance*

My Lady Caroline

"A truly remarkable story." —*Publishers Weekly*

"A bewitching ghost story . . . This is an author to watch!"
—*Romantic Times*

Emily's Secret

WINNER OF THE PRESTIGIOUS "MAGGIE" AWARD FROM GEORGIA ROMANCE WRITERS

"A magnificent novel!" —*Affaire de Coeur*

"Beautifully written and compelling . . . I loved it . . . A must read!" —Heather Graham

"Lovely! It's the book I've always wanted to write."
—Marion Zimmer Bradley

St. Martin's Paperbacks Titles by Jill Jones

EMILY'S SECRET

MY LADY CAROLINE

THE SCOTTISH ROSE

ESSENCE OF MY DESIRE

CIRCLE OF THE LILY

THE ISLAND

BLOODLINE

REMEMBER YOUR LIES

Remember Your Lies

Jill Jones

St. Martin's Paperbacks

This is a work of fiction. Any resemblance of characters to persons living or dead, or events or actions of the plot to real life is entirely coincidental.

REMEMBER YOUR LIES

ISBN: 0-312-97715-8

Printed in the United States of America

St. Martin's Paperbacks edition / March 2001

St. Martin's Paperbacks are published by St. Martin's Press, 175 Fifth Avenue, New York, N.Y. 10010.

10 9 8 7 6 5 4 3 2 1

For Maureen and Joe and "the neighbors . . ."

Acknowledgments

My deepest thanks go to my many good friends in Savannah who helped to bring this story to life: Maureen and Joe Horvath, Kathy and Brian Roux, Alyse and Albert Seidl, Pat Tuttle, Lieutenant Claire McCluskey and Sergeant Jimmy Stevens of the Savannah Police Department, and the rest—you know who you are.

A debt of gratitude goes to Roger Pinckney, author of *Blue Roots*, Llewellyn Publications, 1998, and to John Bennett, author of *The Doctor to the Dead*, University of South Carolina Press, 1995. Both books contributed greatly to my understanding of Gullah traditions and therefore to the creation of this book. I have particularly drawn on Pinckney for the (fictional) excerpts at the beginning of each chapter.

I am also indebted to my critique partners, Pat Van Wie and Karen Hawkins, and to Joanna Shulman, and as always to my editor, Jennifer Enderlin, and my husband, Jerry.

"A long time ago, before yestidy was born, an' before bygones was uster-bes . . ."

—Traditional beginning of a Gullah folk tale

Chapter 1

Everyone knows there be unseen forces afoot playing with our lives an' not caring if we live or die. Hants come an' go an' touch us in th' night, and we must beware not t' set 'em off . . .

—A Gullah conjureman's warning

ANGELA Donahue had forgotten the acrid smells that tainted the air inside a police station. How the burnt brown of old coffee mingled with the sour green of the unwashed bodies of the street people and criminals lounging sullenly on benches or against the cold stone walls.

Or maybe she'd never noticed the stench before, when her visits to places like this had been for business, and she'd been the one wearing a badge.

Today, the rancid odor struck her the moment she entered the building, and a sudden foreboding raised the hair on her arms. She clutched her elbows with her hands, feeling dirty, out of place. Why had she ever agreed to come here?

Behind her, Detective Sergeant Johnny Reilly said, "To your left," and she turned down a long hall. She felt the eyes of all who loitered along the corridor bore into her, and her cheeks grew warm. How had she let herself get into such a predicament?

This was all a misunderstanding, a huge and horrible mistake. But she'd been unable to convince Reilly of that, and rather than make a scene in her place of business, she'd begrudgingly agreed to talk to him at the station house.

The faces of cops and criminals alike blurred as she

walked beside Reilly, who was head of the Savannah Police Department's homicide division. She tried to think about the reason he'd brought her in, but her mind just wouldn't wrap around it.

Murder.

Johnny Reilly was convinced she'd had something to do with a murder—the murder of a man she didn't even know. And everyone knew that Reilly was tough as a bulldog when he had a bone between his teeth.

A man who looked like a street bum approached them from the opposite direction, a curious look on his face. He stopped them and stared openly at Angela, then turned to Reilly.

"Why've you got her in here?" he asked.

The fire in Angela's cheeks burned hotter. She didn't know this guy, but from his tone, it sounded as if he recognized her. From his dress and his familiarity with Reilly, she guessed he was an undercover cop. If so, it was possible he remembered her, although it had been almost five years since she'd left the bureau. Whoever he was, she was horrified that he'd seen her being treated like a common criminal.

"It's none of your business, Turner," Reilly said.

But the man named Turner wouldn't let it go. "Maybe it is. What's the deal?"

Irritated, Reilly gave the man as little as he could to get rid of him. "It's about that floater we found in the river this afternoon. The Slade case. Just got some questions for her, that's all. Now, if you don't mind . . ." Reilly pushed past the man and hurried Angela on down the hall.

Angela looked over her shoulder and saw the man staring after them. Did she know him?

They reached their destination, and Reilly opened the door for her. She stepped inside a small room that was furnished only with a metal table and three hardback chairs. She rubbed her arms as a chill shivered through her. She'd been in interrogation rooms before, when she was with the Georgia Bureau of Investigation, but she'd never been the one in the hot seat.

"Reilly, you're making a mistake," she said at last, wheeling to face him. "A big mistake."

Sergeant Reilly's face was grim. "I wish I shared your optimism," he said. "Sit down."

Angela knew Johnny Reilly from her days with the GBI and remembered his reputation for being tough on the suspects he interviewed. If they did a "good-cop, bad-cop" routine, Reilly was always the bad cop. She also wasn't sure he was a straight cop. Even though he'd survived the scandalous Internal Affairs investigation that had landed a number of crooked cops in jail, he was still a veteran of the old regime. How had he managed to escape? Was he that convincing a liar? Or was he clean?

She eyed him angrily. "Okay, you got me here. Now show me your 'proof' that I know a man I've never heard of." She couldn't keep the irritation from her voice, even though she knew it wasn't a good idea to antagonize a cop like Reilly. But he seemed unfazed by her demand and suddenly in no hurry.

"Want coffee?" he asked as if this were some kind of social event.

"I want to get this over with."

"Want a lawyer?"

"I don't need a damn lawyer," she exploded. "I didn't do anything! I told you, I didn't know—what'd you say his name was?—J. J. Slade, much less murder him. Why on earth are you questioning me?"

Reilly let her rant until she'd used up that round of anger, then he said, "We found a pocket calendar on the body that indicated Slade had a luncheon appointment at the First City Club yesterday at one P.M. It was the last notation he'd written in for the day."

Angela glared at him. "So?"

"So we went there to see if anyone remembered him coming in for lunch. You're a member of the First City Club, aren't you?"

"Yes, but I still don't see what this has to do with me. I didn't know the man."

The policeman produced a piece of paper from his coat pocket and tossed it onto the table. "This says you're lying."

"What's that?" Angela frowned at the slip of paper that resembled a credit card receipt. It looked like the kind of tab she signed for a meal at the private club where she was a member.

"You tell me," Reilly said.

Her earlier foreboding turned to dread that settled heavily in her stomach, and her hands shook in spite of herself as she picked up the paper. It was indeed a tab for lunch at the First City Club the previous day, and it bore not only her signature but also her member number. Angela shook her head and said hollowly, "I didn't have lunch at the club yesterday. I didn't sign this."

"The hostess at the front desk and a slew of waiters and patrons say you did. Angela, don't lie to me. We have numerous witnesses who saw you there with J. J. Slade yesterday around one o'clock. They also said you had a big fight with him."

Angela blanched. "They saw me? But that's impossible." Pinpricks of light danced before her eyes. How could this be happening to her?

Reilly paused and eyed her with skepticism. Then he went on with his unbelievable tale. "We fished his body out of the river this afternoon, and the preliminary guesstimate is that he's been dead about twenty-four hours. You were likely the last person who saw him alive, and from eyewitness accounts of the fight between you and Slade, you made it pretty clear you'd like to see him dead and in hell."

The dread now invaded every cell of her body. "But I swear I didn't have lunch at the club. I wasn't even in Savannah."

"Where were you, then? An alibi would be helpful."

Angela hesitated, realizing her situation had just gotten worse.

"Where were you?" Reilly asked again impatiently.

She raised her head and looked him straight in the eye, as if bold posture would lend credence to what she was about to tell him. "I drove up to Beaufort to meet with a client."

"Can you prove it?"

Angela's pulse beat heavily at her neck, and perspiration simmered on her skin. "Well, not exactly," she admitted, silently cursing Callie Green for having missed their appointment. Angela explained how she'd driven to Beaufort, about an hour north of Savannah, for a two o'clock appointment with a woman who'd wanted to hire Angela's company to handle a large family reunion. "But she didn't show," Angela finished, wishing the truth didn't sound so lame.

"She didn't show . . ." Reilly's tone was just short of sarcastic.

"No, she didn't," Angela snapped, angry at his tone, angry at her vulnerability. "I called her today, and she claims the appointment wasn't until next week." She took a deep breath, trying to calm herself, but she realized how feeble her explanation must sound to Reilly.

Nonetheless, he wrote Callie Green's name down on his notepad. "Guess we can give her a call to verify that. But it still doesn't give you an alibi. Did you meet or see anyone else who could corroborate your story?"

Angela thought frantically and came up with nothing. She'd waited on the woman's veranda for nearly an hour, thinking maybe she'd written down the wrong time, but finally she'd given up. She hadn't gone into any restaurants in Beaufort or stopped for gas where someone might recognize her. She'd just driven straight back to Savannah, furious at having wasted a valuable afternoon.

Suddenly, Angela realized how precarious her position was. Maybe she *should* call a lawyer. Stunned and unable to find her voice, she managed only to give a miserable shake of her head in reply. This was a perfect wrap to the day from hell.

Actually, Angela thought grimly, she'd had two days from hell. Her run of disasters had started yesterday with that fruitless trip to Beaufort that had cost not only an afternoon, but apparently also a much-needed alibi. Then today, the tourism committee she headed had made an arduous pitch for a major convention in Savannah, but in the end had lost out to the city's rival, Charleston.

When she'd arrived back at her shop after that disappointment, she'd had a nasty run-in with Freddie Holloway, a newcomer to the tour business. Too cheap to buy his own advertising, he'd taken to parking his van in front of Angela's shop, giving her customers the impression that he was a driver for her company, Southern Hospitality Tours. He'd even had the audacity to paint the slogan, "THERE'S NOTHING LIKE SOUTHERN HOSPITALITY," on the side of his ratty old vehicle.

Angela had worked too hard to build her business to give even one customer up to the likes of Freddie Holloway.

After being seriously injured in a shootout that erupted during a drug bust gone bad five years ago, Angela had refused the desk job offered by the GBI and had instead embarked upon an entrepreneurial venture. Using some grant money and her love of Savannah's old southern charm, she'd started Southern Hospitality Tours. Although the work was a far cry from law enforcement, it was equally demanding, in some ways more so, for she had no one to count on but herself.

But her dedication and determination had paid off, and her company now boasted a fleet of six shiny, clean buses, two horse-drawn carriages, a souvenir shop, and a reputation for being the premier tour company in Savannah. Freddie Holloway was slime, and if she didn't find a way to stop his intrusion, he'd tarnish all she'd worked for.

But Freddie Holloway was the least of her worries at the moment. Reilly's voice broke into her thoughts.

"You own a gun?"

Angela gave him a withering look. "Of course I own a gun. I'm ex-GBI. I'll always own a gun. Right now, I have a .38 Smith and Wesson revolver in my nightstand drawer. That's where I keep it," she added dryly, "when I'm not out killing strangers."

Her humor was lost on Reilly, who hammered at her unmercifully for another hour, until she thought she was going to lose it. His reputation as a tough interrogater was well-earned, she decided with begrudging respect. She was so unnerved that she didn't hear the door open, and only turned toward it at the sound of an all-too-familiar voice.

"What's going on here, Reilly?"

Angela's heart lurched as a rugged, squarely built man burst into the room. Her eyes widened in disbelief, and then she bit her tongue to keep from swearing. Would the day from hell never end?

Dylan Montana had never seen Angela Donahue look so undone. She sat at the interrogation table, her arms resting on the edge of the tabletop, her hands clutched together. Her face was pale and drawn, her expression tense. Until she saw him. When she turned and discovered who'd come into the room, the tension turned to surprise, then to anger, and then to profound contempt. He'd been prepared for that look, but not for how much it would hurt.

Maybe he shouldn't have come. He'd known he wouldn't be welcomed by either her or Johnny Reilly. But with what he'd just learned, he couldn't *not* come.

Less than half an hour ago, he'd been checking the mooring lines of the weather-beaten motor yacht that he called home and was about to pop the top on a five o'clock beer when his phone rang. He'd expected it to be his boss, Oscar Malone, calling from Miami to brief him on his assignment in the covert DEA operation that had brought him to Savannah. He was anxious to hear from Malone, ready to get this over with and move on. There were too many old ghosts to haunt him in this town.

But the voice on the phone wasn't Malone's. Even after an absence of nearly five years, Dylan had recognized the unique gravelly growl of Scott Turner, a narc who'd been on the Chatham County Counter-Narcotics Team with him the night his world had come crashing down.

Dylan frowned. "Turner? How the hell'd you know I was in town?"

Turner gave a raspy laugh. "I'm not a rookie anymore. I have my sources."

Although he didn't think Turner had been a part of the deceit that had torn Dylan's life apart, Dylan didn't know if he could trust him, and it disturbed him that Turner had so easily located him.

"What do you want?" Dylan demanded. He wondered if Turner was still with the Savannah Police Department, an agency Dylan despised, even though Cecil Clifford, his former boss who'd been responsible for his disgraceful exit from the force, had been sent to prison a few years back.

"Thought you'd want to know Johnny Reilly's got Angela Donahue down here at headquarters," Turner replied, seemingly unruffled. "He's questioning her in a murder case."

"What?" Dylan was sure he hadn't heard right. "He's questioning Angela about a murder?" At the sound of her name, five years melted away, and he was thrust back into a nightmare he'd tried hard to forget. He'd thought he was over it, but he'd been wrong. Five years had not been long enough to erase his feelings for her. Or his guilt over what had happened. Eternity wouldn't be long enough, he supposed. He struggled unsuccessfully for detachment. "Who was killed?"

"A guy named J. J. Slade. Rich. Reclusive. Lived down around Sunhill on a plantation. So far, that's all I know about him. You ever heard of him?"

Slade.

Oh, shit.

Slade was one reason Dylan was in Savannah. He was a kingpin-wannabe who was trying to usurp the powerful drug lord, Lucas Quintos, who'd controlled the drug scene in the Southeast for years. The DEA hoped to take both Slade and Quintos out in the raid that was planned.

Dylan wasn't surprised that Slade had been killed. Lucas Quintos would abide no competition. But that Angela was being questioned in his murder raised red flags all over the place.

"Uh, no," he lied in answer to Turner's question. No one was supposed to know why he was in Savannah. They'd missed Quintos once. Dylan wasn't going to let it happen again by giving away secrets. "What's the real reason you called, Turner? What do you want?"

"Answers," Turner said. "I'm still in the drug-busting business around here, only I'm a little higher in the food chain now. Team leader. Let's just say I find it a little too coincidental that a few weeks after Cecil Clifford is released from prison, you come back to town, and then Johnny Reilly brings Angela Donahue in for questioning in a murder case. There're too many players from that old game board not to make me suspicious. I want to know what's going on."

"Clifford's out of jail? You're just full of good news. How'd that happen?"

"When the Internal Affairs investigation nosed out his

connections with Lucas Quintos, he cut a deal, ratted on his men, and got a short term. We're sure he's gone back to work for Quintos."

The rest of Dylan's conversation with the narc had been brief. He'd thanked Turner for the heads-up and promised him he'd try to find out what was going on and hung up, suddenly terrified for Angela. It didn't take a rocket scientist to figure out what was happening to her. Dylan had heard through the grapevine that Angela was the one who'd instigated the Internal Affairs investigation that had landed Clifford in jail. Clifford didn't forget his enemies, and Dylan figured he'd be out for revenge. Quintos wanted Slade dead and gave the job to Clifford, who'd done it in such a way that it looked like Angela was the killer. How he'd managed it, Dylan couldn't guess, but with Clifford, anything was possible.

The only question in his mind as he'd raced toward the police station was whether Johnny Reilly was on Clifford's payroll.

Reilly jumped from his chair at Dylan's unexpected intrusion and faced him warily, his hand resting on the butt of his gun in its holster.

"What're you doing here, Montana?"

Dylan stared at him for a moment. The policeman's face was lined, and streaks of gray shaded his dark hair. The last five years hadn't been good to him. "Turner called," Dylan replied. "Told me you had Angela in here about the Slade murder. I want to know why."

"Turner! That jackass. This is none of his business. Or yours. Get out."

"Not until I get some answers, Reilly. What have you got on her? Where's her lawyer? Have you Mirandized her?"

Dylan figured he only had a few minutes before Reilly threw his ass out. He was relying on the element of surprise to buy him some time and on his aggressive questioning to at least find out what Angela's situation was.

Reilly scowled at him. "She didn't want a lawyer. And I didn't Mirandize her because I'm not arresting her. She's doing this of her own free will."

"Then let her go. She's innocent. It was a professional hit, Reilly." In his eagerness to wrest Angela from Johnny Reilly, Dylan had blurted out his suspicions before he realized what he was doing. He'd just taken a big chance. If Reilly was a crooked cop, he was up to his eyebrows in Clifford's conspiracy, and now Dylan's life might be at risk as well as Angela's. But if Reilly wasn't crooked, maybe he'd at least listen to Dylan and get off Angela's case. It was a chance he had to take.

Reilly raised a brow. "And just how do you know that, Montana? You've been out of the business a long time."

Dylan clenched his jaw at the man's subtle reference to Dylan's forced resignation from the SPD years ago. "Not out of the business. Just out of here."

Reilly took his chair, turned it backward, and straddled it. His eyes never left Dylan's. "Well then, since you seem to know so much, why don't you tell me all about it?"

"Maybe you already know, Reilly." Again, the words slipped out before he could stop them, and Dylan cursed his quick tongue. He suspected that Reilly was part of the web of lies that was being wound around Angela, but he couldn't prove it, and it was dangerous to even imply it.

But the lawman paid no apparent attention to Dylan's insinuation. "I don't know enough yet about Slade to know if he had the kind of enemies you're talking about. But if it was a professional job, as you say, then Ms. Donahue has nothing to fear. So why does she keep insisting she didn't know Slade, when I have evidence to the contrary? If she has nothing to hide, then why is she lying?"

Chapter 2

You came t' Dr. Lizard t' work some magic for you? You bring money? Okay, then. Let's see here, I have something in my conjure bag that's sure t' fool th' eye . . .

ANGELA bolted from her chair, livid at both men. "I'm not lying! I *didn't* know him!" she yelled. "And I wish the two of you would quit talking about me like I wasn't even here. I didn't know J. J. Slade, I didn't have lunch at the First City Club yesterday, and I didn't kill him."

Dylan turned to her, and the concern in his eyes nearly unhinged her. She clenched her hands into fists. He had no right to be concerned about her. In fact, he had no right to be here. She didn't need his concern, or his interference. This was nothing but a monumental mistake. She had nothing to worry about.

"You sure you don't want a lawyer?" Dylan asked.

"I don't want a lawyer and I don't want you. Now get out."

But Dylan returned his attention to Reilly as if he hadn't heard her. "What makes you think she's lying?"

"I'll make you a deal, Montana," Reilly said impatiently. "I'll answer your question if you tell me why you believe it was a professional hit."

Because he was sworn to secrecy and because he didn't trust Reilly, Dylan had no intention of telling him anything more than he already had, but he took the offer anyway. "You go first. Why do you think she's lying?"

Reilly pushed some papers across the table to Dylan.

"These," he said. "Read them for yourself. They're depositions taken from people who swear they saw Angela at lunch with Slade yesterday at the First City Club."

"They're the ones who're lying," Angela protested.

"Maybe so, but I find it curious to have so many liars under one roof," Reilly shot back. He shoved another paper in Dylan's direction. "But this doesn't lie. It's the member tab Angela signed in advance for lunch before Slade arrived."

Dylan examined the signature on the tab, then looked up at Angela. "Is this yours?"

Angela's knees felt suddenly weak, and she sank into her chair once again, miserable and confused. "No. I didn't sign that, but it's a damned good forgery, and whoever did it somehow managed to come up with my member number as well."

The three were silent for a long moment, then Dylan said, "I believe *somebody* has gone to great lengths to set you up." He carved out the statement slowly, delivering the word "somebody" with deliberate emphasis. She looked up and saw that Dylan had made the statement to Reilly, not her. Was he accusing Reilly of a set-up?

Set-up. The words echoed in her ears. She'd thought this was all a mistake. She hadn't considered that someone had deliberately done this to her. She looked at Reilly, wondering if he'd gotten Dylan's insinuation. He had.

"Exactly what're you implying, Montana?"

Angela heard Reilly's anger. She had to get Dylan out of here. He was only making things worse. But it was too late.

Dylan leaned against the tabletop, jutting his face directly into Reilly's. Dear God, why was he being so confrontational? Angela thought, her panic mounting. Damn him. Hadn't he done enough damage in her life?

"I'm not implying anything," Dylan answered Reilly. "I'm stating it. I believe somebody's setting her up. Look,

Reilly, you've known Angela a long time. You've worked with her, you know what kind of person she is. She doesn't lie, and she doesn't kill. This," he said, raising a handful of the incriminating paperwork, "doesn't make any sense, unless it's a set-up."

Reilly tipped his chair back on two legs to put some space between him and Dylan's determination.

"I agree that none of this makes much sense. But I had to follow up on those depositions." He banged the chair back onto the floor and was suddenly in Dylan's face. "And I still say it's damned interesting that all those people would come up with the same lie. You think she's being set up? You think somebody paid all those people off? C'mon, Montana. Get real. Now, it's your turn. What do you know?"

"I told you, it was a professional hit." Dylan didn't move an inch. "And I believe Angela has an enemy in high places with the power to do exactly that—pay off people to incriminate her."

"You 'believe'? Don't you know?"

"I know. But when you're in the business I'm in, there are things you can't say. You know that. Just trust me, this is not Angela's doing. Slade was part of something much bigger."

Reilly gave him a derisive smile. "Trust you? Why should I trust you, Montana?"

His words had their intended effect, and Angela saw the fury on Dylan's face. She thought for a moment he might punch Reilly out for opening an old and obviously painful wound. But Reilly had a valid point. Why should anyone trust Dylan Montana after what'd happened that night? People had died because he hadn't been where he was supposed to be to make the buy in the drug bust. She'd been shot, and then when she'd needed him most, he'd left. Deserted her. She hadn't seen him for nearly five years, until he'd come barging into the interrogation room a short while ago. She didn't want him here, hadn't asked for his help. Still, a part of her felt sorry and embarrassed for him.

"Okay, don't trust me, then," Dylan said, clenching the muscles in his jaw. He backed away and stood up, folding his arms across his chest. "But tell me her motive."

Reilly's eyes became slits. The two men were back at it, fighting over her as if she weren't there. "Angela's become quite a crusader against drugs in this city since you've been gone," Reilly said. "I can only infer from your mysterious secrecy that Slade was into the drug scene. Who knows? Maybe she lost her head and popped him."

"You're the one who's lost your head!" Angela cried, thoroughly disgusted with Reilly's inane supposition.

Dylan rested a hand on her shoulder, and its warmth comforted her whether she wanted it to or not. "Take it easy," he said, surprising her. He'd been the one doing a lot of the yelling. "We're just starting to get somewhere."

She couldn't see that they were getting anywhere, except maybe closer to securing her a room in the Chatham County Jail. But she didn't argue.

When Dylan spoke again, his voice was low, even, soothing almost. Angela wondered if he'd become a lawyer during the years he'd been gone. He seemed to be manipulating Sergeant Reilly masterfully.

"I don't know how the alleged argument at the First City Club fits into the picture," Dylan said, "but this has to be a case of mistaken identity. That wasn't Angela at the First City Club. It was somebody who looks like her."

"And who just happens to have the same handwriting?" Reilly added dryly. But he turned to Angela with a look of curiosity, and she was encouraged that Dylan seemed to have managed to get him to consider the possibility that someone had purposely impersonated her. "Do you have any relatives in the area, a cousin maybe, who looks like you?"

Angela shook her head. "I don't have any relatives at

all that I know of, except my mother." And then she remembered her mother's call. She looked at her watch. "Oh, damn."

"What's the matter?" Dylan asked.

"Mom called earlier. Said she was real sick. I . . . I was supposed to go by her house and check on her."

Dylan frowed at the mention of her mother, and she guessed that the old enmity between the two people she'd once cared for most in the world was alive and well. Well, screw him. If she'd listened to her mother's warnings about getting involved with him all those years ago, she wouldn't have gotten hurt. Physically or emotionally.

Dylan turned to Reilly. "You don't have enough on her to arrest her," he said. "Let her go for now. Do your homework. Find the real killer. I'll help if I can."

Reilly eyed Dylan for a long moment, and Angela supposed Dylan had pissed the cop off again. Oh, great. She wondered if the jail cells had fleas. She sat very still, holding her breath, praying that Reilly would be reasonable. But before he could answer, a deputy hurried into the room.

"This just came over from security at the bank," he said, handing Reilly a videocassette. "It's a dub of their original. The guy said it's queued to the time you requested."

"Thanks," Reilly said. When the deputy left, he turned to Angela. "I'm going to let you go for now, but first, we're all going to take a look at this. It's a copy of the surveillance tape recorded at the bank yesterday afternoon. One of their cameras is mounted above the front door and is pointed at the elevator. Anyone coming or going to the First City Club should be on here, unless"—he paused—"you took the fire stairs."

Angela glanced at Dylan and then at Reilly. "I didn't take the fire stairs, Reilly, because I wasn't there. And you're about to prove it."

She watched as the tape rolled and saw people going in and out of the busy bank building. They were mostly professional men and women, hurrying about their business. She thought she recognized a couple of her friends. She breathed a little easier. Reilly would soon know just how off base he was.

Then the image of a familiar-looking woman caught her eye. She entered the bank and went quickly to the elevator, where she turned, her face fully toward the camera and clearly identifiable. Angela covered her mouth with the back of her hand, staring at the screen in horror and disbelief.

The woman on the videotape was her.

Chapter 3

Here, child, drink this an' ease your mind. Some evil be too dark t' look at . . .

VERONICA Slade awoke in the dark. She lay very still on the bed, trying to remember where she was.

She attempted to sit up, but her head hurt, so she lay back against the pillows. The room was warm, the air permeated with a cloying scent. Gardenias. The aroma brought her instantly to her senses.

She was at Marguerite's. It always smelled of gardenias at Marguerite's. She closed her eyes and rubbed her temples. Okay, so she knew where she was. But how did she get here? How long had she been here? What time was it? What day, for that matter? She lay still, listening to the wind blowing fiercely through the eaves, listening to her heartbeat, trying to remember.

Nothing.

After a few minutes, she managed to push herself off the bed and stumbled, naked, into the tiny bath that adjoined the room she considered hers. She didn't live here, of course, but she'd spent many a night at Marguerite's shambling old Victorian house that stood at the far perimeter of Paradisia Plantation, where the piney woodlands sloped down into treacherous marshes.

She ran cold water from the tap and splashed it on her face, then looked in the mirror and scared herself.

Her hair hung like a dark brown mop that did not quite reach her shoulders. Her bangs were pasted to her wet forehead, and dark circles bruised the skin beneath her eyes.

Her face was mottled with unattractive blotches.

Veronica leaned over the sink and threw up. Then she sat on the toilet, her body shaking as memory began to seep back.

It had started with the file she'd found several weeks ago in her father's desk when she'd broken into it searching for money. A file containing photos of a girl who looked just like her, but with pretty golden curls instead of plain, straight dark hair. There were clippings of events in this girl's life as she was growing up.

Angela Donahue, tennis champion.

Angela Donahue, valedictorian.

Angela Donahue, Phi Beta Kappa.

And stories of her as an adult, lots of clippings dated about five years ago, when this golden girl, who'd been an agent for the Georgia Bureau of Investigation, had nearly been killed in the line of duty. But of course, she'd emerged a heroine.

Veronica swallowed over the sour taste in her mouth.

Angela Donahue.

Veronica had discovered her father's secret bastard daughter.

A knot of rage tightened in her belly at the thought that her father had cared enough about this other girl to keep those mementoes. The father who'd never cared for Veronica at all, who in fact had made it frequently clear he wished she'd never been born.

"Damn him," she cursed into the darkness, blocking whatever other memories might be waiting to torment her. "Damn him to hell."

She forced herself to stand and go into the shower, wanting to wash it all away. When she was finished, she went into the bedroom and flicked on a small lamp. Her watch and earrings lay on the bureau. Her clothes were strewn across the room. Silk blouse. Conservative skirt. Navy jacket. Pantyhose. Heels.

No. Not her clothes. Her costume. Seeing them released more memories.

She recalled meeting her father for lunch at the First City Club. Even though the luncheon had been part of the plan to do away with him, Veronica had also wanted to shock him and hurt him by dressing to look like his other, favored, daughter, the daughter he thought she didn't know about. But things had backfired, and she'd been unprepared for the horrible words he'd said to her. The humiliation of his scorn.

Damn him.

She remembered going to pieces, screaming at him, calling him every vile name she could think of and wishing him dead and in hell, then running out of the private club. That performance, too, had been part of the plan. She just hadn't known the scene would be so real. Or hurt so much.

Veronica frowned, working to remember what had happened after that. Had she gone through with the rest of the plan? Had she killed the son of a bitch? But her mind seemed to have closed up. Try as she might, she had no recollection of anything except her father's blistering, degrading abuse and her desperate need to escape it.

She picked up the watch. Eight-fifteen. Her eyes wouldn't focus enough to read the date. She wondered again how long she'd been here. She went to the closet where she kept a few extra clothes and slipped into something she found more to her taste—tight-fitting black pants topped with a sweater that clung to her curves. High-heeled come-fuck-me shoes. Ronnie's clothes, not Veronica's. Clothes her father hated as much as he hated her nickname.

She smiled feebly at her image in the mirror and felt a little better.

Her stomach grumbled, and Ronnie realized she was ravenous. She couldn't remember the last time she'd eaten. Certainly it hadn't been at lunch. Opening the door to her room, she stuck her nose into the hallway. A delicious aroma wafted past her, making her stomach growl again. She hurried down the stairs and toward the enormous old-fashioned kitchen at the back of the house. At any hour, Ronnie and the others who visited Marguerite's place could count on finding something good to eat in the kitchen. Gloria, the short, round woman with glistening black skin who cooked for Marguerite, seemingly never slept. This evening, she stood at the stove frying a skillet full of large shrimp. Veronica's mouth watered.

Marguerite Domingo sat across the room in a high-backed rattan chair by the fireplace, looking like some kind of exotic queen. Ronnie grimaced slightly when she saw the woman's pet iguana hunkered down on the hearth next to her. Ronnie found the lizard a disgusting creature, but Marguerite seemed quite fond of it. This room was Marguerite's personal kingdom, and no one dared criticize anything about it, including her choice of pets. As was her custom, Marguerite wore an expensive caftan of brightly colored silk. Enormous beaded earrings shimmered against her shoulders. Her hair was covered with a white turban sprinkled with glittering silver stars, which added height and elegance to her demeanor. Her face was serene and relaxed, her skin smooth and unlined. Ronnie had no idea how old she was. Nor was she ever quite certain what was going on behind her eerie blue eyes.

She had first met Marguerite Domingo when she was a child and had run away from Paradisia during one of her parents' vicious arguments. Later as a teenager, when she'd been thrown out of boarding school for smoking pot and had ended up once again at Paradisia, Ronnie had quickly learned that Marguerite's house at this far corner of the marshlands was a haven from a hostile world, a world that had no love in it for her. Her visits here had become her closely held secret.

Although Marguerite had light skin and haunting blue eyes, she claimed her ancestors had been among the first to arrive on the Georgia coast aboard the slave ships from Africa over two centuries before. She was white, from generations of dilution of her family's blood by white slave owners, sometimes by rape, occasionally by her ancestors' consent. But she was black as well, and her life was a strange mix of the two cultures. Maybe that was why it didn't seem strange to Ronnie that Marguerite Domingo's house seemed to be a crossroads to people of all breeds and creeds.

Ronnie had been warned never to question Marguerite about the melange of people who dropped in from time to time. They were old and young, black and white and in between, mostly the misfits of the world. Like herself. Although some of them knew one another, most kept to themselves, conducted their private business with Marguerite, maybe had a meal, spent a night, and moved on. Ronnie was no more inclined to ask what their business might be than she was to reveal her own business with Marguerite.

It was enough that, as she did with them all, Marguerite accepted Ronnie without question. She'd been there for her when no one else wanted her, giving her comfort and taking away her pain. She was like the mother Ronnie longed for, a friend she could trust who wouldn't belittle and criticize her. Marguerite wasn't exactly warm and fuzzy, but she'd never let Ronnie down. Not all of Marguerite's favors were free. There had been some paybacks along the way, but the exchange had been worth it.

Ronnie would do anything for Marguerite Domingo.

"Evenin', Ronnie." Marguerite's enigmatic gaze met Ronnie's, sending a little chill down her back. "You sleep well?"

Ronnie smiled at her uncertainly and nodded. Although she wasn't sure how she'd gotten into bed, she *had* slept well. Probably as a result of one of Marguerite's famous potions. Her herbal brews were strong and effective. Ronnie knew from experience that they could induce an abortion, put one to sleep, make one forget. Maybe that's why Ronnie's memory was clouded at the moment. Marguerite's "magic" was powerful. "How long . . . ?"

"Since this time yesterday. You were in such a state when you got here, I gave you a little somethin' extra." Marguerite's expression shifted from serene to troubled. "Come to me. Are you sure you're all right?"

Apprehensive now, Ronnie crossed the room and took Marguerite's extended hand. "I'll . . . be fine," she said, then cleared her throat. What kind of a state had she been in? She was suddenly desperate to remember what she'd done the previous afternoon.

"You don't have to talk about it if you don't want to. I know what happened," Marguerite said quietly. "I just want to know if you are okay with it now?"

Ronnie's misgivings deepened. "Okay with what?" What had she done? Had she killed her father?

Marguerite eyed her for a long moment. "You don't remember . . . ?"

Ronnie withdrew her hand and rubbed her fingers. They were cold as ice. "Remember what?"

Ronnie had wanted J. J. Slade dead and had participated in an intricate plan to murder him that would throw the blame on the bastard daughter. But Ronnie had balked at doing the actual killing. She hated the sight of blood. Was that why she couldn't remember what had happened? Had she gone through with it after all? Suddenly, the thought made her almost physically ill.

Marguerite didn't reply directly. Instead, she reached for the remote control of the large television that took up one corner of the spacious room where she spent most of her hours. She clicked on the VCR and looked at Ronnie. "I taped a segment of the evening news broadcast. I thought it would . . . interest you."

Ronnie watched as the newscaster began her lead story: "The body of reclusive millionaire J. J. Slade was found earlier today in the shallows of the Wilmington River, just south of Thunderbolt. He apparently died of a gunshot wound." A photo of Ronnie's father filled the screen as the announcer droned on. "Police say they have no suspects in the case at the moment, although they are following several leads. Slade was a resident of Paradisia Plantation in Liberty County." The camera returned to the newscaster. "Tune in to the eleven o'clock news for the latest developments in this unfolding story. In other news . . ."

Ronnie's heart nearly stopped beating. "Play that again."

Marguerite obliged. Ronnie watched with growing alarm as the announcer's words sunk in. Her father was dead. He'd been murdered. She turned to the older woman. "Do you think they'll find out who killed him?"

The exotically dressed woman measured her with a guarded look. "Probably. Where were you yesterday afternoon, Ronnie?"

"I . . . I don't know. I can't remember." Alarm turned to panic. What if she'd killed him, but the plan hadn't worked? What if the police came after her? "I met him for lunch, but it . . . didn't go well, and I left. That's all I can remember."

"You don't recall comin' in here late yesterday cryin' and screamin' that you hoped your father was in hell?"

Ronnie shivered. "N-no." she murmured. "I don't remember anything."

Marguerite paused, then smiled and said in a soothing voice, "Why, that's good, child. That's real good."

Chapter 4

Some come t' Dr. Lizard t' cure th' ailing body, and for them I can give a potion an' chew a root. But curing th' sickness of th' soul, now that be another matter . . .

ANGELA was still in a state of shock as she and Dylan made their way along the corridors toward the front door of the police station. She was unaware if anyone was staring at her now. She didn't care. All she could see was the image of her face on that videotape.

She'd been too stunned to speak or try to defend herself when Reilly had frozen the frame for them all to study. It couldn't be her, but there she was. Navy suit, sensible shoes and all. Whoever had impersonated her had paid a great deal of attention to detail. The thought that someone had been watching her, observing her actions and manner of dress in order to copy them so exactly horrified her.

Despite this new evidence, Dylan had managed to get Reilly to release her as promised, but the homicide investigator had done so begrudgingly and had given her a terse warning not to leave town. He also exacted a promise that she would bring her gun to him in the morning.

Angela was grateful that Dylan had managed to spring her, at least for the time being. But her gratitude ended there. She didn't know why he'd come to her rescue, but she wanted nothing further to do with him.

It had been five years since he'd walked out on her, betraying her in every way imaginable. She'd thought she'd never see him again. Didn't want to see him again. But after recovering from her initial shock, she was dismayed to recognize that he still managed to pull her heartstrings. And that frightened her as much as Reilly's suspicions.

She didn't know much about Dylan Montana anymore. With his shoulder-length brown hair and faded jeans and T-shirt, he still looked like a scruffy street dealer, and she guessed from what he'd told Reilly that he'd remained in the undercover business. Looking down at her own conservative clothing, she realized how far apart their worlds had spun. She'd heard he was freelancing. Living on a boat. Being the rogue she knew he was.

Angela had no room in her life anymore for a rogue.

As many questions as assailed her about him, about why he'd left her, about why he'd come back, she told herself she didn't want to know the answers. All she wanted was to put distance between them, fast.

Dylan seemed to have fast on the mind, too, as with a hand at her elbow he propelled her swiftly down the hallway, away from Reilly's office. She was glad to get out of there, but she refused to run. She wasn't guilty. "Slow down," she said, pulling her arm from his grasp. She stepped away from him, glaring at him, struggling to control her conflicted emotions.

"I appreciate that you helped me, Dylan," she said, breathless from the near-sprint down the hall and her own runaway heartbeat. "But I can manage my own life. Please, leave me alone."

His expression remained impassive. "You have no idea what you're involved in, Angela."

"And you do?" She bristled at his tone.

"Part of it."

"But you can't tell me," she replied bitterly. "I'm no longer an insider." She turned her back on him and strode to the front door. A sharp pain shot through her knee, as if to remind her of one more reason to get away from Dylan Montana. Damp weather always aggravated the old gunshot wound she'd suffered the night Dylan had betrayed them all.

Outside, a cold October rain pelted the streets. She swore under her breath at yet one more downturn in the day. Wrapping her light jacket around her, she started down the steps, but Dylan caught her arm.

"Let me take you home."

"No." She jerked away. Dylan Montana would never take her home—or anywhere else—again. "My car's in the lot. Goodbye, Dylan."

She dug her keys out of her purse, then turned and dashed through the rain toward her car, not giving him a backward glance, although her pulse was racing. She unlocked the mid-sized Honda and jumped in, slamming the door against the drenching downpour.

Cursing the rain and Dylan Montana and her own still-vulnerable emotions, Angela turned the key. A weak buzzing sound faded to nothingness as the battery was drained of its last drop of energy. Damn. She'd been so unnerved when she'd followed Reilly here, she must have left her lights on. She tried the ignition again, but all she got this time was a slight clicking noise.

She jumped at the sound of a knock on her window and turned to see Dylan standing bareheaded in the rain. She cracked the window just enough to shout out to him. "Go away."

"I'll take you to your mother's."

Those were the last words Angela would have expected to hear issue from Dylan's mouth. He hated her mother as much as Mary Ellen hated him. He'd always believed, maybe rightfully so, that Mary Ellen had done everything she could to sabotage the relationship that had sprung up between him and Angela. Mary Ellen, on the other hand, had been convinced that Dylan, like most men, was no good, certainly not good enough for her daughter, and had told Angela so at every opportunity. Angela had often felt like a rag doll being pulled apart by those who claimed to love her most.

"I don't think so," she replied. "I'll get one of my friends at the station to take me."

"Who? Reilly?"

He was right, Angela realized with dismay. She had no friends on the SPD. Dylan stood motionless, his face dripping, his hair soaked, his dark eyes never leaving hers, and to her consternation, a jolt of attraction tightened her stomach. Damn him. "Oh, all right," she said crossly, getting out of her car, knowing she was making a colossal mistake.

He opened the passenger door of a beat-up old Camaro parked nearby, and she slipped inside. Dylan had driven rust-buckets the entire time she'd known him. It was part of the image. It came with the job, and he was apparently still at it. Things may not have changed in his life, but they had drastically changed in hers. She had no desire to go back to the world of darkness and violence that she'd once thought she could fix as a law enforcement officer. She was crusading in a different way now.

Lightning lit up the sky as he got into the car, outlining the strong features of the face she'd once loved more than life itself. When he'd left without so much as saying goodbye, she'd wanted to die, because the physical pain from the gunshot wounds that had torn through her body was nothing compared to the emotional agony that had ravaged her heart.

Suddenly, anger surged through her again, and she found she did want answers. She wanted an explanation for what he'd done. She deserved to know the reason why he'd deserted her then, and why he'd come back now. But she bit her lip and straightened her spine. She'd be damned if she'd give him the satisfaction of letting him know how much she'd cared, or how badly he'd hurt her.

Or that her heart felt as if it were bleeding even now.

They rode in silence to a quiet suburban neighborhood

of houses that had been built in the fifties. As they pulled into the driveway, she inhaled a deep breath, summoning control, damping her fury. "Thanks for the lift. I'll take Mom's car and pick mine up in the morning. It should be safe for the night at headquarters." She knew she was babbling.

He didn't say a word, but switched off the engine, got out, and came around to open her door. Startled, she looked up at him, then frowned. She didn't want him to be nice to her. "You didn't need to do that." He just shrugged.

She got out and headed up the sidewalk, and to her horror, he followed. She wheeled around. "You can't come in here. Mom would freak."

"I'm not leaving you alone until we have a chance to talk. I can't tell you everything, but I can tell you enough to let you know what you're dealing with."

His words disturbed her, in more ways than one. Angela was alarmed by the tacit warning in his voice. But it also perturbed her that she was disappointed his interest in her seemed to be purely professional. "Oh," was all she said. She started to suggest that he wait in the car, but he was soaked and shivering, and he had, after all, come to her rescue.

Against her better judgment, she added, "Okay, you can come in. But stay in the living room, and if you see Mom, for God's sake don't mention anything about all this to her. You . . . well, you know how she is. I'm sure Reilly will find out who's impersonating me, and this will all blow over. There's no reason for Mom to know what's going on, now or ever, unless the papers get hold of it. Let's hope it doesn't come to that."

Mary Ellen Donahue lived in the house she'd bought almost thirty years before with the life insurance money she'd received when her husband, Jake Donahue, Angela's father, was killed in an automobile accident. Angela had been only five at the time, so she'd grown up here. It was a small, brick bungalow with green shutters and white trim, modest but neat. Mary Ellen's prized roses swayed in the wind as Angela and Dylan went up the stoop and onto the concrete front porch.

Angela used her key, but before opening the door, she knocked loudly. "Mom, it's me. Angela," she called, not wanting to alarm her mother.

Inside the small entry hall, she could see a light on in the kitchen at the back, but otherwise, the house was dark. "Mom?" Angela called again, softer this time. She heard a low moan from the bedroom. Motioning for Dylan to step into the living room, she tiptoed down the hall and around the corner to Mary Ellen's bedroom.

"Mom?"

"I'm all right, honey." Her mother's room was in semi-darkness, illumined only by the faint light that made its way from the kitchen. Angela knew at once she wasn't all right and felt guilty it'd taken her so long to get here.

"Oh, Mom, I'm so sorry I'm late. Why didn't you tell me you were this sick?" Angela's eyes adjusted to the dark, and she made her way across the room and sat on the edge of her mother's bed. She laid her hand on Mary Ellen's hot forehead. "How're you feeling? Maybe we should take you to the hospital."

"No." Her mother's reply was barely audible. "No hospital. I'll be fine. Just a touch of the flu." She reached for a tissue and wiped her eyes, then blew her nose. "There, that's better." She laid her head back and gave Angela a faint smile. "Don't worry about me. I'll be fine," she said again.

Angela recognized her mother's "martyr mode." Mary Ellen Donahue loved her daughter, but she was a master at making Angela feel guilty. Being "just fine" was her way of rebuking Angela for not having come sooner. Sometimes her manipulation angered Angela, but not tonight. Mary

Ellen Donahue was ill, and Angela *should* have come sooner. She silently cursed Johnny Reilly.

"I'm going to fix you that chicken soup I promised," Angela said, rising. "Have you taken any medication? Aspirin? Tylenol?"

"No. I don't want soup, or anything. I . . . my stomach feels queasy . . ."

"You stay quiet. Let me bring you a little soup. Maybe it'll settle your stomach."

Angela went into the living room where Dylan stood looking out of the window, his hands in the pockets of his jeans. Her heart skipped a beat as her gaze took in the square cut of his shoulders, the muscular arms that had always made her feel so secure. She frowned and reined in her fickle emotions. Those arms had held false security, she reminded herself. If she couldn't keep that in mind, then she'd better send him on his way before she made a royal fool of herself.

"Mom's pretty bad," she told him. "I'm going to make her some soup. You go on. We can talk later."

Dylan turned, and the fierce look on his face frightened her. Something was terribly wrong. "I'll wait," he said, and from his tone, she knew there was no use arguing with him. "Need some help?" he added.

Angela shook her head, her earlier dread spreading through her again. What did he know? "It's just a matter of opening a can. I won't be long. Make yourself at home."

"Yeah," he said with a short, mocking laugh. "Right."

Angela realized Dylan would never make himself at home at her mother's house. Nor would Mary Ellen want him to. In fact, she'd have a fit if she knew he was here right now.

Hurrying into the kitchen, Angela tried not to think about the animosity between Dylan and her mother. Or about the grim expression on Dylan's face, or about Johnny

Reilly's suspicion that she'd committed a murder. It was all too much.

Instead, she focused on the chore at hand. Doing something normal, like making chicken soup, grounded her in a world that had suddenly become shaky and uncertain.

As she busied herself warming the soup, Angela's thoughts turned again to the face on the videotape and the signature on the restaurant tab. Was she losing her mind? Could that have been her? She knew better, but it made as much sense as anything else.

Angela hoped that Reilly would get to the bottom of the mystery before her mother found out about it. Angela was afraid it might trigger one of her bad "spells."

Growing up with Mary Ellen hadn't been easy, although her mother had worked hard to give Angela a good life. Mary Ellen, however, bitterly resented the fate life had handed her and often expressed that resentment in fits of temper. Angela had been the prime target of her mother's anger, and she'd learned early on how to placate her so as to avoid the "spells." When she was grown and in a psychology course in college, Angela had decided that being raised by Mary Ellen had been rather like being the child of an alcoholic parent. She'd learned to read her mother's moods and tiptoe around them.

She was, it seemed, still tiptoeing after all these years.

Angela brought a small cup of soup to Mary Ellen, who managed to sit up and take a few sips before pushing it away. "Thanks, Angela, but now I want you to go home. I'm okay, and I don't want you to catch whatever this is."

Angela tried to protest, but Mary Ellen insisted. "I need rest, that's all, and I won't rest if you're here fussing over me. Now go."

Angela knew better than to argue. Mary Ellen Donahue could be the most stubborn woman on the planet. She brought her mother's portable phone to the bedside, watched her take something to reduce the fever, and made her promise to call if she needed anything at all. "I can be here in under ten minutes." Then she kissed her mother on the cheek and went into the living room, enormously relieved that Dylan's presence had gone undetected.

She was surprised to see him studying a framed black-and-white photograph he'd taken from the top of Mary Ellen's entertainment center. "What are you doing?" she asked sharply. Angela didn't particularly want him snooping around her mother's photos, as most of them were of Angela in various stages of growing up. Dylan had long ago forfeited any right to such intimacy.

"Just killing time," Dylan said. "Is this your dad?"

Angela was in no mood to reopen that old story, and she was anxious to leave. "Yeah. I don't know why she keeps that picture around. She's looked at it every day for thirty years, as if she could will him back to life. Come on. Let's go."

But Dylan seemed fascinated with the image. "He was a handsome man. I see a lot of him in you," he said, raising his gaze from the photo to her face.

Angela was about to order Dylan to return the photo to the shelf when she heard a slight noise behind her. She whirled around and swore under her breath.

Mary Ellen Donahue stood in the doorway, and it seemed to Angela as if she radiated wrath from every pore. She clenched her fists and waved one at Dylan. "What the hell's he doing here?"

Chapter 5

There be lovers needing a cure for that old hex. Here, sprinkle this "Follow Me" powder under her porch steps. This love charm never fails.

OUT of the corner of his eyes, Dylan caught sight of Mary Ellen Donahue as she shuffled into the living room, and he regretted they hadn't left immediately. Angela's mother didn't appear to have changed much since he'd been gone. She was now in her mid-fifties, he guessed, and he remembered her as an attractive, if slightly plump, matron. Angela had told him once that Mary Ellen was proud that she'd managed to get a degree in accounting after Jake Donahue's death, and that she'd worked hard to attain her present status—vice president of one of Savannah's leading banks. In her field, image was important. That's why Dylan knew she must be sick.

Mary Ellen stood before them in a ratty old robe, her hair askew and her face pale without makeup. Her eyes were wild, red-rimmed, and livid.

"What the hell's *he* doing here?" Her gaze was riveted on Dylan but her question was directed to Angela. Dylan clenched his jaws. Nope. Nothing about the old biddy had changed.

"Mom, you shouldn't be out of bed." Angela rushed to Mary Ellen, but the older woman resisted her.

Mary Ellen took another step toward Dylan. "Keep your hands off my things," she barked, indicating the photograph.

"Mom!" Angela exclaimed. "Don't be rude."

"It's okay, Angela," Dylan said, replacing the photo on the shelf. "I certainly wouldn't want to do anything to upset your mother, her being so sick and all."

Mary Ellen glared at him. If thoughts were daggers, Dylan knew he'd be a dead man.

Then Mary Ellen turned her angry look on her daughter. "What's this all about? You're not going back to him, are you?"

Dylan saw bright red spots appear on Angela's cheeks. "My battery was dead. He offered me a ride over. That's all, Mom," Angela replied in clipped tones. "Now, go back to bed. Do you want more soup?"

"I want you to stay away from him. You know what happened last time. I'm warning you . . ."

"Let's go, Angela," Dylan broke in, furious at this woman's domineering attitude toward her daughter. He turned to Mary Ellen, and unable to help himself, added, "I wouldn't want to keep you from your deathbed."

"Get out of my house."

"My pleasure. C'mon, Angela."

Angela looked from him to her mother and back, vacillating, clearly ambivalent, then took the familiar path. "Maybe it'd be better if I stay here for a while. I'll take Mom's car home."

Dylan had had enough of Mary Ellen Donahue's manipulation, and he wasn't going to let her jeopardize what might be his only chance to warn Angela of the danger that surrounded her. "We have to talk," he said emphatically to Angela. "I'm not leaving until we do." He gave Mary Ellen a challenging look, then shifted his attention back to Angela. "In private, unless you want to—"

Darting him a warning look, Angela touched her mother's shoulders and steered her toward the bedroom.

"Go back to bed, Mom. Call if you need me. You have my cellular number. It makes more sense for Dylan to take me to get my car. Otherwise we'd have to figure how to get yours back, and with you so ill . . ."

Mary Ellen glowered over her shoulder at Dylan, and he saw the rage on her face that he'd succeeded in getting her daughter to defy her. Not giving Angela time to change her mind, he took her elbow and headed for the front door.

"Good night, Mrs. Donahue," he called as they left. "I hope you feel better tomorrow."

Angela locked the door behind her and walked in stony silence to the Camaro. She said nothing as Dylan maneuvered his way back into the heart of historic Savannah, and he knew he was in deep shit. He shouldn't have taunted Mary Ellen, but damned if that woman didn't bring out the worst in him.

But Dylan had other more important things to talk to Angela about than her mother. "Angela, listen, I need to tell you—"

"Shut up, Dylan. You've caused enough trouble."

"But you need to know . . ."

Angela turned to him with fire in her eyes. "Just take me to my car. I'll find somebody to jump the battery for me."

Dylan bit back his reply, aware that his own fury at her stubbornness was about to get him into even more trouble. They were both too angry to talk at the moment, but he wasn't going to let her go until she clearly understood the danger she was in.

By the time they reached police headquarters, the rain had ceased, at least for the moment, although thunder rumbled in the darkness. The parking space directly in front of Angela's car was empty. "I have cables," he said, pulling into the slot and popping the hood before she could object. She got out and went to her car. Moments later, the Honda was running. He went to the driver's side and knocked on the window, as he'd done before.

"I'll follow you home," he said.

"No." Her voice was tight.

"Look, Angela, I'm sorry, okay?"

Silence. Then, thinly, she said, "Leave me alone, Dylan."

"No. I won't leave you alone. I need to talk to you."

"Goodbye, Dylan." She put the car in reverse and backed out of the parking space with a jerk.

He followed her anyway. Angela lived in a large old Victorian home in the heart of what was politely termed an "emerging" neighborhood, where houses like hers, bought cheap and lovingly restored, stood elbow to elbow with others that remained derelict. Drugs, and the crimes related to them, were no strangers to these streets.

He parked his car behind hers and walked briskly to catch up with her before she got to the front door. He must warn her about her predicament, but also he wanted to apologize. He wanted to say something that would make her forgive him. For everything. But he couldn't imagine what that would be, for his crimes were enormous, and he wasn't that good with words.

The thunder grew louder, announcing the approach of another line of storms. On the porch, she didn't speak to him, acted as if he weren't there. She fumbled to unlock the door and dropped her keys. He bent to retrieve them, then stood again and took her hands in his, gently closing her fingers around the keys. Touching her again after all this time sent what felt like an electric shock through his entire body. God help him, he wanted more than just to hold her hand. He placed a finger beneath her chin and raised her face to his. Only then, in the light of the porch lamp, did he see she was crying.

"Oh, God, Angela, I'm so sorry. I never meant for things to turn out like this."

A tear eased from behind her closed eyelashes and trickled down her cheek. She didn't speak. He brushed the tear away with a rough knuckle, then buried the fingers of one hand in her tawny hair. He lowered his face, drawing hers closer. And then he kissed her. Not a tentative, apologetic kiss, but a deep, desperate, hungry kiss. He'd dreamt of this moment for five long, agonizing years.

And then it was over. She stiffened and drew away, gazing up at him with haunted, confused and angry eyes. Then she slapped him fiercely across the cheek.

"You've got a lot of nerve, Montana. Go to hell."

Inside the dark protection of her house, Angela leaned against the door, shaking violently. What the hell was wrong with her? She should never have let *that* happen.

She rubbed her arms and inhaled deeply, thinking that her day from hell hadn't ended with her encounter with Freddie Holloway. Or with Sergeant Reilly. Or even with her volatile mother. It had ended with the most passionate of kisses, a kiss that to her horror she realized she'd returned. That kiss threatened her more than all the other woes combined.

Pushing away from the door, Angela made her way up the stairs, her knees shaking. She should listen to her mother. Mary Ellen had been right about Dylan all along. *Don't trust him.* But his kiss had totally undone her, and she'd be lying to herself if she didn't admit that she still wanted the man, damn his hide.

Outside, the storm intensified, and rain pelted noisily on the metal roof of the old house. The lights flickered, and the brittle windowpanes rattled in the wind. Angela's room was on the second floor at the back of the house. It was her sanctuary, a place where she could shut out the world when it became too much. After Dylan had made it clear he wasn't going to show up in her life again, she'd decorated it to please only herself. It was feminine without being frilly, draped and hung with pale peach window treatments and bedclothes in shades of peach and green. Very Southern. Very Savannah. As if it mattered.

She noticed that her hands were shaking as she peeled off the dark skirt, silk blouse, and pantyhose she'd donned more than sixteen hours before. Her conservative mode of dress served her well as a businesswoman, but right now, all she wanted was the comfort of her white cotton nightgown, the protection of her favorite robe and slippers. That and a cup of hot chocolate to calm her nerves, and somebody to tell her everything was going to be all right.

But nobody could promise her things would be all right, and she didn't have the energy to go downstairs to the kitchen for hot chocolate, so instead she plopped into the old overstuffed rocking chair in one corner of the room and tucked her knees beneath her chin, hugging her legs and feeling unsettled and vulnerable.

She closed her eyes, and Dylan's face was right there. She felt the prickle of tears and shook her head to dispel them before they spilled. She had to quit thinking about Dylan. But the tears weren't just about Dylan, she realized. She was frightened, too. She shouldn't be; she'd done nothing wrong. And yet, Reilly's questioning had been dead serious, and she remembered the look on Dylan's face, his intimation that he knew something about the murder, and that she was in terrible danger. She kicked herself for not letting Dylan talk on the way back from her mother's house. Now she'd have to face him again. She didn't want to, but maybe his information would help make some sense of all this.

He'd mentioned a set-up to Reilly, and at the time it had seemed ludicrous. But she'd been in too great a shock to think clearly. Now she saw his point. As he'd said, somebody seemed to have gone to great lengths to impersonate her and throw suspicion on her. Somebody had learned her member number at the First City Club. Somebody had been stalking her, learning her every move and habit. She shuddered as that reality slammed through her again.

Somebody had worked hard to make it look like Angela

Donahue, who'd never so much as received a parking ticket in her entire life, was a murderer.

Who could have such a vendetta against her? Somebody she'd sent to prison?

Thinking hard, Angela began to recall the strange incidents that had taken place over the past few weeks. People had remarked that they'd seen her in places she hadn't been, just like at the First City Club. Being at the forefront of the Savannah hospitality scene, Angela was well-known by hotel managers, bartenders, restaurateurs, and shopowners. Several of these people who knew her well had claimed she'd frequented their places of business when she hadn't. Whoever was posing as her must bear a remarkable resemblance to her.

And then she remembered the registered letter, containing nothing. It had seemed a harmless mistake when it happened, but now Angela knew it had been a calculated plan on the part of the killer to obtain her signature. She had signed for the letter and returned the receipt to the postman before opening the envelope and finding it empty. Her signature had been on its way back to the killer, and she'd never suspected a thing.

She rocked, eyes closed, and shifted her thoughts to the man she was supposed to have killed. J. J. Slade. Reilly had shown her a photo of him taken before his body was shipped to the ME in Atlanta for the autopsy. The face seemed vaguely familiar, but she didn't know him. He'd looked like a man who was weighed down with the worries of the world, and she'd felt oddly sorry for him.

J. J. Slade.

Who the hell was J. J. Slade? And what did Dylan know about him?

There was Dylan again at the front of her mind. She let out a heavy breath. Good grief, what was happening to her? When she'd gotten out of bed that morning, she'd never dreamed she'd end up at the police station being questioned in a murder. Neither had she given any thought whatsoever to Dylan Montana. Time had taken care of that. Or so she'd thought. And now, here she was huddled in her room, wondering if she'd spend her next night in jail and shaking from the unexpected impact of Dylan's kiss.

Angela rocked slowly and steadily back in forth in the heavy old chair, breathing deeply and trying to clear her mind of all thought. After a few moments, she managed to pull herself together and decided that hiding out in her room solved nothing. She was tired and hungry. Maybe a bite to eat would help steady her nerves. She stood up and was about to go downstairs in search of a sandwich when she remembered her promise to take her gun to Johnny Reilly the next day.

Angela had a love-hate affair with guns. She hated them, because to her they represented violence and all that was wrong with the world. But as a law enforcement officer, she'd had to make friends with guns. She'd discovered that she was a crack shot, and her natural talent in marksmanship had empowered her in a way that nothing had before. Still, she remained ambivalent. Guns had saved her life, and a gun had almost taken it.

At the moment, she hated guns. She wished she didn't own one, because it gave the police something else to support their false suspicions of her guilt. But she had to take it in. It would look bad if she didn't voluntarily turn over the gun to Reilly, even though it wouldn't do the investigator much good. He'd told her the coroner thought Slade had been killed with a .38 or 9mm, but they couldn't convict her just because she owned a .38. Lots of people owned both kinds of guns. Also, the slug that had killed Slade had gone all the way through his body, and they hadn't found it, so they had no bullet to use to compare the firing patterns with her own. Still, it was better to cooperate.

A brilliant flash of lightning suddenly exploded into a power line nearby, immediately followed by a deafening crack of thunder. Already on edge, Angela let out a small scream as the lights went out. With a shudder at being suddenly plunged into total darkness, she felt her way to her nightstand where she kept the gun. There was a flashlight in the drawer as well.

She opened the drawer and reached inside, expecting to find the gun at the front where she kept it. But where she'd anticipated the feel of cold metal in her hand she found only air. She groped around the small drawer, coming upon the flashlight, but the gun wasn't there.

Angela clicked on the flashlight and peered inside the drawer. Except for a roll of Tums, a ballpoint pen, and some tissues, the drawer was empty.

Angela sank onto the bed and tried to think. Where could it be? Had she left it at the firing range? She didn't think so, but it was a possibility. She enjoyed an afternoon at the range from time to time. But she hadn't been in several weeks. She made a note to call the manager in the morning and see if anyone had turned it in.

But in her gut, she knew she hadn't left the gun anywhere other than in this drawer. An ominous thought brought nauseous saliva to the back of her throat. Had someone stolen the gun? Had someone, the person who'd been imitating her, managed to get into her house and taken the weapon? An even worse notion occurred to her.

Had her gun been used to murder J. J. Slade?

Shaking harder than the leaves in the storm outside, Angela made her way downstairs, suddenly anxious to check the locks on the three doors that allowed entry to her house. Except for the occasional flash of lightning and the beam of the flashlight, everything was pitch-black. She headed toward the cabinet where she kept extra candles, telling herself to calm down. She couldn't allow fear to consume her, or she would be lost.

The doorbell rang, sundering the darkness with its metallic shrill. The noise shattered her nerves all over again, and she nearly jumped out of her skin. Reflexively, she shone the flashlight's beam toward the front door, then realizing she was exposing her whereabouts, she clicked it off. Her heart pounded heavily. Who would be ringing her bell at a time like this? The wind was howling, and the porch was dark. She crept closer and peered out through the curtain lace. A large, dark figure stood there being assaulted by the storm.

"Who's there?" she called out, hoping it was one of her neighbors coming to check on her.

"Open up. It's freezing out here."

Angela didn't know whether to be relieved or terrified. On the other side of the door, a pizza box in one hand, a six-pack in the other, Dylan Montana stood shivering in the cold.

"I won't touch you," he called out over the storm's fury. "I promise. But we need to talk. Can I come in?"

Chapter 6

There be hants in our houses whether we like it or not. The spirits live with us, good uns an' bad uns. Dr. Lizard knows th' way t' keep th' hants and hags calm, all except th' hant in th' mirror . . .

"IT's hard to believe he's gone." Elizabeth Slade's voice was hushed, and her hand shook as she brought the wine-glass to her lips. She sat in front of a flickering fire but didn't feel its warmth.

Outside, a storm lashed the old live oaks that graced the manicured lawn of Paradisia Plantation and bent the marsh grasses to the surface of the normally placid river that flowed just beyond. The turbulent weather mirrored her mood.

Across from her, seated in a matching armchair, Harlow Bertram nodded in agreement and swirled what was left of his favorite single-malt whiskey in a crystal glass.

And both of them knew that neither was sorry that J. J. Slade had passed on.

Elizabeth had called Harlow when the police arrived earlier in the afternoon with the news of J. J.'s murder. He was their family lawyer and a longtime friend. He was also Elizabeth's lover. At Elizabeth's request, he'd gone to Savannah to identify the body.

Harlow stood up to make himself another drink. "I might not have believed it if I hadn't seen him with my own eyes."

Elizabeth had known the police would come when J. J. was killed, but she hadn't expected them so soon. Ricky

Suarez was a very efficient man. She'd had little time to compose herself for the performance that was demanded of her when the local sheriff, Bobby Keilor, had rolled through the gates of Paradisia, bringing with him the homicide detective from Savannah. But she believed she'd pulled it off.

To her amazement, when they told her what had happened, she'd actually felt the blood drain from her face. She'd experienced the shock, the disbelief, the horror, all those things a woman suddenly widowed should feel. Maybe because it was so final.

J. J. Slade was dead.

After all these years, she was free. It was a heady thought. Surreal. And hard to believe. Arranging for his demise was the bravest thing she'd done since she'd married him, and she didn't regret it.

Neither did she regret that she'd married him in the first place, for that alliance had served its purpose. But twenty-nine years was long enough to put up with his greed. His insatiable ambition. His neglect. Still, she would never have considered killing him, or rather having him killed, until Suarez had contacted her with his offer, and she'd discovered the extent of her husband's avarice. And his duplicity.

The police had questioned her for over an hour, trying to get an idea of who might have wanted her husband dead. Did he have any personal enemies? they'd wanted to know. *Oh, just his wife and daughter and most likely everyone else he came in contact with.* "Not that I know of," she'd told them.

Business associates or employees that he'd recently crossed? She'd repeated her answer, shaking her head as if she hadn't the slightest notion why her husband had been murdered.

"I'm afraid I'm not going to be very helpful, Sergeant Reilly," she'd told him, choosing her words carefully. "It's painful for me to admit that J. J. and I have long been . . . personally estranged, even though we lived under the same roof. I don't know much about my husband's affairs. He is . . . was . . . a very private man."

"Has he had any unusual visitors in the past week?"

Ricky Suarez was about as unusual as they get. "No. Not here at Paradisia. But J. J. was gone a lot. That's why I didn't think it strange he wasn't home last night. He never tells . . . told me when or where he was going or when to expect him back."

The police wanted to know her whereabouts at the time of the murder. Luckily, she'd been playing bridge all afternoon at the country club. It had never crossed her mind that she might need an alibi. She didn't know where Veronica had been, nor did she mention her to the police. Obviously, they hadn't yet learned that J. J. Slade had a daughter residing at Paradisia. She saw no reason to bring her up unless the police did.

"I'm glad Veronica wasn't home when the police came," she said now to Harlow, "but I'm worried about her. I haven't seen her for two days."

"Like that's unusual?" Harlow's tone was unsympathetic. Elizabeth knew he was not fond of her daughter. Nobody was fond of Veronica. Poor Veronica. If she just weren't so damned . . . difficult.

Poor Veronica. Elizabeth sipped her wine and thought about her daughter. Even though Veronica professed to hate her father, Elizabeth knew that the opposite, in fact, was true, and that a lot of her problems stemmed from her longing for the one thing she could never have . . . her father's love. Veronica must never know what Elizabeth had done, for now J. J.'s love would be totally and forever beyond her reach.

Chimes from the front doorbell startled her. She frowned and looked across at Harlow. "Who could that be out in this weather?"

Both turned and looked expectantly in the direction of the large doors that enclosed them in the parlor. In a few moments, the Slades' aging servant Bridget Means knocked and opened one door a few inches.

"Sorry to disturb you, Mrs. Slade, but that policeman's here again. The one from Savannah. Says he needs to speak to you."

Elizabeth grew immediately uneasy. She was irritated as well. She had no desire to perform the role of the grieving widow again today, but she supposed she must face the man. "Bring him in, Bridget." She glanced at Harlow. He knew nothing about Ricky Suarez or the deal she'd made, so he couldn't tell the detective anything. There was a lot Harlow didn't know, and Elizabeth intended to keep it that way. Sometimes Harlow's mouth got in the way.

Sergeant Reilly entered the room, his trench coat dripping from the rain. "I'm sorry to bother you again so soon," he said, "but we've learned a little more about your husband's death since this afternoon, and we want to get to the bottom of this as quickly as possible."

"Of course. Please sit down, Sergeant. Would you care for coffee? A glass of wine? Bridget, bring a towel."

He accepted the towel but declined her other hospitality and got directly to the point. "We found a pocket planner on your husband's body, Mrs. Slade. As best we can tell, he was last seen alive at the First City Club in Savannah around one o'clock yesterday afternoon in the company of a young woman."

Elizabeth's hackles rose. That bastard. Did he have to make a fool of her in such a public place? And how young was the woman? She said, "That surprises me. Not the part about the young woman, but that he was in Savannah. He never went to Savannah. J. J. hated the place."

Reilly took a seat, reached inside his coat and brought out an envelope. Inside was a black-and-white photograph, which he handed to Elizabeth. "Do you recognize this woman?"

Elizabeth stared at the photo, and something inside of

her went cold. It wasn't Veronica—the hair was lighter, the style curlier, and it appeared the eyes were lighter than Veronica's—but otherwise the resemblance was undeniable. Harlow had come to look over her shoulder. Before she could reply, he said, "Well, I'll be damned. That looks like Veronica."

"Your daughter?" Johnny Reilly asked quickly.

Elizabeth panicked. Damned Harlow. She'd hoped to keep Veronica out of this. Now, it was too late. "Veronica is my daughter, yes, Sergeant," she said stiffly, "but this is not Veronica. My daughter is younger, has straight brown hair and brown eyes. There is a faint resemblance, I suppose, but I don't know this person. Who is she?"

"Her name is Angela Donahue," the officer replied. "She runs a tour company in Savannah. Witnesses say she argued violently with your husband before storming out of the club. Told him she wished he was dead. At the moment, she is our prime suspect, but we will also need to speak to your daughter. Does she live here?"

Elizabeth shifted in her seat. "Yes, Veronica lives here, but she isn't home."

"Do you know where we can find her?"

She flushed slightly, embarrassed that she didn't know the whereabouts of her daughter. "No, I don't." She should know, especially now. In fact, Veronica should be here, at Paradisia. She didn't even know about J. J.'s death.

Or did she?

A sudden terrible suspicion washed over her. In her mind's eye, she could easily see Veronica causing the scene at the First City Club. Veronica owned a gun. Veronica was mentally unstable. Veronica thought she hated her father.

My God, Elizabeth wondered numbly, had Veronica beaten Ricky Suarez to the draw?

* * *

Two men in a blue van hidden near the entrance to Paradisia exchanged glances when the Savannah police car arrived. They'd learned earlier from their boss that the body of J. J. Slade had been found in the river, and they'd seen the first visit from the local sheriff several hours ago. The police scanner was on, but out here in the boonies, all they were picking up was a lot of static.

"I'd give my right arm to know why the Savannah police have come calling, especially this late at night and in a howling storm," Ricky Suarez said. "I don't like it."

Joe Delano ground out a cigarette and rubbed his stubbled jaw, but he didn't reply. Joe was good at a lot of things, but talking wasn't one of them.

Suarez was worried. Things had not gone as planned, and he wasn't sure what to do next. The boss had told them to keep an eye on every movement at Paradisia, which wasn't easy, since the place was surrounded by a tall fence and the gate was manned.

They had a problem, but none of them was sure exactly what it was. Or rather, who. Suarez had assured his boss that Elizabeth Slade was proud and greedy enough to go along with the plan and keep her mouth shut, but now he wasn't certain. Was she double-crossing him? Was she at this very moment spilling her story to the police, handing over the information that was so vital to their success? Were their months of preparation for the takeover about to go down the toilet?

They must be extremely careful these next few days, his boss had warned him. Lay low. Keep an eye out. The game could still be on, but with Slade off the board, they had to know exactly which players remained before they decided upon their next move.

Chapter 7

Th' hag be th' worst kind of spirit. She comes in th' house and roosts on th' bedpost, and at night she rides you till you get so poorly you want t' up and die. Ain't nobody sees her, but she feels like a piece of raw meat. It takes big magic from th' conjureman t' send a hag on her way . . .

ANGELA opened the morning paper and stared in disbelief at the image that met her eye. There on the front page her own face smiled up at her, topped by the headline, POLICE QUESTION LOCAL BUSINESSWOMAN IN SLADE MURDER.

She groaned as her knees gave way, and she sank into a chair at the kitchen table. Across from her, Dylan looked up sharply from his coffee. "What's wrong?"

The storm of the previous night had passed, but Angela's personal storm continued to swirl around her like a hurricane. Like a fool, she'd let Dylan come in out of the rain the night before, but she'd managed to keep her emotional distance from him as they ate the pizza and drank the beer he'd brought, mainly because he'd been all business.

And he'd scared the bejeesus out of her when she realized that she might be the pawn of the drug lord, Lucas Quintos, and his right-hand man, Cecil Clifford. She knew both of them from her days with the GBI, and she knew they played a deadly game. With her gun missing, Angela had felt exposed and unprotected, and when Dylan had started to leave, she'd impulsively asked if he would stay the night on her sofa. By the light of day, she realized it had been a mistake, and she was about to ask him to leave when she saw the newspaper.

Instead, she shoved it across the table to him. "This is what's wrong."

"Those damn media sharks," he uttered when he saw the headline. "They ought to be sued for this." She saw an odd look cross his face, and he got up suddenly and went toward the front of the house.

The phone rang. Angela hesitated before answering, knowing instinctively it wasn't someone she wanted to talk to. Even so, she picked up the receiver. "Hello?"

"You will burn in hell for what you did, you murdering whore." The voice was guttural, like a snarl. "God will strike you down and a thousand curses will plague you, daughter of Jezebel. Repent now and beg forgiveness of your maker, for unless you do, your soul belongs to the devil." The caller hung up abruptly, leaving Angela too dumbfounded to be frightened.

She heard a commotion at the front door and ran to see what was going on. Dylan's back was to her, and he was shouting at someone. "Get out of here. You're trespassing on private property," he ordered and stepped out onto the porch.

"Dear God," Angela murmured and dashed into the parlor at the front of the house. Peering out of the window, her eyes widened, and she covered her mouth with her hands.

A crowd had gathered in the street, and reporters and photographers, armed with microphones and cameras, had pushed through her gate. She saw Dylan fending them off at the front steps.

As Angela looked out on the scene in disbelief and horror, a van from a local TV station pulled up. She saw her neighbors standing at their doors, some of them coming onto their porches, eyeing her house with open curiosity. All that stood between her and this madness was Dylan.

She sank into a nearby armchair, feeling suddenly lightheaded as she realized what was happening. She'd seen this before, when she'd been involved in sensational criminal cases with the GBI. The reporters were like vultures, ready to pick clean any bones, innocent or guilty, that were thrown in their direction. Panic enveloped her. The allegations against her were a lie, but those revolting carrion seemed not to care.

She looked out the window again and was relieved to see that Dylan had managed to get them to move outside her gate. He came back inside the house, his face nearly purple with rage. He jerked his cell phone from its holder at his waist and angrily punched in some numbers. "Reilly, what the hell's going on? Angela's yard is covered with reporters. It was a little premature to feed this to the media, for God's sake."

His expression grew even darker as he listened to the reply, and Angela heard the fury in his voice when he said, "Yeah, yeah, I understand. But you're the one in charge. Your people broke it, now you fix it. She's not guilty, Reilly, and this smacks of pure harassment. Now get some uniforms over here to control this situation. Angela doesn't deserve to be held hostage by these creeps." He listened for a few moments longer, grunted a couple of times, then disconnected the call and rubbed his eyes.

Watching him fight for her, Angela remembered how things had been between them all those years ago, how she'd depended on Dylan to be there for her, how he always had been, until that night . . . Why hadn't he shown up to make the buy? And what had she done that had caused him to leave her after that? She wanted to ask him that, and why he was here now, but instead, she asked something safer. "What did he say?"

"He claims he didn't say anything to the media, that someone in the department leaked the story, but I don't believe him. I'd like to choke the sorry bastard."

Struggling to control her emotions, Angela stood up. "It's okay, Dylan," she said. "They would have found out sooner or later. And I'm not letting anyone hold me hostage. I've got to get ready for work."

"I wouldn't go in today if I were you," he said quickly. "Think about it. They'll follow you like a pack of hound dogs. It wouldn't be good for your business."

She did think about it. And it infuriated her. The whole monstrous affair infuriated her. And terrified her at the same time, for she remembered with a sickening jolt that a killer had deliberately picked her out to take the hit for this murder. And if what Dylan had told her was true, this wasn't any normal, run-of-the-mill murder.

"So what am I supposed to do? Sit here and wait for the hangman?"

"Let me protect you."

"You, protect me? You're about five years too late, Montana." The old rage flared violently before she could suppress it, but she immediately regretted her outburst when she saw the bleak look that fell across his face.

"There are things you don't know," he said quietly, but made no effort to explain or defend his actions.

Angela let out a long breath and pushed her unruly curls away from her face. "I'm sure there are. But that's history. We don't need to go there. Sorry."

"Yes, we do need to go there," he replied. "But not now."

His pain took her by surprise, and she swallowed hard. What things didn't she know? Was there some explanation for his actions that night she could accept that would redeem him?

She wasn't sure she wanted him to be redeemed. She was still too hurt. "I can protect myself."

Dylan's face hardened. "Maybe so. But Quintos or whoever is behind Slade's murder has, for whatever reason, gone to a lot of trouble to point the finger at you. He blindsided you once. He'll do it again if it suits his purposes. He will, in fact, probably try to kill you if the police don't make this stick. He'll make it look like an accident, a car wreck or something. Or else you will simply disappear. If Reilly is on the take, he'll close the case and that will be that. You know how it works."

His words sent a chill down Angela's back. Yes, she knew how it worked. Cops on the take, owned by the drug dealers. She'd hoped she'd helped rid Savannah of all that. But she wasn't naive. Good cops, underpaid and overworked in a hazardous job, were vulnerable to the big money that was waved beneath their noses by the drug dealers. For every bad cop who'd been sentenced to prison in the upheaval at the SPD, there was a replacement who might end up doing exactly what had sent his predecessor to jail.

Still, she argued with Dylan. "I don't need a bodyguard. Nobody's going to gun me down in City Market. You said you thought Slade was in a battle for control of the distribution of drugs in the Southeast. It stands to reason he was killed by his enemies. Quintos most likely. But why would Quintos want to pin it on me? I'm not GBI. I'm just an average citizen."

"Like I told you last night, I think it may be Clifford out for revenge. But Quintos might not mind seeing you dead, either. You're not an average citizen, Angela, even if you aren't in law enforcement anymore. Your SOS teams and Judge Brown's sentences have made a real dent in the trafficking in the area. If Quintos could knock off Slade and blame it on you, he'd get rid of two enemies at the same time. He'd smear your good name, while he walks away clean."

Angela could hardly believe what he was saying, or that he knew so much about her activities. It made her uncomfortable. Had he been spying on her? She wondered where he'd been for the past five years. She'd believed he'd left

Savannah. Now she wasn't sure, because he knew what she'd been up to.

SOS stood for Save Our Streets. It was an aggressive, hands-on, proactive neighborhood organization that Angela had formed three years before, after a young tourist on her honeymoon was caught in a crossfire between gang members fighting over drug turf and was killed. Angela's own nearly fatal experience in the failed drug bust, followed so closely by the second tragedy, had convinced her that something drastic had to be done if Savannah's beautiful, historic streets were to be made safe.

Savannah was her home, and she loved every inch of its creepy charm and delightful decadence. Angela made her living showing off the quiet tree-shaded squares, elegant houses, and moss-enshrouded cemeteries that were steeped in history older than the country itself. She'd been instrumental in promoting the new convention center and marina across the river, was knee-deep in tourism, and she could not stand by and let the drug dealers turn Savannah's streets into a war zone.

But she knew the cops, or at least a substantial number of them, couldn't be trusted. So she'd urged her boss at the GBI, Vincent Howard, to seek an Internal Affairs investigation. And she'd started SOS to reclaim her own neighborhood. It had experienced an amazing groundswell of support throughout the city since then.

Vigilantes, some might have called her volunteers. Caring was what she called them. Working in teams and armed only with radios and flashlights, neighbors patrolled their own streets. They didn't make arrests. They simply made life too difficult to be profitable for the street-corner vendors of crack cocaine, the most widely available drug in Savannah.

Still, she found it hard to believe a drug lord like Quintos would find her threatening. Sure, her SOS teams were valuable in the fight against drugs. And Judge George Brown was known as the "hanging judge" when it came to handing out sentences to those dealers unfortunate enough to end up in his courtroom. But between them, she thought they were still small potatoes in the effort to rid Savannah of drugs.

"I find it difficult to believe I'm a target for the likes of Lucas Quintos," she said, "but say I am, why do you think you're the man to protect me?" The unspoken implication—*you let me down before*—stretched between them like a chasm.

Dylan looked at her for a long moment before answering, and his expression seemed suddenly sad and tired. "It's been a long time, Angela," he said at last. "There's a lot you don't know about me. A lot I can't tell you. You'll just have to trust me when I say you're in terrible danger, and because of what I know, I think I can keep you out of harm's way until . . . some things happen."

"Because of what you know. Are you DEA?"

Silence.

"Talk to me, damn it," she yelled, losing her temper at last. She wanted to shake him and make him tell her everything. Who he was now. Why he'd come back into her life. Who was trying to kill her. But most of all why he'd left in the first place.

"Yes," she hissed, "it's been a long time, and I by God deserve some answers. You left me, Dylan. I was dying and you left me. And now, out of the blue, you show up on my doorstep wanting to protect me. I want to know why, Dylan. You owe me that much."

Jeremiah Brown slammed his locker, twisted the combination lock a couple of times, then dashed like the star quarterback he wanted to be down the corridor and out of the front door of the middle school. He hoped to catch up with Orinda Stevens, another sixth-grader whose pretty eyes and sweet smile had caught his attention on the first day of school and held it firm ever since.

Outside, the air was cool and fresh, as if it had been cleansed by last night's storm. Only a few cars remained lined up at the sidewalk, waiting for late-comers like himself. Jeremiah looked both ways, and to his dismay, saw Orinda's parents' car just pulling out of the driveway. He waved, but she didn't see him. He barely caught a glimpse of her face before the car turned into the busy street and disappeared.

Darn! If only his teacher hadn't made him stay those extra few minutes after school . . . But he supposed he deserved the punishment. He knew better than to pass notes in class. Jeremiah kicked at a rock and headed for home, a few blocks away.

Just outside the schoolyard, he rounded a large bush and ran squarely into the solid chest of a much larger boy whose body blocked his way.

"You in a hurry, man?" the older boy asked, a challenging, cold smile on his lips.

"I didn't mean nothing," Jeremiah said, too frozen with fear to run back to the school. "I . . . I'm sorry." He tried to pass, but another boy slipped from behind the bush and barred his way. A third joined the other two who stood shoulder to shoulder, and Jeremiah had the fleeting notion he was a quarterback facing the three biggest linemen in the universe. He knew he was about to get his butt whipped. "Let me go."

The first bully just shook his head. "Oh, I don't think so, Jeremiah. We have big plans for you."

"Plans? What plans? I don't even know you."

Before he knew what was happening, Jeremiah felt himself being lifted and carried to a car that stood waiting at the curb. He was shoved roughly into the back seat, where a fourth youth waited with handcuffs and a bandana for a gag. Jeremiah kicked and tried to scream but was easily overpowered by the older, larger boys.

"Hit it," one of them told the driver, and with a screech of tires, the car lurched forward.

The first boy he'd run into turned to him from the front seat and gave him a toothy smile. "Don't you worry none, you freakin' little runt. Nobody's going to hurt you. In fact, we're taking you some place real nice. Sort of an early Halloween treat, wouldn't you say, boys?" The others laughed.

In one last attempt to reclaim his freedom, Jeremiah kicked his closest captor in the shins. The boy cried out in pain. "Shit! You dumb little shit!" He pulled something out of his pocket and lunged toward Jeremiah.

The last thing Jeremiah remembered was a cloth closing over his face, and a sweet but medicinal odor snaking through his nostrils and into his brain.

Chapter 8

Gunpowder mixed with whiskey will calm th' heart and fill it with power . . .

ELIZABETH stared intently at her computer screen, trying to decide if it made sense to learn to trade stocks herself rather than using a broker. J. J. had always managed her substantial investments, but with him gone, and his own fortune coming her way, she'd decided she'd better learn to fend for herself.

They'd signed a prenuptial agreement when they'd married, before it had been a common practice among the wealthy. Her father had insisted upon it, as he took J. J. for an opportunist. She laughed to herself. What an understatement.

But the prenuptial had been a good idea, and it had worked well for them both. Because of it, each had their private and separate monies, and she'd hired J. J. to manage hers. He'd done a splendid job. She was a wealthy woman in her own right. If there was one thing her husband had been good at, it was making money. He'd also done some excellent estate planning. His fortune would come to her and Veronica as beneficiaries of the trust he'd set up years ago. They wouldn't even have to go through probate.

Elizabeth sensed a presence and looked up to see Veronica lounging in the doorway. Her daughter wore tight, black leggings and a sheer blouse over a black lace bra. Her straight brown hair was disheveled, her face pale, her eyes large and hollow. Bright red lipstick clung to the fullness of her mouth. Anger at the image she presented tainted the relief that flooded Elizabeth at seeing her daughter.

"Where the hell have you been?"

Veronica sauntered into the room on backless high-heeled shoes. "I'm happy to see you, too, Mother."

Elizabeth shivered involuntarily, suddenly aware that she was just a little afraid of her daughter. Veronica could be so cold. So hard. Abusive to others as well as herself. Elizabeth knew about Veronica's drug use, but she could only speculate as to the rest of her activities, for Veronica was very secretive. She looked like a hooker and probably was. The suspicion revolted Elizabeth and roused her anger all over again. Veronica was an embarrassment to the family name.

She regarded her daughter coldly and tried to remain unemotional. "I've been worried sick about you. The least you could do is give me a call when you plan to be gone so long."

"I'm not a child, Mother. I'm twenty-eight. It's none of your business where I go or what I do."

Elizabeth thought of the picture of the woman the police called "Angela Donahue." It was very much Elizabeth's business if Veronica, a.k.a. "Angela," had taken a new identity in Savannah and ultimately had killed J. J. Slade. In spite of her daughter's wild, amoral behavior, Elizabeth would do anything to protect her, and the family name, from scandal. But first, she must learn the truth.

"Sit down, Veronica," she said more gently. "I'll have Bridget bring us some tea."

"I'd rather have a drink."

Elizabeth refused to rise to her daughter's bait. Veronica's habitual substance abuse was the source of constant and continuing conflict between them. It was a serious problem, but today, they had something even more serious to discuss. "Very well. What would you like?"

"Jack Daniel's. On the rocks."

Elizabeth thought she detected a flicker of surprise on

Veronica's face that her request was being met with no resistance, and it gave her a certain sense of satisfaction. She called Bridget on the house phone and asked for the drinks to be brought to them, then came to sit on the white brocade sofa that faced the graceful fireplace. She motioned for her daughter to sit in a nearby chair.

"I don't mean to pry, Veronica," she said, studying her daughter and trying to imagine her with light-colored, wavy hair. A wig? "But I do worry about you."

Bridget arrived with their drinks, tea for Elizabeth, Jack Daniel's for Veronica. It gave Elizabeth time to consider how to broach the subject she dreaded. She settled on a direct approach.

"There's something I have to tell you . . ." she started, but Veronica interrupted.

"I already know. Father was killed a couple of days ago." Veronica's voice was toneless. The only emotion Elizabeth could detect was a slight shake of her hand as she brought the drink to her lips.

"I see. How did you . . . ?"

"I saw it on television."

Elizabeth marveled at Veronica's ability to hide her emotions. Learning of her father's murder on television must have been traumatic. *Unless she already knew he was dead because she'd killed him.* It was difficult for Elizabeth to continue, but she knew she must. "Then I guess you have also heard that the police have a suspect. A woman named Angela Donahue."

"That's what they're saying." Again no emotion.

Elizabeth cleared her throat. "The police showed me a picture of her. Veronica, she . . . uh . . . looks very much like you, only her hair is lighter."

Veronica's head jerked up. "What are you saying? You think I killed Father?"

Elizabeth set her teacup down with a clatter. "Of course not. But I was shocked, to say the least, when I saw the resemblance between you and the woman in the picture." She saw a distinct look of contempt pass over Veronica's face and wondered why.

"Maybe Father had a thing for women who looked like me," Veronica said acidly. "He couldn't stand me, but he had an affair with my lookalike. Pretty kinky, don't you think?"

"Veronica, I want you to be honest with me. You are safe here. I'm not your enemy. I want to help you. Where were you when J. J. was killed? And who is Angela Donahue?"

But Veronica was a closed door. She shrugged. "Like I said, it's none of your business where I was."

Elizabeth wanted to shake her. "The police sergeant investigating the murder wants to talk to you. You'd better have a good story to tell him." Suddenly, she was overcome with anxiety. "Veronica," she asked, lowering her voice, "do you have an alibi?"

Veronica gave her a disdainful look. "I didn't kill him, Mother, although I'm glad the son of a bitch is dead." She tossed back the rest of her drink, stood up, and headed for the door. "I'll tell the police where I was. If they ask. It's still none of your business." She turned before leaving the room and added, "I suppose you can prove where you were that day, Mother dearest? And how about good old Harlow? I'm sure he's not sorry Father's gone. Why are you always so quick to blame me?"

Elizabeth stared after her for a long moment. Why *had* she been so quick to suspect Veronica? Just because she hated her daughter's lifestyle? That had not been Veronica in the photo. Maybe J. J. did have a perverted attraction to women who looked like his daughter. But Veronica hadn't killed him. It was Ricky Suarez who'd put that bullet through his heart.

But deep down, a dark worry niggled at her. After Veronica left the room, she went to the phone and dialed Harlow.

"Veronica's just come home. She won't tell me where she was when J. J. was killed." Her voice quavered as in her mind's eye she saw Veronica pulling the trigger. She saw the headlines when the truth was discovered, and her gut tightened in dread of the scandal that would surely ensue.

After all she had done to secure Paradisia and Veronica's place in society . . .

Get hold of yourself. She took a deep, steadying breath.

"You don't really believe she killed him?" Harlow sounded incredulous.

"I don't know what to believe. Veronica is furious with me for insinuating that she might have murdered J. J. She implied that her father had a thing for women who looked like her. I doubt it, but it could be. Before this goes any further, I want to know all about this Angela Donahue woman. Does she even exist? Or was it Veronica in disguise? Do you know a good private investigator? Well, find one, damn it, and get him out here right away."

Ronnie was shaking when she left her mother. Shaking with both fury and fear. Elizabeth had seen Angela Donahue's picture. She'd seen the resemblance. And instead of considering that J. J. had been unfaithful to her and had sired an illegitimate child, her first thought had been that Veronica had pretended to be Angela and killed her father.

It didn't matter that Elizabeth was close to the truth, or at least the way it'd been planned. It pissed Ronnie off that her mother always found a way to place the blame for whatever went wrong in this godforsaken household on Ronnie. Well, if Elizabeth was too stupid to figure out that Angela Donahue was J. J.'s bastard daughter, Ronnie wasn't going to be the one to break it to her. Let her stumble across it when she finally got around to going through J. J.'s files.

Or better yet, let her hear it from the Donahue bitch herself from the witness stand or in the newspapers. For the truth would come out. Sooner or later, Elizabeth would know just how deeply J. J. Slade had betrayed them both.

In the meantime, Ronnie intended to have as little contact with her mother, and the police, as possible. But she had a story ready, in case she needed it.

She still couldn't remember where she'd been the afternoon her father was murdered. She honestly didn't believe she'd killed him, but just in case, she'd pleaded with Marguerite to help her come up with an alibi. Marguerite agreed but had made it clear she didn't want the police nosing around her place. She didn't like police. So they'd come up with a story, and witnesses, that would prove Veronica had been far from the crime scene that day. All it took was money.

Still, Ronnie's stomach was in knots. She needed another drink.

Going into the billiards room, the one room of this wing her father had frequented from time to time, Ronnie went to the bar and poured herself a second Jack Daniel's, not bothering with the ice. It went down hot and steadied her at last. She poured another.

Ronnie was not certain whether she'd killed her father, but she *was* certain of one thing. She was glad he was dead. He deserved to die for all he'd done to her. *For all he hadn't done.* Sudden tears burned in her eyes, and she raised her glass to her father's invisible presence. "I hope you rot in hell, you miserable bastard."

By the middle of the third drink, her spirits were somewhat restored, her courage renewed. Why did she care whether she'd been the one who pulled the trigger? He was dead, and the plan had worked. It was good she couldn't remember. She'd probably even be able to take a lie detector test if she had to. She had an airtight alibi, and someone else was being blamed.

She smiled. It had all worked out so well.

Veronica was familiar with her father's will and the way the estate was planned, and she knew that soon a large portion of his lovely millions would be rattling around in her bank account, ready to set her free again. She hoped Harlow would waste no time in settling her father's affairs. She was ready to get out of Paradisia, out of this stinking armpit of coastal Georgia, and on with her life. She raised her glass again, this time making a bitter toast to the one who had made it all possible. "Here's to you, Angela Donahue. You fucking daddy's girl." Veronica finished the drink, threw the Baccarat crystal glass into the fireplace, and left the room.

Yes, she thought, it had all worked out so well.

Mary Ellen Donahue sat in her favorite chair in the living room, staring out the window but not seeing her beloved roses blooming in the small entry yard. Not seeing the brilliant blue sky above or the leaves beginning to wisp down from the old trees that gnarled their way up through the sidewalk.

Instead, in her mind's eye, she saw her daughter being locked in jail. She heard the clang of the cold metal, caught the odor of what she imagined a prison would smell like. Felt the stares of the other inmates slicing hatefully into Angela. Pain seared her heart, and tears swelled her already puffy eyes. She reached for a tissue and honked into it, then hiccoughed.

Why on earth were they questioning Angela? Mary Ellen dissolved into miserable tears. It was shocking and unfair, but she didn't know what to do about it. She had never felt so helpless.

Mary Ellen heaved herself out of the chair, shuffled over to the sofa, and picked up one of the newspapers that littered the room, and her grief shifted to anger. All those stories focused on Angela as the murderer. Why weren't they questioning his wife? What about his daughter? Families were usually prime suspects, weren't they? Why were they hung up on blaming Angela?

She gazed at the photo of the dead man, and her throat tightened painfully as she asked herself again . . . why?

Desperately in need of divine direction in resolving this unhappy turn of events, Mary Ellen went into the spare bedroom. This had been Angela's room when she was growing up, and for the most part, Mary Ellen had left it as it was before her daughter went away to college. The only change she'd made was to set up a small altar on Angela's dresser.

She lit a candle and gazed up at the crucifix that hung on the wall above. Mary Ellen was a devout Catholic. She believed that God heard prayers, and not always, but sometimes, He answered them.

She took out her rosary and began to pray like she'd never prayed before.

Chapter 9

This goofer dust comes from th' devil's own grave, but th' conjureman mixes it with sulphur t' make it even stronger, for th' evil spirit in it has much work t' do . . .

TWO good things happened to Angela that day. First, she passed the police polygraph test, and second, a sensational news story broke that sent the media scurrying in another direction. She felt terrible about what took them away, however. Jeremiah Brown, Judge George Brown's twelve-year-old son, had been kidnapped from his schoolyard.

She'd been in Reilly's office when she'd heard the news and her mind flashed to Dylan's earlier comments about SOS and Judge Brown. She knew immediately that this kidnapping had something to do with Lucas Quintos, just as Dylan had convinced her she might be being set up by Cecil Clifford, but she didn't say a word to Reilly. Dylan didn't trust him, and neither did she.

Wally Padgett, one of the officers assigned to the Brown case, recognized Angela and shot her a sympathetic look. "I'm real sorry about what's happened to you, Ms. Donahue," he said. "It's a set-up, no doubt. Reilly here'll figure it out in no time."

Obviously Padgett was a new hire. But she appreciated his concern. "Any leads on the kidnapping?" she asked. Angela had been involved in a number of kidnapping cases when she was with the GBI, and they never failed to get to her.

She'd never had children of her own, although at one

time, she'd wanted a child badly. Dylan's child. But that dream had turned to dust, and her desire for a family had dissolved into bitter disappointment when he'd disappeared from her life that fateful night.

Still, she loved children, and kidnappings had been the most difficult cases for her to handle. The GBI had often turned to her, however, because she seemed to have a way with kids. They trusted her and would talk to her when they wouldn't talk to other adults. She'd done quite a few post-case interviews with young victims that had shocked her and left an indelible imprint on her heart.

"A neighbor saw it happen," Padgett answered her. "Jeremiah was just leaving school when three thugs jumped him and threw him into a car. Unfortunately, the neighbor didn't get the tag number. She wasn't even sure what kind of car it was. 'Old and gray, like me,' she said." Padgett gave a short, unhappy laugh at the witness's attempt at humor.

He turned to go, and Angela stood up. "Wally, if I can help . . ."

He nodded. "The GBI is already on the case, and since Brown is a federal judge, the FBI is coming in on it as well. But if we need help, we'll call. I know you and Judge Brown are friends."

The bad thing that happened to Angela that day was that she had no gun to turn over to Reilly. She'd called the firing range, but her gun had not been found on the premises. She'd searched her house high and low and come up with nothing. "I swear the last time I saw that gun, it was in my nightstand drawer," she'd said desperately. "Someone must have stolen it."

From Reilly's expression, she knew he didn't believe her. "And just who do you think did that?" he asked dryly, examining his fingernails.

Angela's cheeks burned. "The same person whose picture is on that videotape. The person who is setting me up."

Her voice edged up a notch, as if an increase in volume would make him understand. "I did not shoot J. J. Slade, and that polygraph should prove it. You're wasting the taxpayers' money, Reilly."

He eyed her evenly. "Maybe. You can go for now. But don't think for a minute you're off the hook."

She gave him an angry look but left before she said something else she'd regret.

Outside, the fresh air and sunshine improved her mood, and she paused at the top of the steps of the precinct building to decide what to do next. She'd managed to convince Dylan that she would be safe enough at police headquarters, and he'd begrudgingly left her off there earlier in the day. He was supposed to check in with her later, but she hadn't heard from him all day. Maybe that was just as well.

Angela's initial anger at Dylan and his sudden and disturbing reappearance in her life had abated somewhat, for she truly appreciated that he'd tried to help her. But she was still ambivalent about letting him too close to her. She'd tried to assure him that his fears for her safety were groundless, but both of them knew better. The truth was, she was frightened. She wanted to say, "Go away, I don't need your help. I can take care of myself." But for the first time in her life, she wasn't sure it was true. What if the police were in on this? What if the drug boss was, as Dylan believed, pissed at her for calling in the GBI on his friends in the police department and for starting SOS? She'd heard of people being killed for lesser reasons.

Angela pulled the collar of her jacket closer to her neck. She ought to go see her mother. Mary Ellen, who was still sick, had not taken the news well when Angela had called to warn her about the headlines. She had, in fact, become nearly hysterical. Angela had wanted to go directly to her house to assure her in person that things would work out all right, but Dylan had been right in urging her not to sic the media onto her mother. And right now, after the grueling hours she'd spent at the police station, Angela just didn't feel like dealing with her emotionally mercurial mother.

She looked at her watch. Five-thirty. Still time to pop into her office and see how things were going. With all that had happened in the past two days, Angela had completely neglected the business that was her joy as well as her source of income. She was glad her friend Connie, who managed the store for her, was so dependable. Unfortunately, it looked as if Angela might be missing a lot of work if this thing wasn't resolved soon.

She drove the short distance to the shop which served as both booking office for her tour business and a place where her customers could buy souvenirs. She parked in a reserved space behind the building, aggravated that she had to sneak around her own place of business, but still wary of roving reporters. Letting herself in the back door, she crept past the boxes of extra merchandise that were stored in the gloomy corridor and entered her office. The light was off, and she was able to look out into the store unobserved. A couple browsed at the far end, and Connie was behind the register. Otherwise, the large room itself was empty. But to her horror, through the plate glass windows at the front, she saw a news crew shooting what surely must be an update about her involvement in the Slade murder.

Angela lost it. Without thinking, she stormed through the store, ignoring the customers and Connie's alarmed expression. She burst through the door and went directly to the young woman who was speaking in front of the camera.

"Get out of here," Angela demanded, and put her hand over the camera lens. But the cameraman was too quick for her. He backed away and refocused his shot, which now included Angela hassling the newswoman. "This is my place of business, and I'll not have you spreading your lies from here. Get out."

The newswoman recovered quickly and spoke rapidly

into the mike, addressing the newscaster back at the station. "Bob, we've just been accosted by Ms. Donahue, and although we are on city property, we're being asked to leave the premises. More on this later. Now back to you . . ."

Angela suddenly became aware that she was in the center of a small crowd that had gathered to watch her attack on the news crew. The camera was still rolling. But she was not intimidated.

"You may be on city property, but you are definitely interfering with my right to earn a living. Any more of this and I'll sue your station to its last nickel. Now get out."

This time, the young woman wasn't so brave. She glared at Angela, then motioned to the cameraman to follow her back to the van. As she walked away, Angela overheard her say, "I thought she was innocent, but after that, I don't know . . ."

Angela's heart plummeted. What had she just done? She looked into the faces of the people whose curiosity she'd rewarded with a dandy scene and cursed her quick temper. "I'm sorry," she stammered. "Please, all of you, just go."

She wanted to run away and bury herself somewhere but found she was unable to move, as if her feet were glued to the pavement. As the onlookers at last began to thin out, from somewhere she heard the sound of one person clapping. She jerked her head toward the singular applause and wasn't surprised to find Freddie Holloway leaning against his bus, watching her with amusement. He was tall and angular, with curly red hair and an attitude.

"Go to hell, Freddie."

"Hey, don't be mad at me. I'm a fan."

His nose seemed more beaked than she remembered, his red hair more clownlike. "You're as big a vulture as they are. You can't wait for them to throw me in jail. Have you already made arrangements with the landlord to take over my lease?"

Holloway's eyebrows lifted. "No, but now that you mention it . . ."

The bastard wasn't worth her time. Angela turned and went back into the store from which all potential customers had by this time escaped. "Close up early, Connie," she said, heading straight for her office. She was on the brink of tears, and she wanted no witnesses if she broke down.

She heard the front door of the store slam shut, the lock turn. But then she heard Connie's footsteps approaching. Angela fought for composure. She wished Connie had gone home, but she really needed to speak to her, find out what sort of day they'd had. And besides, Connie was a good friend. By the time her manager reached the office door, Angela had pulled herself together, but she knew she wouldn't fool Connie.

"Hi," she said.

"Hi yourself," Connie replied. "Want a Coke?" Having a Coke was Connie's answer to all of life's problems.

"Sure." Angela could use an answer to her problems, but she doubted it came in a red aluminum can. "How'd we do today?" she asked as Connie withdrew two frosty soda cans from the small refrigerator at the back of the office.

"You aren't going to like this, but we had the best day we've had in months."

Angela took a Coke and popped the top. "Why wouldn't I like that?"

Connie drank deeply before replying. "Because, most everyone who came in here came to see you, the famous criminal."

Angela felt hollow, as if she were no longer inside of her own skin. "A freak? Is that what I've become? A sideshow attraction?"

Connie didn't answer. She didn't have to. Between the gossip that must be flying locally and the lies printed and broadcast in the media, her life as she knew it had been destroyed. Today had been a good day at the store, but how long would it be before the novelty wore off and customers and friends alike began to avoid her and the enterprise she'd worked so long and hard to create?

Angela could almost feel the prison walls closing in around her. She hadn't even been arrested, and yet it was as if she'd been tried, convicted, and sentenced by a community that had once supported and encouraged her. That was what hurt the most.

"I didn't do it, Connie."

"I know that. Everyone knows that. Your friends think this whole affair is appalling."

"I'll bet they do." Angela's friends would find anything this sordid appalling, but to have one of their own suspected of murder was unthinkable. She figured she'd soon know who her *real* friends were.

She made a sudden decision. "I'm going to stay away from the store for a few days, Connie," she said. "Give this time to blow over. Can you handle it?"

"Of course. Don't you worry."

"You've got my cellular number in case of emergency. I'm hoping like hell the cops will figure this out before the business goes down the tubes."

Connie leaned across the desk and patted her hand. "It's going to be okay. I promise."

The warmth of her friend's touch and her words of encouragement almost sent Angela into a tailspin again. She had to get out of there. "Thanks," she said, rising abruptly and making for the back door. "I hope for both our sakes you're right."

Outside, the afternoon had faded into dusk, and the air grew chill. Angela buttoned the light jacket she wore and strode to the driver's side of her car. She knew something was wrong before she opened the door. A large scratch stretched from the rear panel across both doors and ended just above the left front tire. She swore under her breath. Someone had keyed the paint job.

Then she opened the door and a small scream escaped her lips.

Chapter 10

Th' magic of th' conjureman be ancient as ole Africa herself. Th' secret of th' root crossed th' big water long ago, and th' mantle was passed down t' them who got th' magic. White men don't understand th' power of th' root. That be good . . .

DYLAN screeched into a parking space near Angela's shop just as Johnny Reilly and the police photographer were finishing recording the incident. Her call had been brief—"You want to protect me? Get your ass over here, now!"—and her voice frightened. He was relieved when he saw her with Connie at the far side of the lane that ran behind the shop. Her face was pale and drawn, and she looked as unhappy as he'd ever seen her, but she was alive and in one piece.

"What happened?" he asked, bolting toward her. As he passed the open door of her vehicle, he glanced inside . . . and stopped in his tracks. The body of a black cat, its fur soaked in blood, lay on the front seat. Next to it was a bundle of twigs tied together with black twine, and a low mound of dirt.

"What the hell?"

"Reilly says I've been 'rooted,' " Angela said, giving him a confused look and a little a shrug of her shoulders.

Dylan frowned at her. "Excuse me?"

Reilly answered for her as he peeled off the rubber gloves he'd been wearing. "Rooted. It's a voodoo thing."

"Voodoo?" Dylan stared at Reilly, thinking the man had lost his mind. Of course there were local rumors that practitioners of the ancient African religion still operated in the area, but he suspected those stories were mostly for the benefit of the tourists.

"In fact, it looks like we've got a real 'blue root' going here," Reilly added, his lips curving upward slightly at Dylan's obvious discomfort. "C'mon, Montana. You've been around a long time. You know about this stuff."

"No," he said, glancing at Angela, who appeared more bewildered than frightened, "I don't. What the hell's a 'blue root'?"

It seemed to him that Reilly puffed up a bit as he launched into an explanation. "It's a 'power root,' if you will. Black cats, or parts thereof, are used by the conjure-man in casting the most potent hexes." He held up the bundle of twigs. "The ends of these have been chewed to make the spell even more powerful. And the goofer dust, well, that depends on whose grave it came from and when it was gathered. If it came from a good person's grave and was collected before midnight, it would be a 'good root.' But my bet is this came from an evil man's grave and was gathered after midnight."

"I've heard of voodoo, of course," Angela said, "but I've lived in Savannah most of my life, and I've never heard the term 'root.' "

Reilly leaned back against the car, looking at them as if he couldn't believe they didn't know this. "A 'root' is nothing more than another name for a spell, a charm, a curse. Some call it mojo, gris-gris. Hoodoo. Voodoo. They're all basically the same," he said, gesturing with his hands. "My great-uncle who lived up near Beaufort told me that the expression 'root' came from the herbal remedies used by the primitive slave doctors. A lot of the medicines back then were made from roots. But the old Gullah cures involved a lot more than herbs and roots."

"Like what?" Connie asked eagerly.

Reilly removed his glasses and wiped them with a handkerchief. "According to my uncle, root doctoring involves the spiritual belief system of the people," he went on. "If a man who believes in voodoo thinks he has been 'rooted,' all kinds of bad things are likely to happen to him. He might come down with a disease, or have a traffic accident, or a dog might bite him. Psychologists call it a self-fulfilling prophecy. Others call it autosuggestion. Basically, voodoo works because the people believe it works."

Reilly's stock went up a notch with Dylan. "You learn all that from your uncle?"

The sergeant nodded. "He was deputy to a sheriff up in Beaufort County, old J. E. McTeer, who was probably the most effective lawman in this century around here, because he respected the voodoo tradition. McTeer became a white root doctor and used his knowledge of the old superstitions to maintain law and order in his jurisdiction. I grew up hearing stories about him. When I became a cop, I ran into enough crimes blamed on root hexes that I decided I ought to at least read up on it."

Reilly was smarter than Dylan wanted to give him credit for. And he seemed surprisingly altruistic about being a cop. Maybe he *wasn't* in Quintos's pay. The jury was still out on that one. "So, why do we have this voodoo stuff in Angela's car?" Dylan asked.

Reilly frowned and rubbed his temples. "Probably one of two things. This could be the work of a prankster, somebody wanting to scare you . . ."

"I'd say he's succeeded," Angela broke in. "But why would someone want to scare me like this?"

"It's like that hate call you got. Some people get a perverted pleasure out of kicking others when they're down. If it was a prankster, he's probably watching us right now and laughing his head off."

Angela darted a glance up nervously at the second floor of the townhouse that backed up to the narrow lane that ran behind her store.

"Is that who you think did this, a prankster?" Dylan didn't like the edge he heard in Reilly's voice.

"Let's hope it was a prankster. Otherwise, I think we have a serious situation on our hands, whether it's an authentic voodoo curse or a warning couched in voodoo terms. A bloody black cat is bad enough, but combined with the twigs and the goofer dust . . . well, I'd say somebody wants Angela dead."

Angela was too stunned to talk as she and Dylan drove to a restaurant he'd suggested for dinner. It was out of the mainstream, he'd said, a place where Angela wouldn't be recognized. She hated that she had to skulk around like a criminal on the run, but the voodoo incident had shaken her worse than the media circus on her front steps.

Someone was following her, watching her. Waiting to kill her?

Even though she was still wretchedly uncomfortable around him, a part of Angela was glad Dylan had insisted on becoming her protector, and she had to admit she'd been very relieved to see him when he'd arrived at the shop. On a personal level, things would never be the same between them, because she could never trust him again with her heart. But she did trust his experience and skill as a cop, or ex-cop, or deep-cover narc, or private investigator, or whatever the hell he was now. He'd never answered her question about that. Or the rest of them, for that matter. But with him, she felt safer, less vulnerable, although if a drug lord like Lucas Quintos wanted her dead, she probably didn't have a chance.

They entered Teeple's, a small, unpretentious seafood shack frequented mostly by shrimpers and the locals who worked at the nearby shipyard. Dylan went directly to a table at the back, where he took the seat facing the door. The waitress brought menus and large glasses of ice water, but if she recognized Angela, she didn't show it.

After a few minutes, Angela began to relax a little as she studied the menu. Sitting in a restaurant, deciding on what to order, she felt deliciously normal.

Normal. All she wanted was for her life to return to normal.

She bit her lower lip. There was nothing normal about any aspect of her life at the moment. Maybe there never had been. Or ever would be. What was normal anyhow? She wasn't sure she knew anymore.

"I should have been there." Dylan's voice startled her, and Angela looked up. She heard the quiet guilt behind his words, and she wondered if he was speaking of today or of that night long ago. "You can't follow me around all the time," she said, although until the real killer was found, she wouldn't mind if he did.

"I thought you were going to call me. Since I hadn't heard from you, I assumed you were busy. I didn't want to bother you."

Dylan raised his head, and his dark eyes seemed tormented. "I want to be bothered."

Unsettled, Angela looked away. "Maybe this bodyguard thing isn't such a good idea, Dylan. I mean, I'm a big girl. A trained law officer. Now that I know what I'm dealing with, I can take care of myself." Even as she said it, Angela knew she didn't mean it.

"Don't even think it," he said with a scowl, "not after the phone call I got this afternoon."

His tone of voice made her apprehensive. "Who called?"

"A lawyer named Harlow Bertram. He was looking for a private investigator to do a job for one of his clients. He said I was referred by an old friend of his, a retired criminal defense attorney, who got my name from one of his contacts on the police force."

The hair stood up on Angela's arms. After what had happened in that long-ago drug bust, she doubted anybody on the SPD who would recommend Dylan for dogcatcher, much less a real job. She also knew he was supposed to be undercover. There was only one cop who knew Dylan was back in town. "Reilly?"

"No. Turner. The guy who called me to tell me Reilly'd brought you in."

Angela had forgotten about Turner. The derelict she'd seen in the corridor, the one who'd recognized her. "How do you know him?"

"He was a rookie on the Counter-Narcotics Team back then . . ."

He broke off, and Angela ignored his reference to a time she guessed they both wished they could forget. But she was alarmed. "How did Turner know you were back in town? Did you call him?"

Dylan shook his head. "He's a team leader on the CNT now. I suppose he got a tip from someone that I was headed back this way. There's a network among undercover cops. It wouldn't be hard for him to find out." He gave her a small grin. "Don't worry. I don't think he's on the wrong side. He did me a favor in calling and letting me know Reilly had you on the hot seat."

But Angela wasn't convinced. "Are you sure? Hasn't he blown your cover by giving your name to this lawyer?"

But Dylan waved off her concern. "Turner's okay. And I think he's done me another favor. You'll never guess who the lawyer's client is."

"Who?"

"Elizabeth Slade, the wife of the man you're accused of murdering."

Angela's heart nearly stopped beating, and her palms grew damp. "Don't you find this a bit much, Dylan? I mean, you've been out of town for five years. Your return has something to do with Slade, who gets bumped off right after your arrival. I'm accused of his murder, and the next thing you know, an 'old friend' contacts you about what's happened to me. Then a day later he steers Elizabeth Slade your way. Give me a break. I wouldn't say this Scott Turner is *okay*. I'd say he's been spying on you."

"Maybe. More likely, he's using me to get information he wants. But like I said, he's done me a favor. My . . . ah . . . client wants me to find out if Slade's family knew about his plans to oust Quintos, and if they are involved in any way. I was wondering how I could pull off showing up at Paradisia Plantation and asking a lot of questions without raising suspicions. Now, they've invited the proverbial camel into their tent."

Angela wasn't at all sure Turner had done Dylan a favor. And she wondered who Dylan's "client" was. The DEA? If so, Dylan was once again involved in a dark and dangerous game, and a small shiver inside let her know how worried she was for him. "What does Elizabeth Slade want from you?" she asked.

"Bertram wouldn't talk about it over the phone. I have an appointment to meet him and Mrs. Slade at Paradisia tomorrow morning."

This just didn't feel right to Angela. She started to reach across the table to touch his hands, to try and convince him not to trust Turner, but she caught herself just in time. Embarrassed, she clenched her fingers together and said, "Be careful, Dylan. This could be some kind of trap."

He'd seen her gesture and gave her a curious look, as if he wanted to say something, then thought better of it. He took a sip of his water instead. "I suppose it could be," he replied at last. "But his call played right into my hands."

"Supposing this is all legitimate, which I doubt, are you going to tell them you know me?"

He gave a short laugh. "I don't get paid big bucks for being a fool."

"I'm sorry. That was a stupid question. But maybe they already know that you are my . . . uh . . . friend. Maybe that's why they've called you."

Dylan's dark gaze penetrated hers. "Are we friends, Angela?"

She shifted in her seat and looked away. "Just be careful, Dylan. You might be walking into an ambush of some kind."

The waitress returned and took their order. She passed on the appetizers, but Dylan ordered "gator bites," small chunks of fried alligator meat. Angela wrinkled her nose at eating alligator. "How gross."

"Not at all," he grinned. "It tastes just like chicken."

He convinced her to try one when they were served, and although she didn't find it repulsive, neither did she have a desire for a second.

"Don't want to ruin my appetite," she apologized. And when the main course was served, she was glad she'd held off.

It was one of the best Lowcountry boils she'd ever eaten. They devoured the succulent shrimp, sausage, corn on the cob, and potatoes that were boiled up together in spicy water and served on newspaper. The shrimp peels and other inedibles went into a trash can via a hole in the center of the table. Rustic, but fun. Angela had heard of Teeple's. It'd been around for years, but she'd never been here. She made a mental note to add it to her list of suggestions for visitors who wished to experience authentic Lowcountry cuisine.

If, that is, she had a business when this was all over. If indeed she were still alive.

Chapter 11

Most folk don't know they can pick up evil just by walking on it. Ain't no protection for it, except being aware and watching where you walk . . .

AFTER dinner, Dylan urged Angela not to return to her house, offering his boat as temporary sanctuary. "You aren't safe staying alone in that rambling old house," he said.

"You sound like my mother," she protested. But she knew he was probably right. She resented having to hide out when she'd done nothing wrong, but she wasn't an idiot. Somebody was out to get her, and she didn't intend to make herself an easy target. As much as she hated having to depend on someone else, especially the man who'd broken her heart and shattered her dreams, she actually considered taking Dylan up on his offer. It would be the last place in the world someone would think of to look for her.

But she was nervous about being in such close quarters with him. "Let me think about it." She checked her watch. "I should have brought my own car. I have to look in on Mom again tonight. Will you take me back to the shop?"

As they left the riverside restaurant, Angela expected Dylan to turn right to take the bypass that would lead them directly into the heart of Savannah. Instead, he turned left. "Where are you going?" she asked.

"To look in on Mom."

Mary Ellen Donahue looked no better than she had the night before. She was still clad in the tattered robe, with her hair unbrushed. Angela was shocked and immediately regretted she hadn't been able to help her mother more during her illness.

"You need to go to the hospital," she insisted.

"No, I don't," Mary Ellen replied, glaring at Dylan as he followed Angela into her living room. "I'm getting better."

Angela had tried to persuade Dylan to leave her, just for half an hour, but he'd been adamant that he accompany her. She couldn't fathom his reasoning. He disliked Mary Ellen with a passion, and Angela didn't think anybody was going to harm her on her short visit to her mother's house. But she was learning it did little good to argue with Dylan Montana when his mind was set on something. It was a little detail about him that she'd forgotten.

Angela went into the kitchen and saw the chicken soup still sitting in the pan she'd used to heat it. "Good grief, Mom, you haven't eaten a thing." She turned and placed both hands on her hips. "You have to eat or you'll really get sick."

"I haven't been able to keep anything down," her mother admitted, dropping wearily into a chair.

"Then we'd better get you to the emergency room. You're probably dehydrated."

"I'm not going to any damned hospital."

Angela could be as stubborn as Mary Ellen if need be. "Eat, or go to the hospital."

Mary Ellen's gaze challenged Angela for a long moment, but at last she looked away. "Okay, okay," she said. "But I wish you hadn't brought *him* along." She tilted her head toward the living room where they'd left Dylan. "Even though he looks like a street thug, I'm embarrassed that I'm still in these rags. Let me take a shower first."

Angela thought that was a positive sign. "Fine." She looked into the fridge, which held few options for a quick meal. "Scrambled eggs okay?"

"Whatever."

After she left the kitchen, Dylan ambled in. "Do you think she's getting any better?" he asked. "She still looks pretty bad."

"We'll see when she comes out of the bathroom. Maybe just getting cleaned up will help her feel better."

"I'll do those." Dylan took the carton of eggs from her. "Why don't you straighten the living room? It's a trash heap in there."

Angela eyed him skeptically. "Since when did you become Martha Stewart?"

He shrugged. "Living on a boat makes you change your habits. Leave a few things out and the place looks like a dump." He cocked his head and gave her a lopsided grin. "Remember that if you stay with me."

At his smile, Angela's stomach did a strange little flip-flop, and she flushed. Damn. "Sure. You bet." She quickly headed for the living room before he tried to push her again to stay on his boat.

He was right. The room was a disaster. Newspapers were strewn everywhere, all turned to stories about the murder of J. J. Slade. She saw her own photo several times, and the pictures brought back the horror of her predicament. Reilly had let her go again, but at any moment he might knock on her door with a warrant for her arrest. She cursed the media for propagating lies, cursed Johnny Reilly for believing them, and cursed Lucas Quintos and Cecil Clifford, whom she believed to be behind the scheme.

She was also concerned that the stories were obviously troubling her mother. Was her anxiety for Angela the real reason Mary Ellen hadn't been eating? Angela picked up one of the papers and scanned the story and its many sidebars. She hadn't taken time to read the newspapers since this nightmare began. Or maybe she hadn't had the stomach to face them. She was suddenly curious. Her eye caught on a short article her mother had marked in red pencil. It was a background piece about J. J. Slade. Angela took the paper back into the kitchen.

"You probably know all this, but I know nothing about the man I supposedly killed," she said, then read the meat of the article to him:

" 'Slade moved to Paradisia Plantation in 1971 upon his marriage to the heiress of the property, the former Elizabeth Mayhew, daughter of Angus and Caroline Mayhew, now both deceased. Their only child, Veronica Anne, was born the following year shortly after the tragic death of Mrs. Slade's father in a hunting accident.

" 'Little is known about the reclusive Slade, other than that his worth is reputed to be in the multiple millions. Upon the death of his father-in-law in 1972, he assumed management of the dwindling Mayhew fortune and staged an impressive turnaround. Today, the known assets of the Slades include a shipping line based in Dade County, Florida, a luxury hotel in Palm Beach, Florida, a dog track in Daytona Beach, Florida, major interest in a paper mill near Brunswick, Georgia, and the vast agricultural enterprise on Paradisia Plantation, near Sunhill, Georgia.' "

Angela let out a low whistle. "Man, when I kill somebody, I go for the top, don't I?"

Mary Ellen appeared at the door, dressed in slacks and a fresh blouse. "Don't talk like that, even if you're kidding." She looked at Dylan. "*He* might have to testify that you said you killed him."

"Mother, don't be paranoid." Angela didn't think she could take it if Mary Ellen went into one of her spells right now. In the past, whenever Mary Ellen brooded on life's unfairness in taking away the man she loved, she would lash out at whoever was handy, which most of the time was Angela. Now, she was obviously brooding on what had unfairly happened to Angela and was ready to vent her wrath on Dylan. It was Mary Ellen who was being unfair, and Angela wouldn't have it.

"Leave him alone, Mother. He's not the enemy."

"Supper's on," Dylan interrupted them, sliding the fluffy yellow eggs onto a plate and adding a couple of pieces of toast.

Her mother muttered something about Angela's bullet wounds being Dylan's fault, but she took a seat anyway and began to eat the food as if she were genuinely hungry.

Dylan excused himself and went into the living room. Angela knew her mother's words had stung, because rude as they were, they spoke the truth. Angela closed her eyes against the wave of emotion that tightened her throat. God, how she wished none of that had happened.

But it had. And so had this miserable mess she now found herself in. She felt a renewed urgency to get it sorted out before she found herself liking Dylan again.

As she busied herself cleaning the kitchen, Angela watched her mother out of the corner of her eye. She wanted to talk about the murder and reassure Mary Ellen that things would turn out all right. But she couldn't lie. She wasn't at all sure things would get better.

"I think you should sue the bastards," Mary Ellen said suddenly.

"What? Sue who?"

"The idiots at the newspaper. They've got it all wrong, and it's hurting you. Have you thought about hiring a lawyer?"

"I don't need a lawyer. Dylan's helping me." She hadn't meant to let that drop, but there it was.

Mary Ellen looked up at Angela and said sarcastically, "Like he helped you before?"

"Mother, stop it." Angela had reached the limit of her patience with Mary Ellen. "He . . . has some idea who is behind this and contacts who can help me. I don't need a lawyer, because I didn't do anything. I just want to get to the bottom of this so I can get on with my life."

Mary Ellen said nothing. She looked at Angela as if her

daughter had taken complete leave of her senses. Angela knew that look. It was generally followed by a lecture, and she didn't want to hear it. She finished drying the skillet and replaced it in the cabinet. "I have to go now. Will you be all right?"

"Fine," Mary Ellen said crossly. "I'll be just fine."

A few minutes later, Angela and Dylan were headed toward the marina. She turned in her seat to face him. "Thanks for preparing Mom's supper. And for not getting into a fight with her. She can be so rude sometimes."

Dylan gave her a sidelong glance. "Actually, I'm quite proud of myself."

"For cooking the eggs?"

"No. For not lacing them with arsenic."

Chapter 12

When th' evil spirit comes t' roost inside a man or a woman, that hant take them over and they become evil in th' flesh. It takes great magic t' remove th' hant, and sometime that don't work either . . .

THE music that emanated from the expensive sound system was rich and rhythmical, exotic, heated. Ronnie closed her eyes and swayed in time to the beat, the silk of her chemise brushing erotically against her breasts. She'd inhaled the line of cocaine that had been laid out for her on the dresser, and she was feeling good. The line was her "treat" from the man who lay naked on the bed, watching her. Although she was afraid of him, for she had known the pain of his cruelty and had seen him inflict it on others, she didn't mind fucking him. He was a good lover, always giving her pleasure before taking his own. And he was generous with his treats.

Besides, she owed him a lot of money. This was one way of working off her debt. Although that debt was so high now, it would take a chunk of her upcoming inheritance to take care of it in full.

Ronnie didn't know his name. His skin was tan, as if he spent a lot of time in the sun. His hair was dark and wavy, his eyes like midnight. He wasn't tall, but he was built like a bull. His body was hard, his sex demanding. Just the way she liked it. He asked for her whenever he came to town on business, and she always did everything he wanted her to.

"Hey, baby, let me see that beautiful little ass now," he

said. "Take your clothes off for me, and do it real slow." He spoke with a heavy Spanish accent.

Ronnie liked this part. It turned her on that a powerful man like him found her beautiful. That a man who was old enough to be her father wanted her body.

Moving seductively in the low light provided by several candles placed around the room, Ronnie slipped one strap from her shoulder and ran her hands sensually down the length of her torso. Her nipples stood erect, and she fingered them, feeling the hot juices gathering between her legs. She removed the second strap and dragged it slowly down the length of her arm, baring one breast in the process.

"Oh, baby, you're so good."

Ronnie squinted out of one eye and saw the man stroking himself as she danced. "Don't get too far ahead of me, lover," she said, her voice husky. She was on fire, and she needed him to quench the exquisite desire that mounted with each move she made.

She brought the chemise down to her waist and taking her breasts in both hands, rubbed their ample curves together. "You like this, lover?" she said, licking her lips slowly with her tongue.

"You know it. Don't stop. Dance for me."

Ronnie raised her arms high overhead and danced toward him, rotating her hips and caressing her body. The chemise slipped inch by inch down her torso, past her navel, past the dark triangle at the juncture of her legs, past her hips, and fell into a puddle on the floor.

"Now," she said, flinging one leg over him and settling against his erection, "let me show you how I can really dance." Splaying her fingers across his hairy chest, she moved her hips until she brought him into the hot wetness of her, and she smiled in pure pleasure as his hardness filled her. His hands stroked her breasts roughly, and she tossed her head back in ecstasy. She rode him with silken strokes until she felt her insides begin to go into meltdown.

"Now," she said again, this time with urgency. "Now!" she cried out, wanting the fierce passion she knew he could give. "Now, for God's sake, now!"

He moved on top of her and slammed into her with brutal force. His fingers dug savagely into the flesh of her hips as he ground himself against her. She loved the pain. It made her feel dirty, like the whore she was. She deserved the pain. "More," she whimpered as she approached climax.

His hands moved to her throat and tightened around it, cutting off her breath, but she wasn't afraid. It was part of their game. He'd taught her how it worked. Bright sparkles danced before her eyes, and the sensations became too exquisite to bear. She shook violently when she came, and he released her from his death grip. The air rushed into her lungs, and with it came the indescribable sensation that every cell and fiber of her body was climaxing. God, was he good.

Afterward, she lay in his arms, her breasts pressed into his chest, trying to catch her breath. But he was impatient. He brought her hand down to cover his still-hard cock. Nearby, the sex toys he preferred were lined up and ready. She'd had her fun. Now she had a job to do.

And the night had only just begun . . .

The original antebellum house on Paradisia Plantation, like those on all the neighboring plantations, had been burned to the ground by Sherman in his march to the sea at the end of the Civil War. The structure which was now known as the "Big House" had been built a decade after the war by Elizabeth Slade's great-great-grandfather, a carpetbagger who had married her great-great-grandmother, a Southern belle with a good family name and not much else other than title to the sprawling but despoiled plantation.

To his credit, Josiah Mayhew had managed to bring the property back from the devastation it had suffered during the war and built a substantial but gracious house to replace the earlier structure. Paradisia was the name he chose for his estate, for he'd claimed he had truly arrived in paradise, or so the family story went. Elizabeth had often doubted it, for she knew that malaria was ever-present in those days, making the area nearly uninhabitable during the summer months. But regardless of her ancestor's excessive romanticism, Paradisia, and her family name, meant everything to her, and she would do anything to protect them both.

Anything.

She looked at her watch. It was just after nine A.M. The private investigator wouldn't be here for another hour. She rang for coffee, then settled behind her desk to take care of some pressing business matters. She heard the telephone ring and waited to see if it was something she needed to attend to, or if Bridget would be able to handle it. Seconds later, the intercom buzzed. "It's an Anthony Spriggs, ma'am, calling from Atlanta. Says he's an attorney with the law firm of . . . let's see, I wrote it down . . . Stearns, McIlheny, and Forrester.

Elizabeth frowned. She didn't like lawyers. They only brought bad news. That's why she'd insisted they use Harlow for their legal matters. He was safe. Like family.

"What does he want?" she asked Bridget, thinking it was some kind of solicitation call from a legal shark hoping to make a buck off the grieving widow.

"Just a moment." She put Elizabeth on hold, and moments later came back on the line. "Says it's something to do with Mr. Slade's will."

Mr. Slade's will? Impossible. It, along with the papers concerning the trust, was securely tucked away in a lock box at the Lincoln County National Bank. Something fishy was going on here. "I'll take his call."

Anthony Spriggs sounded young and confident. "Good morning, Mrs. Slade. I'm calling to extend condolences from our firm over the death of your husband. We just learned of it this morning."

"Thank you, Mr. Spriggs. What do you want?" Elizabeth had no patience for fools.

Spriggs cleared his throat. "Well, uh, you see, Mrs. Slade, last week, your husband visited our offices here in Atlanta. He executed a new will and attended to other legal matters."

Elizabeth's skin turned ice-cold and her stomach clenched. "I believe you must be mistaken, Mr. Spriggs," she said, working to keep her voice from shaking. "Mr. Slade's attorney is Mr. Harlow Bertram, who drew up both of our wills, which are secured in a bank vault in a nearby community."

"I know this is difficult, Mrs. Slade, but the fact of the matter is, your husband signed a new will in my presence and in the presence of two partners in the firm just last Thursday."

Elizabeth closed her eyes. *Please, dear God, let this be some kind of hoax.* "Mr. Spriggs, I find this all most unbelievable. Perhaps I should have my attorney call you."

"That would be fine." He gave her the number, which she scribbled on a note pad. "I was given the directive by Mr. Slade to set the reading of the will within a week from the date I learned of his death. That means I need to do it by next Thursday. Under the . . . uh . . . circumstances, I would be happy to come to Paradisia for the reading. What day would be convenient for you?"

"That is very kind of you, Mr. Spriggs. I can't say when would be best. I will discuss this with my attorney, and he'll get back to you." She hung up without another word, then dropped her head into her hands.

Could this be for real? Why would J. J. do such a thing? Harlow had always been their mutual attorney. Harlow had drawn up a will for each of them with terms of which the other approved. They'd established a trust to protect their assets. Even though their personal relationship was distant, Elizabeth had always trusted in their agreements concerning financial matters. At least up until she'd received the phone call from Ricky Suarez.

A shiver passed through her. Had J. J. learned what she'd done? Was that why he'd changed his will? She tried to convince herself that it was impossible, both that he'd learned about her deal with Suarez and that he'd changed his will. But J. J. was both slick and wily. Maybe he'd had their phones tapped.

Panicked, she picked up the phone and dialed Harlow's number, but there was no answer. He was probably already en route to Paradisia for the meeting with the private investigator. Elizabeth stood and paced the floor, her mind racing. She didn't frighten easily, but at the moment, she was alarmed. Had the bastard done something to compromise her ownership of Paradisia? He knew this plantation was her Achilles' heel. If he wanted to hurt her, that's how he'd do it.

Gazing out of the window, she saw Veronica's new BMW convertible skid to a halt in front of the house. The car had been a birthday present from her parents, an extravagant gift designed to assuage some of their daughter's anger at them for keeping her on a tight financial leash.

It was one of the few times Elizabeth and J. J. had agreed on something that concerned their daughter. Putting her on an allowance had been for her own good. Veronica had some very nasty habits, some very *expensive* nasty habits, and she'd managed to run through her substantial trust fund in spite of J. J.'s best efforts to keep her from touching the principal. Elizabeth suspected she'd done it for spite as much as anything, knowing how much it would disturb her father, whose entire existence centered around the building of wealth.

Wealth.

J. J. had built an impressive fortune. What had he done with it?

She saw Veronica get out of the car and slam the door, and winced to see the garb the girl wore. As she had yesterday, she looked as if she'd come straight from the red-light district. Elizabeth knew Veronica had a closet full of decent clothing upstairs. Expensive, tasteful clothing. She could look like the heiress she was when she wanted, but she often chose instead to look cheap and shabby.

It occurred to her that Veronica liked to masquerade as something she wasn't. Had she posed as Angela Donahue? Was she still posing? Was Angela Donahue real or some kind of alter ego for Veronica? She couldn't wait to talk to the private investigator Harlow had lined up.

In the meantime, Elizabeth decided not to mention anything about Anthony Spriggs's phone call to Veronica. Not until Harlow had time to investigate it.

Elizabeth heard the front door slam and her daughter's footsteps echoing in the hall. They stopped outside the parlor door, and she halfway expected Veronica to open the door, if for no reason other than to flaunt her disgusting attire.

But she didn't, and Elizabeth released her breath when Veronica went on. She didn't want to see her right now. Or talk to her. She didn't want to know where Veronica went when she wasn't home, or why she donned her disguises.

Or if she'd killed her father.

Chapter 13

Ain't no one can learn you how t' be a conjureman. It's something you just know. Same with casting a spell. Ain't no one can write down th' spells, because they're all different. They come from th' magic only th' conjureman knows . . .

DYLAN turned into the driveway of Paradisia Plantation and stopped to identify himself to the guard at the gate. He was a few minutes early. Would he mind waiting? the guard asked, giving his old Camaro a skeptical once-over. Mrs. Slade insisted that guests not arrive before their appointed time.

Oh, brother, he thought, but steered the battered car into a parking space alongside the gravel drive. At least this gave him a few minutes to study the house and perhaps form an initial perception of the people who lived there. The panorama before him looked as if it were straight out of a movie.

The drive curved graciously toward the house and was lined with ancient live oaks with limbs that twisted and turned in the macabre fashion of their species. The house stood like a majestic jewel box at the far end. Three stories tall, with Doric columns that extended the full height, it gleamed white and pristine in the morning sun.

There were two cars parked in front of the house, a blue Volvo and a red BMW Z3 convertible with the top down. Another driveway split off to the right and led behind the house. Dylan assumed the Slades' cars and those of the staff were garaged back there somewhere. He'd expected the lawyer Harlow Bertram to be present—guessed the Volvo was his—but he wondered who owned the second car.

He picked up his camera and snapped off several shots, including a close-up of the two cars, capturing both license tags. A knock on his window startled him. He turned to see the scowling guard waving him through. Dylan started the car and proceeded. He supposed Mrs. Slade didn't like her guests to be late, either.

He was greeted at the front door by a short, middle-aged woman with graying red hair and mottled skin. She wore a black uniform and white apron. "This way," she said, and indicated for him to follow her.

His gaze swept the enormous hallway, sizing up the wealth displayed on wall and floor. Portraits and landscapes, Oriental rugs, crystal chandeliers and sconces, marble tables. The place reeked of money. He followed the serving woman to the second set of doors on the left. "They're waiting for you," she said, as if scolding him for being late. She opened the door and announced him to the two people who stood close together in the room.

The man approached with a solicitous smile. The woman, looking drawn and dubious, remained where she was. Dylan could imagine what she thought when she saw him. Although he'd tied his long hair at the nape of his neck and wore a dark blue shirt under a sports coat, he still looked the role of a sleazy PI. He was certain he wasn't exactly the type that called frequently at Paradisia. With an effort, he repressed a grin.

"I'm Harlow Bertram," the man said, extending his hand. "Thank you for coming."

Dylan shook the fleshy hand. Harlow Bertram was not a tall man, but he had a distinctive presence. He was well-dressed in suit and tie. His thick, white hair was neatly trimmed, and he was clean-shaven. His eyes were a faded blue behind the thick lenses of his glasses. His smile appeared overeager but genuine.

Dylan was introduced to Elizabeth Slade, who made no effort to greet him other than to nod in his direction. She was taller than Bertram, slender and obviously well-bred. Her hair was silver rather than gray, her clothing impeccable. Dylan noticed her fingers were long and graceful, as if she were a pianist or an artist.

"Please have a seat," Bertram said. The trio sat stiffly on separate chairs before the unlit fireplace. "As you can surely understand, my client is very distraught at the moment, Mr. Montana. This whole business has been most . . . unpleasant."

"I understand." Elizabeth Slade struck Dylan as the type to find the murder of her husband unpleasant, rather than devastating.

"To get to the point and the reason for my call, it's not just the murder, you see. We trust the police will handle their investigation appropriately. It's about the . . . girl. Angela Donahue. We want to learn more about her."

All of Dylan's senses went on red alert. "I read in the newspapers that she runs a tour business in Savannah," he said cautiously.

"That's just it," Elizabeth said, coming to life at last. "J. J. never went to Savannah," she said. "He hated Savannah. Or at least that's what he always told me." She raised her chin, and Dylan saw that her eyes suddenly gleamed with unshed tears. "We didn't have the greatest of marriages, Mr. Montana, but in my own way, I . . . I loved him. And now . . . he's dead." Her voice caught on her words.

It was a good show, but Dylan wondered how deep her emotions went.

She swallowed and took a deep breath, then went on, her voice more solid now. She gazed at him without flinching when she said, "I want to know who this woman is, this Angela Donahue. I want to know why she killed J. J."

Dylan remained cool beneath her malignant regard. He instinctively didn't like Elizabeth Slade. "From what I hear, Mrs. Slade, the police have found nothing conclusive that would prove that Angela Donahue killed your husband. In fact, I believe she claims she didn't even know him."

"She's lying," Bertram stated flatly. "Everybody saw them together."

Dylan remained unruffled. He was certain Slade had been killed by his enemies in the underworld. But he was uncertain whether these two had been involved. That was what Oscar Malone wanted him to find out. Were they part of Slade's action? Or were they in with Lucas Quintos, the man Slade had sought to oust as kingpin of the drug business in the area? Or had they plotted against Slade to take over things from Quintos themselves? To look at them, they appeared unlikely candidates for being involved in the drug scene at all, but the kind of money involved made for very strange, and deadly, bedfellows.

Whatever, he suspected they knew who killed Slade and were involved in setting Angela up to take the blame. He guessed they wanted to hire him to keep an eye on how the case against her was progressing, to give them a little advanced warning in case they needed to make another move to insure the success of their scheme. He doubted if either of them had actually pulled the trigger, but he decided to yank their chains just a little to see if he could find out who'd made the hit.

"I've spoken to the detective in charge of this case, Mr. Bertram, and he's inclined to believe Ms. Donahue, unless something more substantial comes up. Identities can be easily mistaken. Signatures forged." He watched their expressions closely. "And he has found nothing to link Ms. Donahue romantically to Mr. Slade. Frankly, I think she's innocent, and you'd be wasting your money and my time to send me chasing after her. I'd be of more value to you in helping find the real killer."

Bertram's face turned pink. Elizabeth's went white. His hunch had been correct. Elizabeth Slade did not want him to find the real killer.

"That's not why we asked you to come here, Montana." Harlow said. "We want to know about Ms. Donahue, regardless of your personal opinions. If she wasn't his lover, then she must have been involved in some kind of business deal with him."

"Do you have any idea what that business might have been?" Dylan asked mildly.

"I'm sure you've read in the papers about his enterprises. Most of them are in other states. Other countries even. They're probably legit, but . . . who knows?"

"Harlow!" Elizabeth glared at him.

He shrugged. "Don't be naive, Elizabeth. We don't know what all J. J. was involved in." He turned back to Dylan. "Have your detective friend look into Ms. Donahue's 'tour business.' It's possible J. J.'s money is behind it. Maybe he called her loan, and she killed him."

Dylan raised his eyebrows. Bertram sounded convinced that Slade knew Angela. So maybe he and Elizabeth *hadn't* been involved in Slade's activities. But Dylan was still suspicious.

"I thought he never went to Savannah." He looked at Elizabeth. She averted her eyes.

"Like I said, he told me he hated Savannah. But maybe he was lying. He did that a lot," she added bitterly.

Dylan let it drop and moved on. "So I take it he was often away from Paradisia? How did he travel?"

"He had a private plane, of course," Harlow said, as if it were the most ridiculous question. "There's an airstrip on Paradisia. He employed a full-time pilot, Bob Greer." He paused. "Come to think of it, I wonder what's happened to Greer? Have you heard from him since J. J.'s death?" he asked Elizabeth.

She shook her head. "No. But then, I didn't know the

man well. I'm not sure I'd recognize him if he walked into the room."

Harlow's mention of J.J.'s pilot caught Dylan's attention. It was possible that he'd killed Slade, if they'd been running drugs together or some such. He pressed for more information, although it was tangential to his real purpose. "You said his name is Bob Greer? Any idea where I might find him?"

Harlow thought a minute. "I think he lives in Savannah. I remember once that J. J. wanted to go somewhere, and he was pissed that he had to wait for Greer to drive down here."

J. J. Slade must have been quite the tyrant, Dylan decided. A liar. An estranged husband. Merciless boss. How was he at being a father? Where was Veronica Slade in all this? he wondered suddenly. Malone had specifically wanted to know if and how she was connected to Slade's businesses.

"What about your daughter, Mrs. Slade?" he asked.

"You leave her out of this!" Her reaction was fierce. An overreaction.

Now we're getting somewhere. This wasn't about Angela Donahue. It was about Veronica Slade. Was Mommy trying to cover for her? He'd bet money on it. He looked around the room, hoping to see a photo of the daughter, but to his surprise, there were no pictures of anyone evident on the bookshelves, tables, or the desk. Being a member of the family, Veronica Slade was an obvious suspect. Why hadn't Johnny Reilly interviewed her? Or had he? Dylan made a mental note to check that out as soon as he left here.

"We want you to investigate Angela Donahue," Bertram growled, recapturing Dylan's attention. "You interested or not?"

Dylan shrugged. He wasn't quite ready for the interview

to end. "Maybe. I just think you're barking up the wrong tree."

Elizabeth spoke, her voice cold. "We are a very private family, Mr. Montana. And a very wealthy one. We must protect ourselves from predators such as Ms. Donahue. She was involved with my husband. I want to know how. I want to know everything about her, so that if the time should ever come, I will be better able to deal with the scandal."

Dylan understood her clearly. She wanted to know all about Angela so she could do everything in her power to see that Angela was convicted of the murder. Elizabeth Slade was right about one thing. Hers was a wealthy family. And a powerful one. And there was no doubt in Dylan's mind she would use all those resources against Angela in order to protect Veronica.

He stood. "I'm sorry, Mrs. Slade, Mr. Bertram, but like I said, I think you'd be wasting your money hiring me. If it's scandal you're worried about, I can't help you. There's little you can do to keep this mess out of the papers. You'd be better off hiring a good PR firm. One that specializes in spin control."

Dylan took the steps two at a time. He couldn't get away from this place fast enough. Elizabeth Slade made his skin crawl, and he was more worried than ever for Angela's safety. He hadn't taken their job, but they would find somebody else who would. Somebody who was willing, for a buck, to try to prove an innocent person was guilty.

If that was unsuccessful, he feared that Slade's calculating widow might seek her own personal, private revenge against Angela. A chill passed over him.

Dylan got into his car and started the engine, but before pulling away, he glanced back at the house. To his surprise, he saw a woman standing on the second-floor balcony, gazing down at him. He could not see her face clearly, as it was in the shadow of the roof, but he could see she had dark hair and fair skin, and that she was dressed in black.

Then suddenly, to his shock, she pulled her sweater over her head, baring her breasts to him and anyone else who might be looking. She must have seen the startled look on his face, because she leaned her head back and laughed before stepping inside and disappearing from sight.

Dylan blinked, wondering if his eyes were playing tricks on him. But he knew that wasn't the case.

He shifted into gear, certain that he'd just met Veronica Slade.

Chapter 14

T' find something that's lost, take a shiny penny and put it in your right shoe. Hold th' rattles from th' rattlesnake and shake them three times, then throw them into th' air. When they land, they'll point you in th' right direction . . .

ANGELA looked at her watch and wondered how long Dylan was going to be at Paradisia. She wished like hell she'd made him take her to get her car before he'd left. At least she could have gone to the grocery store or something. Like a caged tiger, she paced the long hallway that ran through the center of her house. Tension knotted the muscles at her neck as she thought about who he was visiting, and she wondered again whether Scott Turner had set some kind of a trap for him.

After leaving her mother's house last night, Angela had opted not to take refuge aboard Dylan's boat. But he'd refused to let her stay home alone. Taking his role of bodyguard seriously, he'd once again slept on the couch in the parlor. What was she going to do about Dylan? Angela wondered as she paced. His presence, although appreciated for security, was also disturbing. At one time, Angela would have welcomed him into her house. Into her bed. Into her body. At one time, she'd thought they would marry and that at long last, she'd have the normal life and family she'd always longed for.

Normal. There was that word again.

Had her life ever been normal? From the time her father had left, it seemed like Angela's life was different from the other kids she knew. There was no father to come home from work, only a tired and angry mother who seemed unable to get over her husband's death. Angela had grown up faster than her friends, because she'd had to. When her mother had one of her spells, Angela had had to cook dinner if she wanted to eat, wash clothes if she wanted something clean to wear to school.

All she could remember wanting as a child was for their life to get back to normal. After she got over being sad about her father's death, Angela had begun to hope that her mother would find her another father, but Mary Ellen refused to even consider dating other men.

Her mother, in fact, had burned candles for Jake Donahue at Mass every week for years after he was killed. At first, Angela had thought she was praying for his soul. But one day, Mary Ellen had told her that she was praying for a miracle, for Jake to come home to them. She intimated that she thought he was still alive, and with new hope of having a father, like Nancy Drew, the preadolescent Angela had started looking for him.

For years she'd tried to find her father, or at least to obtain solid proof that Jake Donahue was dead, so her mother might consider getting remarried. But she'd been unable to accomplish either. Of course she couldn't find him, because he was dead. But the body had been charred beyond recognition, and in her grief, Mary Ellen had fully cremated it when it was returned to her. She'd taken the ashes and spread them on the ocean. Thirty years later, perhaps DNA testing could have proven the body was that of Jake Donahue. But there was no body to test.

Although she'd long ago given up her search, Angela's youthful quest for her father had led to an interest in law enforcement, which she eventually pursued as an adult. It was as an officer of the law that her path had crossed Dylan's. She'd fallen in love with him from the moment she'd met him. And as their relationship blossomed, she'd dared to hope her dreams of marrying and having a family of her own would at last come true.

But it wasn't to be, and her mother's constant and harsh admonishments against Angela's giving her heart to any man had come home to roost. She'd loved Dylan, given herself fully to him, and he'd walked away from her and all they had shared.

Angela drew in a deep, heavy breath and went into the kitchen to make some coffee. She'd given her heart to Dylan once. She wouldn't make that mistake again.

She poured a cup of steaming brew and sat down at the kitchen table, where the morning paper lay open. Angela glanced at it and saw a story on page one about the kidnapping of George Brown's son. Suddenly, she was ashamed that she'd become so self-absorbed that she'd nearly forgotten about it. She picked up the phone and dialed Judge Brown's house, but her call was answered by a machine. They were probably dodging the media too.

She dialed the Savannah PD. "Wally Padgett, please."

She heard two rings, then: "Padgett." The officer answered his own phone. Angela liked that.

"Hi, Wally. It's Angela Donahue. I was just wondering if there's anything new and hopeful on the Brown kidnapping."

"Oh, hi. I'm glad you called, Ms. Donahue. Unfortunately, I have nothing either new or hopeful to tell you. The feds are checking out the judge's current caseload to see if this might be directly related to anything on his docket. They're also looking into the boy's activities to see if he was involved in anything shady."

"Judge Brown's son? I'd find that hard to believe."

"Me, too, but you know these days, anything's possible."

Unfortunately, Padgett was right. The problems of drugs and gangs weren't confined to society's lower echelons.

"So what are you doing in the meantime?" she asked.

"Besides chewing my nails?" he said unhappily. "We've stretched our personnel resources pretty thin searching for him throughout the county. I was going to start a neighborhood canvass, but we don't have much manpower."

"I thought the witness said he was abducted in a car. Will a neighborhood search turn up anything if he's been taken somewhere else? I mean, he could be miles away."

"That's true," Padgett replied. "We're not expecting to find him or even come up with any other witnesses. All we're hoping to learn is if there are any gangs operating in the area near his school. We haven't heard of an organized group in that part of town, but it's possible. We're looking for anything that will give us a lead. You mentioned you wanted to help, Ms. Donahue. We could sure use your experience."

"Of course, Wally," Angela said, her heart going out to the young boy and to his parents who must be suffering the torments of the damned. "And please, call me Angela. What's the plan?"

"There's a meeting of volunteers here at the precinct this afternoon at two. If you know of anyone else who'd be willing and qualified to help, bring them along. We'll brief everyone and give you instructions. We've got to get a break on this thing."

Angela guessed he was under a lot of pressure to find Jeremiah Brown. The kidnapping of the son of a federal judge was a big deal. But to Angela, it didn't matter whose son it was. A child was a child. Jeremiah was an innocent caught in the middle of a dangerous game. An innocent, like herself.

"Count me in, Wally. See you at two."

Ricky Suarez snapped a shot of the old Camaro as it departed through the wide gates of Paradisia. He couldn't imagine who had come to call in such a jalopy, but he was sure this one would interest the higher-ups.

Suarez was taking a lot of heat from his boss, who wanted answers he didn't have. Their whole carefully conceived, long-planned operation had turned to shit. Upon Slade's death, Suarez's men had moved quickly to secure Slade's businesses in Florida, only to find them all shut down, including the shipping line that had been in the Mayhew family for generations. The offices had been cleaned out. Not even a shred of computer paper was left behind. Then they found out that Slade's offshore accounts had been closed as well.

His boss wanted to know what had gone wrong, and how to fix it, fast. He was growing impatient with Suarez and Joe Delano, who had been charged with finding out who had so royally screwed them.

Suarez wasn't certain, but he thought he might have an answer. It had arrived at Paradisia in a red BMW convertible the afternoon after Slade's body had been found, and it was in the form of a dark-haired young female who drove the car like a madwoman. Her breakneck approach caught him by surprise, and he'd been unable to photograph her before she careened through the gates, but he surmised instantly that it was Veronica Slade, the daughter of the deceased. They'd known Slade had a daughter, of course, but thinking her unimportant to their plans, they mistakenly hadn't bothered to check her out carefully.

But when Ricky saw her, he knew intuitively they'd been wrong. This was no mealy-mouthed, overprotected little rich girl. The top had been down on her car, and he'd seen the set of her jaw, the aggression in the way she drove. He'd phoned his boss to see what they had on her, but as he'd suspected, it was very little. His boss had set things in motion to find out more about her, but in the meantime, Ricky had orders to keep a close eye on Veronica Slade.

That had proven easier said than done. Suarez was having one hell of a time staying up with her. Veronica was slippery as the very devil, and, he suspected, equally as wicked. She was also the wild card in the deck, the unknown quantity who might have blown everything . . . or, if they were very lucky, who still might deliver what they were after.

It depended on whose side she was on.

Obviously, Slade had learned about Suarez's deal with Elizabeth and had moved to protect his assets. Every company whose records she'd given him was now defunct. Here today, boom, gone the next. Who had warned him? And why? Unless it had been Elizabeth herself, which he thought unlikely, the informant must have been someone very close to her, someone who could have overheard her or seen her copy the files from the computer. It had to be either family or staff, because they knew the files were kept somewhere in the Big House.

Veronica?

Did she know anything about her father's line of work? Was she loyal enough to daddy to rat on mommy? Did she even live at Paradisia? Would she have had the opportunity to overhear anything? He didn't know jackshit about Veronica Slade, and he was too impatient to wait for his boss to get back to him.

"Let's go," he said to Joe, who grunted and put away the Western novel he was reading. "This is getting us nowhere." Suarez started the engine and headed the old Ford van in the direction of the nearby town.

It was actually no more than an intersection along what used to be the main thoroughfare between Savannah and points south, where a few meager businesses struggled to survive against the competition of the newer franchises out on the interstate. He pulled into the parking lot of a ramshackle diner that advertised home-cooked food. Joe said nothing, but eagerly got out of the van and headed for the door. Suarez's stomach growled. Surveillance work sucked. He looked forward to a decent meal.

The waitress who served them appeared to be in her

fifties, with faded, overpermed hair and a sallow face. She was pleasant, however, and more important, talkative. If she noticed the scar that dissected the upper left side of his face, she didn't let on. Her name was Grace.

Suarez told her he was a writer, and that he and his friend, Joe, a photographer, were in the area doing a travel piece. Would she mind if they included her diner in their article? Grace brightened perceptively. Each time she visited their table, Suarez gained a little more of her confidence, asked more questions, until he was able to get to the heart of the matter.

"We heard about the murder of that guy Slade up in Savannah," Suarez said casually as she refilled their mugs with steaming coffee. "He was from around here, wasn't he?"

"Not originally. Nobody knows exactly where he came from," Grace replied, a shadow of disapproval crossing her plain, weathered face. "Nobody'd ever heard of him until all of a sudden, he up and married Elizabeth Mayhew. Most folks around here took him for a freeloader, you know, marrying a woman he thought had money. Ha! That was back when the Mayhews were about as poor as the rest of us. They just didn't show it. Then old man Mayhew died in that accident and Slade took over, and . . . well, the rest, as they say, is history."

"What do you mean?"

She shrugged. "Word was that Mayhew was a drunken gambler and had just about taken that lovely plantation down the tubes. When Slade got ahold of it, things started turning around. I read in the paper he was worth a kazillion bucks when he died."

"Interesting," Suarez murmured. "Does he have any heirs, other than the widow?"

Grace snorted. "Just a good-for-nothing cokehead daughter."

"Cokehead?" She had Suarez's full attention.

Grace darted a look around, and when she was satisfied that no other customers could hear her, she lowered her voice and said confidentially, "Veronica Slade lives up at the Big House at Paradisia, even though she's in her late twenties. Word is, her momma and daddy keep her on a pretty tight leash financially, because supposedly she blew all her own money on drugs. She's a wild one, that. They've tried to straighten her out. Threw her in rehab a couple of times, but it didn't help."

"How do you know?" Suarez probed. He was learning more about Veronica Slade at this little roadside diner than his boss would find out with all his sophisticated networks and informants put together. Small towns were like that.

She laughed. "Why, my brother's the sheriff, honey. He's picked her up more than a few times when she was so out of it she shouldn't be driving, but . . . seeing as how she's local and all, he takes her home, and the Slades, they promise it won't happen again." Grace paused, then added, "I just hope she doesn't get all coked up and kill somebody someday. She drives like a maniac. Don't know why they let her have that kind of car. We see her go by here doing ninety at least." This time her laugh was derisive. "Like there was someplace important to go around here."

"Where does she get the drugs?" Suarez asked carefully, but he instantly regretted it because Grace's face shuttered. She realized she'd said too much already. She shrugged. "Haven't a clue. Up in Savannah, I guess. Got lots of it on the streets there. Listen, y'all, I gotta get busy now. Can't stand around here chewing the fat all day."

She tore their ticket off her pad and laid it upside down on the table. "Been nice talking to you boys. Send me a copy of your article when it comes out, will you? This joint has been in a lot of stories. Writers like you looking for a nostalgic piece, I guess." She pointed to a wall full of framed newspaper articles. "I like to keep the clippings, y'know?"

Chapter 15

Th' conjureman sees with more than his eyes. He hears with more than his ears, and he knows with more than his mind. Never dare t' cheat th' conjureman . . .

JEREMIAH Brown had been held captive in a darkened room for a long time now it seemed. He'd been fed well. The food, in fact, had been delicious. Nobody had hurt him. He'd seen no sign of the bullies who'd kidnapped him. In fact, he hadn't seen anyone at all other than the woman who brought his meals. She didn't speak to him, and he couldn't say what she looked like. She was like a dark shadow that drifted in and out of the room. He'd been able to stay clean. There was a small bathroom with a shower off his bedroom, and towels were provided. Overall, he hadn't been mistreated.

But still, Jeremiah was afraid, and he wanted to go home. What did they want from him anyway? He was just a kid. He thought of his mom and dad, and a lump formed in his throat. Would he ever see them again?

He didn't know whether it was day or night when at last someone came for him. He was lying on his bed, dozing from boredom, when he heard the door open. He'd been given a substantial meal not long before and wasn't expecting the shadow woman for a while.

He recognized the two young men who entered the room, and fear formed a knot in his stomach. They were two of the bullies who'd kidnapped him . . . how many days ago?

"C'mon, sport. Somebody wants to see you. Somebody important." The boy who'd first accosted him outside the schoolyard appeared to be the leader. He stuck his face into Jeremiah's and gave him a twisted grin. "An' let me warn you, you don't wanna do nothin' to piss him off. This here's one powerful dude. You do as he says and you won't get hurt. But if you don't . . ."

Jeremiah's eyes were wide, and sweat turned his skin clammy. He was too afraid to talk, but he nodded vigorously. They placed a blindfold around his eyes, and he stumbled as they led him roughly out of his little prison.

Outside, the air was chill and damp, and Jeremiah could smell the primordial soup of the marshes. He'd just learned that term in science class. He was fascinated that life had evolved from the very kind of wetlands that had surrounded him his whole life in the low country of south Georgia. From the scent, he figured he must not be far from home. His throat tightened. He wondered if he would ever go to science class again.

He was shoved roughly into a car and driven a short distance. "There he is," the older boy said, his voice barely above a whisper. Jeremiah heard the awe in his tone and wondered who "he" was. Jeremiah felt that way about his own father sometimes, when he was allowed to go into the courtroom and sit in the back row. Judge George Brown was a tall, imposing man, a former football star, who when he entered the courtroom in his black judge's robe, his face stern and serious, looked to Jeremiah like God Himself.

Jeremiah worshipped his father and knew that George Brown's personal mission was to rid his city of criminals, especially those who dealt in drugs. And Jeremiah believed his father was doing everything he could at that very moment to find his only son. He just hoped the judge wasn't too late.

The smell of wood smoke wafted in the air, and Jeremiah could hear the low murmur of voices nearby. The sound ceased as he was led in that direction. When his blindfold was at last removed, he found himself at the edge of a fire circle where flames crackled brightly and sparks rose swiftly into the darkness. Around him, seated on logs, a dozen or more people stared at him. He blinked and stared back. They were mostly young, both men and women, some white, some black, some obviously mixed. They appeared more curious than afraid. He stared at one young woman for a moment, thinking she looked familiar.

He heard a noise, the sound of a footstep nearby, and turned toward it.

There was nothing unusual about the man, really. He wore a black suit, a white shirt, a black tie, and on his head a black felt hat. Jeremiah had seen men dressed like this often, at church or in the courthouse. But there was something different about this one.

Maybe it was the strange blue sunglasses he wore, even though it was night. Or maybe it was the putty gray of his skin, which gave Jeremiah the impression that he was newly removed from the grave. Behind him, clucking and fussing in a cage, was a chicken.

"Good evening, Jeremiah," the man said. His voice was neither deep nor high-pitched. It neither threatened nor assured. And it made Jeremiah's skin crawl.

He struggled for an answer. "Hello," was the best he could find.

"Do you know who I am?" the man asked.

"N-no, sir."

"I'm known as Dr. Lizard, Jeremiah. Does that mean anything to you?"

"No, sir." Jeremiah wondered briefly if he'd been somehow dropped into a sci-fi comic strip or something. Dr. Lizard?

"Well, it will, I assure you," said Dr. Lizard. He took a step closer to Jeremiah. "I hear your father is Judge George Brown."

Jeremiah froze. What did this have to do with his father? He wanted to lie, to protect his father, but he guessed this man already knew who his father was. "Yes, sir."

"Well, now," said Dr. Lizard, looking around the circle at the others. "We got ourselves a celebrity here." Jeremiah's cheeks burned, and not from the heat of the fire. He didn't know what was going on, but he knew it wasn't good.

"Come here, Jeremiah." Dr. Lizard extended his arm. Reflected firelight flickered in the blue glasses that shielded his eyes, giving him the appearance of some kind of devil. Jeremiah didn't move.

"Don't be afraid, Jeremiah. No one is going to hurt you."

Jeremiah felt a hand at his back, and he was thrust forward toward Dr. Lizard. "What do you want?"

Dr. Lizard gave him the creepiest smile Jeremiah had ever seen, and Jeremiah shuddered. He also didn't like the look of the sinister-looking black leather gloves he wore. The strange man reached into his pocket and brought out a piece of candy. "I want to give you this. Trick or treat, Jeremiah. It's almost Halloween."

Jeremiah heard a trickle of laughter pass around the circle, and he recalled the bully who'd captured him saying they were taking him for an early Halloween treat. He didn't want the candy, but Dr. Lizard placed it in his hand. "Taste it. It won't hurt you."

Jeremiah looked at the candy in his hand. He loved sweets, and he hadn't had anything sweet since he'd been captured.

"Go on," Dr. Lizard urged, putting his hand on Jeremiah's shoulder. "It's a reward, for being so patient with us. You've been a very good boy. If you do as I say tonight, you'll get to go home soon."

Jeremiah's hopes soared. "Yes, sir. What do you want me to do?"

"Eat the candy."

It tasted a little like root beer, kind of like licorice, maybe like strong, sugared coffee. But it was sweet and not altogether unpleasant. In a moment, Jeremiah felt a warm glow suffuse him, and he smiled up at Dr. Lizard. What had he been so afraid of?

"Feel better now?" Dr. Lizard asked.

"Yes, sir. It's good candy."

One side of Dr. Lizard's mouth turned up. "Only the best for our guests." Then he went to the chicken cage and beckoned for Jeremiah to join him.

Jeremiah's legs felt a little unsteady, but he did as he was told. His vision was kind of blurry, and the world seemed to move in slow motion around him as he approached. Bright spots shot through his vision like rocket ships. Beautiful rocket ships. It was all very strange, but he wasn't afraid.

"Jeremiah," Dr. Lizard said solemnly, "you've been allowed into a very elite circle. But you must prove you are worthy to be a part of it. Are you ready to show Dr. Lizard your loyalty?"

Jeremiah's head was buzzing now, and he felt relaxed and happy. "Yes, sir." His words seemed to come from outside his body. He looked around to see if they were floating on the air.

Suddenly, an ax was shoved into his grasp. He stared at it dumbly, hardly registering what it was. Dr. Lizard reached into the cage and brought forth the chicken. Jeremiah looked at it in a detached manner, wondering what a chicken had to do with this loyalty thing.

"Kill it, Jeremiah."

He looked up at Dr. Lizard and frowned. Even in his dazed state, he knew right from wrong.

"What for?"

Dr. Lizard lowered his face until it was level with Jeremiah's. "Because I told you to. If you wish to remain alive, and if you were sincere in wanting to prove your loyalty, kill the chicken, Jeremiah." He paused, then added, "It's the bird's life . . . or yours."

Jeremiah had never killed anything before other than a bug. He tried to focus on the chicken that was frantically trying to escape, and he began to cry for its desperation. It was trapped, just as he was trapped. He thought of his mom and dad, how they would feel if he never came home again. He wondered if the chicken had a father and a mother.

Around him, he heard a low chanting that grew louder and louder with each passing moment. The people who were gathered around the fire were humming and repeating strange words that he didn't understand, saying them over and over and over until he wanted to cover his ears. But he couldn't. He held an ax in his hands.

"Do it, Jeremiah," Dr. Lizard commanded. "Kill the chicken now. Or you will be killed."

The tone in his voice led Jeremiah to believe this wasn't a joke. Nothing about this was funny. Dr. Lizard held the bird by its feet and extended his arm toward Jeremiah.

Maybe if I just turn it loose, he thought, then remembered the second part of what Dr. Lizard had told him. *Or you will be killed.* Jeremiah grasped the animal firmly by its neck. The feathers were warm and damp, and he could feel the bird's fear, see it in the bright, beady little eyes. He closed his own eyes and prayed to Jesus to forgive him for what he was about to do.

Dr. Lizard continued to hold onto the chicken's feet, and he lowered his hand until the bird was suspended over the stump of a tree. Jeremiah understood clearly what was expected of him. He brought the bird's body down until it rested on the stump. The creature seemed to also understand what was about to take place, and stilled in terror. The chanting voices swirled in the darkness behind him.

"Now, Jeremiah," said Dr. Lizard. "Now. I command you."

With tears streaming down his cheeks, Jeremiah raised

the ax. He brought it down clumsily, almost hitting his own hand, but only nicking the neck of the chicken. He looked hopefully at Dr. Lizard, praying that this demonstration of his willingness to do as he was told would be sufficient, and that the weird man would let them both go free.

Dr. Lizard shook his head solemnly, then looked from the ax to the chicken, which was now struggling vigorously and squawking loudly. Jeremiah's heart pounded so hard he thought it might come out of his chest. What if he killed the chicken, and they still killed him? This crazy guy meant business.

Giving up hope, Jeremiah raised the ax again and this time brought it down squarely across the chicken's neck. Blood squirted on his face. Dr. Lizard let go of the chicken's feet, and the headless body righted itself and began a dizzy dance on the tree stump. Jeremiah's eyes widened. The chicken wasn't dead? He looked at the bird's head in his bloody fingers. It was impossible! He turned to Dr. Lizard, who was giving him that creepy smile again.

"Very good, Jeremiah. Very good." He touched the chicken's body with his gloved hand, and it ceased its dance. It fell into a lump of bloody white feathers and lay still. Dr. Lizard placed a finger beneath Jeremiah's chin and forced the boy to look at him. "You see the power of Dr. Lizard, Jeremiah?" His voice was very low. "Do not ever doubt my power. You have shown your loyalty with this sacrifice. I expect you to continue to show it in your deeds and actions." He dipped his finger in the chicken's blood, made an *X* on Jeremiah's forehead, then smeared it on the boy's cheeks as well.

"You have become one of us, Jeremiah. Never forget that. You will always remember this night. And you must always remember to do exactly what I ask of you. Do you understand?"

Jeremiah wanted to throw up. He wanted to run away from this disgusting man and his wickedness. He believed he was in the hands of the devil himself, but he was also terrified. He had no doubt that if he didn't do as Dr. Lizard said, he would be killed, just like the chicken.

"Yes . . . sir," he managed through a painfully constricted throat.

"That's good, Jeremiah. Very good."

Chapter 16

Th' word from th' mouth has great power. Be careful what you say, and remember your lies . . .

At ten o'clock the following morning, Angela and Dylan were knocking on doors and interviewing residents, trying to get a lead on the young punks who'd kidnapped Jeremiah Brown. Dylan had been against Angela's involvement in the search, thinking it might put her at unnecessary risk, but when he'd seen she was determined to participate, he'd insisted on joining her.

As if his physical presence could protect her from a shooter's bullet.

Still, she appreciated his concern, especially after what he'd told her about the Slade family.

He'd returned from his interview with Elizabeth Slade and her attorney seething and worried at the same time. He was convinced that Mrs. Slade was out to get Angela, and that she was protecting someone, probably her daughter. He'd called Johnny Reilly the moment he got back to Angela's house, turning on the speakerphone so she could hear.

"You talked to the Slade daughter yet?" Dylan barked.

"As a matter of fact," Reilly said, sounding impatient, "no. Her mother claims she hasn't seen Veronica since Slade's death, and we haven't been able to locate her vehicle."

"She's at Paradisia, or at least she was around noon."

"What were you doing out there?" Reilly sounded angry.

"Looking for answers. Look, Reilly, don't get pissed.

We're on the same side here. I'm just in the . . . private sector." He explained being summoned by Harlow Bertram and shared most of what he'd learned. It seemed to appease Reilly somewhat.

"Are you sure Veronica Slade is there?" Reilly pressed.

"She wasn't in the meeting I had with Elizabeth Slade and her lawyer, but as I was leaving, I saw a woman about her age . . . uh . . . standing on the upstairs balcony, and there was a red Beamer convertible in the driveway. I got a photograph of the license tag if you need it."

"No. That's her car. I'll get a man on it. But, Montana, stay out of my way. I warn you. If you do anything to screw up this investigation, I'll have your ass."

Dylan bristled. "If anything happens to Angela because you aren't doing your job, I'll have yours."

Reilly slammed the phone in their ears.

"Wrong move," Angela said, worried at antagonizing Reilly. "We need him on our side."

"I don't know whose side Reilly's on," Dylan growled. "He could be on Quintos's side, and so could Veronica Slade. Maybe that's why he hasn't interviewed her yet."

Dylan looked at her, and his expression softened. "Don't worry. I'm not going to do anything to undermine him. When this is all over, unless he's on the take, I'll make sure he's the hero."

That had been early yesterday afternoon. They hadn't heard from Reilly since. In the meantime, Angela and Dylan had focused their efforts on the kidnapping. If nothing else, it gave her something to think about besides the peril she was in.

Around eleven o'clock, Angela's cell phone rang. "Hello?"

"Angela, it's Wally Padgett. We're calling off the neighborhood canvass. Jeremiah's home."

She turned to Dylan and gave him a thumbs up. "Wally, that's great! Is he all right?"

"He seems to be fine, just a little dazed. He's on his way to the hospital as we speak to get checked out. We'll know more in a few hours."

"Do you have any idea what happened to him?"

"Not yet. His mother called just a few minutes ago. Seems Jeremiah just wandered into his house a little while ago, but he claims he can't remember where he's been or how he got home."

"That doesn't sound good. Please keep me in the loop. I want to know what happened to him."

"You got it."

Angela hung up the phone and told Dylan the good news. "But I'm worried about Jeremiah," she said. "I've interviewed children who'd been kidnapped who were abused so badly during their abduction, they're likely scarred for life." She wrung her hands, feeling helpless. "I wish I could talk to him."

"Any leads on who snatched him?" Dylan asked.

Angela shook his head. "Padgett says Jeremiah hasn't been able to tell them a thing."

"My money says Quintos is behind this," Dylan said, thinking out loud.

"If he is," Angela added, picking up his train of thought, "and if he killed Slade and is trying to pin the murder on me, I'd say he's sending us a rather strong message—'Don't mess with me.' "

Dylan only nodded grimly in answer. They got into the Camaro, but instead of heading back to police headquarters to turn in their reports, as she'd expected, Dylan turned south.

"Where're you going?" Angela asked.

"To the hospital. You said you wanted to talk to Jeremiah."

Ronnie awoke earlier than usual and couldn't fall back asleep. She checked the clock. Ten A.M. Covering her head with a pillow, she tried unsuccessfully to block out all that had transpired in the past twenty-four hours. The scenes kept running in her mind like a videotape.

Yesterday morning, after returning to Paradisia from her night with the man-with-no-name, she'd tiptoed up the stairs, avoiding her mother. It always took some time to pull herself back together after being with him. This time, it had been particularly stressful, because after the sex, he'd wanted to talk about her father.

Ronnie knew he was interested in Slade's business, and she'd often done him small favors that she supposed amounted to spying on her father—she'd put a bug on his phone once, copied some papers from time to time, even fucked J. J.'s pilot to learn her father's travel plans—but it had never bothered her. In fact, it had given her a delicious sense of revenge.

Now, with her father dead, she found she didn't want to oblige the man by answering his questions. But she'd been forced to. He reminded her of the money she owed him and told her that as soon as she received her inheritance, he expected payment. Until then, she *would* continue to do whatever he asked, whenever he asked. The bruises on her arms told her he meant business.

The police had come to Paradisia in the early afternoon. Even though Marguerite had rehearsed her over and over, Ronnie was nervous about the story they'd made up. Wanting to impress the investigating officers with her station in life—because people like her simply did not commit murder—Veronica dressed in silk slacks and an expensive sweater. She brushed her hair until it shone and dashed on some light pink lipstick. When she entered the parlor to face the cops, Ronnie looked like the rich, well-bred heiress she was.

Two men awaited her. She was introduced to Nate Johnson, a detective with the GBI, and Sergeant Johnny Reilly from the Savannah police. Johnson mostly observed and took notes while Reilly asked questions. She began the interview feeling calm and collected, but by the time Reilly had finished with her, she felt like hammered spaghetti. It wasn't that he'd been mean to her. He'd just questioned her relentlessly, and unlike most men, whom she could easily manipulate, he hadn't seemed to notice her not-too-subtle overtures.

"Where were you on the afternoon of Monday, October second?" he'd asked.

"Why, I drove up to Hilton Head, Sergeant, to meet a friend for lunch."

"Who did you meet?"

"An old friend of mine, Charlotte Magnetti." Out of the corner of her eye, she saw her mother frown. She knew her mother had never heard of Charlotte Magnetti. But then, her mother hadn't heard of a lot of her friends.

"I suppose you can put us in touch with Ms. Magnetti?"

"Of course." Veronica handed him a slip of paper with her "friend's" name and a telephone number on it. It included a Hilton Head area code.

The sergeant copied the information in his notebook, handed the paper back and asked, "How long were you there?"

"Oh, it was a long lunch. Three, maybe four hours." She gave him her most flirtatious smile. "We had a lot of catching up to do. You know, girl talk. I hadn't seen her since we were in boarding school together." There. That ought to answer her mother's questions. Elizabeth Slade had never bothered to meet any of her friends from those awful schools where they'd sent Ronnie. Her mother would never know there was no such person as Charlotte Magnetti.

In answer to another question from the policeman, Veronica gave him the name of the small bistro where they had lunched.

"What time did you leave the restaurant?" he pressed. He was making her very nervous.

"Oh, I'd say around three o'clock."

"What did you do then?"

She laughed and gave him her best Southern belle reply. "Why, we went shopping, of course, Sergeant. Shopped all afternoon. We were so tired, we just crashed at the condo she'd rented, and I spent the night." She gave her mother a triumphant look, but Elizabeth's face remained impassive. Ronnie didn't know whether she believed her or not. Neither did she know if she'd convinced the cops. Perspiration broke out on her skin, but she refused to give in to her fear.

She had thought the interview was over, when suddenly the GBI officer asked, "Did you love your father, Ms. Slade?"

She stared at him as the words slammed into her, and it took her a long moment to answer. When she did, her voice trembled, and she despised herself for showing such weakness. "I . . . I don't see that how I felt about my father is any of your business, Mr. Johnson. If you're insinuating that I killed him, well, I didn't. Angela Donahue killed him, and you know it. I don't know why you are even here."

"See here . . ." Harlow tried to break in, but Nate Johnson continued unperturbed.

"Do you know Angela Donahue, Ms. Slade?"

"No, of course I don't know her. All I know is what I've heard on the news." A trickle of sweat raced down Ronnie's spine.

Sergeant Reilly took a photo out of his coat pocket and handed it to her. "Have you ever seen her before?"

Ronnie's hands shook as she took the picture. As she stared down at the woman who'd stolen her father's love, renewed hatred boiled within her. "No. Never."

And then Johnson said pointedly, "I find it very coincidental, Ms. Slade, that she looks so much like you."

That's when Harlow had taken over at last. The incompetent pig, she thought angrily. He shouldn't have let the investigator badger her like that.

"That's enough, Sergeant. I'm her attorney, and you've stepped over your boundaries. I'm asking you both to leave. If you want to talk to Veronica further, get a subpoena."

The two men hadn't argued. They'd stood and said their polite goodbyes. Reilly had taken the picture from Ronnie, replaced it in his pocket, and they'd left without a backward glance.

And that's when all hell had broken loose.

Ronnie's head still hurt to think of it—her mother yelling at her, Harlow yelling at her mother. And then the bombshell.

"I don't suppose you know anything about your father changing his will?" her mother had shrieked. And the room had gone silent. Elizabeth bit her lower lip. Harlow swore. And Ronnie stared at them both, stunned.

"What did you say?" she managed at last.

Harlow spoke in a quiet voice, trying to appear calm. "Your mother got a call from an Atlanta attorney. He said your father came to them last week and drew up a new will. I did some checking. The firm is not only legit, it's one of the most prestigious white-shoe firms in Atlanta. I'm afraid we have a problem here."

As Ronnie recalled the horrible scene, even from the distance of nearly twenty-four hours, nausea sent hot saliva to the back of her mouth.

Your father . . . drew up a new will.

Fuck him!

Veronica rolled over in bed and pounded the pillow. What had the bastard done? Had he cut her out of his will? She'd thought everything had been arranged through that new trust Harlow had set up, but the way her mother and Harlow were acting, she could tell they were worried. She trembled. What would she do if she didn't receive the money she'd been so desperately counting on? If she didn't get it, what would they . . . he . . . do to her? She closed her eyes and felt the sting of tears.

For the first time since the plan had been devised to take revenge against her father and speed up the inheritance she knew awaited her, Ronnie was afraid. Everything seemed so out of control. She couldn't even remember if she'd killed her father, for God's sake. It had been part of the plan all along, but she wasn't at all sure she'd done it. But the gun she'd stolen from Angela to use in his murder had disappeared. Had she shot him and thrown the gun away? Would somebody eventually find it covered with her fingerprints? Or had she worn plastic gloves, like she'd meant to? She remembered nothing about that afternoon, and that scared the shit out of her. Was she losing her mind? Had the drugs erased part of her brain? What else couldn't she remember?

Ronnie lay on the bed, sobbing quietly. All she'd ever wanted was to be accepted, to be loved by her family. When she'd realized that was never going to happen, she'd taken solace in the fantasy of drugs. Now that escape seemed to have destroyed her mind, and unless she received her inheritance, the debt she'd incurred in pursuit of that fantasy would cost her her life.

She curled up into a fetal position, considering taking an overdose and ending it all. But then she remembered she didn't have anything to overdose with, and no money to buy it.

Damn. Couldn't she do anything right?

Chapter 17

Fear is sometimes all that warns us when th' evil spirits be about. Th' hants be invisible t' th' eye, but th' fear sees them all th' same . . .

ANGELA had been unable to see Jeremiah at the hospital, as he'd been undergoing a barrage of medical tests, but she'd talked to his mother, Camille, a soft-spoken woman with eyes that still reflected the terror of her family's recent ordeal. Camille knew Angela because of SOS, and also, unfortunately, because of the recent headlines. But she seemed glad that Angela wanted to help Jeremiah. Since no one had been able to reach beyond the boy's memory block, Camille had agreed to let Angela try, and they'd scheduled her visit to Jeremiah's home on Saturday morning.

Judge and Mrs. George Brown lived in a genteel neighborhood of older two-story brick homes that lined a quiet boulevard. The center median was landscaped with azaleas that in the spring blazed in brilliant pinks, reds, and whites. Now, in the fall, the scenery was more sedate. Still, the wide lawns were well-kept, and the branches of mature trees overhung the street in graceful arches. Angela found it a pleasing neighborhood, one that would seem safe from the horror the Browns had just endured.

No place was safe anymore, it would seem. And no one.

At that desolate thought, Angela rang the bell. She glanced over her shoulder, wishing for a fleeting moment that she'd let Dylan accompany her after all. He'd been furious with her for insisting on coming alone, but she'd explained that his presence might intimidate Jeremiah. She'd also insisted on taking her own car. She was tired of being his virtual prisoner.

Camille answered the door with a tentative, almost shy smile. "I'm glad you've come. I'm afraid we're getting nowhere with Jeremiah." She closed the door behind Angela. "He's . . . he seems so . . . afraid."

"I can't promise I'll have any better luck, but I'll do my best."

Angela entered a small foyer that led into a main hall. On the left, accessed by a wide arch, was a dining room. On the right, beyond another arch, was the living room. Both were graciously but not ostentatiously furnished.

"Would you like coffee?"

"No, thanks."

"Then why don't you wait in there?" Camille said, indicating the living room. "Jeremiah's upstairs in his room. I'll go get him." Almost as an afterthought, she said, "I'm sorry George isn't here. He had an emergency to attend to. He might be back in time, or not." She gave Angela an apologetic look and hurried up the stairs.

Angela wondered how George Brown was holding up, and if he suspected a connection between Slade's murder and his son's kidnapping. Brown was shrewd and savvy to what went on in Savannah's underworld. Angela wished she could talk to him.

Camille returned with Jeremiah, a boy almost as tall as she was. Handsome and well-built, he looked at her out of large, distrustful eyes. Angela's heart wrenched. What had happened to this poor child?

"Hi, I'm Angela," she said, smiling but not acting overly eager. "I'm a friend of your dad's. How are you feeling this morning?"

Jeremiah shrugged. "Okay, I guess."

Angela turned to Camille. "Would it be all right if I spoke to Jeremiah alone?"

Camille Brown looked at her son, then nodded toward Angela. "Talk to her, Jeremiah," she pleaded softly. "She's here to help." She turned and left the room, and Angela looked up to find Jeremiah staring at her, a strange look on his face, as if he feared her.

"Is something wrong, Jeremiah?"

"No, ma'am."

She didn't believe him, although she had no idea why he would be afraid of her. Maybe the trauma that he'd experienced made him a little afraid of everything right now. Angela wished she could hold him and comfort him, but not only was she a stranger, he was twelve years old, way too mature for such childish things. So instead, she held out her hand toward the comfortable-looking sofa. "Here, come sit down and visit with me for a few minutes."

He sat as far from her as he could, at the end of the long sofa, and Angela shifted sideways to face him. "Please don't be afraid of me, Jeremiah. I'm here to help you."

He looked doubtful and said nothing. His face had lost all expression. He appeared to be completely emotionally shuttered. Searching for a way to reach him, Angela tried to put herself in his place. What would it take to get her to reveal terrible dark secrets to a stranger?

If that stranger revealed her own terrible dark secrets first.

But did she have any secrets to exchange? Angela thought back to the time in her childhood when a terrible thing had happened to her. It wasn't the same as Jeremiah's ordeal, but it had been devastating nonetheless. And she'd never really told anyone how she'd felt about it. It wasn't much of a secret, but it was all she had. She allowed herself to step back into that time, when she was a child of five and there was a policeman at her door. A surprising lump of emotion tightened her throat.

"Jeremiah," she said, clearing her throat, "I know how you must be feeling. Scared and uncertain and distrustful of strangers, and I don't blame you. I remember when a bad thing once happened to me, and I felt the same way."

She saw him glance at her, but then he looked quickly away again.

She hesitated a moment before continuing, thinking about that lump of emotion. Where'd that come from? She'd had those memories hidden away for so long, she couldn't imagine there were feelings still attached. And yet, suddenly she was inexplicably reluctant to dig them out of the dark cellar of her mind.

But a deal was a deal. If she wanted to know his story, she had to tell hers.

"I wasn't kidnapped, like you, but I know what it feels like to be frightened and think you'll never see your father again." She stared into space, seeing the policeman's face as if it were in front of her. But her story started before that terrible day.

"I was just a little kid, a lot younger than you, when my father left us to go to Alaska, where he'd decided he could make his fortune working in the oil fields." Her memories of her father were fuzzy, but she tried to summon him from her past. "I remember him as a tall man, but I can't remember his face very clearly," she told Jeremiah, only just realizing it herself. "He had thick golden hair on his arms that I liked to run my fingers through. He was a working man, and I remember the way he smelled when he got home at night. It was a good smell, like the outdoors where he worked."

At that, tears caught Angela unaware, and she blinked them away. What was this? She'd never cried before when she talked about her father. At least, not after she'd grown up. But suddenly she remembered all the times she'd cried herself to sleep in the first years after he'd been killed. She'd been angry with him for leaving them. Angry that he'd died. And frightened to learn that life could be so uncertain. One day he was there, the next day he was gone.

Angela fought to override her surprising emotions and go on with her story. "The night he left, he came into my bedroom and kissed me goodbye. I felt his hand move under my pillow, and after he'd gone, I found a fifty-cent piece he'd left there for me." Another memory out of the forbidden box. And this one elicited anger, not tears. Had he thought money could take the place of a father?

Get a grip, Angela told herself, amazed at the feelings that were surfacing after all this time. Still, she realized how much she'd missed having a father, even though she could hardly remember the one she'd had. How she'd wanted her mother to remarry, and how Mary Ellen had steadfastly refused, saying that women were too dependent on men and that she'd never put herself in that position again.

"It's funny, Jeremiah," she went on, forcing those thoughts from her mind, "but I knew when he left that he wasn't coming back. I just felt it, and when the police came to our house a few weeks later to tell us he'd been killed in a car accident, I was almost expecting them. Still, it made it real that he wasn't ever going to come home again. That's when I felt like I think you feel now. I was scared. I no longer trusted the world to be a safe place. Strangers had come to my house and told me something that changed my life forever. I was frightened and sad and lonely, and my mother was too upset for me to talk to. I needed a friend, like you need a friend."

She grew quiet, dealing with disturbing thoughts and feelings she hadn't known she harbored. In a moment, however, she composed herself and turned to Jeremiah. She'd told as many of her secrets as she could for the moment. Were they sufficient to get him to share his?

"Let me be your friend, Jeremiah. What happened to me is not the same as what happened to you," she said, "but I was just as scared. And when we're scared, it sometimes helps to talk."

She paused, but he showed no sign that he was ready to

open up. She tried another tack. "Jeremiah, I'm not a cop, but I used to work for the Georgia Bureau of Investigation. Are you familiar with it?"

He shrugged in answer.

"It's like the FBI, only on the state level," she went on. "I've been involved with other kidnapping cases, and I've talked with the kids who were taken, like you were. I've heard their stories. Not always, but sometimes, their stories helped to catch the bad guys who took them away. Almost always, though, talking about what happened helped the kids feel better. Jeremiah, I'm here to listen if you want to talk."

He didn't. In fact, she saw his lips tighten. She let out a deep breath. This kid was hiding something really bad. What had happened to him?

Angela waited in silence for a long time, then reached into her purse and drew out a card. She laid it on the sofa between them. "It's okay, Jeremiah," she said quietly. "I understand. Maybe it's too soon to talk. But I want you to know you have a friend who'll listen if you change your mind. Here are my phone numbers. Call me anytime, day or night."

She stood up, preparing to leave, when the front door opened. Through it strode a tall, handsome, well-dressed man who broke into a broad grin when he saw her.

"Angela! I'm so glad I made it back in time."

"Judge Brown," she said, extending her hand, which he took and shook vigorously. "It's always a pleasure to see you, sir, although I wish we were meeting under happier circumstances."

He nodded grimly. "Thanks for coming. Did you have any luck?"

She turned to glance back at the sofa where she'd sat with Jeremiah and was disappointed to see the boy had gone. She wasn't surprised. But she was pleased to see that he'd apparently taken her card.

"Not directly," she said, encouraged at even that small progress. "But he knows how to reach me. I told him to call me day or night if he wants to talk."

When she turned back to Judge Brown, the look on his face alarmed her.

"I read about the Slade case, of course," he said. "It's absurd to link you in any way to his killing, but . . ." He paused, then lowered his voice. "I've been looking into it, behind the scenes, you know?"

She knew he was referring to his network of political and "practical" connections. She suspected if George Brown wanted to know something, it would be difficult to keep it from him. "Yes?" she replied.

"Seems there's a lot of paybacks going on here. For you. For me."

His words confirmed Dylan's suspicions and sent a chill through her. "What do you mean?"

"We've rocked a lot of boats in the underbelly of our lovely city, Angela. Cleaned up the streets, sent druggies to prison, sent up some crooked cops, too. Word on the street is the dealers want their turf back."

"So what's new?" Angela refused to be intimidated.

"Cecil Clifford's out of prison. He'll never work as a cop again, of course, but my sources tell me he's gone to work for Quintos."

"He always worked for Quintos," Angela said. "He just carried a badge for cover. I suspected that even before he went down in the Internal Affairs investigation. Too many drug busts came up empty-handed. I'm glad he went to prison, but his sentence obviously wasn't nearly long enough."

"That's true," Judge Brown agreed. "But there's nothing we can do about that. He's out, and he's mad as hell. He's dangerous, Angela. Watch your back."

Chapter 18

There was this man who was going to leave his woman for another, and she came t' Dr. Lizard for t' put a root hex on him. Th' conjureman gave her some white powder and instructions and sent her back home. She sprinkled th' powder in th' husband's pants and baked them in th' oven. Then she told her man, "Go, but if you won't be my man, you ain't going t' be a man to any other woman." And he wasn't never again . . .

WORRY for Angela's safety nagged at Dylan as he pulled away from the curb in front of her house, where he'd camped out for the second night in a row. He shouldn't have let her go off by herself, but she'd been adamant that she had to interview the Brown boy alone. He could understand that, but he should have ridden shotgun just the same and waited outside for her. That, or he could have followed her without her knowing.

And if he had, he'd have had hell to pay if Angela found out he was dogging her. She was the most hardheaded woman he'd ever met, except maybe for her mother, and the most fearless, and that was what worried him. Her courage had nearly gotten her killed once.

Her courage, and his mistake.

He hoped he hadn't made another mistake in letting her have her way this morning.

While she was at Judge Brown's house, Dylan was determined to dig deeper into the mystery of Slade's death. He was eager to talk to Bob Greer, Slade's pilot, if he could find the man. He drove back to his boat, showered, changed, and went to work.

There were sixteen listings in the Savannah telephone directory for Greers named Robert or with the initial *R* in their names. Dylan had been around pilots when he was in the military and knew that fliers loved nothing better than to talk about their aircraft and experiences. So he made up a story, picked up the phone and started with the first name on the list.

"Bob Greer? Good morning. My name is Jack Smith. I'm with the Aircraft Owners and Pilots Association, and I'm calling to see if you'd be interested in a special offer . . ."

The first eight calls were short. Two of the numbers had been disconnected, and the other six Greers stopped him at this point, saying something like, "But I don't own an airplane." On the ninth call, he got lucky.

"I don't need any special offers, unless it's a job offer," the man replied gruffly.

"You're out of work, huh?" Dylan said sympathetically while circling the address in the phone book. "Sorry to hear that. What happened? Maybe I can put you in touch with someone."

"Who'd you say you're with?"

Dylan thought he heard a note of hope in the man's voice. "AOPA."

"Know anybody who needs a good corporate pilot? My boss unexpectedly died last week, and I found myself out of a job. I'm type rated on the Citation and the G-4, but I can fly just about anything that'll go in the air."

But Dylan wasn't interested in his credentials. "That's too bad about your boss. How'd he die?"

"Somebody shot him."

Bingo.

Dylan invited Greer to meet him at a sports bar for a Saturday afternoon beer. "I can't promise you I can find you a job, but I'll buy you a beer. I always like hanging out with other airplane people." Dylan was convinced Greer hadn't murdered his boss, but he might know who did. And from the man's openness about his need to find a job, Dylan thought it doubtful that Greer was much of a player in Slade's dark and dangerous game. But Greer had been Slade's transport and was bound to know something about his boss's activities.

Before he left to meet the pilot, Dylan used his computer to scan an AOPA logo out of a magazine and created a business card for himself, just in case.

The lounge was dark and smelled of stale cigarette smoke. A few men sat at the bar, nursing beers and watching the televisions that were mounted at each end. On one, South Carolina was kicking the University of Georgia's butt on the football field. Drivers competing in the Busch Series raced around the other screen.

Dylan watched to see if any of the patrons was keeping an eye out for someone they were supposed to meet, but none seemed the least bit interested in him. He hoped Greer would show.

A few moments later, a man entered the bar and looked around. He was of medium height, with thinning sandy-colored hair and a slight paunch. He looked to be around thirty-five. He wore Dockers and a long-sleeved polo shirt. An aging yuppie.

"Bob Greer?" Dylan said, approaching him.

"Yeah. Hi." He shook Dylan's hand. "I take it you're Jack Smith."

Dylan didn't answer directly. He didn't like to lie. "Glad you could make it. Want to sit at the bar, or shall we take a table where we can talk?"

They moved to a quiet corner of the nearly empty lounge. A waitress brought them a couple of Buds and left them to their business. After some small talk, Dylan cut to the chase.

"So, you said you were a corporate pilot. Who'd you fly for?"

"Well, it wasn't exactly a corporation, but it might as well have been. I flew for this really rich guy, J. J. Slade. You might have read about his murder in the papers."

Dylan leaned forward as if eager to engage in a little juicy gossip. "Oh, yeah, I read about it. That was something, wasn't it? Some people think it was the Mafia or somebody like that who knocked him off. What do you think?"

Greer took a deep drink and set his bottle down heavily on the scarred wooden table. From the way he was acting, Dylan suspected he'd had a couple before coming to meet him. "Could be," Greer said. "Slade had some pretty scary friends."

"That right? You think they were Mafia?"

"I don't know. He never included me in anything. I was just his bus driver." He gave a small laugh. "There was a time when I resented that, but now . . . I'm glad I didn't know anything about his deals."

"Yeah, I can see what you mean," Dylan replied, wondering if the man was telling the truth or if he had been involved in the drug business as well.

Greer gave him a knowing look, then made a serious dent in his Budweiser. Dylan scooted a bowl of popcorn in Greer's direction and signaled the waitress to bring another beer. Greer didn't object.

"I'm not afraid of anybody coming after me or anything," he went on, obviously warming to the gossip. "He kept me pretty much behind the scenes, and I didn't ask questions. He was a real private person, you know what I mean? He had his own airstrip and lived like a recluse, a real Howard Hughes."

Dylan made a mental note of that. Private plane. Private airstrip. Had he been privately importing drugs? Had Greer been part of it? He didn't think so. The man seemed too open, too eager to tell what he knew.

"Was he nuts?" Dylan asked casually, grabbing a handful of popcorn.

"Nah, just rich and eccentric. He wanted me to live in the apartment next to the hangar, so I could be at his beck and call twenty-four/seven, but I wouldn't do it. I didn't want to live out in that backwater. I like a little action, y'know. Some night life. I'm not married, and I'm too young to sit around watching TV every night. Besides," he added, finishing his first beer in time for the arrival of his second, "I didn't want him to think he owned me. He seemed to want to own everybody. A real control freak."

Dylan was getting a pretty clear picture of J. J. Slade and decided he must have been a most unlikable sort of guy. The sort of guy some people might say needed killing.

"So if it wasn't the Mafia who got him, who do you think did?" Dylan asked, as if continuing to press for gossip. "Somebody in his family?"

Greer snorted a derisive laugh. "Could be. I didn't know his wife well, but it was obvious they didn't get along. And his daughter . . . Jesus! What a weird little piece."

Dylan lowered his voice to a conspiratorial whisper. "Yeah? Did you get some of it?"

Greer put his beer bottle down on a cardboard coaster and tapped the glass with his fingertips thoughtfully. "Oh, yeah, I got some. I didn't really want to, although she's a real looker. But she's as scary as her daddy."

"How so?"

"Slade wasn't interested in anything but himself, and Ronnie is just like him. A user. Whatever she wants, she gets. She wanted me. She got me. Whenever she wanted me. That was another reason I didn't want to live out there. She was too close by."

Greer didn't sound happy about being the object of Veronica Slade's affection, and Dylan wanted to know why.

"Most men wouldn't mind a romp in the hay with a good-looking rich bitch like Veronica Slade," he pointed out.

Greer looked up at him. "I told you she was scary. When she came on to me the first time, I told her no, because I didn't want to piss off her old man. She told me Slade could go fuck himself, and then she threatened me. Said that if I didn't . . . uh . . . do as she asked, she'd put some kind of hex on me, and I'd never be able to get it up again." He laughed and finished his beer. "Not that I believed her of course, but then, you never know . . ."

Johnny Reilly found Charlotte Magnetti to be an unlikely playmate for Veronica Slade. For starters, she was black. Secondly, he was sure she was a hooker. But she was where she was supposed to be, in an expensive condo on Hilton Head, and she swore she and Veronica were childhood friends and that they'd spent the day, and the night, together the day J. J. Slade was killed.

After interviewing the Magnetti woman for nearly an hour, Reilly went to the beach bistro. It was almost noon, and the place was beginning to fill up in spite of the cool weather. He identified himself to the bartender, who immediately looked apprehensive.

"I just want to ask you a few questions," Reilly said. He handed him a photo of Veronica Slade. "Do you recognize this woman?"

The bartender looked at it, then broke into a wide grin. "Hell, yes. She was in here most of the afternoon earlier this week with another woman, a black gal. Both of them real lookers. They got shitfaced on margaritas."

"What day was that?"

The bartender thought a moment. "Must have been Monday. In fact, I know it was Monday. That's delivery day. I was having a hell of a time keeping up with serving those two and trying to check in our supplies for the week."

Veronica Slade's alibi had checked out, but something

nagged at Johnny as he drove back to Savannah. Maybe it was the uncanny resemblance between Veronica Slade and Angela Donahue that bothered him. Had the waiters at the First City Club been mistaken? It seemed far more logical that Slade had met his daughter there instead of Angela. Veronica's story had checked out, but she was rich, and people could be bought. It puzzled him that she would choose such an unlikely candidate as "Charlotte Magnetti" to vouch for her.

His cell phone rang, interrupting his train of thought. It was his assistant, Natalie Baker. "We just got the autopsy report. Looks like whoever killed Slade did him a big favor."

"Why?"

"He was a dead man walking. Eaten up with cancer."

Chapter 19

Sometimes, th' good fortune of one be th' bad fortune of another. Only th' conjureman's magic can change that 'round . . .

THE following Wednesday, Anthony Spriggs, accompanied by a paralegal assistant, arrived at Paradisia Plantation promptly at one P.M., as he'd arranged with Harlow. Elizabeth's first impression of him was that he was "dapper." His dark hair was thick and rich and glistened with whatever he used to enhance the shine. His black suit was appropriate for the occasion and impeccable, as was his tie. His shoes gleamed as brightly as his hair. She watched him approach the Big House, and the knot in her stomach tightened. In other circumstances, she might have welcomed his type as suitor to her daughter. But today, he was not welcome at all.

She turned to Harlow and Veronica and saw that their faces were as grim as she felt. "He's here."

Harlow came to stand by her side. "There's nothing to be afraid of," he assured her. "No matter what J. J. did, we can always contest the will. We *will* contest it if it compromises your interests."

Elizabeth wished she had more confidence in Harlow as a lawyer. She saw clearly what a fool she'd been not to have a high-powered attorney protecting her interests all these years. An attorney—and a spy in J. J.'s business. Instead, she'd trusted the bastard, and she knew in her gut she was about to get wiped out.

"Mr. Spriggs is here," Bridget announced as she opened the parlor door.

The attorney and his assistant were ushered in, and coffee was poured. Every Southern courtesy was extended, small talk made, until Elizabeth thought she might scream.

It was Veronica who voiced her exasperation at last, in not-so-Southern-polite terms. "Can we cut the bullshit and get on with it?"

Spriggs looked at her in surprise and amusement. Elizabeth could tell he was attracted to Veronica. Most men were. To her relief, her daughter had chosen a sedate black dress and pearls for the occasion.

The paralegal handed Spriggs a sheaf of papers from the briefcase he'd carried in, and the attorney shuffled through them until he appeared satisfied everything was in its proper order. Elizabeth's heart pounded, and her skin was clammy. She took a seat next to Veronica on the sofa. Whatever their differences, they were family, and whatever this will contained, they would have to face it together. She reached for her daughter's hand and found it was as cold as her own. For once, Veronica didn't pull away.

Before he read the will, Spriggs explained the circumstances under which it was drawn up. "It was rather unusual," he said, "since Mr. Slade was not a client of our firm and the request was made in such a hurry. That's why two senior partners joined me and Mr. Slade for the proceedings. We wanted to make certain that he was of sound mind." He paused and looked at each of them. "I can assure you, there is no doubt that he was fully cogent and aware of what he was doing."

Elizabeth frowned, not fully believing the man. She'd learned from the autopsy report that J. J. had been riddled with cancer. It was likely that the disease had affected his brain. But her husband had also been a master of deceit, the consummate salesman. Even if the cancer had unbalanced him, she believed he would have been capable of convincing the wiliest interviewer of his soundness of mind.

Spriggs cleared his throat and looked at the will. "It's actually quite short and succinct."

Elizabeth tapped her fingers on her knee as he waded through the traditional legal language, until he finally got down to the meat of the matter.

" 'To my wife, Elizabeth, I leave clear title to Paradisia Plantation.

" 'To my daughter, Veronica Anne, I leave clear title to the BMW that is in her possession, and twenty thousand dollars.' "

Elizabeth wasn't certain she'd heard correctly. "Is that all?"

"Ah, I believe so, as far as you're concerned. He bequeathed you these things in lieu of the year's support required by law."

Elizabeth's ears began to ring, and it was hard for her to follow his explanation of the law. She darted a quick look at Harlow and wasn't assured by the bleak look on his face. She glanced at Veronica. Her daughter's face was white but otherwise, she registered no emotion. "Go on," Elizabeth said irritably. "There's a lot of his estate still unaccounted for."

Spriggs cleared his throat and proceeded. " 'To my pilot, Bob Greer, I leave my Citation Four aircraft.

" 'To Bridget Means, for her faithful service to our wretched family . . .' " At this point the young lawyer turned slightly pink and coughed before he continued, " 'I leave one million dollars.

" 'All other monies and assets of my personal estate have been put into a trust, the beneficiary of which shall remain anonymous unless that person chooses to reveal an identity.' "

Elizabeth stared at him, stunned. She brought her hand to her chest, which had painfully constricted, making breathing almost impossible. "But that's impossible!"

Spriggs looked at her regretfully. "No, ma'am. I'm sorry, but these are his last wishes."

From somewhere that seemed far away, she heard Harlow harrumph. "This is total nonsense," he said. "Slade was worth millions that rightfully belong to my client. We'll contest that worthless . . ."

"That's your right, Mr. Bertram, but if you do, your client is at tremendous risk of losing everything. You see, he insisted on including the *In Terrorem* clause."

Elizabeth didn't know what an "*In Terrorem* clause" was, but the very name of it struck fear in her heart. But Harlow knew.

"That bastard," he exploded.

"What . . . what does that mean?" Elizabeth asked, although she was afraid to find out.

"It means simply that anyone who attempts to contest this will is going to automatically lose any benefit he or she has inherited," Spriggs explained.

"Coercion," Harlow blustered. "Somebody made him do it. That secret beneficiary was blackmailing him."

Spriggs shrugged and took two envelopes out of his briefcase. "That's always a possibility," he said without emotion.

He handed one envelope to Elizabeth, the other to Veronica. "He asked me to give these to you after the will was read. I have no knowledge of what is in them. I hope they bring you some solace." Spriggs and his assistant stood, and the attorney gave Harlow a business card. "Call me if you wish to discuss this further. Otherwise, we won't intrude any longer on your privacy. Good day." And with that, they were gone.

Elizabeth stared at the envelope, which bore the embossed return address of the law firm in the upper left hand corner. It was addressed simply ELIZABETH in J. J.'s familiar hand. She heard the sound of paper tearing and turned to see Veronica opening the envelope addressed to her.

Moments later, Veronica dropped the letter and let out a shriek that could have been heard in the next county. "That old bastard! Oh, my God!" Then she crumpled and began sobbing hysterically. Elizabeth put her arms around her daughter, but Veronica seemed not to notice. She wept uncontrollably.

Quietly, Elizabeth picked the letter up off the floor and read it:

Dear Veronica,

Three years ago, you were provided with a trust fund in the amount of five million dollars. I advised you how to invest and turn that five million into a vast fortune, but you chose to spend it instead. Because of your irresponsibility, I consider that trust to have been your inheritance, received before the fact of my death. Therefore, you are now on your own, unless your mother chooses to bail you out again. I have done all I can for you.

It was not signed, "Love, Your father," or even, "Your father." The sorry SOB had signed it as if he were a stranger—J. J. SLADE.

Elizabeth had known J. J. was furious with Veronica, but she'd never dreamed he would inflict such vicious retribution. And the jerk had left it to her to protect their daughter with only her private and separate assets, which although substantial, were nothing to what she had expected to inherit from J. J.'s estate. That he'd left her Paradisia was at the moment little consolation.

She looked up at Harlow. "That bastard," she said in a hoarse whisper. "After all I did for him. He was a nobody when I married him. A nobody!" She felt like joining Veronica in an hysterical breakdown, but instead she stiffened. "He won't do this to me."

She stood and went to Harlow. He might appear to be an upstanding lawyer, but he had some friends in low places. "I don't care how much it costs, or what you have to do. Find out who is the beneficiary of that trust and take care of this problem."

The past few days had been quiet, and although Angela was still keenly aware of the danger she was in, she went back to work. Connie was a good manager, but Southern Hospitality Tours was Angela's company, and she felt an urgency to take the helm again. The business was her only security, and she mustn't let anything happen to it.

Dylan had objected, but he couldn't force her to remain behind the lace curtains and wrought-iron safety bars of her house. Nor would she allow him to station himself as a watchdog on her premises, for the truth was, she desperately needed some emotional space between them.

He'd at last grudgingly agreed to leave her alone, but she'd seen his old Camaro cruise by several times during the day and knew he wasn't far away.

Connie was taking a couple of much-needed days off, and Angela was alone in the shop when a tall, good-looking young man entered. He was dressed conservatively and carried a briefcase.

"May I help you?" Angela asked.

"I'm looking for Angela Donahue," he said, smiling and extending a business card.

Angela looked at the card. The man's name was Anthony Spriggs, and he was with an Atlanta law firm. "I don't need a lawyer," she said, handing the card back to him.

He grinned. "I'm not here soliciting your business. But I do have something urgent I need to discuss with you." He nodded toward the office at the back of the store. "Perhaps we could talk in there, in case customers come in."

Angela had been waiting for the other shoe to drop in

the Slade murder case, and she felt suddenly that it was poised, right over her head. "I suppose so, Mr. Spriggs, but if customers come in, I'll have to excuse myself. Why don't you just say what you have to say right here?"

He shrugged. "Very well. May I . . . ?" He indicated he wished to place his briefcase on a nearby table of merchandise. Angela nodded, her apprehension mounting.

He took out a narrow white folder. "Our firm represents the estate of J. J. Slade," he said. "I . . . know you are aware of his tragic death last week. I offer my condolences." He handed her the folder. "This is a copy of his will that was drawn up shortly before his death. In it, he left the majority of his estate, in the form of an irrevocable trust, to an anonymous beneficiary."

Angela stared blankly at the papers, wondering what all this had to do with her. Spriggs then took out a manila envelope and gave it to her. "These are the papers outlining the trust and naming the trustee he appointed. You, Ms. Donahue, are the beneficiary of that trust."

Dumbfounded, Angela looked up at the attorney, who stood smiling inanely at her. "There is some mistake," she managed at last.

"No mistake, Ms. Donahue. Our firm handled both the drawing up of the will and the formation of the trust. Slade came to us a few days before his death. He told us he had cancer and had only a short time to live," Spriggs said, then added almost as an afterthought, "although I doubt he expected to go so quickly." He seemed to be sizing Angela up, and she realized that he must be aware the police suspected her of killing Slade.

A rock suddenly dropped to the pit of her stomach. Oh, dear God, this couldn't be happening. Talk about motive!

But Spriggs made no mention of the murder. Instead, he said, "Mrs. Slade and her daughter, Veronica, have only this afternoon learned of the changes in his will, and you can safely assume they aren't happy about it. I would advise you to follow Slade's wishes and keep your identity a secret. No one knows you're the beneficiary except myself, two other partners in the firm, and the trustee at SunTrust Bank, who is also executor of Mr. Slade's estate. I have not even confided in my paralegal, whom I've left at a restaurant while I presented this to you. Naturally, no one in our firm would ever reveal your identity without your permission."

Suddenly lightheaded, Angela battled the nausea that washed over her. This had to be a mistake or some kind of sick joke, worse even than the voodoo prank. She shoved the papers back into his hands.

"You are mistaken, Mr. Spriggs. I didn't even know J. J. Slade. And if it's a practical joke, I don't find it funny."

Spriggs looked slightly abashed and put the papers aside on the table. "Mr. Slade made no mention of why he'd chosen you to receive his fortune, but you are the recipient, and it's no joke. You'll find everything is in order. It's definitely your Social Security number on those papers." He paused, then added, "I've read the newspaper accounts of his death, of course, and I'm aware of your . . . uh . . . predicament, Ms. Donahue. I'm sorry to be the bearer of news that, should it become known, is bound to make your situation worse." He gave a short laugh at the irony. "If you can call inheriting a fortune bad news."

He seemed ingenuous when he added, "It's none of my business, but if there is any way I can help, I hope you'll give me a call. You have my card." He shut his briefcase with a click. "I couldn't represent you, of course, but I know several excellent criminal defense lawyers."

He shook her hand while she stared at him in shock, unable to find further words. "Good day, Ms. Donahue."

After he left, Angela looked down at the two parcels that lay on top of some Savannah tourist guide books. This had to be a hoax. It had to be. Who could have done this to her?

Only one man she knew of had the kind of power and money it took to set up something like this. Lucas Quintos. And Cecil Clifford was Quintos's man. Judge Brown had confirmed that Clifford was out of jail and bent on revenge. Clifford, who'd been on both sides of the law and knew every trick in the book. Angela clutched her arms and shivered. He was going to kill her. It wouldn't be a sniper. Or an accident. He was going to use the law to destroy her.

Chapter 20

Ain't nothing in th' realm of man or spirit be impossible, this th' conjureman knows for sure . . .

"I can't go to the police!" Angela shrieked at Dylan a short while later.

"If you don't, and Reilly and the GBI find out about this, your sweet little ass is grass, Angela. It would be better to take this to them now than to have them learn you were hiding it."

They stood almost toe-to-toe in the cabin of Dylan's boat, squared off like prizefighters. After Spriggs had left, Angela had closed the store and called Dylan, who, apparently satisfied that she would be all right at work, had finally gone back to his boat to get some of his own work done. He'd insisted on coming for her, but she told him to stay put, that she needed to come to him. "You remember that sanctuary you were talking about?" she'd said. "I think I might be needing it."

She was sure of it now. Her already shaky world was ready to crumble from beneath her, and she was scared. It was bad enough that she'd been stalked, impersonated, and all but accused of murder, but this turn of events left her feeling as if she'd lost all control over her fate.

"I know you're right, Dylan," she said, her head beginning to hurt. "But what if Reilly is Clifford's man? If he is, then I'd be playing right into his hands. He'd throw me in jail the minute the words were out of my mouth. Even if he's not crooked, he probably still wouldn't believe me. He already thinks I'm lying about not knowing Slade."

"Then go to Vince Howard at the GBI. You know you can trust him."

"I will." Angela collapsed onto the settee, feeling uncomfortably confined in the close quarters of the boat. "But I don't want to go empty-handed. You know, Dylan, one reason Vince took on the investigation of the SPD is because I brought him enough evidence that he couldn't ignore it. I may have worked for him and have friends in the bureau, but Vincent Howard and the rest are professionals. They'll want something concrete to go on. Even if they buy into our theory that this is all a set-up, they're going to want to know how I think Quintos got Slade to change his will."

Dylan cocked his head. "And how *do* you think he did that?"

"Spriggs looked legit, but he might not be a lawyer at all. This whole thing," she said, indicating the papers that lay on the table nearby, "could be phony. Or Spriggs could be a crooked lawyer on Quintos's payroll. Maybe Slade didn't change the will at all. Maybe Quintos paid Spriggs to do it, knowing he was about to knock Slade off. With Slade dead, it'd be hard to prove he didn't make out the new will. Or maybe Quintos sent an imposter to Spriggs's office, somebody posing as Slade, like somebody's been posing as me." The possibilities spun in her head. "I don't know. But Quintos has the money and the contacts to buy off attorneys. It's the only thing that makes sense."

She stretched her legs across the settee, suddenly exhausted and overwhelmed by the whole thing. "I just can't believe he'd want to get me that bad. Spriggs told me the trust was worth a fortune."

"There's one thing we can check out," Dylan said, picking up the envelope concerning the trust. "The trustee." He opened the envelope and re-read the papers concerning the trust fund. "SunTrust is an old and respected bank," he said at last. "It'd be hard to believe they'd become involved in something dirty. It could bring the bank down."

Angela phoned the bank and asked to speak to Quinn Parker, the man whose name was recorded as being the trustee. He was in and available, so she made an appointment to see him, gathered all the papers into her purse and said, "Let's go."

Mr. Quinn Parker was a gentleman who appeared to be in his seventies. He greeted Angela politely but cautiously in the bank's reception area. After he examined the paperwork she'd brought with her, he asked her for two forms of identification. She showed him her driver's license and Social Security card, which seemed to satisfy him. "I'm not at liberty to discuss this trust with anyone except the beneficiary and the attorneys involved," he explained politely. "I'm sure you understand our need to positively identify you, Ms. Donahue."

By the time she'd completed her meeting with Parker, from which Dylan had been expressly excluded by the banker, Angela was convinced the trust was legitimate, and that she had indeed inherited J. J. Slade's fortune.

"Now what?" she sighed as she sank into the Camaro. "We're back to square one. How did Quintos get Slade to change that will?"

But neither had an answer they could take to the GBI.

As he drove back to the boat, Dylan thought out loud. "Let that go for a while, and think about the woman who impersonated you. She must look a lot like you. I mean, copying your style of clothing, even using a wig, wouldn't be enough to fool people who know you well."

"Go on," Angela said, desperate for answers to all the mysteries that threatened to destroy her.

"Do you have any relatives, a distant cousin maybe, that Quintos could have found and paid off to pretend to be you?"

"I don't have any distant cousins," was Angela's first thought, then she realized she didn't know whether she had cousins or not. "At least none that I know of."

"It's worth looking into. Does your mother have any siblings?"

"Two sisters and two brothers, but I haven't seen them since I was a kid and we moved to Savannah after dad died."

"Your mom's a serious Catholic," he pointed out. "Her siblings likely had large families. Maybe you have a lot of cousins. Where did your aunts and uncles live?"

"In Florida. Jacksonville. That's where I was born. My father was from there, too. They were both from poor families. That's about all I know."

"Did your dad have any sisters and brothers?"

Angela thought about it and couldn't come up with an answer. "You know, I don't know. That's pretty bad, isn't it, that I know virtually nothing about my dad except that he died?" It seemed sad to Angela that she knew so little about the man who'd sired her. Except for those few moments when she'd been talking about him to Jeremiah, her father had been little more than an abstract in her mind for most of her life.

"Maybe you should ask your mother," Dylan urged. "Find out if you have any female cousins. I'll try to track them down to see if any of them look like you. Quintos would have the resources to dig up someone he could pay to impersonate you, and if she came from a poor family, she might have been made an offer she couldn't refuse."

Angela groaned. She didn't want to ask her mother about her family. For some reason, Mary Ellen had cut those ties long ago. Maybe because they brought back painful memories of Jake Donahue. Maybe because her family reminded her of the poverty she'd come from. But Dylan's suggestion made sense. "I suppose I could talk to her."

Dylan was silent for a long while, then he said, "We're making the assumption that Quintos and Clifford are behind this. Let's consider something else. What if Slade was some distant relative of yours, your dad's cousin maybe? He'd be about the right age."

"Get real, Dylan." Angela recalled how Dylan's brainstorming had brought new thoughts to old theories on that long-ago case, but this was too much.

"Stay with me," he urged. "From what I've learned about Slade, he was a control freak and eccentric to the max. He demanded complete loyalty from his family and employees. What if, say, his wife or his daughter betrayed him somehow and he found out? Maybe they sold him out to Quintos? It would have to be something really big. And maybe he was quirky enough to leave his fortune to you, a remote relative, just out of spite. Stranger things have happened."

Angela shot Dylan a scathing look. "Name one."

Ronnie's head felt as if a bass drum were pounding inside it, and her eyes burned despite the few hours of tranquilizer-induced sleep she'd had since Anthony Spriggs had torn her world apart. Her worst nightmare had come true.

She rolled over and managed to sit up on the side of the bed. Fresh terror washed over her as she thought of the consequences of the change in her father's will. The man-with-no-name would kill her. If she couldn't pay him, he wouldn't think twice about getting rid of her. She'd managed to keep him at bay by being his sex slave whenever he came to town, and by doing his dirty little errands and spying on her father. He'd given her credit against her expected inheritance for all the cocaine she'd craved, but now . . . there would be no inheritance, at least not enough to save her.

Ronnie fought back the hot tears that threatened to resurface and for the hundredth time cursed her father. She threw her pillow across the room. She wouldn't let him get away with this. She wouldn't!

Rage and determination replaced her fear. She would not let her father win this one. Nor would she let that bitch make off with her father's fortune, for Ronnie was certain Angela Donahue was the secret beneficiary of the trust. Ronnie would find a way not only to set things right, but also to take her revenge. It was too late to hurt her father, but Angela Donahue was another matter.

She wished she could talk to Marguerite, because the woman was clever and would know exactly what to do, but Ronnie didn't dare. Marguerite had already stepped in once to cover Ronnie's ass. It was time for her to think for herself, to take matters into her own hands.

She turned on the shower and stepped inside, letting the hot water beat on her body as thoughts tumbled in a torrent through her mind. Reasoning had never been her strong suit. She'd always managed to get her way through manipulation. Who could she convince to help her get to the bottom of this? She certainly wasn't going to wait around for Harlow to take action. And besides, she wanted to be the one to get Angela Donahue.

The attorney? Although at first she'd wanted to scratch out his eyes and ruin that handsome face forever for what he'd done to her, she reminded herself it wasn't his fault. He'd done nothing except convey her father's latest betrayal.

Don't kill the messenger.

Use him.

Ronnie lathered her hair, thinking about the attorney. Spriggs knew the identity of the beneficiary of the trust. Although Ronnie suspected that her father had left his fortune to Angela Donahue, she had to be certain. She wasn't sure what she'd do about it, but once she knew for sure who had inherited her fortune, something would come to her.

She toweled off, then tied the towel around her wet hair,

and put on a robe, still lost in thought. Spriggs knew, but would he talk? Ronnie trusted her ability to seduce men, but what if it didn't work with Spriggs? He could be gay, for all she knew. It was too important to take a chance. No, she had to find another way.

She lit a cigarette and went out onto the balcony. It was dusk, and the cool air awakened her skin and cleared her thoughts. She inhaled deeply and freed her mind of all but thoughts of Anthony Spriggs and Angela Donahue, and after a few moments, the answer unexpectedly came to her. It happened so suddenly, she caught her breath and choked on the smoke. Then she smiled, elated that she'd managed to solve the problem on her own. She didn't need Marguerite to think for her after all.

Crushing out the cigarette, she rushed back into her room. She took a small suitcase out of the closet, then carefully considered what she would need to pull this off. She threw in her costume, and her gun. Her heart was beating hard with excitement. It felt good to take matters into her own hands.

She threw everything she needed into the bag, then crept down the back stairs and made her way out of the house unnoticed. Harlow's Volvo was still parked in the drive, alongside her Beamer.

Harlow.

She shuddered in disgust. If he'd been half a man, any kind of lawyer at all, this wouldn't have happened. She despised the fat old man and felt sorry for her mother, who had taken him as her lover. Ronnie knew her parents hadn't slept together in years, but no one should have to be that desperate. Once, when she'd been angry with her mother, she'd seduced Harlow out of spite. He was like a hog in bed, grunting and snuffling, and he snored loudly after the sex.

Ronnie jumped into her car and put the top up, as if she

could hide beneath it. It was nearly dark when she roared past the iron gates of Paradisia and turned down the lane, headed for the interstate. She never noticed the blue van that wheeled from its hiding place and fell in behind her.

Chapter 21

When evil abides a long time in a place, it takes over th' souls of all who live there. Th' hags hang out in every room and ride th' folk at night. Th' hants walk behind them in broad daylight, and th' evil breeds more evil unto th' next generation . . .

"I'D kill the son of a bitch if he wasn't already dead," Harlow Bertram said. He was on his fourth or fifth scotch—he wasn't sure—and Elizabeth was deep into her wine as the afternoon wore into evening. Thankfully, at Elizabeth's suggestion, Veronica had taken a couple of tranquilizers and gone to bed. Harlow could hardly abide being in the same room with Elizabeth's daughter.

After Veronica had departed, Harlow had plied Elizabeth with alcohol to get her mind off killing Slade's secret beneficiary. He'd done a lot of shady things in his life, but murder wasn't one of them. He hoped that by morning, Elizabeth would come to her senses.

Elizabeth's only reply to his pronouncement was a loud sniff. She'd said very little since the Atlanta attorney had left. She'd opened the envelope Spriggs had handed her, read Slade's final message, and cried for most of the afternoon. She wouldn't tell Harlow what Slade had written, but it had deeply upset her. She wasn't one to drown her sorrows in a wine bottle, in spite of Harlow's encouragement.

Harlow felt sorry for her, although he was tempted to say I told you so. He'd never understood what Elizabeth saw in J. J. Slade, or why she'd married him instead of Harlow. It had happened nearly thirty years ago, but he remembered everything as if it were yesterday.

Elizabeth had gone to Las Vegas in pursuit of her dissolute father, Angus Mayhew, to try to dissuade him from gambling away what was left of the Mayhew fortune, including Paradisia, in a high-stakes poker game. Slade had been a blackjack dealer at one of the casinos, and according to Elizabeth, they'd been immediately attracted to one another. She'd told him her problem, and he'd given her an answer.

The old man had been unable to continue the game, because she'd followed Slade's suggestion and liberally laced his drink with a powerful laxative.

The three of them had returned to Paradisia in a few days, where Angus made a fast recovery from his bout with "food poisoning." Elizabeth and J. J. had been married shortly thereafter.

Sure, Slade had been a handsome devil. Tall, athletic, nothing like the stocky lawyer she'd left behind. But Harlow knew that Slade had never loved Elizabeth. He'd seen her money, and his opportunity, and he'd taken both.

Absently, Harlow poured himself another scotch and refilled Elizabeth's wine glass. She was beyond conversation, and he was content to continue to reflect on the past and the events that had led to this tragic day.

He'd never liked Slade, but after Angus Mayhew's death, Harlow had come to respect Slade's ability to manage money. In just a few short years, he'd turned the dwindling Mayhew fortunes around. Harlow had been happy for Elizabeth, until he saw how Slade had treated her when she became pregnant with Veronica. He'd even seen Slade backhand her when she refused to have an abortion. Slade claimed a child had never been part of their "agreement," which is how Elizabeth's husband viewed their marriage. Harlow had half expected them to divorce, but Slade loved Elizabeth's money too much to leave her, and she must have loved him, because they'd stuck it out.

When Veronica was born, bad had turned to worse, and the child herself didn't help matters. She was a pain in the ass from the beginning, colicky and unhappy in spite of Elizabeth's best efforts to comfort her. Veronica grew up knowing her father wished she'd never been born, and over time, her bad temper worsened. She became bitter and hateful, petulant and willful. Harlow had felt sorry for the young Veronica, but even more so for Elizabeth, who couldn't be faulted for doing all she could to appease the girl, but who had only succeeded in spoiling her beyond reason.

His pity for the girl changed the day he'd allowed her to seduce him. Harlow's face grew hot with shame at the memory. He must have been out of his mind to fall for her blatant overtures, and he'd been terrified ever since that she'd tell Elizabeth. But if she had, Elizabeth had never brought it up to him.

Harlow believed Veronica was the devil's own daughter, and it wouldn't surprise him to learn she'd murdered her father. And except that it would destroy Elizabeth, he wouldn't mind seeing Veronica hang for it.

The alcohol was making him melancholy. He had to pull out of this funk. He rang for Bridget, who seemed not to understand she was a millionaire and who'd gone about her duties as usual after Spriggs had left. He ordered a light supper for the two of them, to be served by the fire in the parlor. When the maid had departed, he knelt next to Elizabeth and took her hand. "Please don't worry, my darling. We'll contest that *In Terrorem* clause, and then we'll contest the will . . ."

Before he knew what had happened, she slapped him across the face. "No!" she hissed. "We will not contest the will."

Harlow drew back in astonishment. *She must really be drunk.* "But, I thought . . ."

"You thought wrong." Elizabeth's hands were shaking

as she picked up the envelope containing Slade's letter. She creased the fold of the flap with her nails.

"I don't understand."

She raised her swollen, bloodshot eyes and looked at him with a fierceness that almost frightened him. "No, you don't understand, Harlow, and you never will. I've changed my mind. I don't want you to do anything about this. Don't even try to find out who he left his money to. I have plenty of money of my own, and I have Paradisia. We will not contest J. J.'s will. Don't ask me about it again. Just leave it alone."

Harlow had always found women confusing, but Elizabeth's sudden change of mind concerning Slade's will threw him completely off. Bridget arrived with a tray of soup and sandwiches, but Elizabeth ordered her to take them away.

"Mr. Bertram was just leaving," she said coldly.

Bridget removed the tray without a sign that anything was out of the ordinary. When she was gone, Elizabeth said, "Go home, Harlow. I want to be alone with my daughter. I need to talk to her."

Knowing Veronica's penchant for drugs, Harlow figured she'd taken enough tranquilizers to sleep through the night. Even if Elizabeth succeeded in awakening the young woman, he doubted whether she'd be very coherent. But he picked up his hat and coat and made his way toward the front door, giving in to Elizabeth's wishes. He'd always acquiesced to her. Maybe that's why she'd never much respected him.

At the door, he turned and watched as Elizabeth slowly climbed the stairs. He could understand her desire to spend some time with her daughter. It was only human nature. But he hated being dismissed as if he were one of her servants.

He'd waited thirty years for her. J. J. was gone now, and things were going to be different between them. He'd give her time to get over the shock of all that had happened. After that, she would never dismiss him again.

He turned the door handle and was about to step out into the cool night air when he heard her call out his name. "Harlow!" He turned and ran up the grand staircase and found her leaning against the doorway to Veronica's room. The light was on, the bed unmade. And Veronica was gone.

"We have to stop her," Elizabeth said, her voice edged with panic. "She's bound to do something foolish."

Harlow took both of her hands in his and forced her to look at him. "Elizabeth," he said, slightly impatiently, "this is not unusual. Veronica comes and goes like the wind."

Elizabeth jerked her hands away from his. "You idiot. Veronica is as greedy as her father. Do you think for one minute she's going to give up without a fight?"

"If she wants to contest the will, it's her right. But she'd better be careful how she goes about it, or she'll end up with nothing."

Elizabeth's face had turned gray, and she put her hand to her throat. "You don't know the half of it . . ."

"Hold on," Ricky Suarez told his sidekick when he saw the red BMW coming through the gates of Paradisia Plantation. "She's not going to get away from us this time." He started the engine, threw the van into gear, and turned onto the lane in time to eat a healthy portion of her dust. "Shit!" he said, rolling up the open window.

She was driving at her usual reckless speed, but the size and condition of the small road made it possible for Suarez to stay up with her in his cumbersome vehicle. He followed her to the interstate, where she turned north, heading toward Savannah. No surprise there.

The surprise came when she reached Savannah. Instead of taking the freeway into town, she took I-16 in the opposite direction. The brightly lit green highway sign read MACON. "Where the hell's she going?" Suarez said, barely managing to stay with her as she accelerated the sports car and threatened to disappear into the darkening night.

She steadied her cruising speed at around eighty, and Suarez managed to stay up with her, although he wondered if the utilitarian van could keep up the pace. It rumbled on faithfully, however, and he instructed Joe to phone their boss in Miami and let him know what was up.

When they reached Macon, she turned onto I-75 and headed northwest, but shortly afterward pulled into a busy truck stop. Suarez eased off the freeway right behind her and decided to get a closer look at his prey. He pulled up to the gas pump behind her car and got out. She was struggling with the nozzle, and being the hero that he was, he saw his opportunity.

"Need some help?"

She looked up at him, and he saw the usual reaction in her eyes. Alarm. Ricky Suarez was built like a linebacker, with a square face and a heavy jaw. His skin was swarthy, his dark hair slicked back. A scar ran from his left eyebrow to what little remained of his left ear, a reminder of the price one paid for the violent business he was in.

Veronica Slade, on the other hand, was small and pretty, with full lips and dark eyes. Her dark hair brushed across her face in the light wind. She sized him up quickly, then batted her lids and handed him the hose. "Sure. Thanks."

He guessed she went for the dangerous type. As he began filling her tank, he gave her a small smile. Something about her seemed very familiar. He'd seen her only from a distance, but her features reminded him of someone . . .

"You think it's safe for a woman to be traveling alone this time at night?" he asked.

"Why wouldn't it be? What are you, some kind of male chauvinist?"

He laughed. "I guess you could call me that. I just like to take care of women, that's all."

He could see she was interested.

"Oh? And just how do you take care of us poor little helpless creatures?"

It occurred to Suarez that he could have this one in bed in no time, and he wondered briefly if she were a hooker. It seemed unlikely, a rich chick like Veronica Slade. But her clothing and mannerisms bespoke a woman of the night. She was probably after drugs. A part of him felt sorry for her. He wondered how she fit into Slade's operation.

The gas gurgled as it reached the top of the tank, and Suarez replaced the nozzle in the holder. "I just pump gas, ma'am. That's all."

She looked disappointed. "I see. Well, thanks a million." She got in her car and moved it to a parking space by the convenience store. He watched as she got out again and entered the store, heading for the rest rooms. He took the opportunity to fuel his van, using a credit card to pay at the pump, then removed his vehicle to a darkened corner of the parking lot where she wouldn't notice it when she came out. When she emerged again, she paused at the door of the store, obviously looking for him, but when she didn't see him, she shrugged, got back into her car and pulled into the northbound lane of the interstate.

Suarez and Joe Delano followed Veronica to Buckhead, an exclusive area of Atlanta, and watched as she drove up to the front entrance of the Grand Hyatt. She had only one small bag, but she tipped the bellman to carry it for her, while a valet parked her car.

Suarez and Delano settled in for the night. The van was parked where they could easily keep an eye on her car. Delano took the first nap while Suarez picked up a Savannah newspaper that'd been lying around the van. He turned to the story of Slade's murder, and Angela Donahue's picture seemed to jump out at him. Using his fingers to frame down the photo, he covered her hair and looked at only the face. "Well, I'll be damned," he murmured. He could have been looking into the face of Veronica Slade.

* * *

The following morning around nine, Delano spotted the valet going for Veronica's car. Suarez pulled out his powerful binoculars and focused on the woman waiting for the car at the main door to the hotel. It didn't look at all like the woman whose gas he'd pumped the night before. This one wore a dark navy business suit, white blouse, and sensible navy heels. Her hair wasn't dark or straight. Instead, it was strawberry blond and wavy.

He whistled softly. The woman who was getting into the red BMW wasn't Veronica Slade. It was Angela Donahue.

Chapter 22

There was a dead husband hantin' this woman, and she came t' Dr. Lizard and she said, "Cast a spell and bring my husband back." But he be dead, and ain't no spell going to bring him back, an' so I said, "Foolish woman, find yourself another husband. This one used up . . ."

THE smell of the Chinese takeout filled her car, making Angela's mouth water. She was on her way to her mother's house. Mary Ellen was feeling stronger, but she still hadn't returned to work, which doubled Angela's anxiety for her. Mary Ellen's work was her life. For her to miss so many days was unthinkable, unless she was very ill. Angela wished she'd made her go to the hospital last week when the flu first hit.

Angela was nervous about the little mission she was on. She wished she and her mother could talk heart-to-heart, like other mothers and daughters did, but she'd never shared that kind of closeness with Mary Ellen. Theirs had been an arm's-length relationship, emotionally speaking. Mary Ellen had devoted her life to Angela, but she'd never let Angela too close. She'd given her daughter everything she could, demanding only her loyalty in return. And Angela had been loyal. She'd learned to overlook her mother's quirkiness, forgive her fits of temper, and ignore her overzealous Catholicism, because her mother was the only family she had. Besides, Angela loved her. Dylan was the only person who'd ever come between them, and Mary Ellen had made no secret of the fact that she was glad he was gone when he'd walked out on Angela. It'd seemed to Angela that her mother wasn't just happy to have her daughter all to herself once again. Mary Ellen was obviously gratified that he'd proven her right. She'd always told Angela that you can't trust men.

When she reached her mother's house, Angela was happy to find that Mary Ellen was up and dressed and wearing makeup, looking much like her old self. "You're looking spiffy, Mom. I hope this means you're feeling better."

"Thanks, I am," Mary Ellen replied, taking the bag of Chinese food from her and heading toward the kitchen. "A lot better."

"Great. It's been a pretty rough week for you, hasn't it?"

Mary Ellen didn't answer right away, and when she did, her voice was tight. "Yes, it was a very rough week. I'm glad it's over." Angela realized she was referring not only to her illness, but also to what had happened to Angela.

There was a lot Mary Ellen didn't know, and Angela intended to keep it that way. Her mother's fragile emotions would never be able to handle the idea that her daughter was being targeted by a drug lord.

After her lengthy conversation with Dylan about the possibility that the impersonator might be a relative, Angela had decided to gut up and ask her mother about her family. That's why she'd brought in lunch. This was probably going to take a while. Even if Angela hadn't been trying to find out why Slade had left her his fortune, when she'd realized how little she knew about her family, especially her father's side, she'd suddenly become eager to learn more.

Angela had always wanted a family of her own, but her mother had discouraged any of Angela's boyfriends who'd shown signs of getting too serious. Mary Ellen had persuaded Angela to remain single and independent, when in her heart of hearts, Angela desperately had wanted to fall in love, get married, and start a family. She'd thought that might happen with Dylan, but he'd fulfilled her mother's every prediction when he'd walked out on her.

Since then, Angela hadn't dared to have that dream again.

She might never have her own family, but maybe today she could learn more about the one she came from. Angela made hot tea to go with the food, and she and Mary Ellen attacked the meal with relish. Angela was happy to see that her mother's appetite had returned.

When they'd almost finished, she dared to ask her first question. "Mom, whatever happened to Aunt Janet and Aunt Sandra?"

Mary Ellen's head jerked up. "What?"

Angela shrugged and took a sip of tea. "I don't know. I was just curious about them, I guess. And your brothers, too, Paul and Bill. Why didn't we keep up with them?"

"Why should we?" Mary Ellen replied crossly. "They've never had anything to do with us."

"That's a two-way street. Did you ever have anything to do with them?"

Mary Ellen didn't answer. In fact, she finished her lunch in silence before she said, "Why all the questions, Angela? What's going on?"

Angela wasn't about to tell her that her questions stemmed from Dylan's suspicions that a lookalike cousin had set her up. It was a nebulous theory at best. Instead, she told the truth.

"I'm just curious. It's occurred to me that I know very little about my family, and I'd like to know more."

Mary Ellen frowned and cleared the table, but she remained silent. Angela had known this wasn't going to be easy, but she'd expected a little more cooperation than this. "Why haven't you stayed in touch with them?" she pressed.

"You're all the family I need," Mary Ellen replied sharply. "Want dessert? I have some Weight Watchers eclairs in the freezer."

"No, thanks." Angela could tell that her mother was getting upset. Angela had spent a lifetime trying to avoid upsetting Mary Ellen, and yet at the moment, her need to know was greater than her need to keep her mother on an even keel. She took a deep breath and continued. "Mom, do I have any cousins?"

"For crying out loud, Angela, what's this all about?"

"Mom, I'm thirty-five years old, and it's occurred to me I know virtually nothing about the people I'm descended from. You've never told me anything or been willing to answer my questions before. Why?"

But again Mary Ellen remained silent. Angela could almost feel her mother's temper starting to percolate, but she'd come this far. She wasn't going to stop now. Determined to get answers at last, she refused to give in. "Do I have any cousins, Mom, on your side or on my father's?"

"This is nonsense," Mary Ellen grumbled. "I'd like to know who put this in your head." She said it as if she suspected Dylan.

"What about photo albums? Do you have any pictures from when I was small?"

"I never kept any pictures. What good are pictures? They just remind you of things you'd rather forget."

Angela went into the living room and brought back the photo Dylan had been looking at a few nights before. "You have this one," she said, placing it on the table between them. "You've looked at it every day for thirty years. I've seen you."

Mary Ellen shot an angry look at her daughter, but she didn't say anything. Angela held her gaze and didn't blink. "I want to know about our family, Mom. I deserve to know about my people."

As Angela watched, Mary Ellen's face lost its rigidity, and her eyes filled with sadness. She slumped back against her chair and stared at her tea cup. "They aren't people to be proud of, Angela," she said, her voice barely above a whisper.

"Mom, I don't care," Angela said, taking her seat again. "I just want to know."

"All your people, on both sides, were poor Irish Catholics. Your father and I grew up in a slum neighborhood in Jacksonville. Our fathers were fishermen. My mother worked in a diner. His took in laundry."

"That's nothing to be ashamed of," Angela said. She reached across the table and touched her mother's hand. "I know you had two brothers and two sisters. Did Dad have any?"

"Only one. An older brother. Your dad's mother nearly died giving birth to Jake, so there weren't other children. She confided in me once that she felt guilty because she was relieved not to have to bear more children. Her mother had nine and went to an early grave."

"What was Dad's brother's name?"

Mary Ellen thought for a long moment, then shrugged. "I can't remember. I didn't know him very well. Charles maybe. Why does it matter?"

Angela squeezed her hand. "It doesn't. Like I said, I'm just curious." She paused, then dared to push her mother further still. "Will you tell me about my dad?"

Mary Ellen's eyes took on a faraway look, and she didn't speak for a long time. When she replied, her words were dreamy, girlish. "He was the best-looking boy in the whole school. I can't remember a time when I wasn't in love with him. He was older and didn't pay me much attention until we were in high school. Then, things changed, and . . . well . . . we both thought we were grown up."

Suddenly, Mary Ellen sat up straight in her chair, returning to her adult self, and her voice hardened. "I made a terrible mistake getting involved with Jake Donahue. I was young and impressionable, and I fell for his line like I was some kind of whore. I got pregnant. Jake married me, but only because our mothers pressured us into it." Her lips became a tight line.

Angela stared at her. "I was your terrible mistake?"

"I didn't mean it like that, honey," Mary Ellen said quickly. But her words had already left their mark on Angela. It hurt to think she'd been unwanted by both her parents. She tightened her jaw against the pain that caught her by surprise.

"It doesn't matter," she lied. "Please, go on."

"My family hated Jake," Mary Ellen said bitterly, "and they made it clear he was an unwelcome addition. They made it so hard on him that finally he'd had enough. Before you were born he left me and joined the Navy." Mary Ellen's voice cracked, but a moment later, she resumed her story. "He'd already told me he resented being tied down, so his leaving shouldn't have come as a surprise. He was so full of dreams. He swore he was going to be a rich man one day, that he would never be like his father, enslaved to poverty."

Angela was startled to see tears running down Mary Ellen's cheek, but she didn't interrupt her story. "I had no money, so I had to move back into my family's house, but they all treated me as if I was trashy for having gotten knocked up." Mary Ellen sniffed. "My sisters were such self-righteous little prigs. I hated them." She stifled a sob before continuing. "When you were born, things got a little better, until Jake came back."

Angela shifted uncomfortably in her seat. It was easy to understand now why her mother hadn't wanted to keep up with the family that had so mistreated her. Or talk about them. "What made Dad change his mind and come home?"

Mary Ellen blew her nose. "That was God's doing," she said. "I was so miserable at home, I prayed and prayed for Jake to return and take me away from there, and one day, my prayers were answered. I looked up and there he was, tall and handsome as ever, standing in the doorway of my folks' house. It was the happiest moment of my life. He told me he was sorry and asked if he could come home again. And when he saw you, his eyes lit up like I'd never seen them. Jake wasn't very demonstrative. He didn't let people close to him. But I saw in that minute you were different. Special to him."

"Not a mistake?" Angela heard the bitterness in her question.

Mary Ellen was silent a long time. "You were never a mistake, Angela. When Jake left for the Navy, I realized God had sent me a most precious gift. An angel. Jake's child. If I never saw him again, I had you."

Her mother's words brought tears to Angela's eyes, and she was having trouble controlling her emotions.

Mary Ellen went on. "He tried, he really did, to settle down and make a life with us. But we continued to live with my folks because Jake seemed unable to find work he was happy with. My family nagged and nagged at him about getting a job and going to church. The more they ragged on him, the more sullen and unhappy he became." She paused and dropped her forehead into her hands.

"It was horrible. He began to spend all his time reading books and magazines about people who'd made it rich. He was always scheming ways to hit the jackpot, looking for the quick buck. Sometimes he'd take money we couldn't afford and play the ponies. Most always he lost. About the only really responsible thing he ever did was to buy that life insurance policy." She stopped to wipe her eyes. "Little did he know how important that would become.

"Finally," she said, letting out a deep breath, "my family once again managed to drive him away. He claimed he'd come up with a plan that would free us from them once and for all. He was going to Alaska, where men were making big money on the pipeline. He was going to save all his money, then send for us. But the day he left, I wondered if I'd ever see him again. He hated my family, and he didn't really love me. But he loved you, Angela. My only hope was that he would send for us because of you."

She grew quiet, and Angela didn't press her for more. They both knew the end of the story. But in a few minutes, her mother added the final chapter.

"When Jake was killed, instead of being supportive, my family made it clear they were glad he was gone for good. That's when I took the life insurance money and left them forever. Jake may not have loved me, but he left me that final gift that ironically gave me what he'd promised, a new start. With it, I had the means to get out of that awful place and make a better life for both of us. I wasn't able to provide for you in quite the style he'd imagined, but I tried my best."

Angela wondered briefly if Mary Ellen realized she'd done the same thing to Angela when Dylan had left as her parents had done to her when Jake was killed. But it didn't matter anymore. She stood and came to her mother. "You did a great job, Mom," she said, leaning down and kissing her cheek. "I didn't mean to upset you. I didn't know . . ."

Mary Ellen waved her away. "Well, now you do," she replied abruptly. "I suppose I should have told you this before now." She turned her face to Angela. "I'm sorry, but I'm not feeling well. I think I should go lie down."

Angela regretted that she'd drained her mother's limited energy, but she didn't regret learning the truth. She picked up the fading photo of herself with her parents. "Thanks for telling me about him, Mom. I know it was painful for you. But Dad's been dead for a long time. Isn't it time you let him go?"

Chapter 23

Th' mojo be th' charm that makes things happen. When th' mojo be worked right, wishes be granted and fortunes changed . . .

RONNIE pulled into the parking lot of the law offices of Stearns, McIlheny, and Forrester and gazed at the impressive red-brick, Georgian-style structure in front of her. The firm appeared to be exactly as Harlow had described it—one of the largest and most prestigious in the city. Well done, Daddy, she thought bitterly. You always went for the best.

The best daughter?

Ronnie bit her lip. She couldn't think about that now. She had to focus on carrying out her plan that would restore the fortune she so desperately needed.

She looked down at her costume. For this to work, she had to look and act every inch like Angela Donahue. She glanced in the mirror, and Angela's face peered back at her. It was a pretty enough face, certainly the hair was attractive, but something was missing. The image was a little too plain for Ronnie's taste. Not wishing to go out in public looking so . . . modest, she fished in her purse and brought out her favorite bright red lipstick. Her hand was poised ready to apply it when she remembered that Angela wore little or no makeup.

Shit. Like it or not, today everything about her had to imitate Angela in every detail. With a silent curse, she put the cap back on the tube and dropped it in her purse.

The receptionist appeared to be a no-nonsense type in

her thirties. She wore a conservative dress, and her hair was neatly pulled away from her face. She looked up at Ronnie through wire-rimmed glasses. "May I help you?"

Ronnie gave the woman her most innocent smile. "Good morning. I'm sorry to drop in without an appointment, but . . . I really must see Mr. Spriggs. Is he available?"

The woman eyed her with curiosity. Ronnie imagined that very few clients came into these offices unannounced. "Your name?"

"Donahue," Ronnie said. "Angela Donahue. I met Mr. Spriggs yesterday. He . . . uh . . . brought me some rather surprising news, and I . . . I have a lot of questions, now that I've had time to think it over."

"Have a seat," the woman said, nodding toward a comfortable-looking waiting area. "I'll see if he's in."

Ronnie sat in a large leather wingback chair and crossed her legs, exposing their long length, then remembered who she was supposed to be and assumed a more demure posture. Her heart was thundering. Could she pull this off? She was betting heavily on the unknown.

She'd figured that after he'd left Paradisia, Anthony Spriggs must have called on the secret beneficiary to deliver the good news. If Angela Donahue was that beneficiary, Ronnie reasoned, Anthony Spriggs would see her immediately. He couldn't afford to ignore such a valuable client. If she wasn't, Ronnie would be shown the door. It was that simple.

"Ms. Donahue, what a pleasant surprise." Anthony Spriggs's cheery voice greeted her, and he hurried into the waiting area, his hand extended to shake hers. "I didn't expect to see you again so soon."

In spite of her suspicions, this confirmation of her father's ultimate betrayal turned Ronnie to stone. She fought back the hard, cold rage that engulfed her. She mustn't let her emotions jeopardize this performance. Her very life depended on it. She thought of Angela Donahue's hands on all that money. *Her* money. And she smiled sweetly at Mr. Anthony Spriggs. "Thank you for seeing me on such short notice."

In his office, she refused coffee, wanting to get this over with as quickly as possible. "I'm afraid there's been a huge mistake, Mr. Spriggs. That's why I came to see you in person. I'm not a member of the Slade family, and I didn't know Mr. Slade. I cannot imagine why he left that money in trust to me."

Spriggs took the seat beside her and grinned broadly. "It's hard to believe, isn't it, Ms. Donahue?"

"Please, call me Angela."

"Angela. Pretty name. But as I told you yesterday, there is no doubt that he intended it for you."

Ronnie shook her head. "But I don't want the money. It doesn't belong to me. It should go to his rightful heirs. He must have been out of his mind."

Spriggs shook his head. "No, that's not the case. I must have failed to tell you yesterday that we had two other partners sit in . . ."

Yeah, yeah, yeah, Ronnie wanted to say as she listened to him explain how sound of mind her father had been when he'd drawn up his new will. She'd managed so far to fool Spriggs; she mustn't lose her cool now. She was so close to the money she could taste it. What could she do to convince him to divert it back to where it belonged?

"You apparently didn't hear me, Mr. Spriggs," she said when he'd finished. "I said I don't want the money."

"Why?"

Ronnie stared down at her nails and realized to her horror they were painted red. Angela Donahue didn't wear nail polish, either. Damn. She folded her fingers into her palms to hide her mistake.

"I think you have an idea," she replied to his question. "You must know that the police suspect me of killing Slade. If they find out I'm the secret beneficiary in his will, they'll never believe I didn't kill him." She hadn't thought about that before the words tumbled out of her mouth, but she found it a marvelous notion.

"Did you kill him?"

Spriggs's blunt question caught her off guard. She squirmed slightly in her seat and plucked at her sleeve. *Had she killed him?* Ronnie didn't know for sure. She still couldn't remember what had happened that day. "No!" she said, tossing her head back. She felt the wig shift slightly. Alarmed, she pretended to fuss with her bangs to make sure it hadn't gone too far askew. "Not that it's any of your business. I told you, I didn't know the man, and I have no idea why he left that money to me. Do you, Mr. Spriggs?" Ronnie's hands were sweaty and cold.

Spriggs got up and walked to the window where he stood with his hands clasped behind him as he spoke. "He told me he wanted to do something to settle an old debt." He turned and eyed her shrewdly. "If you'll pardon me, Angela, I must say you bear a strong resemblance to Slade's daughter, Veronica. Are you sure there's no family connection?"

Ronnie felt her face flush. "I know what you're suggesting, Mr. Spriggs, and you're out of line. Don't look for answers where there are none." His proximity to the truth was unnerving. She had to divert his thinking. "I repeat, I don't want that money. I want to turn it down, legally."

Spriggs looked at her ruefully, a slight smile edging his lips upward. "I must admit I've never had a client make such a request. But by law, you have nine months to file a disclaimer to decline the trust."

Ronnie's hopes shot up. "What would happen to the money if I do that?"

"It would go to the secondary beneficiary."

"Is it a secret beneficiary as well?"

Spriggs shook his head and looked slightly abashed. "No. In case you disclaimed the inheritance, Mr. Slade made provisions for the money to go to the . . . ah . . . National Rifle Association."

"What?" Ronnie stiffened in her chair. The NRA? That shitty bastard. "Why would he do that?"

Spriggs shrugged. "It was his money. I guess he could give it to whomever he wanted. And so can you. If you don't want the money, you can do just what he did and give it away, although the tax man will get another hefty chunk of it." He laughed. "But I'd be happy to take the rest of it off your hands."

Ronnie's look squelched the laughter on his lips. Clearing his throat, he said, seriously this time, "At the very least, you should draw up a will, in case, God forbid, something should happen to you. That's a hell of a lot of money to give to the government if you were to die without a will."

If something were to happen to you . . .

This man was just full of good suggestions.

The last bell rang and the quiet halls of Harmony Middle School exploded with the energy of hormonal teenagers who'd been cooped up too long in the classroom. Jeremiah Brown waited until the rest of his class had left the room, then he picked up his books and headed for his locker. He didn't want anyone to see the federal marshal who was waiting outside, the bodyguard who'd been assigned to keep an eye on him since the kidnapping. He was embarrassed that he was being treated like a baby.

His parents had wanted to transfer him to a private school, but Jeremiah hadn't wanted to leave his friends. So his father had insisted on federal protection for him. But Jeremiah knew that neither changing schools nor being babysat by a bodyguard would matter. The marshal couldn't be with him twenty-four/seven. Sooner or later, Dr. Lizard would find him alone. And Jeremiah would have to deliver.

Dr. Lizard was *his* problem, not his father's, not the marshal's. Jeremiah was afraid, but no longer terrified.

It had taken him several days to decide what to do about the instructions Dr. Lizard had given him. He knew the things demanded by the voodoo man would be used to hurt his father, but he also knew if he didn't deliver them, he would be killed. It was the kind of dilemma that a movie hero would face, and Jeremiah had thought and thought about what Will Smith would do if he were in his shoes.

Will Smith was smart. Jeremiah was awestruck by how Smith had managed to get the bad guys to kill each other in *Enemy of the State*. It had been a brilliant resolution.

Jeremiah needed one equally brilliant.

He'd watched the movie over and over until a plan had formed in his mind. It was risky and dangerous. But then, everything about this was dangerous. Jeremiah wanted more than anything to be brave, like his father. Like Will Smith. He would be brave. And he wouldn't let his father down.

Dr. Lizard had ordered Jeremiah to take pictures of his family's house, especially the rooms frequently used by his dad. He was also supposed to make a record of his father's daily activities. Jeremiah felt bad that he'd lied to his parents, but he hadn't known how to explain the picture-taking. He'd told them it was a school project, and, ever-supportive, they'd bought him a new camera to use.

Jeremiah had also been commanded to collect a snip of his father's hair, and a clipping from his nails, along with something personal, like a belt or a sock. Jeremiah was no dummy. He'd read up on voodoo immediately upon his return home, and he knew that Dr. Lizard wanted these items so he could cast an evil spell on Jeremiah's father.

The hair and fingernails would have been almost impossible to gather, if he'd actually attempted to do it. But Jeremiah hadn't even considered it.

The plan Jeremiah had devised involved "disinformation." He liked that word. He'd learned it from the movies, too, when double agents deliberately gave out wrong information to throw the enemy off.

So he'd snipped a lock of his own hair and clipped his own nails. If Dr. Lizard tried to use them to cast an evil hex against George Brown, it wouldn't work, because the hair and nails didn't come from his father. Jeremiah didn't think such a hex would harm him, either, because it wouldn't be cast at him.

The photos were another matter. The camera didn't lie. He wasn't sure why Dr. Lizard wanted pictures of the house anyway. They weren't traditionally used in casting spells. But just to make sure they'd be as useless as possible, Jeremiah had deliberately underexposed the shots, and when he'd taken them to the drug store to get the film developed, he'd requested that the negatives be printed backward.

He didn't know if his disinformation would work. But it was the best plan he could come up with. He hoped it was up to Will Smith's standards.

Jeremiah was relieved to see the bodyguard wasn't waiting in the hall by his locker as he'd expected. He opened the combination lock and lifted his backpack off the hook. He'd secreted the items Dr. Lizard expected him to deliver inside one of the zippered pouches. He was ready, and nervous, and he wished they'd just get it over with. He wondered if they would be bold enough to confront him on school property.

They were.

Jeremiah had just entered the boys' rest room when he was dragged into a stall by a boy he didn't recognize. He appeared to be about his own age but was bigger and stronger. He held a knife to Jeremiah's throat.

"You scream, I cut. You understand?"

Despite his determination to be brave, Jeremiah's blood ran cold. He couldn't find his voice, so he only nodded. He wished he weren't such a coward. Wished he could be a hero, like Will Smith, or even Indiana Jones. In his mind, he kicked the boy in the groin, then hoisted him over his head and slammed him—BAM—onto the concrete floor. In reality, he quaked with fear.

"You got the goods for Dr. Lizard?"

Jeremiah held up the backpack, hoping the thug would take the whole thing and leave him alone. Instead, he made Jeremiah take the things out and transfer them to a brown paper sack. "You didn't talk, did you, boy?"

"No. I didn't say anything."

"That's good. Dr. Lizard told me to give you this." He pressed a small object into Jeremiah's hand. "It's a reward." He placed another object in his other hand. "And this one's a reminder. You don't ever mention him to anyone or you'll end up like this. Now count to a hundred before you leave, and don't come looking for me."

Jeremiah looked down at his hands. The reward was a piece of the candy Dr. Lizard had given him before. The reminder was a tiny skull, the head of a small animal. Feeling sick, Jeremiah flushed both down the toilet.

Chapter 24

Folks ask th' conjureman, "How I do know I been rooted?" and th' conjureman says, "Any bad things happen t' you lately . . . ?"

AFTER lunch, back in her office, Angela tried to concentrate on business, but her mind wouldn't slow down long enough to get anything done. Her nerves felt like electric wires humming with tension, and a headache played at her temples.

She'd called Dylan and told him what she'd learned from her mother about her family, and he'd immediately taken it upon himself to try to find any long-lost cousins, in case one of them happened to be the lookalike imposter. It was such a long shot. She believed he was wasting his time, but at least it gave him something to do that kept him from hovering over her.

Toward late afternoon, the sky grew overcast and the wind picked up, tearing the dying leaves from the trees across the street in one of the city's oldest squares. The Spanish moss that draped from the gnarled live oaks waved like somber gray bunting, and a few spots of rain dashed to the sidewalks. No tourists browsed the nearby store windows nor did any customers darken her door. Angela wondered if the business she'd worked so hard to build was going to end up down the tubes.

By five o'clock, she was a basket case. She needed to do something besides brood on her situation or she'd lose her mind. Looking at her calendar, she saw that this was the evening when the Chamber of Commerce held its monthly event they called "Business After Hours" and decided on the spot to go. Under normal circumstances she enjoyed these informal social gatherings, where members chatted over cocktails, networked for business and made bets on the upcoming football games. Tonight, she needed to go to touch base with reality and to reconnect with her friends.

Her friends.

She hadn't heard from many of them lately. Did she still have any friends? Would she be welcome at the party? Or was she now a social pariah? Would a suspected murderer bring shame and scandal too close to their doors?

No, she thought, picking up her coat and heading for the door. They wouldn't be that shallow.

The meeting was held in the lobby of a newly renovated historic hotel on Broughton Street, and Angela lucked out in finding a parking space on a street nearby. She hadn't been inside the hotel since the renovations had been completed, and she was eager to see for herself the transformation she'd heard was so spectacular.

She wasn't disappointed. The once-dowdy, rundown property sparkled like a polished gem, with gleaming marble floors and richly colored walls hung with dramatic works of art. The hotel had volunteered to host the event to show off its renaissance in hopes of gaining word-of-mouth recommendation from Savannah's business community. Waitstaff in tuxedoes moved among the crowd, offering champagne and canapes.

Angela looked around and couldn't stem the swell of pride she felt. For all of its dark side, Savannah was a city with a deep reverence for its history, and it was fighting as a community to resurrect the grace and dignity of days gone by. The renovation of this hotel was but a single example of the hundreds of projects underway that were slowly but steadily bringing the old city into the new millennium while retaining its historical integrity. She was proud to be a part of it, for the effort was embraced by rich and poor, black and white, poet and politician. It made all that she'd endured in her crusade to make the streets safe worthwhile.

"Evenin', Angela. Glad to see you could make it." A masculine voice broke her reverie, and she turned to see who had approached her.

Her euphoria dissolved immediately. "I'm surprised to see you here, Freddie," she replied, "considering that it costs money to join the Chamber."

"Hey, I'm coming up in the world. I've even got a little office now. Don't have to work out of a pay phone anymore." He gave her a taunting grin.

"That's nice," she said coolly. "Glad to know you won't be hanging around stealing my customers." She turned her back on him and pushed through the crowd. She hadn't come here to schmooze with the likes of Freddie Holloway.

Those she did schmooze with greeted her with varying degrees of enthusiasm. Some were friendly, openly curious, and supportive. Others quickly and pointedly steered away from her. One, a reporter for the newspaper, wouldn't leave her alone and kept asking annoying questions to which she didn't respond. Finally, she'd had enough and decided to skip out early. She was supposed to have dinner with Dylan aboard his boat. It had come as a pleasant surprise to learn that somewhere over the past five years he'd learned to cook.

It was growing dark when she left the hotel and walked the short distance to her car. The wind whipped her hair, and she smelled a storm in the air. She wondered what it was like to be on a boat in a storm.

Angela waited for a green light, then stepped out into the street, bent on getting to her car before the rain started. She hardly saw the oncoming vehicle as it rounded the corner. Later, she vaguely remembered hearing the squeal of tires as it veered into the wrong lane, struck her, and sent her sprawling onto the pavement.

* * *

The scene was painfully reminiscent of another night of horror long ago as Dylan raced across the parking lot and through the hospital doors. At least this time Angela was in the emergency room, not intensive care. But that she was in the hospital at all, when he'd vowed to protect her, was unthinkable.

Johnny Reilly and a couple of uniforms waited in the ER lobby, and Reilly motioned to Dylan when he came in. "She's going to be all right," he said, swirling coffee in a plastic cup, "but they won't let us in to see her just yet."

"What happened?" Dylan had been making sure the lines of the boat were secure in preparation for the approaching storm when Reilly had called him. The cop hadn't told him much, just that there'd been an accident, apparently a hit-and-run, and that Angela had been taken to the hospital.

"We don't know much more than what I told you. Witnesses said a car was speeding down Broughton Street and took the corner too fast, hit Angela, and kept on going. Nobody got a tag number. The vehicle was a nondescript gray sedan."

"Was it intentional?"

Reilly looked discouraged and uncomfortable. "I don't know. It could have been. Remember what I told you after the voodoo incident?"

Somebody wants Angela dead.

"Yeah," Dylan said. *And I've let her down again.*

"I've already got an APB out for the car. If it was an accident, we'll find the guy. If someone did it intentionally, you can bet that car's already in a chop shop."

Dylan's guts told him they'd never find the car. This smacked of Clifford's handiwork, and Dylan knew Quintos's organization had plenty of resources to take care of things like getting rid of murder vehicles.

Clifford. The name made him want to chew nails. Dylan's former boss had been well aware of Dylan's feelings for Angela and had used them against him five years ago. If he knew Dylan was back in town, he would no doubt relish a form of revenge against Angela that would also torment Dylan. Like a near-hit with a vehicle. Dylan had to find the asshole and stop him before he could attack Angela again. Next time, she might not be so lucky.

Dylan turned to Reilly, still unsure of whether the sergeant was trustworthy. But he'd given Dylan a call to let him know about Angela's accident, and Dylan owed him the benefit of the doubt. He hadn't told Reilly his suspicions that Cecil Clifford had been the one to try to set up Angela, but he needed to know what Reilly knew about Clifford's activities. He approached the subject cautiously. "I heard Clifford's out."

Reilly's expression turned grim. "Yeah. He's around. Word on the street is he's in with Quintos and out for blood."

He'd known it, but hearing it confirmed by Reilly sent a shiver of trepidation down Dylan's spine. "Angela's blood?"

"And George Brown's, and Vincent Howard's, and others in the GBI. He has a rather long and impressive list, so I hear."

"Do you think he orchestrated the kidnapping of Jeremiah Brown?"

"Probably, although I don't understand why he let the boy go. I'm afraid we're not finished with that one." Reilly shook his head. "With Clifford out of jail and acting as his lieutenant, I think Quintos is gearing up to wage war to get his streets back."

Dylan was not at liberty to tell Reilly anything about his own assignment, but he silently added Slade's name to Clifford's hit list. Slade had been a fool to think for one minute he could oust Quintos. Only one thing would accomplish that—a well-aimed bullet. And Quintos had proven an evasive, almost invisible target.

A nurse pushed through the swinging doors that separated the waiting area from the ER, spotted Reilly, and headed their way. "You can talk to her now, Sergeant," she said. "She's got some cuts and bruises, but miraculously there's no broken bones or internal injuries. She's suffered a mild concussion, but nothing serious. We can release her tonight, but someone needs to be with her to keep her awake and monitor her condition for the next few hours."

Dylan took off through the doors before the nurse could stop him. She hurried after him, protesting that he wasn't allowed in the area unless he was a cop or next of kin. He wheeled around and stuck his face squarely into hers. "I'm her brother. So show me where the hell she is."

The nurse turned to Reilly, who'd followed them. He grinned and nodded. "I can wait." With a suspicious frown, she grudgingly led Dylan to a bed partitioned by curtains. His heart wrenched when he saw Angela lying pale and bandaged against the white hospital linens.

She smiled when she saw him. "Sorry I'm late for dinner," she said weakly.

He went to her bedside and took one of her hands in both of his. "Oh, God, Angela, I'm so sorry. I should have known better than to let you out of my sight for one minute."

"You aren't Superman, so quit feeling guilty," she scolded him. "Besides, I won't be your prisoner, and I won't be treated like some porcelain doll."

He leaned over and brushed her hair away from her face, and all the torment, pain, and guilt he'd carried for five years surged through him again, carrying with it a mounting rage against those who'd done this to her. He'd let her down then because he hadn't listened to his gut instincts. He'd let her down today for the same reason.

Those instincts were shrieking at him now, and this time,

he was listening. There was only one way he could ever truly protect her.

"I'm going to get Quintos and Clifford," he promised her. "I'll kill the bastards barehanded if I have to."

Chapter 25

Now Dr. Lizard said t' this young woman, take this "Adam and Eve Herb" and this "Love Balm" and mix them together with th' juice of th' apple, and when your man comes, entice him t' drink, and when he does, he be yours . . .

ANGELA looked up into Dylan's handsome, tormented face, and was filled with despair. At the moment, she didn't care about Quintos and Clifford. They would be caught in the end. What she cared about was the man standing over her who was seemingly obsessed with only one thing . . . revenge against his enemies.

Angela was afraid she might cry. She didn't want to hear a commitment from him to bring two felons to justice. She wanted to hear this man say he still loved her. For she loved him, in spite of everything that had gone bad between them. She wanted to deny her feelings, but she couldn't. After all these years, her love for him was still there, perhaps stronger than ever. She could've been killed tonight, could be killed any time Quintos or Clifford took the notion, and she didn't want to die without Dylan knowing how she felt.

His pulse beat steadily against hers where their fingers entwined. His gaze seared her with intensity. Her heart raced and her face grew warm. Without thinking, she drew his hand toward her and placed it on her breast. "Kiss me, Dylan," she begged.

The taste of his lips was sweet, the scent of his skin familiar. Ignoring the pain of her bruises and stiff, sore muscles, she encircled his shoulders, her arms and hands remembering the strength of his body, the firmness of his muscles. Deep inside, an old familiar fire flamed, filling her with an ache only he could heal. His kiss reminded her of all the good things they'd once shared, of all the love and laughter, all the hopes and dreams. Her heart felt as if it would break. God, how she wanted it all back! How she wanted it to be the way it had once been between them. But could he love her? And could she take the risk of finding out?

She knew better than to set herself up for heartbreak all over again, but her reason wasn't in control at the moment. She didn't want to beg him, but it seemed her heart was willing to do anything for a second chance. Gathering all her courage, she touched his cheek. "Could we . . . I mean, maybe we could . . . try . . ." Her words were cut off as her throat tightened with emotion. Her pulse raced with fear that she would be rejected again.

Dylan's expression was as enigmatic as it was intense. "To start over?" he asked.

She nodded and closed her eyes, and a tear trickled over the edge and ran down her cheek. Dylan wiped it away gently and kissed her again.

"Let's get you out of here," was all he he said, and then he left her to take care of the paperwork so she could leave the hospital.

In his absence, Angela tried to answer Johnny Reilly's questions coherently, but her thoughts were on Dylan and her miserable attempt to get him to love her again. Her cheeks burned in humiliation.

Thirty minutes later, she was released from the hospital. Although she protested, hospital rules dictated that she must be taken to the curb in a wheelchair. Perhaps it was just as well, she thought as she sank into the chair. Her knees were weak, and she would've had to lean on Dylan for support. His detached response to her overture had left her cold and empty, and she didn't want him close, not even to help her to the car.

The nurse saw them and raised an eyebrow as they passed her on the way out. "Her brother?" she remarked to Dylan with a sardonic smile.

Angela guessed that's who Dylan had told her he was. Next of kin. Maybe, she thought glumly, that's how he felt toward her. Brotherly.

Outside, rain fell in sheets. Reilly stayed with her beneath the portico while Dylan sprinted to the Camaro. "Mind if I smoke?" Reilly asked.

"No."

The sergeant lit up. "I can get the GBI to put you in a safe house."

His unstated implication was that she might not be safe with Dylan. It was probably the truth, but she understood another truth as well. "No place is safe from Quintos." With sudden clarity, Angela knew that her best, maybe her only chance of survival was to bring the drug lord to his knees. She took a leap of faith and decided to trust the cop who stood next to her. "We have to get him, Johnny."

"Yeah, I know. The problem is how. He owns a lot of people in Savannah."

She raised her chin and looked directly at him. "Does he own you?"

Reilly lifted one side of his mouth in a mirthless grin. "I won't take offense. It's a fair question. And it's your call as to whether you believe me or not. But no, Quintos doesn't own me. I have a wife and kids I want to protect from scum like him and Clifford. It's the main reason I stay in this crazy business."

Angela wondered how many others in the SPD she could trust. "What do you know about Scott Turner?"

"As far as undercover cops go, Turner's one of our best. Squeaky clean. You know him?"

"Actually, I've never met him, except briefly the day

you brought me in for questioning. I didn't know who he was then. I think he and Dylan go back a ways."

Dylan pulled his car under the portico and got out, heading toward Angela. Before he reached them, Reilly dropped his cigarette and mashed it out with his foot. "For what it's worth," he said so only she could hear, "Montana's okay. He got a bad rap back then."

Taken by surprise, Angela wanted to ask him what he meant, but Reilly was already halfway to a waiting police car.

"You okay?" Dylan asked, and she nodded a reply, although suddenly every muscle in her body seemed to ache. He helped her into the low-slung car and drove out into the downpour. The wipers beat a steady rhythm on the windshield, scarcely clearing it enough to see. "You sure you're okay?" he asked again, irritating Angela.

"I'm fine. I just want to go home."

"Your house or mine?"

"You don't have a house."

"No, but I have dinner waiting."

Angela didn't reply. She stared out the window into the rain-swept darkness, feeling a bone-deep exhaustion settle over her. She didn't really care where she went. At the moment, all she wanted to do was sleep and forget about Dylan and her hurt feelings and her sore body and the dangers that loomed around her. Maybe she should have taken Reilly up on the offer of a safe house, where she could hide out from Quintos and her own foolish emotions concerning Dylan.

Dylan drove to her house. "It's your choice. Stay here, and I'll make a run for a pizza or something. Or you can grab some clothes and things and spend the night on the boat, where I must say a damned decent dinner awaits you. Either way, you're stuck with me. The nurse made me promise I'd keep an eye on you, and," he added with a twinkle in his eye, "she was bigger than me."

Angela's house was chilly and for once uninviting. And she found she didn't want to be alone. "Wait just a minute. I'll get my things."

The rain had abated by the time they reached the marina, and Dylan parked in a handicapped slot close to the dock. "You'll get a ticket," she warned.

"I know a cop who'll fix it," he replied with a grin, helping her out of the car and down the dock to his boat that bore the unlikely name, *Midnight Lace*.

The vessel was more than just a boat. It was a forty-foot motor yacht that Dylan had told her he was trying to restore. He said he'd bought it from a man who'd made his fortune in the lingerie business. Apparently, it had been quite a party boat, and it needed extensive repairs. He was going to change the name, he'd assured her, but not until he was able to afford to have the boat's entire hull painted.

Where before Angela had found its limited space confining, as she went into the warmth of the cabin below, she welcomed the boat's cocoonlike feeling of security. And her stomach growled at the smell of whatever Dylan had cooked for dinner.

"You can have the aft stateroom," Dylan said, motioning her toward the back of the boat. "You're in luck. I changed the sheets this afternoon. There's a bathroom back there, and I'll get you some clean towels. Why don't you take a shower and change while I move the car?" he suggested, then added with a small lopsided grin, "I really don't make a practice of parking in handicapped spaces."

Angela looked down at the skirt and jacket she'd been wearing all day. They were wet and torn and embedded with dirt from the street where she'd fallen when the car struck her. Reilly had asked her to save the clothes for forensic examination. She hoped they'd find them helpful, because that was about all they were good for now. She rubbed her arms, feeling the dampness soaking through to her skin. "Good idea," she said.

She went into the master stateroom at the stern of the boat, normally Dylan's domain. It was smaller than a bedroom in a house, but large enough to hold a queen-sized bed, built-in hanging lockers, drawers, and a small desk, all made of teak that Dylan had refinished and varnished to a high sheen. She was impressed that the bed was made. The bathroom opened off the stateroom and included all the comforts of a landside home—a tub and shower, toilet, and vanity. The tub looked very appealing at the moment.

Shedding her clothes, Angela ran water into the tub and added a dash of her favorite perfume in lieu of the scented bath salts she used at home. She settled her aching body into the warm water with a sigh and leaned back, closing her eyes. From somewhere that seemed very far away, she heard Dylan's footsteps as he came back aboard from moving his car, but she let her mind drift, releasing all thoughts of lost love and drug lords and hit-and-run drivers.

Chapter 26

Th' spirits in th' grave be dangerous if disturbed. Th' wise man knows not t' disturb them before midnight, when they make their rounds anyway. If a plateye or other evil hant be cursing you, leave something on th' grave t' appease him. Th' plateye be especially fond of whiskey . . .

DYLAN turned the stove on to warm the hearty stew he'd prepared earlier and put a CD he knew Angela liked on the sound system. He waited for her to come back into the main cabin, but after half an hour, he began to worry. Since he hadn't heard the sound of running water, he figured she must have drawn a bath. She was probably enjoying a much-needed soak which would be good for her aches and pains. But by now, the water must have grown cold. He went to the door of the stateroom and knocked softly. "Angela?"

No answer.

Suddenly he remembered the nurse's warning. *Don't let her go to sleep.* She'd suffered a mild concussion, and she wasn't supposed to go to sleep for several hours.

"Angela?" he called louder.

Still no answer.

He turned the handle and eased the door open, expecting to find her asleep on the bed. But she wasn't there.

"Angela?" Alarmed, he went into the bathroom where he discovered her sound asleep in the tub. Thank God, her head was above the water. Dylan stared at her for a long moment, knowing he should awaken her immediately, but instead, gazed at her for a long moment, wanting to imprint the beauty of her body on his mind. She lay with her legs to one side, exposing her exquisitely rounded derriere to his hungry gaze. The taut nipple of one breast barely broke the surface of the water. Her arm floated at her side, glistening with moisture.

Dylan felt himself growing hard, as he had at the hospital when she'd nestled his hand over her breast. God in heaven, how he ached for her, and after she'd told him that she wanted them to try again, he'd allowed a spark of hope to ignite in his heart. But then he'd stared into reality. Angela was hurt—again. Could have been killed—again—because he wasn't where he was supposed to be. Angela's life had been on the line back then and was in jeopardy now. As much as he longed for a return to the intimacy they'd once shared, he couldn't afford to let it happen. At least not now. He had to finish what he'd started five years ago. He had to get Quintos, and Clifford, and anyone else who threatened Angela.

Then, maybe, they could start over.

He knelt by the tub and touched her face lightly. Her skin was cool. "Angela? Angela, wake up. You're not supposed to go to sleep just yet."

Her eyes fluttered open, but he could see it was a struggle. She turned her lips toward his hand and nuzzled the back of his fingers. "Dylan?" she murmured.

"Yes." His heart pounded at her touch. "I'm here. You're safe. But you've got to wake up."

Slowly, she regained consciousness. "Where am I?"

"On the boat. In the bathtub," he answered, unable to keep his eyes from wandering down the length of her naked body. She was so beautiful. "It's time to get out," he said, forcing himself to pay attention to the matter at hand. "The water's cold, and you're getting pruny."

She closed her eyes again and groaned. "I ache all over," she said a moment later. "And I'm so sleepy."

"You can't go back to sleep. Nurse's orders. C'mon, I'll

help you up." He slipped his arm around her and eased her into a sitting position, but she remained groggy and made no attempt to get out of the tub. Dylan stood and took her hands, pulling her upward while he encouraged her to make the effort on her own. At last, she was standing on the bathmat, dripping wet and shivering. Dylan grabbed a towel and began to dry her skin, acutely and uncomfortably aware of the effect she was having on him.

"Let's get you into some warm clothes," he said gruffly as he ran the towel over her backside and down her legs. No man should ever have to show this kind of restraint, he thought.

In the stateroom, she pulled a long white gown from her small bag, and he helped her into it.

"I'm so cold," she said, shaking involuntarily. And equally involuntarily, he took her in his arms and held her against him until he felt her trembling start to ease. Strains of a romantic oldie sung by Harry Connick Jr. drifted in from the main salon, and without thinking, Dylan began to rock gently from side to side, holding her, breathing in her perfume, wanting her.

She encircled his waist with her arms, tucking her thumbs under his belt, and began to move with him in time to the music. Five long years dissolved into nothingness. They danced as if they'd never been apart. He remembered every nuance of her body, the way it moved against his, the way her breasts pressed against his chest, how he could rest his chin on top of her head.

He should break the embrace, but he couldn't. He should push her away, put a safe distance between them. But he knew there was no safe distance.

Instead, he gently raised her lips to his and kissed her long and tenderly, unable to help himself, and knowing it was the worst thing he could possibly do.

* * *

The storm that battered the windows of Paradisia reminded Elizabeth Slade of the night she'd learned that J. J. had been murdered. That had been less than two weeks ago, and in that time, her life had been all but destroyed. The devastation would be complete, unless they found Veronica in time.

"You watched the house all day?" she asked Harlow, who sat across the gleaming mahogany table from her. They were alone in the large, gloomy dining room. Candles burned in the elaborate candelabra, and a fire crackled in the hearth, but Elizabeth couldn't seem to shake the chill that had enshrouded her since J. J.'s death. It wasn't a chill of grief, but rather of premonition.

Harlow pushed at his food with his fork. "I parked across the street and down two houses, and I was there from eight o'clock this morning until just after six. If Veronica lives there, she didn't come home today."

"That doesn't mean it isn't her house," Elizabeth snapped irritably. Maybe she was unnecessarily concerned, but she had to know for certain that there really was a woman named Angela Donahue, and that it wasn't Veronica operating under an alter ego. When Dylan Montana had refused the job, Elizabeth had asked Harlow to play private eye for a day and stake out the house listed under "Angela Donahue" in the phone book. Veronica obviously loved to masquerade, and her mother thought it entirely possible that she could be living a double life. It would explain her extended absences from Paradisia. It would also confirm her suspicion that Veronica had killed J. J.

Every time she thought of her daughter, the expression "loose cannon on deck" came to mind. Right now, Veronica might well be her worst enemy, primed to destroy her without ever knowing it. "I want you to go back tomorrow," she demanded. "Stay there until you find her. I want her back."

"No," Harlow replied wearily. "I'm not going back

there. It's not Veronica's place. Angela Donahue is for real, and you're paranoid."

Maybe so. But Elizabeth was also terrified. "Don't question me, Harlow. I know what I'm doing."

To her amazement, Harlow Bertram stood up and tossed his napkin on the table. "I don't know that you do, Elizabeth. First of all, what you're asking of me is nothing short of kidnapping, even if she is your daughter. I know you think it's in her best interest to hide her away until this blows over, but it's not right. If Veronica killed her father, she must pay the price. But I don't think she did it. Why would she?"

Elizabeth glared at the old fool. "For the money, of course. She thought she would inherit millions."

Harlow shook his head. "I suppose. But frankly, my dear, I don't think Veronica is smart enough to have masterminded a plot such as you're suggesting. She's just too stupid." With that, he turned and left.

Elizabeth stared after him in disbelief. Harlow had never spoken to her like that. And he'd never walked out on her. Rage flooded through her. After all she'd done for him! But his words echoed in her mind. Maybe she *was* just being paranoid. Maybe Veronica *wasn't* smart enough to have murdered J. J.

She didn't want to admit how much she'd been depending on Harlow, not just for legal advice, but for moral support as well. Now, that support had clearly been withdrawn, and Elizabeth was surprised at how betrayed and forsaken she felt. She rose slowly from her chair and left the room.

The men in her life had always forsaken her.

She entered the hallway that divided the mansion in half. Her eyes took in the sweeping staircase, the gallery of expensive portraits and landscapes that hung on the walls. Ironic, she thought, wandering aimlessly down the hall, how desolate one could be amidst so much, and she wondered if all she'd done to preserve and maintain this plantation had been worth it.

She paused in front of a portrait of Angus Mayhew, her father. The artist had charitably painted a decent nose on him, not the red, bulbous, veined beak he'd had as an old, alcoholic man. In this painting, his face was kind, his eyes bright.

What a flatterer the artist was, she thought in disgust. Angus Mayhew had been mean, arrogant, alcoholic, and stupid. She wondered why her beautiful, gracious mother had ever married him. But then, hadn't she married a man very much like him? Except that J. J. had been neither alcoholic nor stupid. And instead of dissipating the family fortune, he'd re-created it. She had much to thank him for, she supposed, although at the moment, her life and everything in it seemed the color of ashes.

Elizabeth stared at the portrait of her father and thought about the letter the lawyer had given her. It shouldn't have come as a surprise that J. J. would make such a move. She'd made a mistake in selling those files to Suarez, although at the time, she'd thought J. J. had betrayed her by excluding her from the offshore accounts, and she'd wanted nothing more than to destroy him. But now she knew the truth, just as J. J. had found out the truth of what she'd done. He'd set a trap for her, and there was no way out other than to let his odious will stand.

"Damn him," she cried, clutching her arms tightly around her. He had power over her even from the grave.

Chapter 27

Th' hants don't always look like you expect th' spirits t' look. Sometimes a hant comes from th' past, and you don't recognize it. Sometimes it looks like a fearsome beast, and it breathes fire and follows you at night. Sometimes th' hant looks like old Jack Mullater, all lit up out there in th' swamp. And sometimes it looks like your luck be going from bad t' worse, and it ain't never going t' change . . .

MARY Ellen Donahue had been away from the office for almost two weeks, but even though she was feeling better, she had little spirit for going back to work. As much as she loved her job, she didn't particularly look forward to the questions and gossip about Angela she knew she'd encounter in the office. She'd hoped the police would have gone after the Slade daughter by now, but if they had, there'd been nothing about it in the newspaper.

Pouring herself a second cup of coffee, Mary Ellen sat back down at the kitchen table and gazed at the small black-and-white photo that had remained there since Angela's visit two days ago. Jake's youthful, handsome face stared back at her.

Angela had told her it was time to let him go. Mary Ellen took a deep breath and steeled herself against the emotions that always seemed to ambush her when she thought about the man who'd deserted them. Emotions that ranged from fury to bitter grief.

Angela was right, she decided resolutely. He was dead, and the time *had* come to say goodbye.

With hands that shook in spite of her resolve, Mary Ellen carried the photo into the bedroom and laid it on the carefully made bed. She went into her closet, where she reached for a small metal box that rested on the back of the top shelf. It was old and rusted, and the lock no longer worked. Not that it mattered. The contents were valuable only to her.

Placing the box on the bed, she opened it and gazed inside. There wasn't much. A few old postcards, a dried rose—the only flower he'd ever given her. Some more photos and a small brown envelope. Funny, once these mementoes had meant everything to her. In fact, in those early years, they'd been all that had kept her going. Now, touching them was like sifting through so much dry sand in an emotional desert. She reached for the photo, placed it in the box, and closed the lid. So much for that.

But the snap of the lid changed nothing. She regarded the box for a long moment. No, she thought with a sigh, just hiding his picture away wasn't enough. If she wished to let Jake Donahue go, she had to *destroy* all these things that reminded her of him.

But not today.

She just couldn't bring herself to do it. Standing abruptly, she returned the box to its obscure hiding place. Angela had never known about it, and Mary Ellen didn't want her to find it now. She'd deal with it another day. Another day real soon.

In the meantime, she had something she must do. She'd come up with an idea she thought would steer the Slade murder investigation away from her daughter.

Straightening her shoulders, Mary Ellen studied herself in the bedroom mirror and swore beneath her breath. The woman whose image looked back at her appeared haggard and worn, and had puffy, swollen bags beneath her eyes.

This would not do.

If she wanted to be successful in her venture, she must

look the part. It was one of her cardinal rules, and it had served her well. Professional armor was what she needed today, for today she was going into battle to save her daughter's life.

Two hours later, dressed to kill in her most expensive suit, her hair freshly coiffed, her makeup perfectly applied, Mary Ellen Donahue pulled into a parking space in front of the office of Savannah's largest newspaper. She looked up at the gray stone building as if it were a dragon to be slain. In a way it was. Or at least the people inside were, those who kept making those ridiculous claims about Angela.

First, she'd set them straight, then she'd do the same with the Savannah police.

She looked at her watch and frowned, suddenly realizing that it was Friday the thirteenth. Mary Ellen wasn't particularly superstitious, but she wished she'd thought of this yesterday. Drumming her nails on the steering wheel, she considered waiting a day, but then decided her errand couldn't be put off even another minute. She picked up the manila envelope that lay beside her on the seat. It wasn't heavy artillery, but it was ammunition they couldn't ignore. She couldn't understand why they hadn't seen this already.

Inside, she asked to speak to the managing editor, Sid Blackburn. The receptionist took her name and invited her to have a seat. Mary Ellen wondered if she was about to be shunted off to some lesser editor, or worse yet, a reporter. "Please," she said to the receptionist, "tell Mr. Blackburn I'm the mother of Angela Donahue, the woman the police mistakenly suspect in the Slade murder case. I . . . I really must talk to him."

Moments later, she was gratified when Sid Blackburn came into the lobby and greeted her personally. He was a handsome man in his sixties, with silver hair and blue eyes. His face was somber.

"Mrs. Donahue?" he said.

"Yes."

"Please come with me." He held the door that separated the public waiting area from the offices and corridors of the busy newspaper. She accompanied him to his office, where he closed the door behind him. "I'm so sorry about your daughter," he said in a solemn voice.

Mary Ellen huffed. "Sorry? Then why have you been raking her across the coals on the front page of your newspaper?" Without waiting for his reply, she handed him the manila envelope. "Open this, and tell me why you haven't printed any stories about the possibility that Slade was murdered by his own daughter."

Blackburn looked at her with open curiosity. He bent the metal clasp and tapped the contents of the envelope onto the top of his desk. Two pictures fell side by side, both of which she'd clipped from his newspaper. One was Angela Donahue. The other was Veronica Slade.

"See there?" Mary Ellen said, adjusting them slightly. "What did I tell you? They look just alike. *My* daughter did not kill J. J. Slade, Mr. Blackburn. This is a case of mistaken identity, and it's resulted in gross negligence in both your reporting and the police investigation. Any fool can see the resemblance. It wasn't Angela at the First City Club, having lunch with a perfect stranger. It was Veronica Slade, having lunch with her father."

Sid Blackburn took a deep breath and studied the photos. "We've noticed that the two women do bear a strong resemblance to one another," he said at last, "but I'm afraid there's more to this than mistaken identity."

"That's ridiculous. And unless your stories stop falsely accusing my daughter, I'm going to file suit against you and your newspaper."

Blackburn shrugged. "That's your prerogative, of course, Mrs. Donahue, but I must inform you of the phone call I received this morning. Granted, it was an anonymous call, but we're checking it out thoroughly."

"Call?" His tone, and the look in his eye, suddenly filled her with dread.

"Mrs. Donahue," Blackburn said patiently, "the caller informed us that Mr. Slade changed his will just the week before he died. Relatively speaking, he left very little to his wife and daughter. Most of his estate was placed in trust for an anonymous beneficiary. That beneficiary, according to the caller, is your daughter, Angela. If this proves to be true, Mrs. Donahue, your daughter is suddenly worth a fortune, and *that*," he said, "is a pretty strong motive for murder."

Angela awoke to the sound of a telephone ringing. She sat up, momentarily disoriented, until she remembered she was on Dylan's boat. Morning sunlight streamed through the high, narrow windows in the stateroom. She glanced at the alarm clock on the small dresser. Nine-thirty. Good grief. She never slept this late. What was wrong with her? Her whole body ached as if she'd run a marathon, and her head throbbed. And then it all came back. The hit-and-run, the trip to the hospital, and . . . the dancing with Dylan right here in this room.

She closed her eyes and groaned. Why did she let these things keep happening? These things with Dylan. The kiss on her front porch. The slow dance that had led to another, deeper kiss last night. She didn't know why he'd done that, because it was obvious Dylan was not interested in giving them a second chance. Maybe it was just the romance of the moment, the sensual mood, the dreamy music.

The fact that she'd been naked when he'd awakened her in the bath.

Angela shivered, remembering the delicious way his body had felt as it moved next to hers, the taste of his kiss, the scent of his skin. She'd wanted him, and she'd hoped he'd changed his mind about giving them a second chance. But in spite of the lingering kiss, at the end of the song, he'd disengaged her thumbs from his waistband and eased her away from him.

And he'd kept his distance the rest of the evening, damn him. He'd made her eat a bite of the stew he'd made, which he claimed had rabbit in it. "Tastes just like chicken," he'd teased when she turned up her nose at it. But she was too tired to argue. It could have had snake in it for all she cared. He'd probably have told her it tasted like chicken, too.

Like brother and sister, they'd sat up chastely playing Trivial Pursuit until long after midnight. Only when she'd bested him the third time in a row did he decide that she'd sufficiently recovered from her concussion to go to sleep.

After he tucked her in and left her alone in the large bed, Angela concluded that there was to be no second chance for them.

But where had that kiss come from?

She heard his approaching footsteps, followed by his knock on the door. Her heart fluttered in spite of herself.

"You awake?" he said, peering in.

Angela ran her hand through her hair. She must look a fright. "Yeah. Just moving a little slowly."

He opened the door wider. "You need to get dressed. That was Camille Brown, Judge Brown's wife, on the phone."

Alarm shot through her, and she jumped up. "Something's happened to Jeremiah."

"Not exactly," Dylan said, stepping inside the stateroom. "George Brown had a heart attack this morning."

"Oh my God," Angela uttered. "How awful."

"He's going to be okay. Mrs. Brown said the paramedics stabilized him before transporting him to the hospital, and the doctors say it was a mild attack."

"Well, that's good news."

"Yeah. But the bad news is that apparently Jeremiah went ballistic when it happened. He's at the hospital as well, and Mrs. Brown said they had to give him a mild sedative to calm him down. He's in the pediatric ward. They want to keep an eye on him for a few hours."

"The poor kid." Angela thought of all Jeremiah had been through in the past week, and her heart went out to him. She glanced up at Dylan, and his grim look unsettled her. "What aren't you telling me?" she asked.

"The reason Jeremiah is hysterical is that he thinks it's his fault that his father had the heart attack."

"His fault! Why on earth would he think that?"

"That's what Mrs. Brown wants to know. She's asked if you'll come and try to talk to him again. I have his room number."

"In a heartbeat." Angela rummaged in her suitcase for the pair of clean slacks and cotton sweater she'd brought along. Ten minutes later they left the boat.

They found Camille Brown in Jeremiah's hospital room talking quietly to the boy, who sat on the side of the bed with his arms folded across his chest. He was swinging his legs so hard he looked as if he were trying to run.

Camille turned when she heard the door open, and Angela could see she'd been crying.

"Camille?" Angela said tentatively.

Jeremiah's mother stood up and gave her a shaky smile as she extended her hand. "Thanks for coming."

Angela took her hand, but then pulled Camille into her arms and held the other woman as sobs shook her body. "It's okay," Angela whispered. "Go ahead and cry. God knows you deserve it."

Over Camille's shoulder, she saw Jeremiah turn and look at her. His eyes grew wide, and he jumped off the bed, edging away from her. Angela glanced at Dylan, who'd seen Jeremiah's reaction. He frowned and went toward the boy.

"It's okay, Jeremiah," Dylan said softly. "Your dad's going to be okay."

"No," he retorted, and Angela saw his bottom lip quiver.

"He's not. He's going to die. And it's all my fault."

Camille pulled away from Angela and went to Jeremiah's side. "No, sweetheart. It isn't your fault. It isn't anyone's fault. These things . . . heart attacks . . . just happen."

But Angela could see that Camille's comforting words fell on deaf ears. And she was alarmed to see the fear in Jeremiah's eyes when he looked at her again.

"Jeremiah," she said, taking a step toward him. "What's the matter? What are you afraid of?"

He pressed his lips together and shook his head.

"Please, honey, just talk to us," his mother pleaded. "We can't help you if you won't tell us what's wrong."

"My dad's gonna die, and it's all because of me," he insisted. Then he turned accusing eyes on Angela. "And you."

Chapter 28

It's not th' potions that make th' magic. It be th' words that th' conjureman say over th' potions. Th' spirit takes over th' conjureman and causes him t' have fits, and he don't even know it till th' spirit leave him and th' magic be done . . .

DYLAN didn't have much experience with kids, but he could tell that Jeremiah was terrified of Angela, and the boy's accusation stunned him. He was determined to find out what craziness was going on in his adolescent head.

He turned to the women. "Why don't you two go get some coffee?" Going to Angela, he placed his hands on her shoulders, drew her ear to his mouth and whispered, "I don't think Jeremiah wants to talk to you."

Angela backed away, a look of doubt and suspicion in her eye, but she got the message not to push the boy. She turned to Camille and said, "Maybe that's a good idea. I'm sure you'd like to check on your husband, too. Jeremiah's in good hands with Dylan."

Camille shot Dylan an uncertain look, then went to Jeremiah, kissed his forehead, and ran her fingers through his hair. "Will you be okay, baby?"

"I want to see my dad," Jeremiah replied stubbornly.

"Maybe later," Camille told him. "Right now, he's in intensive care. They might not even let me see him. But if they do, I promise you, I'll tell him you love him."

Suddenly, Jeremiah rushed into his mother's arms and held onto her fiercely. Camille rocked him until he relaxed a little and let her go. Turning to Angela, she said, "Maybe I should stay here."

But Dylan shook his head and took Camille gently by the arm. "Please, give me a little time with him. I think he needs to talk, man to man, you know?" He saw Jeremiah straighten and wipe his eyes, attempting to recover his masculine composure and figured he'd scored a point or two with the kid. "He's going to be fine," he assured Jeremiah's mother. "He's just had the emotional wind knocked out of him. It's a lot like what happens physically to a football player in a rough game. I'm not a coach, but maybe I can help him dust himself off a bit."

The two women left, and Dylan turned to face Jeremiah, totally clueless as to where to go from here. He didn't know where the words came from when he asked, "You hungry?"

Jeremiah started to shake his head, then paused and nodded slowly instead.

Encouraged, Dylan asked, "You want to blow this joint and go downstairs for a hamburger in the cafeteria?"

At first he didn't reply, but then Jeremiah reached for his sneakers and put them on. "Sure. But we can't stay long. I don't want Mom to come back and find me gone. She'd worry."

He was a good kid, Dylan thought, and it angered him that the boy had become the pawn in some kind of evil game. It made him more determined than ever to get to the bottom of it all.

To ease Jeremiah's concerns, Dylan stopped by the nurses' station and sweet-talked the nurse on duty into letting him spring Jeremiah long enough for a burger, and she promised to let Camille know where they were if the women returned before they did.

Dylan searched for some common ground between them. He was swimming upstream blind when it came to kids. "You like sports?" he asked as they entered the elevator.

"I'm going to be a pro football player, just like my dad

was," Jeremiah said proudly, then his face fell as he remembered where his dad was at the moment.

"Cool," Dylan said, placing one hand reassuringly on Jeremiah's shoulder. "What position?"

"Quarterback."

They went to the fast-food counter that was part of the cafeteria complex and ordered burgers, fries, and shakes, then sat at a table by the windows. Dylan picked up the conversation where they'd left off. "Quarterback. That's pretty brave. Everyone's out to get the quarterback, you know."

"Yeah, but I'm not afraid," Jeremiah said, taking a big bite out of the burger.

"You don't strike me as the type to be afraid of much."

Jeremiah looked up abruptly, his eyes wide. He hesitated a moment, then looked crestfallen. "There's things to be afraid of," he mumbled.

"Like what?"

Jeremiah put his burger back on his plate and lowered his head. "I . . . I can't tell you."

"Why not? Maybe I can help you."

"What about her?"

"Her?"

"That lady you came in with. She your girlfriend?"

Dylan's gut twisted. "No," he said. It wasn't a subject he wanted to talk about, but Jeremiah was afraid of Angela, and Dylan wanted to know why, so he left it open. "We're just friends."

"How do you know her?"

"We used to be cops together."

"Are you a cop?"

"Not anymore. Neither is she."

"Why not?"

"Needed a career change. It's not important." The kid was getting too close to painful territory. Dylan leaned forward, suddenly anxious to get to the point. "Jeremiah, why are you afraid of Ms. Donahue? And why did you say she was partly responsible for your father's heart attack?"

Jeremiah turned in his chair and looked out the window, but he didn't reply. Dylan could see the boy was torn. He wanted to tell Dylan something, but he was afraid to.

"It has to do with your kidnapping, doesn't it?" Dylan pressed, taking a risk that Jeremiah would clam up altogether.

But the boy turned back to him, a look of desperation on his face. "Can I trust you, man? Or are you one of them?"

Dylan leaned toward him. "One of them? Who do you mean? I told you I'm not a cop."

"It's not the cops I'm afraid of."

"Then who is it?"

"You can't tell anybody."

"I promise."

Jeremiah looked around to see if anyone was listening, then he whispered, "Dr. Lizard."

Dylan stared at him. "Who?"

"You ever heard of Dr. Lizard?"

"No, can't say as I ever have. Who is he?" Was the boy making up tales?

"He's a root doctor. A voodoo man. He made me do bad things." Jeremiah paused and looked as if he were going to lose it right there. But he bit his lip and continued. "He told me if I didn't do as he said, he'd kill me."

Dylan's mind flashed onto the bloody corpse of a black cat on the seat of Angela's car. "A root doctor? What'd he make you do?"

Dylan listened in growing horror as Jeremiah described his imprisonment, how he'd been given strange candy that made him high, how he was forced to kill the chicken. He told Dylan that he'd been instructed by the evil man in blue sunglasses to photograph his home and collect samples of hair and fingernails from his father.

"I thought I had him fooled," Jeremiah said, and explained his attempt at giving Dr. Lizard disinformation in the form of the wrong hair and nails. "But my plan didn't work," he added dejectedly.

"Good Lord," Dylan exclaimed. "You think your father had a heart attack because Dr. Lizard cast a voodoo hex on him?" Whoever he was, this Dr. Lizard had really messed with this kid's mind.

Jeremiah nodded. "It's all my fault, don't you see? My dad's going to die, and it's all my fault." He didn't cry, but his eyes reflected his torment.

Voodoo works because people believe it works.

Dylan looked the boy in the eye and said, "Listen, Jeremiah, you didn't cause your father's heart attack. It had nothing to do with a voodoo hex. He just had something go wrong with his heart. It happens to people all the time."

But he could see Jeremiah wasn't convinced.

Over the boy's shoulder, Dylan saw Angela and Camille standing in the entryway to the cafeteria, looking for them. He discreetly motioned for them to go away. Angela gave him a quizzical look, but after his second gesture, she did as he asked. But seeing her reminded him of why he'd brought Jeremiah here in the first place.

"Jeremiah, I need to know why you're so afraid of Ms. Donahue," he asked again.

Inhaling a deep breath, Jeremiah reached into his pocket. He took out a small white slip of paper and passed it to Dylan. "Dr. Lizard told me that he would kill me if I told anyone about him. But I can't let him go on hurting people like he's hurt my dad. I'm not afraid of dying. I was going to give this to the police if I had the chance. But I trust you. I think you can help me."

Dylan looked down and saw that he'd been handed Angela's card. "Why were you going to give this to the police, Jeremiah?"

The boy hesitated a moment, then said, "Because she was there that night. She's one of them."

Angela paced the floor of Jeremiah's hospital room, on fire to know what, if anything, Dylan had been able to get out of the boy. Camille stood looking out the window, and Angela could see she was tense and worried. "Maybe he got Jeremiah to talk," Angela said hopefully. "They seemed to be having a deep conversation."

"I hope so," Camille replied. "I can't bear that he's suffering like this."

A moment later, Dylan stuck his head in the room. "I need you to leave," he said to Angela. "Go downstairs and wait in the lobby. I'll explain later. Mrs. Brown, could you please wait here? I'll bring Jeremiah back in just a minute."

Camille frowned at him. "What's going on, Dylan?"

But he'd already disappeared. Angela turned to Camille. "Well, I hope he has a good explanation for this." She gave the woman another hug. "I know your husband is going to be fine, but call me if you need anything at all."

Fifteen minutes later, Dylan joined Angela in the lobby. "C'mon," he said, taking her by the arm. "I've got to talk to Padgett and the FBI."

"What's happened?" She had to run to keep up with him as he sprinted for the Camaro.

Once they were headed downtown, Dylan told her the boy's incredible story. Like Dylan, Angela was astonished, especially that Jeremiah seemed to think he'd seen her in the company of Dr. Lizard's disciples.

"Here we go again," she sighed. "It has to be the same woman who impersonated me at the First City Club, which means the kidnapping and the Slade murder are definitely related." They didn't have time to explore the possibilities further because Angela's cell phone rang.

"Hello?" she answered.

"This is Reilly. Where are you?"

"On the way to see you. Why?" The tension in his voice alarmed her. So did his hesitation in answering.

"We got an anonymous phone call a while ago," he said at last. "Angela, we've got more questions with no answers in the Slade case. How long till you get here?"

"We're just around the corner. Johnny, what's this all about?"

"It's about you inheriting all of Slade's money."

Chapter 29

Th' best way t' protect yourself from th' hants and th' hags and th' evil eye is t' paint th' entrances t' your house blue, the color of heaven. T' protect yourself outside th' house, wear blue-tinted glasses. If th' hags still hant you, wear a root bag round your neck till you feel th' spirit give up and move on . . .

MARY Ellen was beside herself with worry. After receiving Sid Blackburn's little bombshell, she'd stalked out of the newspaper office with her back ramrod straight, but inside, she was crumbling. This couldn't be true.

Could it?

She had to find Angela.

Panic frayed her nerves the rest of the morning as she searched for her daughter. It was unthinkable that Angela could be the secret beneficiary of that man's trust fund, but Sid Blackburn had taken that call very seriously. And Blackburn was right about one thing—if by some outside chance Angela was the secret beneficiary, she was in very real danger of being arrested for his murder.

The more Mary Ellen thought about it, the angrier she became. Unfair. Why was everything in life so unfair?

Her daughter wasn't at the tour company, and Connie had no idea where she was. Angela wasn't at her house, either. As loathsome as she found it, Mary Ellen even lowered herself to trying to find where Dylan Montana lived, but to no avail. She didn't want to think that Angela had let herself become involved with him again. He was nothing but a scoundrel who'd pretended to love Angela and left her to die in that shootout.

Mary Ellen's anger flared hotter.

At last, she gave up and went back to her own house. There was one other place she hadn't looked, but she was afraid to call and see if her daughter had been taken into police custody. Instead, she placed a call to Angela's home phone and left a terse message on the answering machine. "Angela, it's your mother. I have to talk to you. It's urgent. Don't do anything until you call me." She was so upset that, out of habit when leaving business phone messages, she left her phone number on the recording.

Distressed, Mary Ellen placed a hand over the knot tightening in her stomach. How could this be happening to her? To Angela? Rational, logical answers eluded her, for there was nothing rational or logical about the situation. It was a cruel twist of fate.

God must hate her, Mary Ellen thought, going into Angela's bedroom and gazing up at the crucifix. What had she done to deserve this? Nothing! She'd done nothing to deserve all the rotten things that had happened in her life. And Angela certainly didn't deserve it. Mary Ellen grabbed the crucifix from its nail and threw it across the room, where the plaster shattered into a spray of shards.

She was through praying.

She was through believing that God cared.

Because there was no God.

Ronnie hummed as she drove the red BMW eastbound on Interstate 16, heading toward Savannah. Marguerite would be proud of her. She was, in fact, proud of herself for once in her life. She'd taken matters into her own hands in going to Atlanta, and thanks to that idiot, Anthony Spriggs, things had suddenly started falling perfectly into place. She had another plan, and this one was going to work. That money was almost in the bank.

She'd executed the first part of the plan after leaving Spriggs's office earlier that morning, when she'd placed two phone calls, one to the Savannah police, the other to the *Savannah Morning News*. By now, the world should know Angela Donahue's little secret. Ronnie grinned at the thought of Anthony Spriggs trying to hold onto that secret when he was questioned by the cops and the media. But she knew he would talk. Spriggs was a prick.

She considered the second part of the plan and grew a little squeamish. Ronnie had managed to sweet talk Spriggs into drawing up "Angela's" new will while she was there, so she wouldn't have to make two trips. But now she had to kill Angela Donahue if she wanted to inherit the money. Suddenly Ronnie wondered if she could do it.

She had to. She had no choice. She'd just have to find a way that wouldn't be too bloody.

She thought about going directly to Angela's house and waiting for her there. She could kill her and put the gun in her hand, making it look like a suicide. Except the gun at Ronnie's disposal was her own and was registered in her name. She still didn't know what had become of Angela's gun.

No, she decided, if she was going to do the suicide thing, she'd have to find another gun.

Ronnie looked at her watch. It was not even three o'clock in the afternoon. She had some time to work this out. Angela normally would be at work at this time . . . if she wasn't already in jail. The cops should have found her sorry ass by now. The thought brought a malicious grin to Ronnie's lips. But then it faded.

If Angela was in jail, Ronnie couldn't kill her. Not easily, at least.

Shit.

Ronnie pulled into a rest area and sat with the engine running. Her heart raced and her breathing was shallow and rapid. What had she done? In her eagerness to incriminate

Angela, had she also made it impossible to carry out the most important part of the scheme?

She slumped dejectedly in the seat. Her father had always told her she was stupid. Maybe he was right. Then she thought about the money, and about the man who would kill her if she didn't get it. She wasn't that stupid, and she would find a way to pull this off.

Ronnie took out a cigarette and lit it with shaking hands. There had to be a way to fix this. There was one person who would know what to do. Marguerite could always find an answer, and she had ways, almost magical ways, of making things happen.

Resolute in her purpose and fueled by desperation, Ronnie returned to the freeway, and when she reached I-95, she headed south.

Ricky Suarez was pissed. Although the blue van had managed to keep up with Veronica Slade the night before, she'd managed to ditch them in the busy Atlanta traffic. He must be losing his touch, he thought sourly. Lacking any kind of sophisticated tracking device on her car, he'd had no choice but to return to the gates of Paradisia and take up his vigil in hopes that she'd show up.

This was getting old. Suarez was ready for some action.

He got it not long afterward when he spotted Veronica's car bearing down the dusty lane at her usual outrageous speed. He expected her to turn into the plantation, but instead, she passed the imposing gates and kept on going. Suarez started the van and fell in behind her, hoping her dust would camouflage the van.

"Where you suppose she's going?" Joe Delano asked, finishing off a banana. "Ain't nothing out here but marsh."

Suarez wondered the same thing. He knew the road ended less than five miles to the east, just at the edge of the swamp. He followed the red sports car at a discreet distance, his curiosity mounting.

At last he saw her turn left and disappear into the woods. He slowed as he approached where she'd turned into an even smaller lane. His eyes widened, and he cursed himself that he hadn't seen this before in his reconnaissance of the area. Set back from the main road, hidden by a stand of trees, was a gate topped with a surveillance camera. A high, thin, electric fence stretched on either side of the gate. He drove past the lane and parked a short distance away where the camera wouldn't detect them. "C'mon," he said to Joe, making sure his gun was loaded. "Let's see what we've got here."

Not wanting to expose their presence to the camera, Suarez followed the fence line, which took them through the woods, right to the edge of the swamp. He couldn't tell what the fence enclosed, for it seemed to be in the middle of the wilderness. Cautiously, he waded into the water and motioned for Delano to follow, and together they managed to slip around the end of the fence.

Once on the enclosed land, they crept through the woods until they spotted an old house through the trees. Suarez stepped behind a tree and peered around it at the structure. There was nothing unusual about the house, except perhaps the paint job. It was traditional in style, two-storied with a gabled roofline and a large porch that ran the width of the front. The house itself was white, although in need of paint. But the trim around all the windows, doors and the pillars supporting the front porch were painted bright sky-blue.

Veronica's car was parked in the front, along with several other vehicles, most of which were as run-down as the house. All except one. A big black Mercedes.

"Whoa, what've we got here?" he murmured. He motioned to Delano to follow him, and the pair slipped around the property to get a closer look. Several decrepit trailer houses hunkered in rusting squalor about a hundred yards away from the old house. Beyond them was the inlet off the river, and there, tied to a rickety dock, were two boats.

Suarez let out a low whistle. "By God, Delano, I think we've hit the mother lode."

One of the boats was a dilapidated shrimper. The other was a sleek dark blue cigarette boat that looked as if it could outrun any vessel the Coast Guard might send after it.

Suarez's pulse pounded. He was certain they'd found what the boss was looking for. Veronica Slade had led them directly to Lucas Quintos's lair.

Chapter 30

A scrap of cloth, a snip of hair be all th' conjureman needs t' cast a root spell. If they can't be had, th' root doctor just conjures them from th' air . . .

"WHY didn't you tell us?" Sergeant Johnny Reilly was livid, and Dylan didn't blame him. But he hoped the investigator wouldn't be too hard on Angela, who sat at the table in the interrogation room looking distraught and defeated.

"I was planning to," Angela told him wearily. "But I wanted to bring you answers, not more questions." She looked up sharply. "I have no answers, Johnny, other than . . . I-didn't-kill-Slade." She said it in a "read my lips" fashion.

"I told you from the start," Dylan broke in, "it was a professional hit, Reilly. Slade was killed by his enemies."

"Since you seem to know a lot more about this than I do, would you mind filling me in on exactly who 'his enemies' might be?" Reilly didn't bother to disguise his impatience.

Dylan hedged. He'd already broken his oath of silence in expressing his theory to Angela that Quintos had killed Slade when he'd found out Slade was trying to take over his operation. Dylan knew more about the story than that, but he couldn't talk. He couldn't risk jeopardizing the operation at this point. Oscar Malone and his buddies in the DEA had worked long and hard to pull this off, and Malone had told him they were getting close to nabbing Quintos.

This time, Dylan wanted to be there for the kill. "You'll just have to take my word for it."

Reilly exploded out of his chair. "Your word! Sorry, Montana, but I can't just take your word that Slade's murder was a professional job. I have a fistful of evidence, and now this . . ." he blustered, waving an arm at Angela, "that says Angela Donahue killed Slade. She has a motive—inheriting Slade's fortune. She had the means—she owns a gun that has mysteriously disappeared. And she had the opportunity, obviously, since she has no alibi. Now, if you can't come up with something stronger than 'take my word for it' I'm going to have to arrest her. The DA is already breathing down my neck to nail someone on this."

Dylan closed his eyes and rubbed his temples. He couldn't get mad at Reilly. The cop was only doing his job. But Dylan had to figure out something, find a bone to throw Reilly to hold him off until the boys in Miami got off their asses and made a move.

The boys in Miami.

What *were* they waiting for? Dylan had been in Savannah nearly two weeks, waiting on orders, and all he'd been told was to be patient.

Well, his patience had just run out. "Excuse me a minute," he said to Reilly. "I have to make a phone call."

Fifteen minutes later he was back. Nate Johnson, the GBI investigator who'd been working on the Slade case with Reilly, had arrived, and Angela looked pale. "Glad you're here," Dylan told Johnson. He turned to Reilly. "Okay, Johnny. You want answers? I'm going to give you some. But I want Vince Howard here, and Wally Padgett, and Scott Turner, if you can find him."

Angela looked up at him in surprise, and he gave her a tight smile. Malone had told him to use his own judgment in bringing these others into the loop. He hoped to God he was doing the right thing. If not, he might blow the entire operation, and because of his mistake, Quintos might get away again. But he was listening to his guts this time, and his guts told him this was the only way to protect Angela.

Because he worked in the same building, Wally Padgett showed up right away. Vince Howard, Angela's former boss, and a third GBI agent came in a short while later. Scott Turner, the undercover narc with the SPD, had been notified but couldn't come in just yet. Well, Dylan couldn't wait for him. He'd have to fill Turner in later.

Dylan took a deep breath and plunged in. "I know because of what happened five years ago, my credibility with you guys isn't all that great, but I'm asking you to trust me anyway. My cover around here is pretty well blown by now, so I just officially took myself off the job I was sent here for."

"Which would be . . . ?" Reilly asked.

Dylan looked at the men assembled in the room, measuring the trustworthiness of each. Vincent Howard and the others with the GBI were safe. So was Wally Padgett. The only question mark hovered over Johnny Reilly. Dylan stared hard at the police sergeant. Was Reilly clean? Was it just Dylan's prejudice against the SPD that was making him hesitate? One look at Angela told him he didn't have a choice. He had to trust Reilly, or she was going to jail.

"To get Quintos," Dylan replied.

"Are you DEA?" Vince Howard wanted to know.

Dylan shook his head. "I work for myself. Guess you'd call me a hired gun. But my client up until a few minutes ago was the DEA. They've been stalking Quintos for years, but as you know, the bastard's like a ghost. They think he's in the area, and I was on standby to block his escape by water." He glanced at Angela. "*Midnight Lace* may not be pretty, but she's fast."

Vince Howard whistled. "What makes you think he's here instead of Miami?"

Everyone in the room knew that although he was based in Miami, Lucas Quintos ran all the drugs in Savannah. He came to town from time to time, but even the sharpest narcs hadn't been able to take him out. "The DEA doesn't know exactly where he is, but they believe what brought him to town was J. J. Slade."

Dylan could have heard a pin drop in the room.

"Slade?" Reilly exclaimed at last. "What the hell did Slade have to do with Lucas Quintos?"

"Slade's been laundering for Quintos for years. He was more or less the chief financial officer of Quintos's entire operation. It was Slade who set up the phony companies, made transactions, kept the computer records, and reported to Quintos about his earnings. And as far as we can tell, Slade kept everything important at Paradisia, where no one else could access it."

"Does Quintos know where the records are?" Howard asked as he furiously scribbled notes on a yellow legal pad.

"He's bound to know. That's why the DEA thinks he's in the area. But they don't know if he'll make a move to get them. He doesn't really need them now, except to protect evidence that might be used against him, because they're records of defunct companies."

Reilly raised his eyebrows. "What happened?"

"Over the years, Slade learned everything about the drug business from Quintos. He was a loyal, and rich, lieutenant. Then his greed got the best of him, and he took his first step across the line. He started running drugs with the Mayhew Shipping Lines. Nothing major, certainly no threat to Quintos's empire. But it led to bolder thoughts, greater ambition. His plan was to oust Quintos and step in as top dog."

Howard grunted. "Poor bastard. I could've told him chasing Quintos is like chasing the wind. I wonder how he figured he was going to pull it off?"

"He started by emptying Quintos's pockets," Dylan told them. "When we found out Slade had been killed, the DEA team in Miami moved in on all his businesses and found them shut down. Same with the offshore accounts. Must have really pissed Quintos off when he found out, but there wasn't anything he could do about it. The money was gone."

"What did Slade do with it?" Johnson asked.

Dylan looked at Angela and saw the truth dawn on her.

"He put it in a trust fund and left it to me," she said grimly.

Angela's whole body began to shake. Dylan had told her that he thought Slade was killed because he was trying to horn in on Quintos, but the rest of the story was news to her. Especially the part about the money she'd mysteriously inherited. It was all drug money! She brushed her hands down her arms, as if to wipe away something dirty.

Wally Padgett spoke up. "This is all very interesting, Montana, but what does it have to do with me?"

"I think the Brown kidnapping and the Slade murder are both linked to Quintos." He looked at Angela. "Tell them what Judge Brown told you."

Angela repeated the judge's opinion that both he and Angela were on Cecil Clifford's payback list. "I believe it's possible that I'm being set up to take the blame for this murder as part of Clifford's revenge for my having instigated the IA investigation," she said, looking at her former boss. "By the way, Vince, you're on his list, too."

Dylan broke in. "Here's our theory. Quintos found out what Slade was up to and told Clifford to get rid of him. But instead of simply assassinating Slade, Clifford orchestrated a rather elaborate scheme to not only kill Slade, but to cast the guilt on Angela. Clifford somehow found a look-alike who staged a fight with Slade in a public place the day he was killed. I think Clifford followed Slade when he left the First City Club, killed him, and threw him in the river, making sure that little calendar book was in his pocket."

Reilly rubbed his jaw. "It would be like Clifford to pull

something like that. He's got a warped sense of humor, and he likes to play with people. But that still doesn't explain your being the beneficiary of that trust fund, Angela."

"Yeah, let's talk about that trust fund," Vince Howard said, obviously intrigued. All eyes turned to Angela.

She swallowed hard, believing she was about to seal her coffin. "A couple of days ago, an attorney from Atlanta showed up in my shop and claimed that Slade had left most of his fortune in a trust fund with an unidentified beneficiary. Then he told me . . . that I was that beneficiary. Unfortunately, it's true. We confirmed it with the trustee."

This information clearly stunned everyone who hadn't heard it. Vince Howard leaned toward her. "Did you know Slade?"

Losing her temper, Angela stood up and slammed her palms on the table. "No, I didn't know Slade. I'm mystified and appalled by all of this. The only thing I can think of is that somehow Quintos is behind this, too. He has the kind of power and money to buy off even the best attorneys."

Reilly shook his head. "I don't think so. That law firm is top-notch, and the attorney, Spriggs, swears it was Slade, not a Slade lookalike, who signed those papers. I'm sure they checked him out thoroughly." Then the sergeant stood up and went to a desk in the corner. "Speaking of look-alikes, Angela, are you aware that Slade's daughter looks a lot like you?"

Angela whirled around, caught off guard. She'd known Slade had a daughter, of course, but she'd never seen a picture of her. "No. I wasn't."

Reilly brought a photo of Veronica Slade to the table and laid it face up for all to see. "This isn't a very good shot of her," he said, pointing to the photo they'd retrieved from the society editor of the Savannah newspaper. "But if you look closely, you'll see a marked resemblance. Look at the eyes, the cheekbones. I've seen her in person, and the likeness is quite remarkable."

Angela stared at the photo in shock. She could be looking at her sister, their appearances were so much alike. "She must be the one who's been impersonating me," she uttered. "But why?"

"Maybe she's involved with Clifford, or even Quintos," Vince Howard submitted.

It was Dylan's turn. "I spoke with Slade's pilot, Bob Greer," he said. "Apparently Veronica Slade was estranged from her father, but from time to time, she . . . uh—" he darted an embarrassed look at Angela—"went after Greer, in bed, I mean. He said she always asked a lot of questions afterward about her father's activities."

Angela was amused at Dylan's embarrassment. As if she'd never heard of anybody screwing someone for information. Then she saw Dylan's expression change, as if he'd remembered something else. "What is it?" she asked.

Dylan scratched his head. "I know this sounds wild, but Greer told me something else I'd forgotten until now. He said Veronica Slade was into some strange things, that she'd threatened to put a hex on him if he didn't . . . 'service her,' was how he put it."

"Hex." Reilly looked from Dylan to Angela.

"Voodoo," Angela said, then looked at Dylan. In unison, they said, "Jeremiah Brown."

"What," Wally Padgett exclaimed, "are you talking about?"

Dylan told the group what Jeremiah Brown had told him earlier that day. "He said he was kidnapped by some kids who took him someplace out in the marshes, where an old voodoo man who called himself Dr. Lizard scared the living daylights out of him." Dylan turned to Reilly. "This is what we were coming to tell you when you called."

"Jeremiah believes he's responsible for his father's heart attack, because he gave the voodoo man some photos of his house," Angela added. "He thinks this Dr. Lizard used the pictures to cast a hex on Judge Brown."

"Judge Brown had a heart attack?" Padgett said. "Why doesn't anybody ever tell me anything?"

"It just happened this morning," Angela told him a little impatiently. Her mind was on other things, like bloody black cats and strange old men in the swamps who kidnapped kids. "There's probably a memo on your desk about it by now. Judge Brown is going to be all right. But right now, I want to talk some more about voodoo."

Chapter 31

Th' conjureman's hex be sure and true, and there be no foolin' him . . .

ELIZABETH Slade was not in the habit of trespassing into the west wing of Paradisia. It had been her husband's domain, and he'd made it clear she was unwelcome there, but she knew her way around. She'd come here a number of times in the past few months when she was trying to break into his computer and copy the files for Suarez.

Although most of the actual businesses J. J. had set up were in Florida, she'd learned to her dismay that he'd kept all the records of his laundering activities at Paradisia. She was appalled when she learned the truth about her husband. She'd thought he was merely an astute investor, that his fortune had been built in the stock and commodities markets.

She supposed cocaine was a commodity, although not one she wished to be associated with Paradisia. That's why she'd decided to come here this afternoon, to get rid of the evidence that would tarnish her family's reputation if the police should decide to look into her husband's affairs more closely. It was bad enough that her daughter was a drug user. Elizabeth couldn't bear it if the world learned that her husband had been associated with a drug supplier.

A sudden shocking thought crossed her mind. Drug supplier. Cocaine was Veronica's nasty little habit. Had J. J. been supplying cocaine to his own daughter? Elizabeth couldn't imagine it, but then, she'd been naive about everything J. J. was involved in.

Elizabeth opened the door to what had been J. J.'s large office. It was dark inside, even though it was the middle of the afternoon. He'd preferred heavy draperies and lamps to natural lighting. She flipped on the switch by the door, and several lamps dispelled the gloom. Her eyes wandered around the room, and she considered the stranger who once had cocooned himself here. The stranger who had been her husband. How little she had really known him.

A large desk occupied a good portion of the room, but Elizabeth doubted it contained what she'd come to destroy. J. J. had been too smart to leave a paper trail. The files she was after were the same ones she'd copied for Suarez, and they were in the computer.

She sat in the chair that faced the computer and turned on the machine. It buzzed and hummed and made waking-up noises as it booted the programs into its electronic brain. As she waited, she thought about her daughter. Veronica had vanished the night after the will had been read. At first, Elizabeth suspected she'd gone to Atlanta to try to contest the document, but after twenty-four hours of worrying about it, she'd at last called the attorney's office.

To her relief, Anthony Spriggs informed her that he hadn't seen Veronica since the day he'd been to Paradisia. The call had given Elizabeth the opportunity to instruct the young lawyer that under no circumstances was he to allow the will to be contested. Although he'd informed her that Veronica was free to hire any attorney to take up that fight for her, he'd assured Elizabeth that if Veronica came to him, he'd do everything in his power to dissuade her.

That had given Elizabeth a little hope, until he'd added, "If the will is challenged, however, I must inform you that we have yet another directive from your husband that we're required by law to honor. He left one more envelope with us . . ."

Elizabeth shuddered. She knew exactly what was in that envelope. Her ruin.

The computer screen was now dotted with icons, ready and waiting for Elizabeth's command, but she found she couldn't concentrate. Her nerves were shot, and the more she thought about Veronica, the more distressed she became. The girl had always been damned difficult, but now she was downright dangerous.

The telephone rang, nearly jarring her out of her skin. She looked at the phone set on J. J.'s desk. The call was on the main line to Paradisia. She didn't want Bridget to know she was in J. J.'s study, so she hurried out of the room and back to "her" side of the house in time to hear Bridget's soft Irish accent on the intercom.

"Mrs. Slade? A reporter from the Savannah newspaper is on line one."

Elizabeth pressed the intercom button. "Tell him to go to hell."

A moment later, she heard Bridget's voice again. "Pardon, mum, but I think you might want to take this. He says to tell you he knows who the secret beneficiary is."

Moments later, Elizabeth returned the receiver to its cradle and stared into nothingness. Angela Donahue had struck again. Angela Donahue, who'd been seen having lunch with her husband. Angela Donahue, who looked a lot like her daughter. Angela Donahue, who supposedly had murdered J. J.

Had she now inherited the fortune that rightfully belonged to her and Veronica?

Or were Angela Donahue and Veronica one and the same person?

Elizabeth's voice was calm when she asked Bridget to bring her some tea to the parlor, but on the inside, she was quaking. She sank into the white damask sofa, forcing herself to consider unthinkable possibilities.

Possibilities such as Veronica, a.k.a. Angela Donahue, conspiring with her father to inherit his full fortune while virtually cutting Elizabeth out of anything other than ownership of Paradisia.

The notion was as unlikely as it was mind-boggling. J.J. had hated Veronica. It didn't make sense that he would provide for her in such a grand and circuitous way, no matter how much he desired revenge against Elizabeth.

Unless . . . Veronica had something on him.

Or unless he'd somehow used her to suit his own purposes.

J.J. had been a user. The latter was the only thing that made sense, although Elizabeth couldn't think for the life of her what purposes could have caused her husband to make such a pact with the daughter he'd never wanted.

Bridget brought in a tea tray with sandwiches and cookies. "Thought you might be hungry," she said quietly.

Elizabeth looked up at the aging servant. "Why are you still here, Bridget?" she asked. "You're a millionaire. You don't ever have to wait on anyone again."

Bridget smiled and shrugged. "It's all I know, waiting on people. And this is my home. Besides, you need me, mum."

Elizabeth shook her head as Bridget left the room. How marvelous to be so simple, she thought, so naive. It made life much easier. But simplicity and naivety weren't in Elizabeth's blood, and her life had never been easy. Yes, she thought, she needed Bridget.

And she needed to go upstairs and finish what she'd started before the phone had rung. No matter what her husband and daughter had done, Elizabeth wanted no part of drug dealing. Without calling the servant, she carried the tea tray herself and returned to the study and the computer. It had been here that she'd set these terrible things in motion when she'd copied the files for Suarez. It must be here that she put an end to it.

Opening the program, she watched the screen for the list of files she'd found there before. There had been over forty of them. It had taken her several days to copy all of them to disks.

Today, only one file showed on the screen. She drew her breath in sharply, for the file name was ELIZABETH. Using the mouse, she double-clicked on it and watched in horror as a message appeared before her eyes:

> You should have waited, my dear, for I would have died soon anyway, and it all would have been yours. Your name wasn't on those offshore accounts because I didn't want Quintos to come after you. By the way, did you know Suarez wasn't my rival? He's DEA. The records you gave him would have sent me to prison for life. Some reward for thirty years of service. Too bad you got greedy, Elizabeth, but then, greed always did run in the family.

Dylan's cell phone rang, interrupting the meeting that had been going on for nearly two hours. He ducked out into the hall to take the call. "Montana."

"We've found Quintos."

Dylan's heart rate soared at Oscar Malone's statement. Then he remembered he'd quit the job.

"I'm off the case, remember?"

"Consider yourself rehired. We need you, Montana. How soon can you get that boat in place? It's about thirty miles south of Savannah."

"I'll need better coordinates than that."

"They're coming. Our surveillance team is giving us a GPS reading as we speak. We think he's holed up in a fenced-in compound on a remote peninsula east of Paradisia Plantation."

Dylan raised a brow. "Slade's next-door neighbor? Did Slade know that?"

"Who knows? We figure Quintos must have been using the place for years. Maybe he was keeping an eye on his bookkeeper. It's the perfect hideout, in the middle of nowhere, with easy access to the ocean. There's a shrimper and a cigarette boat tied up there. We believe it could be Quintos's main port of entry for the area. This is the break we've been waiting for." The excitement in Malone's voice was unmistakable.

Dylan knew that a lot of cocaine came into Savannah by car, with mules on "the pipeline," Interstate 95, stopping in the city that was about halfway between Miami and New York. But it made sense that Quintos would have more than one avenue of supply. The business was just too lucrative to take a chance on being cut off, even for a short time. Dylan shook his head. Why hadn't he thought of that five years ago? They'd been looking in the ghettos, when they should have been combing the swamps.

Malone gave Dylan the coordinates and authorized him to recruit assistance from the local area narcs and the GBI. "Get down there tonight and secure your position somewhere where you can see the action without being seen. There'll be other boats besides yours, but we want to keep the Coasties offshore. They're too easy to identify. You know what to do. We're hoping to take them out landside, but you know they'll run for that cigarette the minute they hear the helicopters."

Dylan took notes as Malone finished briefing him on the details of the operation. When he hung up, he stood alone for a moment in the corridor. Everything was coming full circle, only this time they were closer to Quintos than ever before. Clifford was openly on the other side, and the DEA was running the show. Surely to God they'd get the bastards this time.

And this time, he had to make sure Angela was out of harm's way.

He reentered the room, and all eyes turned to him. "They've found Quintos," he said, "right under Slade's nose. Got a map of Lincoln County?"

Heads together, they studied the topographical map that Reilly produced moments later. Dylan pinpointed the small peninsula using the latitude and longitude coordinates Malone had given him.

"They're supposedly right here, in a compound of some sort, although his surveillance guys say it looks more like a fish camp. There's a shrimper and a cigarette boat at a dock. He expects them, or the big guys at least, to make a run for the cigarette. It's our job to make sure they don't get out into open water. I've got the boat, but I'll need some help. Sharpshooters if you've got them, Reilly. And I want Turner, if he shows up in time."

Dylan's request that Scott Turner go with him had less to do with Turner's ability as a marksman than the fact that Turner was the only one who hadn't turned against him before. He was a team leader in Counter-Narcotics now, and he deserved to be in on the kill.

"What about me?" Angela asked, and he looked up to find her glaring at him.

"Uh-uh," he replied with an emphatic shake of his head.

Angela's eyes flashed. "Why not? I've got as much at stake in this as you. Maybe more, since Quintos and Clifford are out to get me. And you know I'm good with a gun."

"You can't go, Angela. You know that," Dylan tried to reason with her. "You're a civilian. And besides, I want you out of the way, someplace safe."

"Out of the way! Like I was *in* the way before? Like I meant to step in front of those bullets?" She glowered at him, red-faced. "I've worked hard to get rid of Quintos, and I deserve to be there when he goes down."

To Dylan's enormous relief, Vince Howard stepped in. "Dylan's right and you know it, Angela. We couldn't allow you to go along on this. You're a civilian now. Besides, you've been out of the business for a long time. Your training is outdated, and your skills are bound to be rusty. None of us wants to take a chance with your life, and we can't allow you to take a chance with ours."

His words, spoken quietly and with compassion, clearly upset Angela, but Dylan could see that she knew he was right. She knew it, but she didn't like it.

"So it's the good-ol'-boys' game?" she lashed out. She was being unreasonable, but Dylan understood her frustration. "And just what is little ol' me supposed to do while all you testosterone types are out there saving the world?"

Reilly looked up. "I could throw you in jail," he replied with a look that said he was only halfway teasing. "It'd be the safest place for you."

"Go to hell, Reilly."

"Safe house?" he offered.

Dylan heard Angela mumble something under her breath, and he doubted it was ladylike. She picked up her purse and headed for the door. "I'm out of here. You cowboys have fun."

Dylan followed her into the hall and reached for her arm, but she jerked away.

"Leave me alone, Dylan. You've let me down one too many times."

Her shot hit its mark, but instead of letting it hurt him, he got angry. "I'm not letting you down. You know damn well you can't be involved in this. You're not thinking clearly."

She didn't reply, but her eyes were fiery and her jaw was set. He wanted to kiss her. Instead, he asked, "Where are you going, by the way?"

"None of your business."

"Why don't you stay around the station house until we give the all-clear? We don't know that Quintos's men are all out there in the marshes. You might still be in danger."

"I can take care of myself." She headed down the hall.

"You don't have a car." He went after her, thinking he'd at least take her home and try to convince her to lay low.

"I'll call a cab," she said.

He watched her storm toward the door, never giving him a backward glance. Dylan swallowed hard. He was sorry she'd taken this like she had, and he was concerned about her even though it gave him some small comfort that this time she'd be out of the line of fire.

Chapter 32

There be hags, and there be hag-hags, but th' most dangerous hag in th' world be th' slip-skin hag, that evil hant who pulls her skin up over her head so's nobody can see her. Th' slip-skin hag moves through keyholes and under doors, and she comes upon folks without any warning . . .

RONNIE checked her speed as she drove back into Savannah. Marguerite had warned her against drawing attention to herself.

"Be like the chameleon," Marguerite had advised, "and hide yourself by becoming like all the rest." It was difficult not to put the pedal down, though. Adrenaline-laced fear pulsed through her.

Although she hadn't told Marguerite about the glitch in the inheritance, the old woman seemed to know. "You're in grave danger, my child," she'd said as she'd hurried Ronnie into the house. Ronnie had seen her glance over her shoulder at the black Mercedes parked nearby and knew the danger came from the owner of the car, the man-with-no-name. Ronnie had forgotten he was here and had no desire to run into him until she'd accomplished her mission.

Marguerite took her into the back room, where she kept her secret lotions and potions and other bags of tricks. Ronnie had never really taken Marguerite's powers seriously until the night the old woman had conjured up the correct combination to the lock on J. J. Slade's file drawer. Ronnie had been desperate for money, since the man had asked for a goodwill payment. Instead of money, she'd found Angela Donahue.

Now, ironically, she was desperate to find her again, only this time in the flesh.

After appeasing the spirits with certain rather ghoulish offerings, Marguerite had gone into a trancelike state, mumbling words that Veronica found unintelligible. The spirits must have told her something, for when she returned to consciousness, the woman passed along certain instructions to Ronnie, although they seemed a little vague. "You'll know what to do," Marguerite had assured her as she sent her on her way.

The most important thing the woman did was give her another gun to use. Ronnie had hoped she'd also find someone else to do the dirty work, but Marguerite had made it clear the killing was Ronnie's responsibility. Following the first part of her mentor's instructions, she parked the easily identifiable red sports car in the busy supermarket parking lot three blocks away from Angela's house. She checked the gun to make sure it was loaded and slipped some extra bullets into the pocket of her jacket.

Her next stop was the supermarket itself, where she purchased a pair of thin rubber gloves. She threw the packaging away and slipped the gloves into her pocket with the bullets.

Dressed in black, Ronnie moved through the night toward Angela's house, gripping the handgun tightly in her jacket pocket. She knew the neighborhood like the back of her hand from when she'd stalked Angela to learn her habits, but she was still nervous. She shivered involuntarily, frequently glancing around her, half expecting to be attacked by whatever lurked in the thick shadows. She saw a young man loitering on one corner and crossed the street before she reached him. She craved what he was selling but didn't have time for that now.

When she reached Angela's block, Ronnie stopped and

looked at the house from the corner. It was a yellow-and-white Victorian, trimmed with gingerbread and painted accents. The first time she'd seen it, she'd wanted to puke. It was so . . . prissy. Just like Angela. God, she was glad she hadn't had to live with her as a real sister.

Ronnie pulled the rubber gloves over her clammy hands, then cut back to the lane directly behind the house. She came to the gate that opened into Angela's small, hidden courtyard. The windows were dark, and Angela's car was not in the driveway. Ronnie took a deep breath and crept up the steps leading to the back veranda. She found the key to the door exactly where Marguerite had said it would be, under a flower pot. How did the woman know these things?

Angela was either a fool or too trusting for her own good, Ronnie thought as she let herself in. This was a terrible neighborhood. She'd never dream of living here, much less leaving a key to the door in such an obvious place. But tonight, she was glad her secret sister was so trusting.

Once inside the house, Ronnie stopped to catch her breath and realized she was trembling. The gun was slippery against the gloves. She released her grip on it, leaving it in her pocket. She was in such a state, she was afraid she might pull the trigger without meaning to.

At last she calmed down enough to wonder what to do next. Marguerite had agreed that it should look like a suicide and had assured Ronnie that Angela would eventually show up. There seemed to be nothing to do but wait.

Ronnie crept farther into the room, bumping her upper leg painfully on a large piece of furniture. Her heart pounded. As her eyes adjusted to the dark, she made out a small lamp on a nearby table and dared to turn it on even though it might alert Angela that someone was in the house. Ronnie couldn't stand being alone in the dark, especially in a strange place.

The soft light illumined the room, and she immediately felt better. She looked around and remembered the rather old-fashioned furnishings in the dining room. A large oak claw-footed table sat squarely in the center of the room, surrounded by antique chairs. There was a glass-paned china cabinet filled with dishes and glassware. Several small occasional chairs and tables filled the corners of the room, and a fireplace graced the outside wall. A worn Oriental rug lay beneath the table on the hardwood floors. The word that came to Ronnie's mind was "quaint."

How very different from her home, Ronnie reflected. She hated to admit it, but Angela's house was warmer, more welcoming than Paradisia had ever been, even though she was an intruder. Suddenly, she wondered what it would be like to live here. To be Angela, the daughter who had been loved. The one who lived in a warm, quaint place.

Ronnie tried to imagine herself as Angela, pretending that this was her house. Slowly, she began to explore the rooms, touching Angela's things. A teapot here. A book there. A throw pillow on the sofa. In the room adjacent to the dining room, she found a bookcase, and she ran her hand across the spines of the volumes lined neatly on the shelves.

She was Angela, the smart daughter.

She sat in one of Angela's chairs and studied the paintings that adorned the walls. They were lovely, tasteful. Just like her.

She was Angela, the beautiful daughter.

Ronnie felt something soft at her neck and turned to find an angora sweater had been hung over the chair. She slipped it over her back and tied the sleeves across her chest. She could smell a light fragrance in the wool. She hugged herself.

She was Angela, the loved daughter.

Almost in a daze, Ronnie continued her fantasy tour of Angela's house, assimilating the essence of her sister, becoming her sister. Becoming the daughter her father had loved. Becoming the child her mother would be proud of.

Becoming Angela Donahue.

Ronnie had come nearly full circle through the four first-floor rooms at the front of the house and found herself at a desk in the hallway. A telephone sat on the desk, and the blinking red light on the adjacent answering machine indicated there were messages. Who had called her? Ronnie wondered, and pressed the play button.

There weren't many messages. Mostly business calls. Ronnie envisioned herself as Angela the successful businesswoman, and it made her feel good that she was proficient at something.

But it was the last call that grabbed her attention. "Angela, it's your mother. I have to talk to you. It's urgent. Don't do anything until you call me." The woman left a number.

Her mother. Of course. Angela Donahue had a mother, and from the worried voice, she must be a mother who cared about her daughter. Still in a dreamlike state, Ronnie pressed the button to replay the message. She wanted to talk to her mother. She picked up the phone and dialed the number as it was repeated from the tape.

It was answered on the first ring. "Hello, Angela? Is that you?"

"Yes, Mother," Ronnie answered, her voice soft and seemingly far away.

"Mother?" the woman said. "What's the matter with you? You never call me mother."

The sharp voice in her ear startled Ronnie, who suddenly realized what she'd done. "Shit," she swore as she slammed down the phone.

Ronnie was back in her own skin again and suddenly scared witless. What the hell had she been thinking? Obviously, as her father had been so fond of pointing out, she *hadn't* been thinking. And she was a fool to play those pretend games. She didn't want to be Angela Donahue. She hated Angela, and she'd come here to kill her.

The phone rang, shattering the quiet. Ronnie didn't answer it. Whoever called hung up before the machine picked up.

Ronnie darted a glance over her shoulder, half expecting to find someone had been watching her and had caught her in her little game, but the house was empty. Christ, she swore, get a grip. Remembering why she'd come here, Ronnie reached into her pocket for the gun. Stealthily, she returned to the dining room and turned off the lamp, then crouched in the dark and waited for her prey.

It was time for Angela Donahue to die.

Angela slammed out of the doors of the police station and directly into a wall of a man who didn't smell so good.

" 'Scuse me, ma'am," he said, grabbing her arm to steady her.

She looked up into the pockmarked face of a derelict street bum and hastily stepped back in alarm. "No problem," she said and moved to pass by him.

"Angela?"

His raspy voice stopped her in midstride. She turned, suddenly remembering him. "Turner?"

"I didn't mean to scare you." His voice sounded like he'd had a bad tracheotomy.

Angela wasn't afraid of him, but she was curious about one thing. "How do you know me?"

"I was a rookie on the Counter-Narcotics Team five years ago with Dylan. I'm real sorry about what happened to you."

Would this nightmare never end? Everything in her life right now seemed to have to do with what had happened five years ago. "Thanks," she said, then remembered sourly that Turner was invited to the party tonight and she wasn't. "You'd better hurry. Dylan's waiting for you." She pushed past him and started down the steps.

"Angela." He called out her name again, and the urgency in his tone stopped her.

She turned. "What?"

"I know what happened that night."

He seemed to want to talk about it, but she wasn't interested in standing on the street discussing that catastrophe with a man who looked like he'd slept on a park bench last night.

"Montana's a good guy," he said. "I appreciate him letting me in on the action tonight."

"Yeah, well, some of us don't share your sentiments."

Understanding showed in his eyes. "I take it you're not coming along?"

"Certainly not. I'm just a civilian now."

"He *is* a good guy, Angela."

She answered him with a withering look.

"What happened back then wasn't his fault," Turner said.

"I don't want to talk about it."

"He's never told you, has he?"

"He left, and I didn't see him again until he showed up in Reilly's office after you called him." That old pain oozed through her again.

"Everybody blamed Dylan for the bust going bad. Said he didn't show up where he was supposed to."

"That's history."

"But not the right history. History is written by the victors, remember? That particular history was written by Cecil Clifford, Dylan's boss at the time. It was Clifford who sent Dylan to the wrong place. On purpose. Dylan was only following orders. Clifford deliberately queered the bust for his buddy Lucas Quintos. Then when it was all over, he made Dylan the scapegoat and asked for his resignation."

His story didn't surprise her. Angela had suspected as much, especially after Clifford had been indicted, but she'd never known for sure. But that still didn't explain why he'd walked out on her. Or why even now he hadn't told her the truth.

As if he were reading her thoughts, Turner said, "You're asking why he didn't stand up for himself. I don't have an answer for you, except to say that Cecil Clifford is a cruel and ruthless man. He must have threatened Dylan with something pretty powerful to send him running."

As mad as she was at Dylan at the moment, Angela knew he was no coward. She couldn't conceive of him running from anyone's threats, no matter how ruthless. He'd been running from her, from their relationship, pure and simple. But she wasn't about to share that with Scott Turner.

"Thanks for letting me know, Turner," she said, meaning it. It helped to have confirmation that Dylan hadn't been derelict in his duties. "I've got to go."

"Yeah, me, too."

She forced a smile. "Good luck. I hope you nail that bastard once and for all."

She waited for Turner to go inside, then returned to the building herself and called a cab. It was dark when the taxi arrived, and a chill wind whirled the leaves along the street as she stepped into the vehicle. The air was crisp and smelled of Halloween.

Her house was dark when the cab pulled up in front, and Angela made a mental note to check the bulb in the front porch fixture. It was on a timer and should be lit. She paid the cabbie and asked him to wait until she got inside the house.

She turned the lock and opened the door, reaching inside to flip on the switch in the hall. "Thanks!" she called to the driver and waved him on.

The house was chilly, and as she went to adjust the thermostat in the hall, she thought she heard something. She looked up and caught a glimpse of a shadow in the dining room, and adrenalin shot through her. Someone was in the house!

"Who's there?" Angela cursed the fact that she had no gun.

A figure clad in black stepped out of the shadows, a figure who did have a gun. And it was pointed straight at her. To her surprise, it was a woman, and to her even greater surprise, she recognized the face.

Veronica Slade.

Before Angela could pull her wits together, the intruder spoke. "Hello, *sister*. It's about time we met."

Chapter 33

Hants and hags and other evil spirits be known t' come from time t' time and steal good folk and take them t' th' Otherworld. T' keep those spirits away, sprinkle this magic root all round th' yard, over th' doorsteps, and round your bed. Then th' hags'll leave you be . . .

"SISTER?" Angela repeated, stunned and confused.

"That's right," the intruder snarled. "Father's real daughter, not his illegitimate bastard."

Angela took a step backward, her heart pounding. "I don't know what you mean. I don't have a sister."

"Unfortunately, you do. Let me introduce myself," the woman said. "I'm Veronica Slade. The only *legitimate* daughter of the recently deceased J. J. Slade, who you killed so you could steal my rightful inheritance."

The blood drained from Angela's face. What was this madwoman talking about? "I don't know what you mean . . ."

Veronica's face turned red, and she cut Angela off. "Don't act like the innocent with me. You killed my father. It's all over the newspapers. And now you're trying to take what belongs to me." The gun wavered.

Angela held up her hands as if she could fend off a bullet. Cold sweat trickled down her back. "Calm down," she said unsteadily. Was this crazy woman going to pull the trigger? "I'm sorry your father died, but I didn't kill him. I didn't even know your father. And I'm not your sister."

"Millions of dollars recently added to your net worth says you knew my father . . . real well," Veronica said coldly. "I'd just like to know how you got him to sign it all over to you."

Ironically, Angela wished she knew that as well. "I didn't get him to do anything. I never met the man. I never even saw his face until they showed me a photo at the police station."

"And you didn't notice the resemblance?" Veronica clearly didn't believe her. "That your eyes are like his? Your cheekbones the same? Look," she demanded, pointing at a mirror that hung in the hallway. "Look at us."

Angela stepped toward the mirror and could see them both reflected there. Even though she'd seen their photos compared, their resemblance in person was uncanny. Angela had light hair, Veronica dark. Angela's was curly, Veronica's straight. Their eyes were different colors, but the features looked as if they had indeed come from the same mold.

Angela's pulse thundered. "N-no," she murmured, half in reply, half in denial. But suddenly she recalled having felt that Slade had looked somehow familiar when Reilly had shown her his photo.

"Look, Veronica," she said, trying to hang onto her sanity, "this is a big mistake. Your father was not mine. My father died in a car accident thirty years ago."

"Yeah, right," Veronica said. "That must have been the fairy tale your mother made up for you. More likely she had an affair with a married man, got knocked up, and he paid her off. Was there any mention of a large sum of money coming in after the 'car accident,' or has he been supporting her all these years?"

Angela's eyes widened. The life insurance. Her mother had told her that about the only responsible thing her father had done for them was buy the life insurance policy that gave them the chance to start over. Had it been life insurance, or a payoff?

Good God, she thought. Could this be true? *Was* she the bastard daughter of J. J. Slade? It might explain why Slade had left her his fortune. When he'd learned of his terminal cancer, had he lost his mind or suffered a bout of belated guilt and changed his will to provide for his bastard daughter? Every fiber of her being screamed that it couldn't be true.

"You're wrong, Veronica," she said firmly. "About all of this."

"Then why did he keep a file in his desk drawer with photos and clippings of you he'd collected while you were growing up? I must admit I was surprised. I didn't know Father could be that sentimental."

"What are you talking about? This is madness."

"You're damned right it's madness. But it's there. That's how I found out about you."

Nausea rose in Angela's throat as she began to put the pieces together. "You found out your father had another child, and you stalked me, impersonated me, set me up to take the rap for his murder, didn't you?"

"You're pretty smart for a blonde."

"You know I didn't kill your father," Angela said in a low, even tone, "because you killed him yourself and threw the blame on me." She was astounded. The set-up had nothing to do with Lucas Quintos or Cecil Clifford. It was Veronica's crazed revenge against her father. She'd probably also expected to inherit his fortune, Angela realized.

"I didn't kill him!" Veronica screamed, sounding suddenly hysterical.

Again, Angela held up her hands. "Okay, okay. Sorry." She had to think of some way to calm her down. "Veronica," she said slowly, "how old are you?"

"Twenty-eight." Veronica eyed her uncertainly, suspicious of her question.

"How long were your parents married?"

"What? Are you trying to imply my mother had to get married? Well, she didn't. Mother and Father have been legally married for almost thirty years."

"Then do the math. I'm thirty-five. Even if your father was also mine, which is not the case, he wasn't married to your mother when I was born. For all either of us knows, he *was* married to my mother."

But a doubt had been planted in Angela's mind. *Had* her father, Jake Donahue, ever been married to Mary Ellen? she wondered wildly. Or had they been married and divorced? Mary Ellen's faith didn't believe in divorce. It would have been humiliating and degrading. Maybe that's why she'd left Jacksonville and never contacted her family again.

Angela thought back to Mary Ellen's years of rage, of her prayers for the return of her dead husband. Had she believed he might return because he really wasn't dead? Had Mary Ellen made up the whole story so Angela wouldn't know about the divorce? Or worse, that she was illegitimate?

Overwhelmed, Angela fought to keep her thoughts straight and her emotions under control. First things first, she told herself. She had to somehow get the gun from Veronica Slade and get help. Then she could sort out the rest.

"He was never married to your mother," Veronica went on. "You're his bastard, and I want my money."

"Fine. I don't want it. Can we work something out?"

She didn't like the expression that settled over Veronica's face. It was a mean, vengeful look.

"Oh, yeah," Veronica said. "We're going to work something out all right. Get your car keys."

Angela wasn't going anywhere with this nutcase. Hoping surprise would be on her side, she lunged at Veronica, knocking her against the wall. Grasping Veronica's wrist,

Angela tried to twist the gun from her hand. She heard the shot before she felt the rip of pain where the bullet struck her leg. Unable to hold on, she fell away from Veronica, who inched upward, her back still against the wall, the gun still in her hand.

Your skills are rusty. Vince Howard's words echoed in Angela's mind.

"You fucking bitch!" Veronica shrilled, and Angela fully expected her to pull the trigger.

She thought fleetingly of Dylan, of the harsh words they'd exchanged, of the years they'd wasted being apart. Tears welled in her eyes, not from fear, but from regret. She loved Dylan, and now she'd never see him again.

But Veronica didn't shoot her. "I said, get your car keys." White-faced, she waved the gun at Angela. "Do it!"

Numbly, Angela reached for her handbag, but Veronica's voice stopped her before she could fish for her keys.

"Wait! You don't have a gun in there, do you?"

Angela shook her head, but she couldn't speak. The pain in her leg took her breath away. She looked down to see that her slacks were torn and her leg was bleeding. She wondered how badly she was wounded. "I . . . I need to get a towel or a bandage or something," she managed at last.

"Forget it." Veronica motioned toward the door with her gun. "Let's go."

The twin diesels roared as Dylan headed the *Midnight Lace* down the Intracoastal toward the rendezvous point. As hopeful as he was that this time the bust would be successful, that they'd get rid of Lucas Quintos for good, he was also despondent over the fight with Angela. He was relieved to think she was safe, but there was no guarantee he would walk out of this alive.

And there was so much he hadn't said to her.

Such as, I'm sorry.

And, I love you.

Perhaps he should have come back to her when Clifford had been sent up, when her life was no longer in danger from his threats. But by then, more than two years had passed since he'd left, and Dylan had doubted she ever wanted to see him again. She didn't know his reasons for leaving, but he'd believed no woman could forgive what could only be perceived as a brutal rejection.

But only yesterday she'd told him she wanted to try again. Had she meant it, or was it just the bump on the head? He drew in deeply of the dank night air. Maybe she'd meant it yesterday, but he was damn sure she'd had second thoughts today.

Dylan warned himself to stay focused on the job at hand and not allow his problems with Angela to cloud his thinking. Once he'd taken care of Quintos and Clifford, he'd see where he stood with her.

Keeping a close eye on his navigational instruments, he pushed the powerful boat forward into the night as fast as he dared. The channel was narrow in places, and it wound through the marshland like a snake. He had to be very careful to follow the channel markers. The last thing he needed was to go aground.

There were five men aboard the *Midnight Lace*, Dylan, Scott Turner, and three SWAT sharpshooters, armed with night-vision goggles, high-powered rifles, and nerves of steel. They were but a small part of an overall deployment of law enforcement officers that was nothing short of an invasion force, if Malone was to be believed. And Dylan believed the man. He'd been on other assignments for Malone and understood the power the DEA operative commanded. Unlike the rather uncomplicated and unsuccessful bust five years ago, this one had far more going for it. Sophisticated electronics. Linked communications. And an overcast, moonless night. Hopefully, it wouldn't rain.

Scott Turner joined Dylan, a cigarette dangling from his lips. "How's it going?"

On what level? Dylan thought glumly, unable to quit brooding about Angela. "Fine," he answered. "We should be there in about thirty minutes, but the last will be slow going. We may have to turn off the engines and paddle this thing if we want to approach unobserved."

He was half serious. Although he knew nobody could really row a fifteen-ton vessel, he wasn't sure how close the Intracoastal came to the peninsula Malone had identified as their target. Dylan had programmed the latitude and longitude of the area into his electronic navigational charts, but until they got closer and could see things first-hand, he wouldn't know the best way to arrive undetected.

"Hand me a paddle. I've been lifting weights," Turner said, kiddingly offering his muscle for the impossible.

The two men didn't speak for a long while, then Turner broke the companionable silence. "I saw your lady on my way into the station."

"My lady?"

"You know who I mean. Angela."

"She's not my lady," Dylan growled.

"Don't lie to me, Montana. She's always been your lady."

"Yeah, well, that was a long time ago."

"She still loves you, y'know."

Dylan doubted that. "No. I don't know. What makes you say that?"

"I could just tell, in spite of the fact that she was really pissed at you for not letting her in on this. Which, by the way, thanks for giving me the chance."

"You're welcome." Dylan wondered what was prompting this conversation.

"Anyway, after I explained what had really happened in that other deal . . ."

Dylan turned on him. "You did what?"

Turner shrugged. "I figured you'd never told her the truth, and she deserved to know."

Dylan's face grew hot. "What'd you tell her?"

"That you were only following orders. That Clifford gave you misdirections."

"How'd you know that?" Dylan thought he was the only person on the planet besides Cecil Clifford who knew what had actually happened that night.

"I have eyes, man. I saw what happened. I heard him change your orders, and I thought it was strange." Turner gave a low laugh. "You might find this funny, but back then, you were my hero. I was an eager young rookie, you were the best in the business. I wanted to grow up and be just like you. Then I saw what Clifford did to you, and my idealistic world came crumbling down. I was afraid to confront him, because I didn't know what he'd threatened you with. But I swore if I ever got the chance, I'd do what I could to set the record straight. Guess that's why I told Angela about it."

Dylan couldn't find it in him to be angry with Turner. Loyalties like his were hard to come by. But neither could he bring himself to say thank you. He wasn't sure he was glad Turner had told her. What did she think of Dylan now? That he was too big a wuss to fight back?

"There's just one thing I'd like to know," Turner said, breaking into Dylan's morose thoughts. "What did he threaten you with? I know you'd never have left, disappeared so completely, especially not deserted your lady without a damn good reason."

Dylan hesitated. He'd never told anyone this, although now it seemed so far in the past, he guessed it didn't matter. "Clifford told me if I talked, or even showed my face around here again, he'd kill Angela."

"Jesus. And you believed him?"

"Wouldn't you?" Dylan lashed out. "Would you have taken a chance like that? She was already in the hospital, unconscious, her head in a bandage, her leg torn apart by gunshot wounds because of Clifford. I managed to sneak in there, and I saw what he'd done to her," he added, and his mouth went suddenly dry.

"She was lying there so pale I was afraid she was dead. All those monitors beeping and lights blinking scared me. I wasn't sure she was going to make it. Clifford was a ruthless son of a bitch, and I knew he meant what he said, so I decided it was best if I took off and picked up the fight against him and Quintos somewhere else."

His throat ached at the memories. "I never even said goodbye. Clifford's goons were guarding her room. I've spent the last five years regretting what happened and working my ass off to get to tonight, and I won't be happy until I see him and Quintos both go down."

Turner tossed his cigarette out the door and over the side of the boat. "I know the feeling."

Their conversation had ended, but Dylan continued to ponder his decision of that long-ago night. Would Clifford have killed Angela if he'd come back and brought the truth to light? He'd considered returning when he learned Clifford and the others had been indicted, but even with Clifford in jail, Dylan worried that his former boss would use his connections with Quintos to fulfill his threat against Angela. Believing that she probably hated him anyway, Dylan had decided to leave matters as they were.

Now Clifford was out, and clearly he was after Angela. A sudden, almost painful realization rocked Dylan. It hadn't mattered that he'd stayed away. He hadn't protected her one whit by his absence. Angela's life was more at risk now than ever. Clifford wasn't insane, but Dylan considered him to be borderline psychotic, and if he wanted Angela, he'd get her.

Dylan peered into the darkness, and another horrible thought struck him. Was Clifford out here in the marsh with Quintos, or was he in Savannah, watching Angela's every move? The hair rose on the back of Dylan's neck. Watching her go home alone in a taxi? Watching her house? Waiting on the perfect moment, when Dylan let his vigilance down?

"Shit," he said, reaching for the cell phone. In rapid fire, he punched in Reilly's number. "Go get Angela," he barked into the phone. "I don't care if she screams bloody murder, bring her in, lock her up, and keep her safe until we get Clifford."

Chapter 34

There was this man who came home one night t' find his wife had been stolen by th' devil. He took his shotgun down and loaded it, then called his dogs and off they went to th' swamp, where he knew th' devil lived. But th' devil's friends saw him coming and shined their lights t' lure him th' wrong way, and he was never seen again . . .

DEEPLY disturbed by that queer phone call, Mary Ellen picked up her pocketbook and headed to Angela's house. It could have been a wrong number. Angela hadn't answered when she'd called back. But the woman had called her "mother" before she'd hung up. Something wasn't right.

She arrived just in time to see Angela's Honda turn out of the driveway and head down the street in the opposite direction. "What the hell?" She picked up her cell phone and dialed Angela's cell number. Her daughter didn't go anywhere without that phone.

It rang and rang, until at last the cellular service recording informed her that the customer she was trying to reach was not available at the moment.

Something was horribly, terribly wrong.

Mary Ellen cursed, suddenly remembering it was still Friday the thirteenth.

She stepped on the gas, ran a stop sign and a red light until she finally caught sight of Angela's car heading for the ramp leading to the Interstate. As it passed beneath the bright lamps that illumined the freeway, Mary Ellen could see that another woman was in the car with Angela.

Mary Ellen fell in behind them at a safe distance and considered calling the police, but then thought better of it. The police had been useless in protecting her daughter, and besides, she didn't know for sure that Angela was going anywhere against her will. She decided to follow Angela's car and find out what was going on first, and then, if she needed to, she'd call in the cavalry. But Mary Ellen was quite capable of taking care of most things herself.

Leaning over, she pressed the button on the glove box. The door opened, and the small light inside revealed the .38 she always carried for personal protection. In these days of road rage and drive-by shootings, you never knew when you'd need a gun.

Keeping an eye on the road, she reached for the weapon and brought it into her lap. Then she retrieved a box of bullets, shut the glove compartment, and checked her rear-view mirror as she refocused on driving. She hoped she wouldn't need the gun, but she didn't like it that Angela was almost out of Savannah and still headed south. Where could she be going? As the minutes passed, Mary Ellen's apprehension grew, because she became convinced that Angela was being kidnapped.

A light mist began to fall against the windshield, obscuring her view. The wipers only smeared the existing road dirt, making things worse, until she at last managed to clear the window using her washers. In the meantime, Angela's car had gained several lengths on her.

"Oh, no you don't, sweetheart," she muttered, stepping on the gas. It was unlike Angela to speed. It must be the other woman forcing her to go dangerously fast.

The other woman.

Suddenly, Mary Ellen knew who the other woman was—the woman who'd tried to frame Angela. She didn't understand why this woman had chosen Angela for her victim, but Mary Ellen had no intention of letting her harm her daughter. She pressed her foot a little harder on the gas.

Not only would she rescue Angela from the claws of this predator, she'd make the woman pay for all she'd done to hurt her daughter. And it would give her great pleasure to inflict the punishment.

Less than half an hour later, she saw Angela signal that she was taking the Sunhill exit off I-95. She followed Angela's car along the main thoroughfare headed east, to where the road became a much smaller lane. She slowed and turned off her headlights so she wouldn't be noticed. Her heartbeat picked up, and her mouth was like cotton. Where were they headed? They were in the middle of the marshlands, the middle of nowhere. And then Mary Ellen realized with sickening certainty that most likely the kidnapper was going to murder Angela and dump her in the swamp where no one would ever find her.

Mary Ellen had tried hard to be a good mother to Angela, tried to make up for her not having a father. She hadn't always done everything right, she was sure, but she'd done her best.

And now she had to do everything in her power to save her daughter's life.

Elizabeth Slade jumped when the telephone rang. She'd been sitting alone in the darkness of her parlor, lost in sorrow and old memories, worried about her daughter and the fate that awaited if Veronica contested the will. Snatching up the phone, Elizabeth hoped it was Veronica checking in at long last. She halfway expected to hear that her daughter had left the country. Perhaps that would be for the best. If Veronica had killed J. J., Elizabeth would just as soon her daughter disappeared. It was the only graceful way to avoid prosecution if the truth ever surfaced. And she wouldn't be able to make any dangerous waves concerning the will.

Before Elizabeth could speak, she heard Bridget answer the main phone. "Paradisia Plantation."

The voice on the line was low and accented. "Tell Mrs. Slade someone needs to talk to her. It's about Veronica."

Adrenalin charged through her. "I've got it, Bridget," she said, and heard the servant hang up the other phone. "This is Mrs. Slade."

"Good," the man said. "Now I want you to listen real close, Mama. You got something I want, and I got something you want. So I'm going to offer you a deal."

"Who is this?" Elizabeth demanded. At first she thought it was Ricky Suarez calling with some kind of blackmail scheme. But she realized this thickly accented voice was different.

The man laughed. "Let's just say I'm an old friend of the family. Your husband was my man for years, Mrs. Slade, until he got greedy."

Elizabeth's skin turned to ice. This was the man for whom J. J. had done all that dirty business, and from whom he'd stolen a fortune. "What do you want?"

"For one thing, I want my records back. Your husband thought he was real smart hiding everything there in that big old house. He thought I didn't know what he was up to. But he wasn't smart at all. I knew the minute he turned on me, and I watched his every move. I know where those files are, and I want them back. Now, you can either hand them over, or I'll come get them."

"*You* killed him," Elizabeth murmured, hardly hearing what he was saying. She was relieved in spite of the horror of it all. At least she knew Veronica hadn't murdered her father.

His laugh was like a rumble of thunder. "Oh, no. I was going to, but someone beat me to it. Saved me a lot of trouble. Now about those records?"

His words echoed in her ears. *Someone beat me to it.* Veronica? Elizabeth felt suddenly brittle, as if she were coming apart. "Records?"

"The files I was talking about, Mama. The ones that belong to me."

Oh, dear God. Those files had been on J. J.'s computer, and he'd deleted every single one of them. Elizabeth had nothing to give this man. "They're not here," she stammered. "He . . . he had them on his computer, but I went to find them this afternoon, and . . . they're gone. He must have gotten rid of them."

The man swore so loudly that she had to move the phone away a few inches. "That's too bad, Mrs. Slade," he said angrily, "because if you don't come up with them, I'm going to kill your daughter. She owes me a great deal of money, by the way. I want that paid back, too. The files and the money, Mama, or you'll never see your daughter again. I'll be in touch."

He hung up in her ear.

Elizabeth sat staring at the telephone but seeing nothing but her life going up in flames. She began to quake. How could this all have happened? Her husband a drug dealer. Her daughter a user and a murderer. She was glad her mother was long dead so she would never know what a mess Elizabeth had made of her life.

What would happen if she couldn't find those files? Did the man really have Veronica? Would he kill her?

She drew in a deep breath, trying unsuccessfully to stem the wave of despair that engulfed her. Of course the man had Veronica. He'd been supplying her drugs. She owed him a lot of money. She'd killed J. J. to get her hands on her inheritance to pay him off, only to discover she'd been virtually cut out of his will. Elizabeth wanted to deny every sordid thought as it popped into her head, but she couldn't.

She bit her lip. In spite of all Veronica had done, she was still her daughter. Elizabeth couldn't let that man kill her. She had to find those files. And she'd sell some of her stock, all of it if she had to, to pay him off. And then she'd lock Veronica in a rehab center somewhere far away, until her daughter understood that the Mayhew women simply did not behave as she had.

One more chance, Veronica. You have one more chance.

If, that is, I can find the files.

Elizabeth took the gun she kept in her desk drawer and crept back into J. J.'s study, wondering if the man who'd phoned her was somehow watching. Would he try to break into the Big House? Sitting at the computer, nerves on edge, waiting for the machine to boot up, Elizabeth came as close as she ever had to praying. "Please don't let him harm my baby."

She searched through the computer in every way she knew how, but J. J. had been thorough. All that remained was the installed software and the file marked ELIZABETH, which she promptly deleted.

Nothing.

There was nothing with which to barter for her daughter's life. Damn J. J.! There had to be something.

She considered the large desk that had been her husband's workplace. The combination lock on the single large file drawer caught her eye. She looked at the gun in her hand. Elizabeth didn't know the combination, but she was a pretty good shot. It was doubtful that J. J. had been careless enough to leave printed records behind, but it was the only place she had left to look.

Raising her gun and taking careful aim, Elizabeth squeezed the trigger. The shot rang out, and the bullet hit the mark. The small lock popped backward and fell into the drawer.

She heard Bridget's footsteps running toward her down the hallway, but Elizabeth didn't care. She was breathing heavily, hoping against hope she'd find what she needed in this drawer.

"It's okay, Bridget," she snapped when the servant ran through the door. "Please, just leave me alone."

Bridget's eyes grew wide when she saw the gun in Elizabeth's hand. At first she hesitated, but then obeyed and quietly left the room.

Slowly, with shaking hands, Elizabeth opened the file, and her hope soared. The drawer was crammed full. Elizabeth sank into the large leather desk chair and began to pull the files out, going through them one by one. Her optimism was short-lived, however, as she discovered they contained nothing but thirty years' worth of personal and household records. Receipts of paid bills. Stock and bond portfolios. Copies of correspondence having to do with the agricultural operation of Paradisia. Records concerning the airplane.

But nothing to do with the business that had created Slade's wealth, and caused the downfall of them all.

Frantically, she pulled the files from the drawer, scrambling through them, cursing and crying. She reached the last file, every shred of hope dashed. She frowned when she glanced at the tab of the last folder.

"Angela."

Elizabeth Mayhew Slade's world finally fell apart.

She laid the file on the desk and opened it. It contained mostly newspaper clippings, dog-eared and yellowed by time. Each article was about the same person, a girl named Angela Donahue. A bright-haired, pretty girl who, except for hair and eye coloring, looked like Veronica.

Looked like her father, J. J.

Elizabeth realized the reason for Veronica's contemptuous look the day Elizabeth had accused her of the murder. Veronica knew about J. J.'s bastard daughter.

Why are you always so quick to blame me?

J. J. had died at the hands of his daughter, all right, but not his legitimate daughter. Elizabeth had suspected her husband must have had affairs, since their own love life had long ago ceased to exist. But to hide his bastard, and then to leave everything to her . . .

It was J. J.'s ultimate revenge. And it had worked.

Chapter 35

Th' conjureman knows just what t' mix in th' potions and charms. Sometime he uses th' feathers of crow, sometime of buzzard. Th' foot of chicken or salamander also be powerful, but even more th' left legbone of a black cat. Goofer dust costs extra. But everyone knows none of these works without th' conjureman's magic words . . .

JOHNNY Reilly had been uncomfortable when Angela left the security of the police precinct building, but because Dylan Montana had seemed all right with it, he hadn't said anything.

Now, Montana had apparently had a change of heart, and Reilly didn't blame him. No one knew where Cecil Clifford was, or how deeply his desire for revenge ran. He could have been watching Angela all along. That would explain how he'd known she was leaving the hotel the night she'd been hit by the car, which hadn't turned up despite an intensive effort to find it.

Reilly dialed Angela's home number, but it was picked up by the answering machine. He dialed her cell phone. No answer.

Grabbing his trench coat and signaling to another officer, Bryan Seidel, to come with him, he raced out the door. A light rain slicked the streets, and his tires spun as he sped out of the parking lot. This did not feel good.

They drove as fast as they could to Angela's old Victorian home. When he pulled up in front of her front gate, his heart nearly stopped beating. The porch was dark, but a light illumined the hallway, and her front door stood wide open.

"Oh, Christ," he whispered, taking out his gun. He motioned to Seidel to follow him. Creeping down the short walk, he kicked something that lay on the pavement. He bent to see what it was.

A cell phone. Torn apart. It looked as if it had been thrown onto the bricks from a good distance.

No wonder Angela hadn't answered his call.

He closed his eyes. He didn't want to go into this house and find her dead, but he was certain that was exactly what awaited him.

Swallowing his fear, Reilly mounted the steps and pushed the door fully open while keeping his back to the wall. While the other officer stood backup, Reilly melted around the corner and into the house, his gun poised and ready to shoot. Cautiously, he inched into the hallway, then waved Seidel inside. Reilly went into the front parlor while the other cop headed up the stairs.

Five minutes later, a search of the house had revealed no intruder, and to Reilly's intense relief, no corpse. The pair met up again in the main hallway.

"What do you think happened?" Seidel wanted to know.

"My guess is she's been kidnapped," Reilly answered, the weight of the possibility crushing his shoulders.

Seidel placed a hand on the nearby roll-top desk and returned his pistol to the holster. "So what do we do now?"

"Start looking," Reilly said grimly.

Bryan Seidel looked down at the floor. "Uh-oh."

Reilly followed the direction of Seidel's gaze and any doubt that Angela had been abducted disappeared. Between them on the golden slats of the hardwood floor lay a puddle of blood.

"Oh, Jesus," he swore and squatted beside it. Just because there was no corpse didn't mean Angela wasn't dead. However, there wasn't enough blood to indicate that she'd died here. Nor was there any sign that her body had been dragged. In fact, a closer inspection showed a trail of drops of blood leading out of the front door.

Angela had been alive but wounded when she left here.

Reilly called for an investigation unit to seal off Angela's house and search for clues, then hung up the phone, totally disheartened. How was he going to break this to Montana? He decided he wouldn't, not until the night's work was done. Montana needed to have all his wits about him, and Reilly knew the man would come unglued if he thought anything had happened to Angela.

With any luck, maybe they'd find her before Montana came back, but he had no idea where to look. This had to be Clifford's work. Had he taken her himself, or had he sent a henchman to do the dirty work? More importantly, where had he taken her? He was afraid they might find another floater in the river in the morning.

Reilly went out onto the front porch. The rain was coming down steadily now, washing away any traces of mud and blood they might have found useful. Discouraged, he walked to the end of the veranda at the side of the house and noticed that Angela's car wasn't parked in the drive. Neither was it on the streets out front.

Reilly took out his phone again and called headquarters. "I need an APB on this vehicle, license number . . ."

Angela's hands were cold with sweat as she followed her captor's directions, which were taking them deeper into the desolate marshlands south of Savannah. The road had become nothing but a narrow lane, and no lights shone through the misty gloom. Few people lived out here, and no one would hear her cry for help. Even if Veronica hadn't thrown the cell phone out the window, Angela doubted she could have used it in such a remote place. She was driving to her death, unless she could disarm her kidnapper. Maybe when they arrived at their destination, wherever that was, she could try again, although her leg throbbed with pain.

As they drove, Veronica, who had insisted on being called Ronnie, had kept up a running diatribe against Angela and the man she claimed was their mutual father. Angela wasn't sure if she believed that Slade had been her father, but she *did* believe this woman was out of her mind. She had to move carefully, or Ronnie would go over the edge and pull the trigger.

"Where are you taking me?" she finally ventured when Ronnie told her to slow down and get ready to turn left.

"Shut up. Did I tell you to talk?" Clearly, Ronnie was enjoying her power over Angela.

Angela didn't press her further. She'd find out soon enough where she'd meet her fate. They turned down a nearly indistinguishable lane and came to a gate. "Get out," Ronnie ordered, and opened her own door.

Angela's pulse began to beat harder. Maybe this was her chance. Her feet squished in the mud when she got out of the car. Ronnie motioned her toward the gate, which was lit up by the car's headlights. Ronnie stepped up beside her and waved her hands at something perched on top. Then, still holding Angela at gunpoint, she went to a small box and pressed some numbered buttons. The gate creaked open.

"Get back in the car," Ronnie ordered, and Angela cursed herself for missing her opportunity.

Angela drove down the narrow path, unable to see anything but darkness beyond the yellow glow of her headlights. She drove slowly, thinking at any moment she might end up in the swamp. That was probably what Veronica had in mind. A bullet through the brain, her car in the marshes, never to be found again.

Suddenly, she thought she saw lights twinkling through the mist that had thickened into rain. Will-o'-th'-wisp sort of beacons, but Angela knew they weren't swamp gas. They'd reached wherever it was that Veronica Slade intended to kill her sister, or rather half-sister, the total stranger she hated so much. A part of Angela regretted she would never know the truth.

Was she Veronica's secret sister?

If she was lucky enough to get out of this alive, Angela vowed to confront Mary Ellen, who had some serious explaining to do.

The lane ended in a large open area. To her left, Angela saw a large, run-down white house with a sagging front porch lit by a dim bare bulb. To the right, several low-slung old trailers were lined in a row. Lights shone through the windows of two of the trailers. She guessed it had once been a fish camp but doubted very much that Veronica had brought her here to go fishing. What was this place?

"Park there," Ronnie directed sharply, indicating for her to pull alongside one of several nondescript vehicles that were parked haphazardly on the grounds. Then Angela saw one car—a big, black Mercedes—parked near one of the trailers, and suddenly she knew where they were.

This was the compound where Dylan and the others believed Lucas Quintos was hiding out. Quintos . . . and Cecil Clifford. Ronnie wasn't just going to shoot Angela and dump her body in the swamps. She'd brought her to someone else, someone who wanted to watch her die.

Angela's heart sank. She might have had a chance against Veronica Slade. But against Quintos and Clifford, she was a dead woman.

"Go around back," Ronnie said in an elevated whisper. They made their way to the back porch by the dim light coming through the windows. Ronnie didn't knock, but nodded for Angela to open the door. They entered a darkened room, a storeroom of some kind that smelled of herbs and incense and gardenias. Ronnie snapped on the light, and Angela glanced around to see a pharmacopeia of strange bottles lining the shelves along the walls.

Unlit candles in various stages of meltdown were stuck

in odd holders here and there, and bunches of herbs hung upside down from the rafters. A large jar appeared to have pickled frogs in it, another contained what appeared to be the heads of cats. Yet another was filled with snakes. Something skittered across the floor, and Angela looked down and let out a yelp when she caught sight of a large, gray-green lizard peering at her through slitty eyes.

"Shut up," Ronnie told her again. "Turn around and put your hands behind your back, and don't try anything funny."

Angela decided it was now or never. She wasn't about to let Ronnie bind her and serve her up like a trussed pig for Clifford to finish off. She pushed her lookalike back against the shelves, and several jars crashed to the floor. She'd almost made it to the back door, when large hands grabbed her shoulders and threw her roughly to the floor.

"Well, well, look what the cat dragged in." The man's voice seemed familiar. Angela rolled to one side and peered up in astonishment at the face of Freddie Holloway.

"Freddie?" What was Freddie Holloway doing here? It didn't make sense. Maybe she was dreaming. Maybe this whole thing was just a nightmare.

But the ache in her leg and the throb in her head told her this was not a dream. It was very real and very scary.

"Dr. Lizard isn't going to like this, Ronnie," Holloway said, ignoring Angela. "Why'd you bring her here? Couldn't do the job yourself?"

"Shut up, asshole," Ronnie replied. "Help me tie her hands."

Freddie roughly lifted Angela to her feet, where she swayed dizzily, biting back the pain. He tied her wrists behind her with rough twine that cut into her skin. Then Ronnie pulled a cloth tightly around her mouth, gagging her. Angela struggled to breathe.

Ronnie shoved her into a chair. "Wait here. And don't even think about running." She locked the outside door and took the key, then followed Freddie into the house and locked the door behind them. On the other side, Ronnie and Freddie started bickering like two teenagers.

Angela tried to breathe slowly to calm her hammering heart, while struggling to think clearly and sort out where she was and what was happening to her. Freddie had mentioned Dr. Lizard. Looking around, Angela guessed she was in a macabre laboratory of sorts for the voodoo man. Jeremiah had said he'd been taken somewhere in the swamps. It must have been to this place, although he hadn't mentioned this particularly charming little room. She gazed in distaste at the lizard, who'd taken up a position across the room as if it were guarding her.

Dr. Lizard. Jeremiah Brown. Judge George Brown.

Drugs.

Veronica Slade. J. J. Slade. Lucas Quintos.

Drugs.

She began to see the picture. Where did Freddie Holloway fit in? She remembered how Freddie, posing as a tour guide, had dogged her every move. He must have been Quintos's eyes and ears. Or Clifford's. His dilapidated vehicle was his cover, and the "tours" he gave were nonexistent. Most likely, he supplied drugs out of that bus.

Drugs. And a little voodoo hex every now and then. Freddie had been loitering around her shop the night the bloody black cat and other things had been left in her car. He'd also been at the Chamber of Commerce affair, just before she'd been hit by the car.

Had he been the one to run over her?

She didn't have time to wonder about it further, as voices approached and the door was yanked open. The lizard scurried away as a stately, exotically dressed woman stared wide-eyed at Angela. Then she frowned, shook her head and spoke over her shoulder to Ronnie. "Oh, girl, why didn't you do like I told you? Why'd you bring her here?

What if you was followed? Dr. Lizard is going to be very angry."

Ronnie pushed through the door. She'd lost the arrogant defiance Angela had seen. Her face was pale, and she looked extremely nervous. "I . . . I couldn't do it," she admitted. "I shot her in the leg, and I nearly got sick. I . . ." Her voice trailed away.

"You foolish twit. All you had to do was pull the trigger, kill her, and get out of there."

To Angela's amazement, Ronnie cringed. "You know how I am about blood and stuff," she whined. "Nobody saw us. One of the guys can take her out into the swamp and finish her, and no one will ever know."

"The man will know," the woman said, her voice as cold as icy steel. "He doesn't like anyone bringing outsiders here, even if they're never going to leave. You know the rules. You broke them. And now he'll make you pay."

Angela saw Veronica turn white as a ghost. "Does he have to know?" Ronnie begged, grabbing the woman's hand. "Please, Marguerite, help me. Let's kill her now and get rid of her before he finds out. I . . . I didn't mean to . . . I mean, I forgot . . ." Apparent panic stole any further words.

The man. Were they speaking of Lucas Quintos?

Angela dared to hope that she'd actually ended up in the den of the drug lord, because she knew that it was only a matter of time . . . hours, maybe only minutes . . . before Dylan and his DEA friends were going to toast the place.

If she could just stay alive long enough, and survive the attack.

Before the woman named Marguerite could answer, Angela heard Freddie swear loudly from the front of the house. "Hey, you'd better get out here," he called. "We got company."

Chapter 36

St. John th' Conqueror be most powerful when dressed with Hearts Cologne and prayer. Then it becomes High John th' Conqueror, king of th' root world, and there ain't no evil spirit nowhere can defeat him . . .

DYLAN and Scott Turner stared through infrared binoculars at the compound across the creek from where they'd secured the *Midnight Lace.*

"I can't believe it," Dylan uttered, his heart sinking as he watched Veronica Slade force Angela ahead of her at gunpoint. He picked up his phone and dialed Reilly, hoping to learn that she was safe and sound at home and that his eyes had deceived him.

But when Reilly reluctantly filled him in on what they'd found at Angela's house, he knew it was Angela who was being held prisoner in the compound of the drug lord.

He disconnected the call and cursed.

"Guess that answers the question of whether Slade's daughter was involved with Quintos," Scott Turner said. "She must have been the one who sold him out."

Dylan didn't give a damn about who'd sold out whom in the nasty little Slade family. He was mortified that Angela was once again in the line of fire. He had to find a way to get her out before Malone set the operation in motion. He was about to go below to don his wet suit when Turner let out a low expletive. "Oh, God. You're not gonna believe this."

Dylan took up his glasses again and frowned in disbelief.

Another woman had come on the scene. She was short and stocky and clad in dark green sweats, the top of which was decorated with sequins and spangles. She looked like she belonged on a Florida beach at Christmas, not in the compound of one of the most dangerous drug lords in the country. Dylan swore out loud. It was Mary Ellen Donahue. And she was wielding a gun.

"Jesus Christ," he muttered. "What are we going to do now?"

Quickly, he dialed Malone in Miami. "We've got civilians on site," he told the man who was running the operation from a war room hundreds of miles to the south.

"Yeah, we know. Suarez saw them come in. Said it looked like a damned parade. You know who they are?"

Dylan explained about Angela being brought in at gunpoint, and his suspicions about Veronica Slade being in Quintos's ring. "The older woman is Angela's mother," he went on, still in shock. "I always knew she was nuts. I have her in sight as we speak. She's gotten out of her car and is marching right up to the front of the house, gun in hand."

"Stay on the line and await further orders," Malone instructed Dylan.

But Dylan wasn't about to wait around. "Here," he said, thrusting the phone into Turner's hand. "You're in charge. I'm going to get Angela out of there before Malone opens up. See if you can talk him into giving me some time."

"Don't be a fool, Montana," Turner protested. "You don't know what you're up against."

"I know if I don't go, Angela is going to die."

Dylan had been prepared to make the short swim, but he didn't have time to put on the wet suit that would afford him some protection from the poisonous snakes that infested these waters. Besides, he couldn't ask Angela to swim back with him. Obviously, she'd been injured, and blood attracted 'gators.

Going to the bow of the boat, he loosened the line that

held the inflatable dinghy in place. He picked the boat up off the deck and swung it overboard, where it landed with a splash in the water. He grabbed the paddles and swung his body over the side of the larger craft and dropped into the dinghy. As silently as he could, he began to row the short distance to the dilapidated dock on the other side of the creek.

He'd just managed to run the boat up into some tall marsh grass in the shadow of the dock when he heard a woman shout. Her voice was all too familiar.

"I want my daughter," Mary Ellen roared. She'd come up onto the porch and was yelling toward the door.

Oh, God, Dylan thought, she's going to blow it all. Including Angela's life. He ran toward the front of the house, sprinting from tree to tree, his gun at the ready. Crouching behind a large bush, he gained a clear view of the front of the house. He saw Mary Ellen sway slightly as she aimed the gun, arms extended, at someone who stood in the front doorway.

A brightly clad woman emerged, standing tall and regal, looking like some kind of African queen. "Who are you?" the woman demanded in a mellow voice.

"You know darn well who I am," Mary Ellen snarled. "I'm Angela's mother, and I want her back."

"I don't know any Angela," the woman began, but she was cut off when a dark-haired young woman stepped out onto the porch, dragging Angela, who was bound and gagged, with her. Holding the gun to Angela's head, Veronica Slade spoke to Mary Ellen.

"So you're the one who seduced my father and had his bastard kid."

Dylan wasn't sure he'd heard correctly. It certainly wasn't something he expected to come from Veronica Slade. He was close enough he could see Veronica studying Mary Ellen's plump figure. "Funny," Veronica continued with a scornful laugh, "you don't look like his type. Too fat."

Dylan saw fire in Mary Ellen's eyes. He knew the look. She was going to snap any minute now. He trained his gun on Veronica, since she was the one who posed the greatest threat to Angela. But he feared there were others inside who would kill them all before he could get Angela to safety.

"Not your father's type?" Mary Ellen snapped. "No, I suppose I'm not. At least not now. But I wasn't fat when he left me. I was just too much of a burden."

Now it was *her* words that stunned Dylan, and he saw Angela's eyes widen. Mary Ellen went on, seemingly perversely enjoying taunting Veronica. "That was before your time, though, Veronica. That's when your father was Jake Donahue. Before he left me and Angela. The sorry jerk didn't have the courage to divorce me. He just ran away and staged his death, and took on a new identity. Even though the police accepted that he was dead, I always suspected he'd done something exactly like he did." She gave a grunt of a laugh. "I just wonder who the poor bugger was who died in that accident."

"Shut up!" Veronica shrieked. "You're lying. You were never married to my father. Your kid is a bastard. Admit it."

Mary Ellen calmly shook her head, but venom gleamed in her eyes. "I think they call it bigamy when a man has two wives. He knew damned well he had a wife and child when he married your mother. So who's the bastard kid, Veronica? Your mother's marriage was never legitimate, and neither, my dear, are you."

Angela stood frozen to the spot, watching her mother and Veronica sling insults and accusations that rocked her to the core. If she hadn't heard the words issue from her mother's mouth, Angela would have fought with everything she had to deny that her father and J. J. Slade were the same man. But Mary Ellen had just verified it.

Angela was the firstborn child of the man from whom she'd inherited a fortune. The legitimate child of a man she'd never known except as a shadowy memory. Her head was swimming, and she fought to keep her wits about her. She was vaguely aware that the woman named Marguerite had slipped back inside the house, probably to get another gun. But Angela didn't care. She was too intent on hearing the rest of what was being said.

"If my father was your husband, and you didn't think he was dead," Veronica asked Mary Ellen, "why didn't you try to find him?"

"I didn't know where to look or I would have, if for no other reason than to kill the bastard. I didn't deserve what he did to me. Neither did Angela."

"But you did find out he was alive. How?"

"That was your doing, Veronica. Your doing, and a strange twist of fate. I had no way of knowing when I got on the elevator at the First City Club that my prayers for Jake's return were about to be answered. He didn't recognize me, but I knew him instantly. He was older, more haggard, but I knew his eyes. I knew his body. I knew his scent. You see, Veronica, at one time, I loved him very much. Beyond reason. I could never forget anything about him."

As Angela watched, her mother's tough demeanor crumbled. Mary Ellen's eyes filled with tears, and the gun wavered. Angela wanted to shout to her to pull herself together, but all she could get past the gag was a stifled grunt.

Veronica took a step toward Mary Ellen, and in a low, menacing voice said, "*You're* the one who killed him, aren't you?"

Mary Ellen's gaze shifted from Veronica to Angela, who read the awful truth in her mother's eyes.

Oh, my God, no! Angela fought against the bonds that

restrained her wrists and shook her head, screaming into the gag in her mouth. *No! No! No! No! No!*

But Mary Ellen only looked at her sorrowfully. "I'm sorry, honey," she said to her daughter. "When I saw him, I was too shocked to do more than dash out of the elevator at the next floor. But then I got angry. I wanted some answers. I deserved answers. So I returned to the club level and got there just as he was leaving. He seemed terribly upset.

"I followed him when he left the bank building." Her voice softened. "I never meant to kill him. I just wanted to talk to him in private. I wanted to speak to him, to make sure it really was him. And I wanted him to know how much we'd suffered. I guess . . . I wanted him to say he was sorry."

Angela's fingers had been absently picking at the knot of twine all the time she'd been listening to her mother's shocking revelation, and suddenly her bonds fell away. She made no move, however, which would alert her captors that she was free. She stood stock-still and listened in growing astonishment and horror.

"I followed him all afternoon," Mary Ellen continued, her eyes turning glassy with tears. "He just drove around town, aimlessly it seemed to me, and finally ended up at Bonaventure Cemetery. I still don't know why he went there.

"I parked my car when I saw him pull off the road, and I got out my gun. When he reached the bluff overlooking the river, he stopped with his back to me. I . . . I called out his name. 'Jake,' I said. 'Jake Donahue, is that you?' He turned around before he realized his mistake. He saw me. He knew me, Angela. He started to speak to me, which is what I'd wanted. But something inside of me snapped. The only thing I wanted at that moment was to see him die, for him to pay for all he'd done to us. I pulled the trigger before I could think."

Angela watched as her mother lowered her gun, as if in surrender. Veronica saw it, too, and swung her gun away from Angela and toward Mary Ellen. "You killed my father!" she cried.

In what seemed like a horror film run in slow motion, Angela saw Veronica pull the trigger, heard the loud report of the gun. Saw Mary Ellen fall to the floor of the porch, dropping her gun. Angela ducked and dashed to her mother's side as bullets began to fly. She grabbed Mary Ellen and her gun and dragged her mother behind an old stuffed chair in the corner.

Peering around the edge of the chair, she saw Veronica dash inside the house. Across the open expanse of the compound, she could hear the sound of booted feet running toward the trailers. Gunfire lit the night like noisy fireflies, and in the distance she heard approaching helicopters.

Dylan's operation was underway.

Angela jerked the gag from her mouth as she turned to her mother, but her eyes fell upon a figure in the window just above and to her right, and she froze. It was a man, dressed in a black suit and tie, wearing a hat and strange blue sunglasses. His face was long and thin, and he had a flat, reptilian nose. He gave her a skeletal smile and raised his gun.

Angela rolled to one side and aimed her mother's gun just as she heard the sound of a gunshot and shattering glass. A bullet whizzed past her. She didn't ask for a second invitation. She pulled the trigger, felt the familiar kick of the revolver. More glass shattered, and the figure disappeared behind the curtain lace, but she wasn't certain she'd hit him.

"Mom," Angela whispered breathlessly to Mary Ellen, whose body lay too still on the porch floor. She lost all awareness of the firefight that was going on around her. All she could think of was that her mother was dying.

Her mother, who had killed her father.

"Mom," she moaned, gathering the older woman into her arms and crying with grief and pain unlike she'd ever known before. "Please don't die."

Mary Ellen looked up at her. "Forgive me, Angela," she whispered. "I never meant for you to get caught up in my crime. I think Veronica was planning to kill Jake and pin the blame on you. I just happened to get to him first." Her breath was coming in ragged gasps.

"Mom, don't talk. Save your energy."

But Mary Ellen shook her head stubbornly. "It's time for me to go. I don't deserve to live. But you do. You're young and strong, and you know how to make it on your own. Take his money, Angela. You're his daughter. It's your rightful inheritance." She coughed up blood and struggled for air. "I took out a life insurance policy, in case anything ever happened to me. It's nothing compared to Jake's legacy, but . . . I didn't know he'd left you the money."

Mary Ellen Donahue died in Angela's arms. Her daughter crumpled down beside her, behind the protection of the old chair, and wept.

Chapter 37

Th' world be made up of flickering shadows and spirits that fool us when they can. Common folk believe their eyes, but th' conjureman, he knows better . . .

DYLAN had seen Angela take cover behind an overstuffed chair that hunkered in one corner of the porch, but he'd also seen gunfire strike the porch. He knew Mary Ellen had been shot, but he wasn't certain about Angela. He wanted to run to her directly across the yard, but shots exploded around him in the darkness, and he couldn't risk making the dash in the open.

Before the operation got underway, he'd seen Veronica shoot Mary Ellen, then run into the house. He'd heard others inside yelling angrily at her for what she'd done in bringing Angela to the compound. "If that woman followed you, how do you know the whole goddamned world isn't on your tail?" The man's voice sounded familiar, but Dylan couldn't place where he'd heard it before.

Dylan sprinted into the shadows at the side of the house just as all hell broke loose around him. He heard a helicopter overhead, and the nasal sound of someone talking over a powerful loudspeaker. "You are surrounded on all sides. You cannot escape. Surrender now and no one gets hurt. I repeat, you are surrounded. Surrender now. Go to the clearing in the center of the compound. Surrender now."

The reply was the report of a hand-held missile launcher, followed by a fiery explosion as the helicopter was struck.

"Holy shit," Dylan exclaimed, ducking fiery shards as they fell to earth. Moments later, the chopper crashed to the ground in a nearby copse of trees, the fire lighting up the night. He'd been prepared for a shootout, but not an all-out war. He had to get Angela out of here.

He ran to the back of the house, thinking to go around it, out of sight of those inside, and approach the porch from the shadows on the other side of the house. From there he could get Angela into the woods and safety.

But as he turned the corner, he saw Veronica, a red-headed man, and a strange-looking man in a black suit, tie, and hat making a run for the docks. Dylan crouched and shot off several rounds. He clipped Veronica Slade, who fell to the ground with a curse. The red-haired man kept running, but the man in black seemed to melt into the night.

Dylan chased the redhead, overtaking him just before he reached the dock. He grabbed him from behind, and they fell together into the fetid swamp water. Dylan dropped his gun as he tried to wrestle the man, who struggled and twisted in his arms. He managed to kick Dylan in the groin, sending him reeling onto the shore in pain. Apparently thinking he'd defeated his enemy, the redhead waded out of the water and came up to Dylan's side, pointing a gun at his head. "So long, Montana, and this time it's for good."

Dylan recovered enough to roll sideways, knocking the man off his feet and sending his gun flying. It skipped in the mud at the water's edge. They both dove for the gun, and Dylan came up the winner. He sprang to his feet and aimed at the man, who began to back off.

"Okay, asshole," Dylan said, gasping for breath, "the game's over."

And then he blinked. By the light of the fire from the helicopter crash, he could see the man's face clearly. He knew that face. The man gave him a wicked grin and removed the wig that was his shock of red hair. Beneath it, he was bald.

"Clifford!"

He made the name an epithet. The man sneered.

"Go ahead, Montana. Shoot me. Or don't you have the balls?"

"You move one inch and you're dead." Dylan's finger tightened on the trigger. He heard the gunfire all around them and thought of Angela huddled behind that chair. He was wasting time showing mercy to Clifford. But he couldn't just kill him in cold blood. Even though he could get away with it, he couldn't commit murder.

But what was he going to do with Clifford? Stand here and hold a gun on him until things quieted down?

Clifford sensed his hesitation and made the decision for him by turning and running for the cigarette boat. Dylan smiled. "Thanks, asshole," he said, taking careful aim. He squeezed the trigger and shot Cecil Clifford in the knee.

He saw Clifford's leg go out from under him, heard him call to whoever was on the boat to wait, and saw him fall to the dock. Dylan ducked behind the protection of a nearby tree, ready to take another shot if need be. But someone on the boat spared him.

As he watched, a squarely built man with dark hair and a swarthy complexion raised his gun and shot Clifford in the head.

Dylan could guess the man's identity. A drug lord who was taking no chances that his lieutenant would slow him down.

Lucas Quintos.

To Dylan's dismay, Quintos disappeared below the open cockpit of the boat, and the driver revved the engines.

Quintos was getting away!

Dylan stepped from behind the tree and aimed at the driver, but before he could pull the trigger, the man behind the wheel fell forward and slumped over the console. The sharpshooters from *Midnight Lace* had scored their first hit.

Dylan was torn. He wanted like hell to finish off Quintos himself, but if he did, Angela might die. As he hesitated, he saw a figure emerge from the darkness. It was Scott Turner.

"Go get her," Turner barked, as if he'd read Dylan's mind. "I'll take care of Quintos."

Dylan didn't argue. He turned and ran toward the house again, frantic to find Angela. The cigarette boat was in good hands.

He found her still crouched behind the chair, too greatly in shock to speak, almost unable to move. Her clothes were soaked with blood where she'd been cradling the body of her mother.

"Angela," he breathed her name as he jumped over the porch rail and knelt beside her. He put his arms around her and drew her into his embrace. "It's okay, sweetheart. Everything's going to be okay."

The words sounded ludicrous. Everything wasn't okay, and in Angela's life, everything would probably never be totally okay again. She'd witnessed the cold-blooded murder of her mother just as she'd learned that the woman had killed the father she'd never known. It was enough to send anyone over the edge.

He held her and rocked her and kissed her and made reassuring noises, wishing none of this had happened, but thankful that she'd survived. He raised his head to see what was happening on the river, but it was too dark to tell. He heard the rumble of the cigarette boat and guessed Quintos was trying to get away from the dock. Where was Turner?

Then he heard a high whine, like the sound of a rocket on the fourth of July. The force of the explosion that followed nearly knocked them over. Angela jerked and tried to bury herself in his chest.

Flames engulfed the water where the cigarette boat had been tied to the dock. As he watched, Lucas Quintos, his body on fire, staggered to the front of the boat and jumped into the water. Then he saw Turner crouched on the dock, perilously close to the spreading flames. Turner aimed a high-powered rifle into the water and fired twice. Then, apparently satisfied that he'd finished off his target, he ran down the dock toward the house.

"Over here, Turner," Dylan called, risking sticking his head up from behind the chair.

Turner headed his way. "Is . . . Angela . . . ?"

"She's here. She's okay, although she's been through hell. What's happening?"

Even as he asked, the gunfire ceased, and a strange calm enveloped the scene. Fire crackled from the copse of trees behind the trailers and from the direction of the dock. Then from a distance, they heard sirens.

Men dressed in dark clothing began to emerge from the shadows, some of them holding others at gunpoint. They gathered at the center of the clearing and waited. Moments later, police cars, fire engines, and ambulances careened onto the scene and began to bring some order to the chaos.

Dylan carried Angela to an ambulance, and together they made the trip back to Savannah. Angela drifted in and out of consciousness, mostly suffering from shock, the paramedic told him. He assured Dylan that she'd be all right.

Dylan wasn't as confident. The wound in her leg was superficial, but the wound to her spirit might never heal.

Veronica awoke face-down in the mud and sodden leaves behind Marguerite's house, on fire from the bullet wound in her side. Slowly, she managed to roll over, but the pain was nearly unbearable. She broke into a cold sweat, and nausea threatened to wrench her body. She lifted her head and looked around, trying to remember what had happened.

The rain had stopped. Fire burned on the river, and she could see more flames rising from somewhere in the front of the house. She heard sirens and urgent voices shouting orders, but behind the house, there was only darkness. Did anyone know she was there? Panic shot through her. She didn't want to die out here in the swamps.

"Marguerite," she called weakly. "Help me."

And then she remembered what she'd seen just before the firefight began. She'd run back into the house after shooting the woman who'd killed her father and found Cecil Clifford frantically trying to remove the cocaine from its hiding place in the kitchen, tossing package after package out the back door into the woods. He'd yelled at her, saying that this was all her fault for bringing Angela to this forbidden place. She'd turned to Marguerite for help with her defense and saw a transformation that made her blood run cold.

Marguerite, in whose arms she'd found comfort and understanding, stood looking out one of the front windows of the house, her back to the room. Suddenly, she seemed enshrouded in a gray mist, and Ronnie had to blink to keep her in focus. As she watched, Marguerite slipped a pair of glasses from the pocket of her flowing caftan and put them on. Ronnie instantly recognized those blue sunglasses. Then Marguerite had removed the white turban. Ronnie had never seen her without a headdress of some sort.

Beneath the turban, her hair was short, like a man's. With the smooth moves of a reptile, Marguerite took another item from the other pocket and carefully unfolded it, then placed it on her head. It was a black felt hat.

Then, as Ronnie watched in shock, Marguerite unzipped the front of her caftan and slid it off her shoulders. Beneath it, she wore a man's black suit. She turned and saw Ronnie gaping at her. Dr. Lizard smiled, and it wasn't a smile of motherly affection. It was an evil, wicked smile. Ronnie couldn't see his eyes behind the blue lenses of the glasses, but she knew they were just as evil.

"So now you know," said Dr. Lizard. "I'm surprised you didn't guess before." He took a gun from inside his jacket. "Excuse me for a moment. I have a little job to do. And then I have a score to settle with you."

Dr. Lizard turned back to the window, pulled the lace

curtain aside, raised the gun, and fired right through the glass.

Ronnie was so stunned she didn't know what to do. She was afraid of Dr. Lizard, because she'd seen his power. He made people do things they didn't want to do. But she'd trusted Marguerite with her life. Surely, they couldn't be the same person.

Gunfire was returned from the porch, shattering more glass, and Dr. Lizard stepped away from the window. "It's time to become as the chameleon," he said in the mellow tone Ronnie now recognized as Marguerite's voice. Turning, he strode toward the back of the house. "Leave that," he called to Cecil Clifford, meaning the cocaine. "Hurry. Go to the boat."

Clifford was out the door ahead of Dr. Lizard, and Veronica was on their heels. Even though she was afraid of Dr. Lizard, she'd rather escape with him than be arrested or killed. She'd thought they were going to get away when she heard a shot and felt red hot pain rip through her. Now, as she lay alone in the mist, that pain seemed to be her only companion.

She heard footsteps approaching. "Help," she cried again. She knew she was in deep trouble with the law, but she didn't want to die. Anything, even jail, would be better than death. "Help!"

"Over here," a man's voice said. Other footsteps came her way. The man knelt beside her. "It's her. Tell them we've found her."

Ronnie looked up into the man's face. A heavy scar ran down one side, and he was missing most of an ear. He seemed familiar. She frowned, then remembered. The man who'd pumped her gas that night she went to Atlanta.

"You!" she said, and found that it hurt to talk.

"Yeah, me. Don't move. We'll get a medic here in a minute."

"You were following me."

"Yeah."

Ronnie closed her eyes. This man was some kind of a cop, and he'd been tailing her. Was nothing ever as it seemed? Her father was a bigamist, his marriage to her mother a sham. She was a bastard. Marguerite wasn't a woman at all, but a shapeshifter who assumed the form of Dr. Lizard when it suited him. She was aware that the man-with-no-name had used Dr. Lizard, the same as he'd used Veronica. They'd all been his pawns in a game of greed and ambition.

She wasn't so different from her father after all.

Veronica Slade was critically injured and was transported by helicopter, along with others who'd been seriously wounded, to a hospital in Savannah. Ricky Suarez watched the helicopter lift off from a field near the scene of the drug bust and wondered what the poor little rich girl was going to do now.

Chapter 38

Th' conjureman knows th' tricks of th' slip-skin hag, and he uses them if he needs t' slip th' noose . . .

HARLOW Bertram received a frantic phone call from Bridget Means around midnight. "Something's going on down east from here," she told him. "There's been an explosion, and ambulances and fire trucks are coming down the road in droves. I tried to wake Mrs. Slade, but I couldn't get her to answer when I knocked. Both her doors are locked. I . . . I found an empty bottle of tranquilizers in the bathroom. I'm afraid . . ."

Harlow jumped out of bed. "Call 911 and tell them about Mrs. Slade. I'm on my way." He dressed hurriedly and grabbed his cell phone on his way out. He dialed Bobby Keilor, the county sheriff, then drove toward Paradisia as fast as he dared. Keilor wasn't there, and the dispatcher wouldn't tell him anything about what was going on near Paradisia. Damned bureaucrats.

When Harlow had almost reached the plantation, an ambulance sped past him going in the opposite direction down the narrow road. He could see the glow of fire reflected on the low clouds to the east and was tempted to drive on to see for himself what was going on. But Bridget's reference to an empty tranquilizer bottle had him worried.

Bridget met him at the front door. "Hurry!" she said, wringing her hands. "I . . . I don't know what to do. I called 911, but they're not here yet, and I haven't been able to find a key to open her door."

Harlow swore beneath his breath and headed upstairs

toward Elizabeth's room, taking the steps two at a time. He didn't bother looking for a key. Instead, he crashed his substantial body into her door, splintering the molding.

He found her lying against a mountain of pillows, her eyes closed, her hands crossed over her chest. Her hair, normally perfectly in place, was disheveled, as if she'd been running her fingers through it. Although she was elegantly dressed, her face was pale, her cheeks sunken, and her eyes hollow dark circles.

"Oh, dear God," Harlow whispered, walking softly to her bedside. Bridget had turned on a lamp in the room, which cast a soft glow over the pale blue and white satin bedcovers. He took Elizabeth's hand in his. The silken soft skin he'd loved so dearly was cold to the touch, and her hand weighed heavily in his. He laid his fingers against her neck, searching for a pulse and finding none.

"No," he uttered, laying his head against her chest, hoping to detect a heartbeat. "No!"

For the first time since he was a boy, Harlow Bertram cried. He drew Elizabeth into his arms and held her tightly to him, rocking her, pleading with her. "No, don't leave me. Elizabeth, please . . ."

But it was too late. He'd waited for thirty years for her to return to him. Now she was gone forever.

He held her and cried until his tears were spent, at least for now. When his storm of grief had subsided, Harlow released Elizabeth and sat up on the bed. He stood up and reached into his pocket for a handkerchief and struggled to pull himself back together. There was much to be done.

He felt more than heard someone behind him in the doorway and turned to see Bridget, who was sobbing into a tissue.

"She's gone, isn't she?" the faithful servant cried.

Harlow could only nod. A moment later he found his voice. "You said you thought she'd taken too many tranquilizers?"

She pointed to the adjacent bathroom, which Bridget had accessed from the hallway door. Elizabeth had locked the door between her room and the bath. "In there. I found the bottle with the lid off. It was empty. I have no idea how many pills might have been in the bottle."

Harlow looked around the room, searching for a note or something to explain Elizabeth's suicide. There was no note, but on her dressing table he came across a plain manila file marked ANGELA. Next to it lay the letter the Atlanta attorney had given her the day the will was read.

Bridget peered over his shoulder as he opened the file, and she gasped when she saw what was inside.

"It's her, isn't it? The woman who killed Mr. Slade?" she asked in a hushed tone.

Harlow shrugged. "Maybe. I always guessed there was some connection between Angela Donahue and J. J. She looked too much like him for it to be coincidental, but I didn't want to mention to Elizabeth the possibility that Slade had had an illegitimate child. She'd taken enough from Mr. Slade in her life. She didn't need any more. But it does explain how the Donahue woman ended up in his will."

His curiosity getting the better of him, Harlow picked up the letter from the attorney, even though Elizabeth had not allowed him to see it before.

"Dear Elizabeth," it read,

> Because of what you have done, and because of what Veronica is, I have chosen to leave my estate to another, more responsible person than either of you have proven to be. I have taken every precaution in the will to prevent either of you from contesting the will or in any way challenging the trust arrangements.
>
> Ironic that trust should be the issue. I trusted you, Elizabeth, and you sold me out. Now, if you attempt to go against my will, I have made arrangements to sell

you out as well. My attorney is in possession of yet another sealed letter which I have directed him to turn over to the authorities should my will be contested by either you or Veronica. In that letter, I have spelled out in detail the entire story of our arrangement, including the way we murdered your father. I will be dead, so the law can't touch me for the actual killing. But you can and will be tried as an accessory to murder. Trust me, Elizabeth, this *will* happen if you make even the slightest move to contest the will.

Harlow felt the blood drain from his face. *The way we murdered your father* . . . Had Elizabeth and J. J. killed old Angus Mayhew? Harlow stumbled to a chair and fell into it. "Could you . . . bring me a whiskey, please, Bridget?"

Harlow's mind raced back to the time when Elizabeth had first brought J. J. to Paradisia. She'd met him in Las Vegas, where her father's gambling was about to completely wipe out the Mayhew family fortune. She'd followed Angus there to try to persuade him not to gamble away Paradisia in a high-stakes poker game.

It was Slade who'd given her the idea that sent Angus away from that game, landing him instead in bed with severe "food poisoning." It was Slade who'd taken Angus on that hunting trip to Maine not long after. It was Slade who'd called the rural sheriff in Maine and whose word had been accepted that the shooting had been a tragic hunting accident. And it was Slade who'd taken over the Mayhew empire and turned it around.

I trusted you, Elizabeth, and you sold me out.

How had Elizabeth sold him out? Elizabeth, who to Harlow's knowledge knew nothing about J. J.'s business.

Bridget arrived with his whiskey, which he tossed back in a single swallow, needing to feel the burn all the way down to his belly. He remained in the chair for a long time, staring at Elizabeth's silent form on the bed.

He'd thought he'd known her, but apparently there was a dark side to her he'd never suspected.

Still, he'd loved her, and he owed her one thing. It was probably against the law, but he didn't care. Making sure Bridget wasn't around, he stood up and took the letter to the fireplace, where he wadded it into a ball and threw it on the gas logs. He turned on the fire and watched as the paper burned. When he was satisfied that no bit of the incriminating document remained, he turned off the logs and left the room.

Elizabeth Mayhew had been a proud woman, and she'd suffered so much. Harlow guessed that finding Angela's file was the last straw, the final blow that drove her to take her own life. That was punishment enough. No one need ever know about her complicity in her father's death. That much he could do for her.

Chapter 39

That old devil's gone away now, and th' conjureman, too. They've not gone far. They'll be back. Till then, th' hants and th' hags lie sleeping, dreaming up new mischief for another day . . .

ANGELA opened her eyes and gazed around, disoriented and confused. She lay in a narrow metal bed with railings at the sides, and an IV dripped into her arm. A hospital. What was she doing in a hospital? What hospital was it? She looked out of the window into a gray day, but all she could see was the brick wall of the building's adjacent wing and rain falling against it.

She closed her eyes again, trying to figure out what she was doing in a hospital. When she shifted slightly, a sharp pain in her knee gave her the first clue. She'd been shot in the leg. But that had been a long time ago, hadn't it? She'd thought that wound had healed.

Slowly, the pain began to awaken her memory, and she recalled the more recent gunshot wound, although the circumstances surrounding it remained hazy. Inexplicably, a lump formed in her throat, and a heaviness settled in the center of her chest. Tears stung her eyes. She wasn't sure exactly why, but she knew something was terribly, terribly wrong.

She heard someone call her name softly. "Angela?" It was a man's voice. She turned her head toward the sound but didn't open her eyes. Pretending to be asleep, she peered through nearly closed lashes and saw Dylan tiptoe to the foot of her bed. He placed a large covered basket on the chair, then crept to her bedside.

Dylan.

Did she want to see Dylan? Was he going to leave her again? The weight on her chest grew heavier. At least this time, she thought, he'd had the decency to say goodbye.

Her eyes fluttered open, and she looked up at him. She saw a distinct look of relief replace the worry on his face. He leaned over the railing and touched her cheek.

"Angela. Oh, thank God," he whispered, and she saw that his eyes were glassy with tears. A tear escaped from the tail of her eye as well.

"Dylan?"

"Shhh. Don't talk. It's all right. Everything's going to be all right. The doctor says it's just a surface wound this time."

Surface wound. But where had it come from?

"What . . . happened?"

His face clouded, and he ran his fingers gently through her hair.

"Shhhh," he said again. "We'll talk about that later. Right now, you just get well."

It frightened her that she couldn't remember how she'd been shot, and she clutched Dylan's hands fiercely.

"No. Tell me what happened."

She saw that he clearly didn't want to tell her, and her earlier misgivings that something was wrong intensified. She took a deep breath. A part of her didn't want to face what she unconsciously knew was an ugly reality, but she knew that sooner or later, she had to. "Tell me," she demanded.

"We got Quintos," he said at last. "And Clifford."

Quintos. Clifford. The names conjured up a firefight in the night, and her memory flickered. Quintos, the drug lord they'd been after for almost as long as she'd known Dylan. And Clifford, his right-hand man.

"Are they dead?"

Dylan nodded. "I saw them both go down. They're in the morgue this morning."

She was quiet a moment, processing his information. This was good news. Why did she feel so terrible?

"What else?"

He swallowed. "Veronica Slade was injured, but she's going to survive. She's in custody, charged among a lot of other things with drug trafficking, kidnapping, and . . . murder."

Murder.

A dark shadow loomed behind the word, but Angela didn't want to look at it. Instead, she focused on the name Veronica Slade, and in her mind's eye, she saw herself reflected in the old mirror in her hallway, standing beside another woman who looked remarkably like her.

Hello, sister. It's about time we met.

"Veronica," Angela murmured, and cold dread washed over her as she began to remember the horror. "She's the one who shot me."

"Yes."

"She's my sister, isn't she?"

Dylan squeezed her fingers. "We can talk about that later." He released her hand and went to the foot of the bed and picked up the basket. "Right now, we have more important matters to attend to."

Angela was grateful he'd interrupted the flow of memories that threatened to drown her in a flood of darkness. She batted away the wetness in her eyes and swallowed hard over the tightness in her throat. She looked at the basket.

"What's that?"

Dylan placed it beside her on the bed. "A little get-well present."

The basket shifted as if it were alive, and Angela jumped

back a little. "Am I hallucinating, or did it just move?" she asked unsteadily.

"Probably. Go ahead. Open it."

Gingerly, she reached out and drew away the brightly colored cloth that covered the basket. A tiny gray-and-black tabby kitten peeked out at her with large, inquisitive eyes. Startled, she looked up at Dylan. "What's this?"

"A new friend." He reached into the basket and placed the kitten on the bed, and she stroked it with her finger. Its fur was fine and soft, its eyes bright with the promise of new life.

"Does my friend have a name?" Angela asked, touched to the core by Dylan's gift. She only hoped it was a get-well wish and not a farewell present.

"No. That's up to you."

She smiled and picked up the kitten. "I'll have to think about it. I've never had a pet before. Mom wouldn't let me . . ." The last words caught in her throat, and she looked wide-eyed at Dylan. His expression immediately turned grim.

"Mom," she murmured, and the heaviness that had lifted somewhat when she saw the kitten returned, nearly crushing her. Suddenly and without warning, the memories she'd tried to repress roared into her consciousness, and darkness closed around her.

Mom. Her mother.

Her mother was dead. Murdered.

Her mother, who had loved her and who'd tried so hard to give her a good life.

Her mother, who'd also been a murderer.

Angela began to shake convulsively, and she was unaware of anything but a grief so painful she thought she would die. She didn't hear Dylan lower the protective rail, didn't feel him edge onto the bed next to her, but she didn't resist when he drew her against him. She leaned hungrily into his warmth and strength, for they were all she had left.

Her next words escaped her lips before she could stop them.

"Don't go," she choked. She should be ashamed that she was begging him, but she wasn't. He was the only person in her life who mattered now. "Don't leave me."

His arms tightened around her, and he kissed the top of her head. "Don't worry. I'm not going anywhere," he whispered, rocking her gently. "You're stuck with me this time."

Somewhere in a far corner of her heart, she knew he meant what he said. She hiccuped, trying to regain control, but his promise only unleashed more tears. He raised her face to his and kissed her swollen eyelids, and, as if he understood her deepest need at that moment, said, "It's okay. Go ahead. Cry."

Epilog

THE newspapers called it the biggest drug bust in history. The street value of the drugs found in and around the old house at the far end of nowhere in Lincoln County was astronomical.

Local dealers suffered a severe setback when Lucas Quintos and Cecil Clifford died, although because the demand for drugs remained strong, new bosses quickly moved in to lay claim to the territory. For Savannah's Counter-Narcotics Team, the war against drugs continued.

The group of young thugs rounded up in the raid claimed they worked for a voodoo conjureman they called Dr. Lizard. Like Fagin, he used children to distribute the drugs that came into the compound by boat. In return, they were paid well, given lodging in the old trailers on the property, and feasted on meals prepared by Georgia the cook. Most importantly, they were allowed to live. One misstep and Dr. Lizard made sure you disappeared into the swamp forever, they swore.

The youths ended up with new accommodations in various prisons, but neither Dr. Lizard nor the exotic Marguerite Domingo were ever seen or heard of again. During interrogation, Veronica Slade described Marguerite's transformation into Dr. Lizard, and a search of the old house turned up a closet full of both colorful caftans and men's suits and hats like the voodoo doctor wore. Although some of the youths firmly believed the conjureman was a shapeshifter, the general consensus was that he was just a very creative cross-dresser.

Angela was shocked to learn that her redheaded nemesis,

Freddie Holloway, was none other than Cecil Clifford himself. Although she'd been involved in the earlier drug bust in which Clifford had set Dylan up, she'd never met the man face-to-face. After learning the whole truth of what Clifford had done to Dylan, she wished she'd been the one to take him out.

As for her inheritance, Angela wanted no part of her father's dirty money. But Anthony Spriggs convinced her to reconsider. "There's no way to prove that money came from drugs. If there was, the feds would have confiscated it," he pointed out. He suggested that she use the money to fight drugs, and when she found out that if she didn't accept the money, it'd go to the NRA, Angela decided his idea made sense. She hired him to put a foundation together to fund educational efforts to keep kids off drugs.

The most difficult thing Angela had faced, other than attending her mother's funeral, had been cleaning out the small house where she'd grown up. Disposing of Mary Ellen's things had been stressful and emotional, but Angela had done all right until she found the small metal box on the top shelf of her mother's closet.

Her hands trembled as she opened it, as if she knew the secrets it contained. Inside, she found two postcards, one from the Smoky Mountains of Tennessee, the other from the city of Chicago, mailed that fateful summer when her father had taken off. "The world is mine at last," read one. "The city is full of riches, just waiting to be taken," said the other. They sounded to Angela like they'd been written by a man who was obviously glad to be free of his family obligations, and she found them contemptible.

It wasn't the cards themselves, however, that led her to understand why her mother had held onto a thread of hope that Jake Donahue wasn't dead. It was the small brown envelope lying on the bottom of the box. In it, she found a man's wedding ring, inscribed with the date of her mother's wedding anniversary. There was no message in the envelope. But the ring had been sent to Mary Ellen less than a year after Jake Donahue was declared dead, and the handwriting on the outside was identical to that on the postcards.

Her father had been a cruel, cruel man. Somehow, that made it easier to forgive her mother.

As promised, Dylan didn't leave, and in the spring, when the azaleas and quince and flowering fruit trees were in riotous bloom, he and Angela were married in one of Savannah's beautiful historical squares by the Honorable Judge George W. Brown. The wedding party was small, consisting only of Camille and Jeremiah Brown, Connie Perry, Detectives Johnny Reilly, Scott Turner, and Wally Padgett, and one small tabby cat.

Author's Note

WHEN our country was young and men still traded in human flesh, many ships from Angola offloaded their slave cargo in Charleston and Savannah. These involuntary immigrants were purchased by plantation owners along the coasts of Georgia and South Carolina. Although the "Gullah," as they were called, after their native country, brought no worldly possessions with them, they carried a rich and lasting cultural heritage in their hearts, minds, and souls. That heritage was passed in their gently lilting dialect from generation to generation through folk tales and song. Among those traditions handed down was the practice of the ancient African religion know as voodoo.

Unlike the overtly sexual form of voodoo practiced in Haiti and New Orleans, the Gullah religion was a blend of spiritual faith, herbal medicine, and primitive ritual into which they also eventually integrated the white man's Christianity. Over the centuries, practitioners, once called "witch doctors" by fearful white folk, became known as "conjuremen" or "root doctors." They often assumed the name of an animal they felt gave them special powers, such as Beaufort, South Carolina's famous Dr. Buzzard. And they held great sway over their followers, for their magic was known to be potent and sometimes deadly.

Voodoo, hoodoo, conjuration, root work, whatever name it goes by, is still practiced today, but quietly. Voodoo herbal charms such as Love Balm, Jinx Kill, and St. John the Conqueror can be purchased in esoteric stores on certain streets in Savannah. But if you want to consult a root doctor, you have to "know somebody who knows somebody."

For the conjureman's power is strong as ever, and still feared by many . . .